An extraordinary collection of short fiction from Latin America that invites us to voyage into uncharted territory

Organized geographically, this diverse collection includes a number of stories never before published in English, as well as short biographies of the authors that place their works in context. From Horacio Quiroga's "The Dead Man," who is disturbingly alive, to the quintessential feat of magical realism found in Alejo Carpentier's "Journey Back to the Source," *A Hammock Beneath the Mangoes* offers abundant reading pleasure for those simply curious about, or already captivated by, the magic of Latin America's fiction.

THOMAS COLCHIE is a noted translator and literary agent for writers from Latin America, Portugal, Spain, and Portuguese Africa. His translations include Manuel Puig's *Kiss of the Spider Woman*, Marcio Souza's *Emperor of the Amazon*, and Murilo Rubião's *The Ex-Magician and Other Stories*. Now at work on a biography of Jorge Amado, he has also been awarded a Guggenheim Fellowship to translate *The Devil to Pay in the Backlands* by João Guimarães Rosa.

A HAMMOCK BENEATH THE MANGOES

STORIES FROM LATIN AMERICA

Edited by Thomas Colchie

A PLUME BOOK

PLUME
Published by the Penguin Group
Penguin Books USA Inc., 375 Hudson Street, New York, New York 10014, U.S.A.
Penguin Books Ltd, 27 Wrights Lane, London W8 5TZ, England
Penguin Books Australia Ltd, Ringwood, Victoria, Australia
Penguin Books Canada Ltd, 10 Alcorn Avenue, Toronto, Ontario, Canada M4V 3B2
Penguin Books (N.Z.) Ltd, 182-190 Wairau Road, Auckland 10, New Zealand

Penguin Books Ltd, Registered Offices: Harmondsworth, Middlesex, England

Published by Plume, an imprint of New American Library, a division of Penguin Books USA Inc.
Previously published in a Dutton edition.

First Plume Printing, November, 1992
10 9 8 7 6 5 4 3 2 1

 REGISTERED TRADEMARK—MARCA REGISTRADA

LIBRARY OF CONGRESS CATALOGING-IN-PUBLICATION DATA
A Hammock beneath the mangoes : stories from Latin America / edited by Thomas Colchie.
     p.   cm.
     ISBN 0-452-26866-4
     1. Short stories, Latin American—Translations into English.   2. Latin American fiction—
20th century—Translations into English.   I. Colchie, Thomas.
[PQ7087.E5H35   1992]
863'.010898—dc20   92-53571
                                                                             CIP

Printed in the United States of America

A hammock beneath two mangoes
swayed in the dreaming world.

—*Carlos Drummond de Andrade*

CONTENTS

Four. Mexico

Five. The Caribbean

INTRODUCTION

In 1974, a slim volume of eight fantastic tales by a reclusive author named Murilo Rubião was published in Brazil, where it became an unprecedented bestseller. In a country preoccupied with the sordid realities of a military dictatorship, these stories of a helplessly immortal magician and a lascivious kangaroo, of fire-breathing adolescents and amorous time warps, offered unaccountable pleasures. In fact, the fantastic had seldom surfaced in Brazilian letters (unlike elsewhere in Latin America), at least not since the death of that solitary master of the absurd, Machado de Assis.

When a translation was eventually published in the United States, as *The Ex-Magician and Other Stories,* critics understandably turned to Borges and Kafka for comparison. They also remarked upon Rubião's evident debt to Gabriel García Márquez. Yet it is the hallmark of Latin American literature not to be what it seems. For the celebrated author of *One Hundred Years of Solitude* was barely twelve when, back in 1940, his Brazilian herald had begun submitting those dreamlike parables to the literary supplements of Belo Horizonte and Rio de Janeiro. Soon afterward, the first collection of Borges's fictional enigmas would be published in Buenos Aires; and a few years later still, Kafka's tales, introduced to Brazilian readers by the gifted novelist, poet, and critic Mário de Andrade, who compared them—understandably enough—to the works of Murilo Rubião.

It can be difficult at times to situate the Latin American writer. Cortázar, who was born in Brussels and spent most of his life in Paris, *is* one; whereas Lautréamont, who passed all but the final three years of his life in his native Uruguay, is apparently not. It is not a question of language or location. Amado has been accused of being excessively Bahian and Borges of being insufficiently Argentinean, but both are acclaimed as quintessentially Latin American authors.

Matters are not helped by the lack of a unifying Latin American language. Brazilian Portuguese and several varieties of Spanish predominate, but there is also French, English, Dutch, and—perhaps more significant—pre-Columbian languages such as Quechua, Quiché, and Tupi. It is hardly surprising to learn that Carpentier read French at home before learning Spanish or that Scliar speaks and writes with a Jewish "accent." Puig wrote novels in English and in Portuguese, along with those in his native Spanish. Ferré and Ubaldo Ribeiro have translated (or better, rewritten) their own works into English.

The late Uruguayan critic and biographer Emir Rodríguez Monegal suggested that there *is* finally one language that has forged a degree of cultural cohesion in Latin America: "The generation that emerged in the forties and fifties is one for whom film constitutes a veritable lingua franca, the true *koine* of this linguistic Babel in which we live." Given the number of authors in the present anthology who have written for film or about film, or who have in one way or another acknowledged their debt to the cinema, Monegal certainly has a point. As Cabrera Infante once boasted from behind his cigar: "Would you believe it if I told you I went to the movies when I was twenty-nine days old!" Of course the girl he had his arm around at the time was his mother, yet there's no denying the predominant influence of film, not literature, on his texts. Puig sat in the same seat at his local cinema five nights a week for the better part of ten years. Salles Gomes became one of the most important Latin American film critics of the century before sitting down to compose Brazil's funniest piece of fiction.

Film, however, is a language that extends beyond the borders of Latin America. And the question still remains: Is there not some peculiarly Latin American way of looking at the world? Some writers have thought so, Carpentier among them: "For what is the story of [Latin] America if not a chronicle of the marvelous in the real." This rather intriguing notion would seem to have found its fullest expression nearly twenty years later in the "magic realism" of Arenas and García Márquez. Yet other authors vehemently disagree: "There are no miracles to be found, like those in García Márquez," Onetti has said of his own fiction, stressing "the great difference between the north and the south of our continent." Another River Plate writer has put the matter more succinctly: "The world, unfortunately, is real; I, unfortunately, am Borges."

Amado has challenged the very idea of a Latin American literature, declaring it "a false and dangerous concept." He insists "there's nothing more different than a Mexican and a Brazilian," conceding merely that "we are united simply by what is negative— misery, oppression, military dictatorship." Certainly it has been dangerous at times to be a Latin American writer. Brazilian dictators have occasionally trussed them on poles like wild game. In Argentina, they have been "disappeared," to use the vernacular. Fidel Castro has a reputation for sending them off to various camps. And in a curiously Orwellian innovation, Sandinista Nicaragua wholly redefined the meaning of the term *writer*. Through an ingenious amalgam of the Hollywood star system and hammer-and-sickle dialectics, anyone holding public office there suddenly became a "writer"; while anybody who did not hold such a position just as suddenly was not.

Generations of poets have tried to engender a more metaphysical Latin America. In his magnificent but capricious *The Bow and the Lyre,* the Mexican Octavio Paz rummages through everything from the Hindu to the haiku to embody a Latin American poetics. So persuasive is his rhetoric that most readers are willing to overlook the omission of all of Brazilian poetry. The Chilean Pablo Neruda was quantifiably more successful, missing only Costa Rica in his politically charged, monumentally uneven *Canto general,* which, though it often reads like an essay, includes one of the greatest moments in all of modern poetry, *The Heights of Macchu Picchu.*

Fortunately for the present anthology, the Latin American short story—even in its longer guises—has tended to be crafted by less predictable intentions. This may to some extent account for its frequently gifted and occasionally brilliant manifestations. For at the heart of modern Latin American fiction, and the selection that follows, lies an intricate and ambiguous revolution that began with the work of Machado de Assis and Horacio Quiroga. As the age of sailing ships and Victorian ideas drew to a close in the latter half of the nineteenth century, so did the dominance of European thought in the New World. Since it was still considered impolite or bohemian to notice this, a few American writers devised surprisingly deceptive strategies to chart the growing transatlantic fissures. The Brazilian Machado de Assis would take a European idea, turn it inside out, and set it sailing like a paper clipper back across the ocean. "The Psychiatrist" is but the most comically outrageous of these intellectual origamis. Like his North American contemporary Henry James, he normally welcomed passengers aboard with a genteel urbanity that kept them comfortably distracted till they were well out to sea.

In 1900, the Uruguayan writer Quiroga decided to make the crossing himself. He spent only a few hungry, possibly desperate months in Paris, which seem to have left him so disgusted that, when he returned to the River Plate, he could no longer abide even the simulacre of Paris. So he abandoned Buenos Aires and Montevideo for the jungle, a place seldom visited by writers since the time of the Conquest. He went first as a photographer, a fact of no little consequence to his subsequent development as a writer. It may even be claimed that Quiroga's style owed more to photography than to literature. This is not to say he did not understand the difference between taking a picture and writing a story. "The Dead Man" is no less baroque than "The Psychiatrist," precisely because the dead man is so alive.

From these twin summits—Machado and Quiroga—it is possible to map out any number of Latin American literary journeys. I have chosen to emphasize three major landscapes: Brazil, the River Plate, and the Caribbean. Even these are only partial itineraries, for I have not included the French Caribbean, the Brazilian Amazon, or the Paraguayan sources of the River Plate. Yet one of the pleasures of traveling anywhere lies in the anticipation that one will have exhausted oneself, perhaps, but not the place.

From the Caribbean I have included Reinaldo Arenas, Guillermo Cabrera Infante, and Alejo Carpentier (Cuba); Rosario Ferré and Ana Lydia Vega (Puerto Rico); and Gabriel García Márquez (Colombia). From Brazil, along with Machado de Assis's "The Psychiatrist," are texts by Jorge Amado, Lygia Fagundes Telles, Rubem Fonseca, João Guimarães Rosa, Clarice Lispector, Murilo Rubião, Paulo Emílio Salles Gomes, Moacyr Scliar, and João Ubaldo Ribeiro. From the River Plate I have selected, in addition to Quiroga, Juan Carlos Onetti and Armonía Somers (Uruguay); along with Adolfo Bioy Casares, Jorge Luís Borges, Julio Cortázar, and Manuel Puig (Argentina). There are also stories by Isabel Allende (Chile) and Carlos Fuentes and Juan Rulfo (both from Mexico).

I need not point out the somewhat arbitrary, though faintly addictive nature of all anthologies. Like crossword puzzles, like maps, they play with our desire for order and completeness while holding aloft the promise of a discovery. Still, like those equivocal charts that caused the first tentative navigators to stumble upon an un-known continent, even the most pedestrian volume of selected sto-ries can lead to unexpected discoveries.

In the case of the early cartographers, the promise was India, which gave birth to a New World of notable illusions. It was Co-lumbus who first discovered that false India of the Arabian Sea that would turn out to be the Caribbean. And by taking up his pen to persist in observing the India he did not see, throughout his letters and journals from the New World, he set the tone of hyper-bole and prestidigitation for all the narratives that were to blossom from that gaudy landscape. For what he had found was not Ma-harashtra but a mirage splayed by light, heat, and water. And once the false Indians had been exterminated, all that remained of the place were figures of speech, from the flowers of Bestial to Big Mama of Macondo. All was reduced to language, whether it be the laughter of Maracaibo pirates or the imprecations of African slaves, while even dictators were known to talk to themselves for hours at a time. And no sooner had Cabrera Infante set his sonorous Ha-vana to the page, than it was gone . . .

After Columbus had been sent home in chains, Magellan came to sound the upper reaches of that silver mouth of the Ganges known as the Río de la Plata. Of all its fluvial regions, this would prove the most metaphysical. Lying somewhere (but not only) be-tween Montevideo and Buenos Aires, the River Plate has been var-iously described as "a tireless labyrinth, a chaos, a dream," but also a children's game, a movie, a clock. Some have called it "the black hole" of Calcutta. Others know it as Santa María.

No one is certain who first sighted the secret, subcontinental India of Brazil. Even now there are those who wonder if it has been discovered at all. Officially the event occurred in 1500. Yet if we go back to that first global summit of them all—at Tordesillas, in 1494—we uncover more ambiguous mischief than the predict-able division of a brand-new globe into two useless "blocs." Was it the luck, the prescience, or the temerity of the Portuguese to con-vince the Spanish to move the line of demarcation farther to the west—thus obtaining Brazil for themselves, as well as India? The Spaniards, of course, have never forgiven them for it, and to this day certain Spanish-American writers would sooner tell you where to find the Bay of Bengal than the Bay of All Saints.

The very enormity of Brazil is what makes it so elusive. The literary landscape to be found there is as vast and varied as its

geography and population, ranging from the disquieting miniatures of a Lispector to the ubiquitous *sertão* of a Guimarães Rosa.
A single book by just one of its writers—*The Centaur in the Garden*
by Moacyr Scliar—has been called "a comedic novel," "a regionalist novel," "a realistic novel of bourgeois alienation," "a metaphorical novel," and "a fantastical phantasmagorical novel."

I have not slighted the tantric India of Mexico with its "other"
Aztec face, or the misty Himalayan reaches of the Andes—among
the countless Indias of the imagination. I prefer to leave them to
future Latin American anthologies and to the readers who, having
exhausted the present pages, will feel confident enough to make
other journeys on their own.

NOTE TO READERS: *To the extent possible, only titles published in English
translation are cited in the biographies that follow. Unless otherwise indicated, publication dates for works cited are given only for first publication in the original language, not for the English translations whose
dates would be misleading in terms of the writer's development.*

ONE

THE RIVER PLATE

Horacio Quiroga
(1878–1937)

Born in the river town of Salto, the Uruguayan Horacio Quiroga seemed to be haunted by death from the very beginning. His father died in a hunting accident when he was barely a few months old. The family moved to Cordoba, Argentina, and then, four years later, back to Uruguay, when his mother remarried. His stepfather, struck by incurable paralysis, committed suicide.

In 1900, already published pseudonymously in various literary journals, the twenty-two-year-old Quiroga left for Paris, where he settled in the Latin Quarter. Having squandered his money almost immediately, he spent a penurious, disillusioned four months until he was able to borrow enough to return home. Back in Montevideo, he formed a bohemian literary circle and continued publishing his stories with success until 1902, when, in March, he accidentally killed a close friend. Exonerated by the authorities, he left for Buenos Aires to live with his sister. The following year, with the author Leopoldo Lugones, he went as a photographer on an expedition to Misiones in the Argentine jungle. The trip proved to be a revelation, providing the literary landscape for his greatest fiction and a possible refuge from the urban cultural decadence he now rejected.

Over the next decade, he would try several times to settle in the region: producing cotton, charcoal, maté, orange liqueur, and various agricultural products. In 1906, back in Buenos Aires after his first failed attempt to acclimatize himself to the tropics, Quiroga was teaching Spanish in normal school when he fell in love with one of his students. Three years later, they married despite her parents' strenuous objections. They had a daughter and a son, moving to San Ignacio in the jungle, where they lived until 1916, when Quiroga's wife committed suicide.

The author spent the next ten years in Argentina, working at various consular positions and publishing his finest works, in which he masterfully explored Latin America's dark interiors of landscape and psyche. His first collection of stories in English translation appeared in 1921, as *South American Jungle Tales*. In 1927, Quiroga married his daughter's school friend, María Elena Bravo, by whom he had a second daughter before they separated. Then, as a result of a coup d'état in 1933, he soon lost his consular position, an event that—together with an unsuccessful attempt at growing oranges on his farm—brought him close to financial ruin. Through the intervention of some influential friends, however, Quiroga was reappointed as honorary consul.

He was by this time suffering from what would prove to be prostate cancer, for which he was operated on in late 1936. A few months later he committed suicide. Among the anthologies of his work available in English translation are *The Decapitated Chicken and Other Stories* and *The Exile and Other Stories*.

The Dead Man

With his machete the man had just finished clearing the fifth lane of the banana grove. Two lanes remained, but, since only chirca trees and jungle mallow were flourishing there, the task still before him was relatively minor. Consequently the man cast a satisfied glance at the brush he had cleared out and started to cross the wire fence so he could stretch out for a while in the grama grass.

But as he lowered the barbed wire to cross through, his foot slipped on a strip of bark hanging loose from the fence post, and in the same instant he dropped his machete. As he was falling, the man had a dim, distant impression that his machete was not lying flat on the ground.

Now he was stretched out on the grass, resting on his right side just the way he liked. His mouth, which had flown open, had closed again. He was as he had wanted to be, his knees doubled and his left hand over his breast. Except that behind his forearm, immediately below his belt, the handle and half the blade of his machete protruded from his shirt: the remainder was not visible.

The man tried to move his head—in vain. He peered out of the corner of his eye at the machete, still damp from the sweat of his hand. He had a mental picture of the extension and the trajectory of the machete in his belly, and coldly, mathematically, and inexorably he knew with certainty that he had reached the end of his existence.

Death. One often thinks in the course of his life that one day, after years, months, weeks, and days of preparation, he will arrive in his turn upon the threshold of death. It is mortal law, accepted and foreseen: so much so that we are in the habit of allowing ourselves to be agreeably transported by our imaginations to that moment, supreme among all moments, in which we breathe our last breath.

But between the present and that dying breath, what dreams, what reverses, what hopes and dramas we imagine for ourselves in our lives! A vigorous existence holds so much in store for us before our elimination from the human scene! Is this our consolation, the pleasure and the reason of our musings on death? Death is so distant, and so unpredictable is that life we still must live.

Still ...? Still not two seconds passed: the sun is at exactly the same altitude; the shadows have not advanced one millimeter. Abruptly, the long-term digressions have just been resolved for the man lying there; he is dying.

Dead. One might consider him dead in his comfortable position.

But the man opens his eyes and looks around. How much time has passed? What cataclysm has overtaken the world? What disturbance of nature does this horrible event connote?

He is going to die. Coldly, fatally, and unavoidably, he is going to die.

The man resists—such an unforeseen horror! And he thinks: it's a nightmare; that's what it is! What has changed? Nothing. And he looks: isn't that banana grove *his* banana grove? Doesn't he come every morning to clear it out? Who knows it as well as he? He sees the grove so perfectly, thinned out, the broad leaves bared to the sun. There are the leaves, so near, frayed by the wind. But now they are not moving. . . . It is the calm of midday; soon it will be twelve o'clock.

Through the banana trees, high up, the man on the hard ground sees the red roof of his house. To the left, a glimpse of the scrub trees and the wild cinnamon. That's all he can see, but he knows very well that behind his back is the road to the new port and that in the direction of his head, down below, the Paraná, wide as a lake, lies sleeping in the valley. Everything, everything, exactly as always: the burning sun, the vibrant air, the loneliness, the motionless banana trees, the wire fence with the tall, very thick posts that soon will have to be replaced. . . .

Dead! But is it possible? Isn't this one of many days on which he has left his house at dawn with his machete in his hand? And isn't his horse, his mare with the star on her forehead, right there just four meters away, gingerly nosing the barbed wire?

But yes! Someone is whistling. . . . He can't see because his back is to the road, but he feels the vibration of the horse's hooves on the little bridge. . . . It is the boy who goes by toward the new port every morning at 11:30. And always whistling. . . . From the bark-stripped post he can almost touch with his boot the live-thicket fence that separates the grove from the road; it is fifteen meters. He knows it perfectly well, because he himself had measured the distance when he put up the fence.

So what is happening, then? Is this or isn't it an ordinary midday like so many others in Misiones, in his bushland, on his pasture, in his cleared-out banana grove? No doubt! Short grass, and hills, silence, leaden sun . . .

Nothing, nothing has changed. Only he is different. For two minutes now his person, his living personality, has had no connection with the cleared land he himself spaded up during five consecutive months, nor with the grove, work of his hands alone. Nor with his family. He has been uprooted, brusquely, naturally, because of a slippery piece of bark and a machete in the belly. Two minutes: he is dying.

The man, very weary, lying on his right side in the grama grass, still resists admitting a phenomenon of such transcendency in the face of the normal, and monotonous, aspects of the boy who has just crossed the bridge as he does every day.

But it isn't possible that he could have slipped! The handle of his machete (it's worn down now; soon it will have to be changed for another) was grasped just right between his left hand and the barbed wire. After ten years in the woods, he knows very well how you manage a bush machete. He is only very weary from the morning's work and is resting a little as usual.

The proof? But he himself planted this grama grass that is poking between his lips in squares of land a meter apart! And that is his banana grove and that his starred mare snorting cautiously by the barbed wire! The horse sees him perfectly; he knows she doesn't dare come around the corner of the fence since he himself is lying almost at the foot of the post. The man distinguishes her very well, and he sees the dark threads of sweat on her crupper and withers. The sun is as heavy as lead, and the calm is great; not a fringe of the banana trees is moving. Every day he has seen the same things.

. . . Very weary, but he's just resting. Several minutes must have passed now. . . . And at a quarter to twelve, from up there, from his house with the red roof, his wife and two children will set out for the grove to look for him for lunch. He always hears, before anything else, the voice of his smaller son who tries to break away from his mother's hand: "Pah-pah! Pah-pah!"

Isn't that it . . . ? Of course, he hears it now! It's time. That's just what he hears, the voice of his son. . . .

What a nightmare! But, of course, it's just one of many days, ordinary as any other! Excessive light, yellowish shadows, oven-still heat that raises sweat on the motionless horse next to the forbidden banana grove.

. . . Very, very tired, but that's all. How many times, at midday like this, on his way to the house, has he crossed this clearing that was a thicket when he came, and virgin bush before that? He was always tired, slowly returning home with his machete dangling from his left hand.

But still he can move away in his mind if he wants; he can, if he wants, abandon his body for an instant and look at the ordinary everyday landscape from the flood ditch he himself built—the stiff grama grass in the field of volcanic rock, the banana grove and its red sand, the wire fence fading out of sight in the distance as it slopes downward toward the road. And, farther still, the cleared land, the work of his own hands. And at the foot of a bark-stripped post, thrown on his right side, his legs drawn up, exactly like any other day, he can see himself, a sunny little heap on the grama grass—resting, because he is very tired.

But the horse, striped with sweat, cautiously motionless at a corner of the fence, also sees the man on the ground and doesn't dare enter the banana grove, as she would like to. With the voices nearby now—"Pah-pah!"—for a long, long while, the mare turns her motionless ears toward the heap on the ground and finally, quieted, decides to pass between the post and the fallen man—who has rested now.

Translated by Margaret Sayers Peden

Julio Cortázar
(1914–1984)

The Argentine writer Julio Cortázar was actually born in Belgium of Argentine parents who, after the First World War, returned to Buenos Aires. When they divorced, Cortázar remained with his mother. He studied literature at school and in 1935 received a degree in education. He began writing poetry while teaching French at various secondary schools. Then, in 1945, he took up literary translation (works by Chesterton, Defoe, Gide, Giono, and eventually the complete prose of Poe).

During the late forties Cortázar turned to writing short stories, the genre of his finest works, and was discovered by Borges. By the early fifties, because of the political pressures of the Perón dictatorship, Cortázar had quit teaching and begun training as an interpreter, for which he won a scholarship to France. In 1951, he arrived in Paris, where he was soon working for UNESCO as a translator from English and French into Spanish. That year he also published his first collection of short stories, *Bestiary* (1951).

Over the next decade he added two more collections—*The End of the Game* (1956) and *Secret Weapons* (1959)—and a selection from these works eventually appeared in English as *Blow-up and Other Stories,* masterfully translated by the American poet Paul Blackburn. Though Cortázar had already published one novel, in 1961—an allegory of Peronism entitled *The Winners*—his international reputation came two years later with the appearance of *Hopscotch* (1963), a playfully experimental novel that took place simultaneously in Paris and Buenos Aires and was formally inspired by Borges's "The Garden of the Forking Paths."

Like the surrealists, he yearned for a radical fusion of art and life

and so was attracted to revolutionary causes. He frequented
Castro's Cuba (though his books did not), donated his French Prix
Medici for the novel *A Manual for Manuel* (1973) to the United
Chilean Front, and actively supported the Sandinistas in Nicaragua.
The same quest led him aesthetically to the dadaist-inspired, black-
humored antics of *Cronopios and Famas* (1962) and the collage-texts
of *Around the Day in Eighty Worlds* (1967).

In 1981, Cortázar was awarded French citizenship by President
François Mitterand. His other works include the novels *62: A Model
Kit* (1968) and *A Certain Lucas* (1979) and the short fiction of *All
Fires the Fire and Other Stories* (1966), *A Change of Light and Other
Stories* (1977), and *We Love Glenda So Much and Other Stories* (1981).

Axolotl

There was a time when I thought a great deal about the axolotls. I went to see them in the aquarium at the Jardin des Plantes and stayed for hours watching them, observing their immobility, their faint movements. Now I am an axolotl.

I got to them by chance one spring morning when Paris was spreading its peacock tail after a wintry Lent. I was heading down the boulevard Port-Royal, then I took Saint-Marcel and L'Hôpital and saw green among all that grey and remembered the lions. I was friend of the lions and panthers, but had never gone into the dark, humid building that was the aquarium. I left my bike against the gratings and went to look at the tulips. The lions were sad and ugly and my panther was asleep. I decided on the aquarium, looked obliquely at banal fish until, unexpectedly, I hit it off with the axolotls. I stayed watching them for an hour and left, unable to think of anything else.

In the library at Sainte-Geneviève, I consulted a dictionary and learned that axolotls are the larval stage (provided with gills) of a species of salamander of the genus Ambystoma. That they were Mexican I knew already by looking at them and their little pink Aztec faces and the placard at the top of the tank. I read that specimens of them had been found in Africa capable of living on dry land during the periods of drought, and continuing their life under water when the rainy season came. I found their Spanish name, *ajolote,* and the mention that they were edible, and that their oil was used (no longer used, it said) like cod-liver oil.

I didn't care to look up any of the specialized works, but the next day I went back to the Jardin des Plantes. I began to go every morning, morning and afternoon some days. The aquarium guard smiled perplexedly, taking my ticket. I would lean up against the iron bar in front of the tanks and set to watching them. There's nothing strange in this, because after the first minute I knew that we were linked, that something infinitely lost and distant kept pulling us together. It had been enough to detain me that first morning in front of the sheet of glass where some bubbles rose through the water. The axolotls huddled on the wretched narrow (only I can know how narrow and wretched) floor of moss and stone in the tank. There were nine specimens, and the majority pressed their heads against the glass, looking with their eyes of gold at whoever came near them. Disconcerted, almost ashamed, I felt it a lewdness to be peering at these silent and immobile figures heaped at the bottom of the tank. Mentally I isolated one, situated on the right and somewhat apart from the others, to study it better. I saw a rosy little body, translucent (I thought of those Chinese figurines of milky glass), looking like a small lizard about six inches long, ending in a fish's tail of extraordinary delicacy, the most sensitive part of our body. Along the back ran a transparent fin which joined with the tail, but what obsessed me was the feet, of the slenderest nicety, ending in tiny fingers with minutely human nails. And then I discovered its eyes, its face. Inexpressive features, with no other trait save the eyes, two orifices, like brooches, wholly of transparent gold, lacking any life but looking, letting themselves be penetrated by my look, which seemed to travel past the golden level and lose itself in a diaphanous interior mystery. A very slender black halo ringed the eye and etched it onto the pink flesh, onto the rosy stone of the head, vaguely triangular, but with curved and irregular sides which gave it a total likeness to a statuette corroded by time. The mouth was masked by the triangular plane of the face, its considerable size would be guessed only in profile; in front a delicate crevice barely slit the lifeless stone. On both sides of the head where the ears should have been, there grew three tiny sprigs red as coral, a vegetal outgrowth, the gills, I suppose. And they were the only thing quick about it; every ten or fifteen seconds the sprigs pricked up stiffly and again subsided. Once in a while a foot would barely move, I saw the diminutive toes poise mildly on the moss. It's that we don't enjoy moving a lot, and the tank is so cramped— we barely move in any direction and we're hitting one of the others with our tail or our head—difficulties arise, fights, tiredness. The time feels like it's less if we stay quietly.

It was their quietness that made me lean toward them fascinated the first time I saw the axolotls. Obscurely I seemed to understand their secret will, to abolish space and time with an indifferent immobility. I knew better later; the gill contraction, the tentative reckoning of the delicate feet on the stones, the abrupt swimming (some of them swim with a simple undulation of the body) proved to me that they were capable of escaping that mineral lethargy in which they spent whole hours. Above all else, their eyes obsessed me. In the standing tanks on either side of them, different fishes showed me the simple stupidity of their handsome eyes so similar to our own. The eyes of the axolotls spoke to me of the presence of a different life, of another way of seeing. Glueing my face to the glass (the guard would cough fussily once in a while), I tried to see better those diminutive golden points, that entrance to the infinitely slow and remote world of these rosy creatures. It was useless to tap with one finger on the glass directly in front of their faces; they never gave the least reaction. The golden eyes continued burning with their soft, terrible light; they continued looking at me from an unfathomable depth which made me dizzy.

And nevertheless they were close. I knew it before this, before being an axolotl. I learned it the day I came near them for the first time. The anthropomorphic features of a monkey reveal the reverse of what most people believe, the distance that is traveled from them to us. The absolute lack of similarity between axolotls and human beings proved to me that my recognition was valid, that I was not propping myself up with easy analogies. Only the little hands ... But an eft, the common newt, has such hands also, and we are not at all alike. I think it was the axolotls' heads, that triangular pink shape with the tiny eyes of gold. That looked and knew. That laid the claim. They were not *animals*.

It would seem easy, almost obvious, to fall into mythology. I began seeing in the axolotls a metamorphosis which did not succeed in revoking a mysterious humanity. I imagined them aware, slaves of their bodies, condemned infinitely to the silence of the abyss, to a hopeless meditation. Their blind gaze, the diminutive gold disc without expression and nonetheless terribly shining, went through me like a message: "Save us, save us." I caught myself mumbling words of advice, conveying childish hopes. They continued to look at me, immobile; from time to time the rosy branches of the gills stiffened. In that instant I felt a muted pain; perhaps they were seeing me, attracting my strength to penetrate into the impenetrable thing of their lives. They were not human beings, but I had found in no animal such a profound relation with myself. The axolotls were like witnesses of something, and at times like horrible judges. I felt ignoble in front of them; there was such a terrifying purity in those transparent eyes. They were larvas, but larva means disguise and also phantom. Behind those Aztec faces, without expression but of an implacable cruelty, what semblance was awaiting its hour?

I was afraid of them. I think that had it not been for feeling the proximity of other visitors and the guard, I would not have been bold enough to remain alone with them. "You eat them alive with your eyes, hey," the guard said, laughing; he likely thought I was a little cracked. What he didn't notice was that it was they devouring me slowly with their eyes, in a cannibalism of gold. At any distance from the aquarium, I had only to think of them, it was as though I were being affected from a distance. It got to the point that I was going every day, and at night I thought of them immobile in the darkness, slowly putting a hand out which immediately encountered another. Perhaps their eyes could see in the dead of night, and for them the day continued indefinitely. The eyes of axolotls have no lids.

I know now that there was nothing strange, that that had to occur. Leaning over in front of the tank each morning, the recognition was greater. They were suffering, every fiber of my body reached toward that stifled pain, that stiff torment at the bottom of the tank. They were lying in wait for something, a remote dominion destroyed, an age of liberty when the world had been that of the axolotls. Not possible that such a terrible expression which was attaining the overthrow of that forced blankness on their stone faces should carry any message other than one of pain, proof of that eternal sentence, of that liquid hell they were undergoing. Hopelessly, I wanted to prove to myself that my own sensibility was projecting a nonexistent consciousness upon the axolotls. They and I knew. So there was nothing strange in what happened. My face was pressed against the glass of the aquarium, my eyes were attempting once more to penetrate the mystery of those eyes of gold without iris, without pupil. I saw from very close up the face of an axolotl immobile next to the glass. No transition and no surprise, I saw my face against the glass, I saw it on the outside of the tank, I saw it on the other side of the glass. Then my face drew back and I understood.

Only one thing was strange: to go on thinking as usual, to know. To realize that was, for the first moment, like the horror of a man buried alive awakening to his fate. Outside, my face came close to the glass again, I saw my mouth, the lips compressed with the effort of understanding the axolotls. I was an axolotl and now I knew instantly that no understanding was possible. He was outside the aquarium, his thinking was a thinking outside the tank. Recognizing him, being him himself, I was an axolotl and in my world. The horror began—I learned in the same moment—of believing myself prisoner in the body of an axolotl, metamorphosed into him with my human mind intact, buried alive in an axolotl, condemned to move lucidly among unconscious creatures. But that stopped when a foot just grazed my face, when I moved just a little to one side and saw an axolotl next to me who was looking at me, and understood that he knew also, no communication possible, but very clearly. Or I was also in him, or all of us were thinking humanlike, incapable of expression, limited to the golden splendor of our eyes looking at the face of the man pressed against the aquarium.

He returned many times, but he comes less often now. Weeks pass without his showing up. I saw him yesterday, he looked at me for a long time and left briskly. It seemed to me that he was not so much interested in us any more, that he was coming out of habit. Since the only thing I do is think, I could think about him a lot. It occurs to me that at the beginning we continued to communicate, that he felt more than ever one with the mystery which was claiming him. But the bridges were broken between him and me, because what was his obsession is now an axolotl, alien to his human life. I think that at the beginning I was capable of returning to him in a certain way—ah, only in a certain way—and of keeping awake his desire to know us better. I am an axolotl for good now, and if I think like a man it's only because every axolotl thinks like a man inside his rosy stone semblance. I believe that all this succeeded in communicating something to him in those first days, when I was still he. And in this final solitude to which he no longer comes, I console myself by thinking that perhaps he is going to write a story about us, that, believing he's making up a story, he's going to write all this about axolotls.

Translated by Paul Blackburn

Armonía Somers
(1918-   )

There is little biographical information on the reclusive Armonía
Etchepare de Henestrosa, whose pen name is Armonía Somers.
Born in Uruguay, she has had a career in teaching and has written
texts on pedagogy. Part of the "generation of 1945," which included
the late critic Emir Rodríguez Monegal, Somers published her first
novel in 1950 to considerable critical acclaim. Yet her unwillingness
to cultivate publicity has resulted in a rather spotty publishing
history, and her works are often difficult to obtain.

Her fictional world is more freakish than fantastic and seems to
hover somewhere between the subconscious and the oneiric, with
the artist's hand as carefully concealed as her own identity. In the
past forty years she has published only seven works of fiction,
including *Muerte por alacrán* ("Death by Spider") in 1978, from
which the following story has been taken.

Waiting for Polidoro

Our attention was suddenly drawn to that old-fashioned funeral carriage with little black angels supporting its roof, the type drawn by horses, to judge by the shafts. It looked like its butt had got stuck in that deep ditch bordering a large grove of apple trees. And this, at least for the Bergman fans (the dangerously cultivated of our group), distanced us a little from that other image, on a sidewalk and near a streetlamp, which will never be erased from our eyes.

We stopped to look at it more carefully. The angels had birds' nests installed between the palms of their hands and the roof. A heretic baker bird had taken advantage of a corner of the cross as a foundation for his nest. And to measure time better, the branch of an apple tree, entering one side and coming out the other, made the wagon reminiscent of a Chinese print. The man, who had been following us on horseback since the railroad station as a special favor of Don Gallardo, came up to our car to explain the actual fact of the matter: "It's waiting for Polidoro. For almost ten years now the old geezer has been pretending to be absent-minded."

We started going again. The apple trees and sky were of a much too perfect harmony. Art would have to pursue new rules in the face of all this, but the landscape and its carriage were evidently uninterested or blind. A postcard purism was standing firm, while a certain Polidoro was postponing who knows what dangerous date in a ditch.

And one is suddenly stunned to think of what contrasts the black humor of this damned life feeds upon. For the political meeting

17

we had arrived there to attend was called off that spring day due to the sudden death, by apoplexy, of the candidate, whom we didn't even get to meet.

Floating in the innocent air of the village were bubbles of many colors, not visible to anyone, of course. Lies multiplied by other lies, which hadn't been able to be used in the words of the speeches, would somehow have to be changed with regard to energy, which never decreases, as they say. And the best they could do was this, get lost in those species of soapbubbles which were hanging exactly from the place where the change from the festive to the mortuary, or vice versa, had been brought about.

Not quite knowing in what atmosphere to enter (after all, if this guy wanted to die, let the flies eat him up, and also the greedy unions, for which they will thus prepare the way), we asked for the house of a certain Don Polidoro. And we entered into an open courtyard and from there directly into his bedroom. An old though not decrepit man looked at us without a trace of surprise from his double bed in the style of Louis XV, another pure breed who would have nothing to do with functionalism, in which one falls to the ground if one isn't careful.

"Don Polidoro?"

"At your service."

An embarrassing dialogue about his relationship to the carriage and the little angels was about to begin, when an infernal music rebounded from all the walls, furniture and cupboards in the room. Seventy clocks sounding the hour, each in a different voice. And all of a sudden, from the rear, as calm as someone long deaf, clock seventy-one serenely gave out its own retarded news.

"Compadre, beloved and faithful Compadre," the old man said, his eyes filled with sugar water.

There was nowhere to sit. The few chairs were also occupied by these monstrous prodigies, in each of which a different heart was beating, but which were all set up in unison like a planetary system.

"All right," he said, "make yourself comfortable anywhere, on the edge of the bed or on the floor. I've just heard about Don Gallardo's death, if that's what you came to tell me."

"Exactly, we came to give you a hand, and look what happened, a real misfortune . . ."

Aforesaid Gallardo mattered to us no more than that nothingness in which his soul must be floating by now. But the master of the clocks controlled time like a seated Cronus, and we had to await his decisions.

"I told him, with the Compadre I can help you. Your neck is very red, and any day now the vein is going to burst. But to no avail. The man was in a hurry, he wanted to die at the appointed minute."

We grew silent, our eyes on the clock with supernatural powers, unable to avoid a certain gust of sacred terror, as before the birth of a myth. Whereupon, and only in the face of such awe, Don Polidoro gained the confidence to tell his story, the occupants of the room serving as background.

"Twenty years ago, when I became a widower, I needed to fall in love again, damn it. But it turned out to be difficult. They all wanted more than, under the circumstances, one is capable of. And it was during one of those humiliating days that it occurred to me: buy clocks. At sales, at homes where somebody was dying or where their taste had changed, and at stores going bankrupt. That way I would have company, and they required no more than the chain and some other kind of mechanism. Thus I spent my nights with each one until I succeeded at something with the whole bunch, which, as I later came to know, is called synchrony, at least according to Don Gallardo ... Poor man, if only he had paid attention to me. When is the funeral?"

"Tomorrow at five."

The old man brooded as though doubting something. But he didn't pursue the fly in his mind for long.

"No," he said suddenly, "it's better not to think about it, the Compadre would have to have been at the headboard."

The metaphysical virtues of the clockwork kept us in a state of suspense. And even more so the fear that after so much respite the metallic henhouse would start its racket again. But Don Polidoro, slowly and once again in good spirits, continued:

"Until one day I found it in a garbage can. Just imagine. It was sticking half out, as if waiting for me. And then I, who always maintained restraint, nevertheless didn't feel any disgust and extricated it from among the filth. And I took it home. But when I opened the case I discovered it was empty, the wood well polished and the dial and hands perfect. Quite like me, a disaster inside, with none of what those itchy bitches were looking for when they came to bed with me, and then would hang on Don Gallardo, thickening his blood in the process."

"And then what, Don Polidoro?"

"Ah, well, I began looking for clockworks everywhere, but no luck. Until one day I went to Montevideo. And there, near the

University, on a Sunday morning, I was looking and looking, but always nothing. Then I reached a bridge, and imagine, all of a sudden I see a similar clock, almost new. I was carrying mine in a bag. I took it out and compared them. 'I'll sell it to you,' the guy said, 'and you can leave this rotten piece of junk with me and deduct it from the price. Here everything is of use, even a shoe for one foot, as there will always be some cripple in need.' 'What are you proposing?' I asked as though insulted. And, right in front of the boor's eyes, I took apart the new clock he was offering me, and then and there I put his clockwork into my old clock, leaving him the present of his own case, as empty as a recently delivered female."

For a few minutes he seemed to be dreaming. Nobody would ever know the interior trip he was taking.

"Thus *el Compadre* was born," he continued, when he felt like it again. "I gave it that name on the train ride home. But I had no luck when I arrived. He didn't want to synchronize, even by force, with the others. Of course, he was from Montevideo."

Little time was left before the hour would strike. The uproar was going to start again, so Don Polidoro would have to hurry up.

"We saw a funeral carriage in a ditch. How does it fit in with all of this?"

And suddenly, with a force stronger than that inane aviary of clocks, the old man's laughter shook the bed, as if all the village girls were tickling him at the start of his widowhood. Finally he calmed down, coughed, straightened the pillows and told us, as if it were just anything:

"The one that's waiting for me? Well, if you want to know, it's never going to catch me again, not even with a devil between its shafts. For I already died once, here in this bed, and the woman who brings me the food is my witness. And at that moment, at seven P.M., they all started ringing. And, like always, a few minutes later the Compadre . . . And then, it seems, they put a violet pleated paper gown over my robes. They even packed me into the wooden box, to take me to that place you know."

The lunacy of the man was making us suspicious. But a completely unsound mind would not be capable of maintaining the discipline of such a batallion, some of whose chains were being wound every twenty-four hours, others once a week and still others every two weeks. And that's why we waited until the end of his new asthma attack. And there, in the bend, was the Grace, nothing less than the last naked daughter of the sky over the dark earth. And

thus, with her dancing on his nose, Don Polidoro told us everything: "The hearse stopped at the Church, and they took the deceased out for the responsory. And meantime the priest is asking
the woman privately at what exact time it happened. And the
woman giving him this strange answer: 'I don't know, Father, it was
seven on all the clocks, but not yet on the one he called the Compadre.' 'But that cannot be,' the priest whispers, beginning to sprinkle holy water, 'there is only one time to die . . .' And that's when
the hearse, standing at the gate, began backing downhill, dragging
along the horse whose legs had broken. And it didn't stop until it
got to the apple trees. Nobody had the heart to pull it back out."

There, amidst the clocks, like a diorama in its best manner, we
saw the funeral carriage reappear with flowers inside and nests
outside. The old man, meanwhile, had become serious for the first
time. He was one of the few packages returned in such a sinister
state, and there was no longer anything to joke about.

"And so," he said, "I got up out of the box in the middle of the
funeral service, in that scarecrow costume they'd put me in. And
the old boy got up, shooting his mouth off like a bunch of fire-
crackers. There were only the priest and my poor humanity to
embrace each other between one *kyrie eleison* and the next, while
making fun of one another amicably, in order to reassure ourselves
we weren't living a nightmare. Because only this mixture of *kyrie
eleison* and slapping each other on the back was capable of returning to reality a dead man who hadn't died, and somebody who had
been recommending him unwillingly to heaven. And here I am.
Now I know that what happened to poor Gallardo can never happen to me. In the first place, I never accumulated as much money
on as many lies as he did. And then, as long as I remain strong
enough to wind the seventy clocks. And at last, the Compadre . . ."

And so it happened. The scandal of the clocks. And the one that
was late. And Don Polidoro's time, governed only by himself and
the grace of God.

Translated by Klaus Winkelmann

Jorge Luís Borges
(1899–1986)

Born in Buenos Aires into a family whose lineage on both sides traces back to the heroes of Argentina's independence, Jorge Luís Borges was to become the symbol of Latin American literature's coming of age and one of the most influential authors of the century. His father, Jorge Borges, was an English professor. Little "Georgie" learned English (before learning Spanish) from his paternal grandmother. At six he declared his intention to be a writer and by the following year had authored a compendium (in English) of Greek mythology. Inspired by *Don Quixote,* which he had read in English, he composed his first story at the age of eight. A year later he published a Spanish translation of Wilde's *The Happy Prince,* which critics mistakenly attributed to his father.

After his father's retirement due to failing eyesight, in 1914, the family moved to Europe and eventually settled in Geneva. There Borges attended a French school, taught himself German, and read some of the authors who would prove pivotal to his development as a writer. These included Whitman, who would influence his early poetry and offer a telling model for the elaboration of his own persona as a writer; and Schopenhauer, who would provide the philosophical underpinnings of his metaphysical essays on time, space, and identity. In 1919, the family moved to Spain, where Borges collaborated with the poetic avant-garde and discovered the baroque writings of Quevedo. Two years later the Borgeses returned to Argentina, where the author experienced the spiritual rediscovery of the city of his birth. Over the next decade, in succeeding books of poetry that drew upon its history and folklore, he laid the mythical foundations of his hyperbolic Buenos Aires.

These and subsequent works of poetry have been anthologized in his *Selected Poems, 1923–1967*.

In 1930, he met Adolfo Bioy Casares, with whom he would carry on a lifelong literary collaboration, jointly editing an influential series of anthologies devoted to science fiction, the fantastic, and the detective genres. They also co-authored a series of original, comic detective fictions under various pseudonyms including H. Bustos Domecq. A year later, Borges began his long association with the literary review *Sur,* founded by his friend Victoria Ocampo. Throughout the thirties, he explored and expanded the limits of the literary essay as a genre, drawing upon philosophy as "a branch of aesthetics" to prove quite paradoxically the futility of all literary (and philosophical) judgment. Some of these essays were later reworked and incorporated into his most famous collection, *Other Inquisitions, 1937–1952*.

In 1935, he published *A Universal History of Infamy,* a series of pseudo-essays (actually baroquely disguised fictions) on the lives of infamous historical figures. Then, in 1938 his father died and, to earn a living, Borges took a post as assistant librarian in a suburb of Buenos Aires. In December of that year he had a near-fatal accident that left him partially blind from septicemia. In order to test the recuperation of his mental capacities, he decided to attempt something in a different genre than he had ever practiced before and to thereby allay his worst fears of a loss of creativity. The genre he turned to was fiction, and the two collections he produced in the forties—*Ficciones* (1944) and *The Aleph* (1949)—revolutionized the meaning of the term. With their intricate doublings, false attributions, glosses on imaginary texts, and parodies of espionage novels, detective stories, and science fiction, they laid the aesthetic foundations of the modern Latin American narrative.

In 1946, in retaliation for Borges's outspoken opposition to the government of Juan Perón, his mother and sister were arrested at an antigovernmental demonstration, and the author lost his library post and was relegated to chicken inspector of the local public markets. After the fall of Perón, in 1955, he was appointed director of the National Library. With his eyesight failing, Borges turned to the brief verse of his later poetry and to short prose pieces (often relying upon his mother to record dictations until her death in 1975), of which *Dreamtigers* (1960) is the most striking compendium. In 1961, he shared with Samuel Beckett the Formentor International Publishers Prize, which confirmed his growing reputation.

Throughout the sixties and seventies, Borges traveled widely throughout the United States and Europe, giving lectures, receiving honorary degrees, and overseeing the English translation of many of his works. These include *Labyrinths: Selected Stories and Other Writings, A Personal Anthology* (1960), *The Book of Imaginary Beings* (1967), *In Praise of Darkness* (1969), *Dr. Brodie's Report* (1970), *The Gold of the Tigers: Selected Later Poems* (1972), *The Book of Sand* (1975), and a selection of lectures given in 1977 entitled *Seven Nights*. He died in Geneva.

The Circular Ruins

And if he left off dreaming about you ...
Through the Looking Glass, VI

No one saw him disembark in the unanimous night, no one saw the bamboo canoe sinking into the sacred mud, but within a few days no one was unaware that the silent man came from the South and that his home was one of the infinite villages upstream, on the violent mountainside, where the Zend tongue is not contaminated with Greek and where leprosy is infrequent. The truth is that the obscure man kissed the mud, came up the bank without pushing aside (probably without feeling) the brambles which dilacerated his flesh, and dragged himself, nauseous and bloodstained, to the circular enclosure crowned by a stone tiger or horse, which once was the color of fire and now was that of ashes. The circle was a temple, long ago devoured by fire, which the malarial jungle had profaned and whose god no longer received the homage of men. The stranger stretched out beneath the pedestal. He was awakened by the sun high above. He evidenced without astonishment that his wounds had closed; he shut his pale eyes and slept, not out of bodily weakness but out of determination of will. He knew that this temple was the place required by his invincible purpose; he knew that, downstream, the incessant trees had not managed to choke the ruins of another propitious temple, whose gods were also burned and dead; he knew that his immediate obligation was to sleep. Towards midnight he was awakened by the disconsolate cry of a bird. Prints of bare feet, some figs and a jug told him that men of the region had respectfully spied upon his sleep and were solicitous of his favor or feared his magic. He felt the chill of fear and sought out a burial niche in the dilapidated wall and covered himself with some unknown leaves.

The purpose which guided him was not impossible, though it was supernatural. He wanted to dream a man: he wanted to dream him with minute integrity and insert him into reality. This magical project had exhausted the entire content of his soul; if someone had asked him his own name or any trait of his previous life, he would not have been able to answer. The uninhabited and broken temple suited him, for it was a minimum of visible world; the nearness of the peasants also suited him, for they would see that his frugal necessities were supplied. The rice and fruit of their tribute were sufficient sustenance for his body, consecrated to the sole task of sleeping and dreaming.

At first, his dreams were chaotic; somewhat later, they were of a dialectical nature. The stranger dreamt that he was in the center of a circular amphitheater which in some way was the burned temple: clouds of silent students filled the gradins; the faces of the last ones hung many centuries away and at a cosmic height, but were entirely clear and precise. The man was lecturing to them on anatomy, cosmography, magic; the countenances listened with eagerness and strove to respond with understanding, as if they divined the importance of the examination which would redeem one of them from his state of vain appearance and interpolate him into the world of reality. The man, both in dreams and awake, considered his phantoms' replies, was not deceived by impostors, divined a growing intelligence in certain perplexities. He sought a soul which would merit participation in the universe.

After nine or ten nights, he comprehended with some bitterness that he could expect nothing of those students who passively accepted his doctrines, but that he could of those who, at times, would venture a reasonable contradiction. The former, though worthy of love and affection, could not rise to the state of individuals; the latter pre-existed somewhat more. One afternoon (now his afternoons too were tributaries of sleep, now he remained awake only for a couple of hours at dawn) he dismissed the vast illusory college forever and kept one single student. He was a silent boy, sallow, sometimes obstinate, with sharp features which reproduced those of the dreamer. He was not long disconcerted by his companions' sudden elimination; his progress, after a few special lessons, astounded his teacher. Nevertheless, catastrophe ensued. The man emerged from sleep one day as if from a viscous desert, looked at the vain light of afternoon, which at first he confused with that of dawn, and understood that he had not really dreamt. All that night and all day, the intolerable lucidity of insomnia weighed upon him. He tried to explore the jungle, to exhaust himself; amidst the hemlocks, he was scarcely able to manage a few snatches of feeble sleep, fleetingly mottled with some rudimentary visions which were useless. He tried to convoke the college and had scarcely uttered a few brief words of exhortation, when it became deformed and was extinguished. In his almost perpetual sleeplessness, his old eyes burned with tears of anger.

He comprehended that the effort to mold the incoherent and vertiginous matter dreams are made of was the most arduous task a man could undertake, though he might penetrate all the enigmas of the upper and lower orders: much more arduous than weaving a rope of sand or coining the faceless wind. He comprehended that an initial failure was inevitable. He swore he would forget the enormous hallucination which had misled him at first, and he sought another method. Before putting it into effect, he dedicated a month to replenishing the powers his delirium had wasted. He abandoned any premeditation of dreaming and, almost at once, was able to sleep for a considerable part of the day. The few times he dreamt during this period, he did not take notice of the dreams. To take up his task again, he waited until the moon's disk was perfect. Then, in the afternoon, he purified himself in the waters of the river, worshiped the planetary gods, uttered the lawful syllables of a powerful name and slept. Almost immediately, he dreamt of a beating heart.

He dreamt it as active, warm, secret, the size of a closed fist, of garnet color in the penumbra of a human body as yet without face or sex; with minute love he dreamt it, for fourteen lucid nights. Each night he perceived it with great clarity. He did not touch it, but limited himself to witnessing it, observing it, perhaps correcting it with his eyes. He perceived it, lived it, from many distances and many angles. On the fourteenth night he touched the pulmonary artery with his finger, and then the whole heart, inside and out. The examination satisfied him. Deliberately, he did not dream for a night; then he took the heart again, invoked the name of a planet and set about to envision another of the principal organs. Within a year he reached the skeleton, the eyelids. The innumerable hair was perhaps the most difficult task. He dreamt a complete man, a youth, but this youth could not rise nor did he speak nor could he open his eyes. Night after night, the man dreamt him as asleep.

In the Gnostic cosmogonies, the demiurgi knead and mold a red

Adam who cannot stand alone; as unskillful and crude and elementary as this Adam of dust was the Adam of dreams fabricated
by the magician's nights of effort. One afternoon, the man almost
destroyed his work, but then repented. (It would have been better
for him had he destroyed it.) Once he had completed his supplications to the numina of the earth and the river, he threw himself
down at the feet of the effigy which was perhaps a tiger and perhaps a horse, and implored its unknown succor. That twilight, he
dreamt of the statue. He dreamt of it as a living, tremulous thing:
it was not an atrocious mongrel of tiger and horse, but both these
vehement creatures at once and also a bull, a rose, a tempest. This
multiple god revealed to him that its earthly name was Fire, that
in the circular temple (and in others of its kind) people had rendered it sacrifices and cult and that it would magically give life to
the sleeping phantom, in such a way that all creatures except Fire
itself and the dreamer would believe him to be a man of flesh and
blood. The man was ordered by the divinity to instruct his creature
in its rites, and send him to the other broken temple whose pyramids
survived downstream, so that in this deserted edifice a voice might
give glory to the god. In the dreamer's dream, the dreamed one awoke.

The magician carried out these orders. He devoted a period of
time (which finally comprised two years) to revealing the arcana
of the universe and of the fire cult to his dream child. Inwardly, it
pained him to be separated from the boy. Under the pretext of ped-
agogical necessity, each day he prolonged the hours he dedicated to
his dreams. He also redid the right shoulder, which was perhaps de-
ficient. At times, he was troubled by the impression that all this had
happened before . . . In general, his days were happy; when he closed
his eyes, he would think: *Now I shall be with my son.* Or, less often: *The
child I have engendered awaits me and will not exist if I do not go to him.*

Gradually, he accustomed the boy to reality. Once he ordered
him to place a banner on a distant peak. The following day, the
banner flickered from the mountain top. He tried other analogous
experiments, each more daring than the last. He understood with
certain bitterness that his son was ready—and perhaps impatient—
to be born. That night he kissed him for the first time and sent
him to the other temple whose debris showed white downstream,
through many leagues of inextricable jungle and swamp. But first
(so that he would never know he was a phantom, so that he would
be thought a man like others) he instilled into him a complete
oblivion of his years of apprenticeship.

The man's victory and peace were dimmed by weariness. At dawn and at twilight, he would prostrate himself before the stone figure, imagining perhaps that his unreal child was practicing the same rites, in other circular ruins, downstream; at night, he would not dream, or would dream only as all men do. He perceived the sounds and forms of the universe with a certain colorlessness: his absent son was being nurtured with these diminutions of his soul. His life's purpose was complete; the man persisted in a kind of ecstasy. After a time, which some narrators of his story prefer to compute in years and others in lustra, he was awakened one midnight by two boatmen; he could not see their faces, but they told him of a magic man in a temple of the North who could walk upon fire and not be burned. The magician suddenly remembered the words of the god. He recalled that, of all the creatures of the world, fire was the only one that knew his son was a phantom. This recollection, at first soothing, finally tormented him. He feared his son might meditate on his abnormal privilege and discover in some way that his condition was that of a mere image. Not to be a man, to be the projection of another man's dream, what a feeling of humiliation, of vertigo! All fathers are interested in the children they have procreated (they have permitted to exist) in mere confusion or pleasure; it was natural that the magician should fear for the future of that son, created in thought, limb by limb and feature by feature, in a thousand and one secret nights.

The end of his meditations was sudden, though it was foretold in certain signs. First (after a long drought) a faraway cloud on a hill, light and rapid as a bird; then, toward the south, the sky which had the rose color of the leopard's mouth; then the smoke which corroded the metallic nights; finally, the panicky flight of the animals. For what was happening had happened many centuries ago. The ruins of the fire god's sanctuary were destroyed by fire. In a birdless dawn the magician saw the concentric blaze close round the walls. For a moment, he thought of taking refuge in the river, but then he knew that death was coming to crown his old age and absolve him of his labors. He walked into the shreds of flame. But they did not bite into his flesh, they caressed him and engulfed him without heat or combustion. With relief, with humiliation, with terror, he understood that he too was a mere appearance, dreamt by another.

Translated by James E. Irby

Juan Carlos Onetti
(1909–   )

Born in Montevideo of Uruguayan, Brazilian, and possibly Irish
background, Juan Carlos Onetti is still largely undiscovered in
English translation, although he has long been acknowledged
internationally as one of the pivotal masters of the Latin American
narrative. As a child he was a voracious reader of *Fantomas* and
Jules Verne. He never finished high school and began writing
(confessedly in a slavish imitation of his momentary idol Knut
Hamsun) while working at various menial jobs, including janitor
for a dentist and garage mechanic. From 1930 to 1934, Onetti eked
out a living in Buenos Aires by selling calculators, then writing
copy for an advertising firm, publishing an occasional story but
failing to make ends meet. In the meantime he married a cousin,
then divorced three years later to marry her sister. When he finally
returned to Montevideo, he read the Spanish version of Faulkner's
Sanctuary, which, together with Celine's *Journey to the End of Night,*
exercised a profound influence on his future writings.

In 1939, he took a job with the weekly news magazine *Marcha*
contributing prose and fiction to its literary pages, while managing
to publish a small edition of his first novel with a counterfeit
Picasso as the cover illustration. Set in an oneiric Montevideo (and
actually written in a first draft in 1931), *El pozo* ("The Pit"), with its
existentialist overtones, brought its thirty-one-year-old author
something of a cult following among the young intelligentsia of the
River Plate.

Two years later he moved back to Buenos Aires, where he would
spend the next fourteen years working as a journalist. In 1941, he
also published his second novel, *Tierra de nadie* ("No Man's Land").

Inspired by Dos Passos's *Manhattan Tranfer,* it shifted the focus of the Latin American narrative from its traditionally regionalist, provincial confines to the emerging social landscape of the modern, impersonal city—in this case the squalor and sprawl of an immigrant Buenos Aires. In three subsequent novels—*A Brief Life* (1950), *The Shipyard* (1961), and *Juntacadaveres* (1964)—Onetti would fuse the two capitals of the River Plate and the vernacular of their streets into the tough, sordid, often comic milieu of an imaginary town called Santa María. In this trilogy, as well as in the half-dozen or so works to follow, are to be found the narrative seeds that (in combination with Borges) would eventually produce authors like Cortázar and places like Macondo.

Onetti returned to Montevideo in 1954 to work for a publicity firm. There he translated Erskine Caldwell's *This Very Earth* and married Dolly, his fourth and present wife. In 1956 he traveled to Bolivia and the following year was appointed Director of Municipal Libraries in Montevideo.

In the sixties, Onetti attended writers' congresses in New York (held by the PEN Club) and in Chile, and his work began to receive proper recognition at home (Premio Nacional de Literatura, 1962) and abroad (The William Faulkner Foundation Certificate of Merit, 1963). Then, in 1974, he was suddenly arrested and imprisoned for his participation on a jury that awarded—over his own objections on aesthetic grounds—a literary prize sponsored by *Marcha* to a novel whose subject was a thinly veiled account of the sexual involvement of a member of the Uruguayan military with a revolutionary from the Tupamaru National Liberation Front. The government condemned the work as pornography, closed down the newspaper, and apprehended *Marcha*'s editor, the author of the novel, and members of the jury, including Onetti. When he was finally released, because of poor health and in response to an international protest organized by Adolfo Bioy Casares and other writers, Onetti settled in Spain with his wife, Dolly, and his sister. A selection of his stories has been published in English translation as *Goodbyes and Stories.*

The Dog Will Have Its Day

For my teacher, Enrico Cicogna

The overseer, his head bared in respect, was handing the pieces of bloody meat one by one to the man in the bowler hat and frock coat. At afternoon's end, in silence. The man in the bowler waved his arms in a circle above the kennel, and immediately there arose the dark hot wind of the four Dobermans, thin, almost skin and bone, and the blind avidity of their muzzles, their innumerable teeth.

The man in the bowler stood for a few moments watching them eat, swallow, then watched them beg for more meat.

"All right," he said to the overseer, "as I ordered. All the water they want, but no food. Today is Thursday. Let them out on Saturday at this same time, more or less—when the sun sets. And tell everyone to go to bed. Saturday I want everyone deaf even if you can hear it all the way from the peons' quarters."

"Sir," nodded the overseer.

Then the man in the bowler handed the overseer a few meat-colored bills, refusing to hear his words of thanks. He settled his gray bowler lower on his forehead and spoke as he continued to watch the dogs. The four Dobermans were kept separate by wire-mesh fences; the four Dobermans were male.

"I'll be up to the house in a half-hour or so. Have the coach ready. I'm going to Buenos Aires. Business. I don't know how long I'll be there. And don't forget. All his clothes have to be changed afterward. Burn the papers. The money is yours, and anything else you want—rings, cufflinks, watch. But don't wear anything for several months. I'll let you know when. The money is yours," he re-

32

peated."City men always have plenty of money. And his hands—
don't forget about his hands."

Then he was small and strong, dressed now in a gray embroidered shirt, a wide belt heavy with silver medallions, a dark pon-
cho, and a black necktie. The color had been imposed on him
when he was thirteen, and by now he had forgotten why or by
whom. There was a big silver knife, sometimes, for show or for
decoration, and the hat with the brim turned back. His eyes, like
his moustache, were the color of new wire, and they had the same
stiffness.

He gazed at the world without real hatred or pain, looked invariably to other men as though he were sure that life, his life,
would unfold in pleasant routine until the last. But he was lying.
Leaning on the mantelpiece, he saw the room lie: the silk-and-gilt
armchairs he had never allowed himself to sit in, the cabinets and
"curios" with their twisted, elaborate legs, their glass doors, their
shelves full of tea services, coffee services, chocolate services which
probably had never been used, the enormous birdcage with its
dreadful cacophony, the curves of the loveseat, the low fragile tables of no known purpose. The heavy wine-colored drapes shut
out the calm afternoon; all that existed was suffocating bric-a-brac.

"I'm going to Buenos Aires," the man was saying again, as he
did every Friday afternoon, in his slow, solemn, deep voice. "The
boat leaves at ten. Business, that swindle they're trying to pull on
me with those lands of yours up north."

He looked at the bonbons, the thin slices of ham, the little tri-
angles of cheese, the woman pouring tea: she was young, blond,
forever pale, quite mistaken now about her immediate future.

He looked at the six-year-old child, nervous, speechless, whiter
than its mother, always dressed by her in feminine clothes, profu-
sions of velvet and lace. He said nothing, because everything had
been said long before. The woman's repugnance, the man's growing hatred had both been born on that same extravagant wedding
night they had conceived the girl-boy that now leaned open-
mouthed against its mother's thigh, its restless fingers twirling the
thick yellow curls that fell to its neck, to its necklace of little holy
medals.

The coach was a shining black; it gleamed as though it were new-
varnished every day. It bore two great carriage-lamps which years
later would be disputed over by the wealthy of Santa María, who

would want them (with lightbulbs now, instead of candles) to grace
their front porches. The coach was drawn by a dapple-gray horse
that could have been forged of silver, or of pewter. And the coach
itself had not been made by Daglio; it had been brought from
England.

Sometimes with envy, even almost with hate, he marked the
speed, the blind youth of the animal; sometimes he imagined himself infected with its youth, its ignorance of its own future.

But once again that Friday—that Friday especially—he did not
go to Buenos Aires. He wasn't even in Santa María, in fact; because
as he came to the first houses outside Enduro he pulled the young
dapple's head to the left, and the barouche swung around, its
wheels kicking up clods as it spun down a dry-clay road that led
through fields of burned hay and past a distant, solitary tree here
and there, and that continued on toward the dirty beach which
many years later would be a resort that bore his name, with beach
houses and shops and summering people, another humble stone
in the edifice of the achievement of his ambitions.

Farther on, through enormous flatlands, the horse trotted along
a road flanked by the peaceableness of wheat fields, of seemingly
deserted farms, all timidly washed-out, bleached, immersed in the
growing heat of the afternoon.

He halted the coach in front of the largest building in the ramshackle settlement. He did not reply to the murmured words that
greeted his arrival; into the hand of the dark man who emerged
to meet him he counted out ten bills. He was paying for the animal's feed, the stable in the barn, the secret, the silence which both
men knew was a lie.

Then he walked over to a new-looking, whitewashed shack. It
was surrounded by pigweed, and a huge, straight pine planted by
no one half a century before seemed to be what was keeping it
upright.

As always, he knocked imperiously, coolly three times with the
handle of the whip at the flimsy door. Perhaps that too was an
implicit part of the ritual: the woman silent, maybe not even at
home, taking her time. The man did not knock again. He waited
there unmoving, drinking in, with his heavy breaths, this first dose
of the weekly suffering that she, Josephine, obediently and generously served him up.

Submissive, the girl opened the door; hiding the revulsion and
disgust that once had been pity, she unbuttoned her robe, let it
fall to the floor, and turned and walked naked to the bed.

One Friday long ago, uneasy because she was afraid of another man, she had looked at her little clock: she knew, then, that this ritual took two hours. He took off his coat, laid it next to the whip and the hat, and then, trembling, went on folding things across a chair. Then he walked over to her and, as always, began at the girl's feet, sobbing in a hoarse, broken voice, begging forgiveness with incomprehensible moans for some old, old sin still unpardoned, his tears and saliva wetting the girl's red toenails.

For almost three whole days the girl had him underfoot about the place, rolling cigarettes, silent, emptying with no hurry, no drunkenness the big bottles of gin, getting up to go to the bathroom or to come back, furious and docile, to the torture of the bed.

Carried by the seeds wrapped in filaments of white silk, flying on the wings of the capricious air, the news reached Santa María, reached Enduro, reached the little white house on the coast. When the man got it—the horse's caretaker stirred himself to scratch at the door and tell him the news, his eyes averted, his strangled cap in his huge dark hands—he realized that, incredibly, the naked woman imprisoned in the bed already knew it.

Standing there outside the door, his head still bowed from trying to catch the servile, less and less understandable words, the man with the wire-colored moustache, with the gleaming black barouche, with the pewter horse, with more than half the property in the settlement, spoke slowly and spoke too much:

"Fruit thieves. It's for them I've got the best dogs, the most murderous dogs there are. They don't attack. They defend." He looked an instant at the impassive sky, not smiling, not sad; he took more bills from his waist. "But I don't know anything, don't forget. I'm in Buenos Aires."

It was Sunday noon, but the man didn't leave the house until Monday morning. Now the little dappled horse was held back to a trot; it didn't need to be guided; it was trotting back home so rhythmically it had something of a wind-up animal, something of a toy about it.

"A soldier-boy," unconcernedly thought the man when he saw a bored young policeman leaning on the wall beside the great black wrought-iron gate with its ornate doubling swirls of a J overlaid with a P. The young man's uniform had once been blue; it had once belonged to a heavier, taller man.

"The first soldier-boy," the man thought almost smiling, feeling himself fill slowly with excitement, with something like the beginnings of amusement.

"Pardon, sir," said the uniformed young man, looking younger and shyer the closer the older man came, almost a boy at last. "Commissioner Medina told me to ask you to stop by the Station. I, I mean at your convenience."

"Another soldier-boy," murmured the man, his senses entangled in the steam and the smell of the horse. "But it's no fault of yours. Tell Medina that I'm home. I'll be in my house. All day. If he wants to see me."

He ticked the reins imperceptibly and the animal jubilantly drew him past the garden and the arbor out to the half-moon of dry earth and the coach house.

The men who came over to meet him and take charge of the carriage were glum yet experienced; none of them spoke of Saturday night or of Sunday morning.

Petrus didn't smile, because he had discharged his mockery years before, and perhaps forever, into the moustache the color of iron filings. He had a blurred memory of reaching fifty; he knew everything that he still had to do or try to do in that strange spot in the world not yet on any map; it was his opinion that he would never meet any obstacle more stubborn, more viscous and sticky, than the stupidity and incomprehension of other people, of all the other people he'd be obliged to come up against.

And so, that afternoon, when the suffocating heat began to soften a little under the trees, there came Medina, the Commissioner, a man timeless, heavy, and slothful, driving the first Model T Henry Ford had managed to sell in the country in 1907.

The overseer greeted him with a salute too slow and exaggerated. Medina measured him with a wry smile and spoke to him mildly.

"I expect you at the Station at seven, Petrus or no Petrus. It'll be to your advantage to come. I promise you it will not be to your advantage if you make me send somebody to get you."

The man dropped his arm and consented, nodding. He was not intimidated.

"The master said that if you came he was in the house."

Medina walked deliberately, planting his heels in the dried-out earth at each step, swaggering a little, and he went up the granite steps, too wide, too high. "A palace; this foreigner thinks he can live in a palace here. In Santa María."

All the doors were closed against the heat. Medina brushed off his hands as a kind of notice and he stepped into the large parlor with all the glass, all the fans, all the flowers. In a different suit from the morning's, and as neatly dressed as though he were about to go for an evening spin in his barouche, even wearing a hat, sitting with a cigarette in the only chair that looked able to support the weight of a man, Jeremías Petrus dropped onto the carpet the book he had been reading and raised two fingers in a kind of salute, a welcome.

"Take a seat, please, Commissioner."

"Thank you. Last time we saw each other my name was Medina."

"But today I promoted you. I already know what brought you here."

Medina looked doubtfully at the profusion of little gilt chairs.

"Any chair, any chair," Petrus insisted. "If you break it, you'll be doing me a favor. But first, what'll we drink? I'm sick of gin."

"I didn't come for a drink."

"Or to tell me no alcohol while you're on duty, either. No bottles from France have been delivered in months. Some little soldier-boy must be drinking my Moët Chandon in some cathouse some-where. But I've got some bitters—Campari—that I think would be about right for this time of day."

He rang a little bell, and the servant who had been waiting be-hind a curtain came. He was young, dark-skinned, his hair greased down on his skull. Medina knew him; he was reformatory fodder, a messenger-boy for secretive whores—and what woman isn't one?—a petty thief when the opportunity presented itself. He re-membered, looking without triumph into the boy's eyes, the classic, if now butchered, phrase, "I know you, Mirabelles." The boy looked comical in his white waiter's jacket and black bow tie. "He brought furniture, a wife, a whore, and a little horse and buggy from Eu-rope. But I guess he couldn't find an exportable servant. He had to pick one out of the garbage in Santa María."

A parade of memories had filed by—of ruined harvests, stagger-ing harvests, rises and falls in the price of cattle; they had re-minded each other of long-gone summers and winters, so worn and polished by time as to have become unreal, when the bottle showed only two glasses left of the red liquid as soft as sweet water. Neither of the two men had changed, neither showed a trace of mockery or of dominance.

"My wife and the boy went to Santa María. They may go on farther. I mean, you never know with women," Petrus said.

"I beg your pardon, I didn't ask how your wife was getting along," Medina replied.

"No matter. You aren't a doctor, anyway; you came because my dogs killed a chicken thief."

"No, don Jeremías, with respect. I came for two reasons. The corpse we carried away had been disguised. Your peons muddied his face and his hands, they dressed the body in the overseer's clothes, they stole his belongings. Rings—you could see the marks on the fingers. Wash off the mud, and you saw he'd been clean and sweet when he came; just out of the bath. They forgot the cologne, good cologne, as sweet and sissified as the cologne your own wife wears, don Jeremías. A clumsy trick, typical of these peons. But that's enough of that—I know the man's name now. It's very possible that you don't know who he was, or it's possible that you'll place him when I tell you the name or when you see—if you want to be troubled to come to the Station, of course—when you see the file. The dogs mangled his throat, his hands, half his face. But the dead man didn't come to steal your chickens. He came from Buenos Aires, and you didn't go to Buenos Aires on Friday."

A pause chewed over by both men, a shared apprehension.

Petrus smelled danger, but no fear. His peons had been stupid, clumsy, and so had he—he had trusted in them and this grotesque charade.

"Medina. Or Commissioner. I went to Buenos Aires on Friday. I go almost every Friday. I paid a lot of money so that everyone would swear to that."

"Which they did, don Jeremías. No one double-crossed you, no one cheated you out of so much as a single peso. They swore on their fear, on the Bible, on the ashes of their whoring mothers. Although not all of them were orphans. But anyway, and flattery aside, I felt like they were swearing out of some other respect, don Jeremías, something besides money."

"Thank you, " Petrus said without moving his head, a slight line of dry amusement trying to push at his moustache. "The end, story over, case closed, then. I was in Buenos Aires."

"Case closed because the dead man was inside your house, your land, your sacred private property. And because it wasn't you that murdered him. It was the dogs. And I tried, don Jeremías, but your dogs refuse to testify."

"Dobermans," Petrus nodded. "Intelligent breed. Very refined. They don't talk to police dogs."

"Hah. Maybe not out of scorn for them, though. Discretion,

maybe. Anyway—case closed. But there are some things I'd like clear. You weren't around here on Saturday night. But you weren't in Buenos Aires, either. You weren't anywhere, you weren't alive, you didn't exist from Friday to Monday. Curious. A story about a ghost, vanished. No one ever wrote that story, and nobody ever told it to me."

At that Jeremías Petrus left his chair and stood motionless, looking straight and hard at Medina's face, the useless riding-quirt dangling from his wrist.

"I have been patient," he said slowly, as though talking to himself, as though he were murmuring into the magnifying mirror he shaved at every morning. "All this bores me, it befuddles me, it makes me slow, it wastes my time. I want, I *have* to do so many things—there may not be room for them all in one man's life. Because in this work, I'm all alone ..." He broke off. He stood unmoving for a long time in the enormous parlor filled with things—objects born of and imposed by the never-defeated female sex. His voice had sounded, a little, like a prayer and a confession. Now it turned cold; he returned to everyday stupidity to ask without curiosity, without insult, "How much?"

Medina chuckled softly, making his poor hilarity fit the atmosphere of unbearable vitrines, japanned tables, fans, gilt settees, and dead butterflies under domes of crystal.

"Money? Nothing for me. If you want to pay off the mortgage, that's another thing, don Jeremías. It's the Bank's, or nobody's. I always have my cot at the Station."

"Done," Petrus said.

"As you like. In payment, I want to tell you something that will upset you maybe at first, tonight or tomorrow, say ..."

"You always hated to waste time. Me too. Maybe that's why we put up with each other for so many years. Maybe that's why I'm listening to you this minute. Say what you have to say."

"As you wish. I thought a little prologue, between two gentlemen whose hands are clean ... But as you wish. Mam'selle Josefina refused to say or listen to a single word. I beg your pardon, she did say one thing, I didn't quite catch it, just one thing, something like 'say petty car song.' I'm not sure ... She cried a little. Then she scattered a bagful of silver coins all over the bed. They're at the Station, with the file, waiting for the judge. He went to a horse race; he may stop by here on his way back."

"That's fine," Petrus said. "She was heard to say that—no matter.

The money, a little under a hundred and thirty-seven—that's no matter, either, and it's got nothing to do with the case."

"I beg your pardon again," Medina said, trying to sweeten his voice. "Less than fifty."

"I understand. There are always expenses."

"Exactly. Especially for a trip. Because Mam'selle was using the telephone in the train station. You know poor old Masiota, you know how poor old Masiota treats all the women, as long as it's not his, of course, as we all know—all you have to do is look at his left eye on Monday after the conjugal spree every Saturday night. All the women except the one he puts up with and the one that was lucky enough to find him half awake this Monday morning at the train station, when you reappeared. A coin, a smile, a kind word was all it took for him to put all the telephone lines, all the freight cars full of bags and cows waiting on the siding, all the miles of rails going who knows where, the left ones and the right ones both—put all of it at her service."

"And so?" Petrus interrupted him, lashing at his boot with the whip impatiently.

"I was taking my time getting there because I thought we were gentlemen. I apologize. I know we don't like to waste time. So: Mam'selle must have worn out our station-master's batteries. But in an hour or two she got what she'd wanted. Train, hotel, ship for Europe. I learned all this a few minutes ago. There's never a want of a drunk or some layabout on a train-station bench."

Petrus had been nibbling at the whip-handle, pensive, all desire to lash out at something now gone, as Medina, not at ease, not entirely inattentive, rubbed his thumb over the trigger of the pistol at his waist. Without prior agreement, his mouth and his thumb, both slow, drew out the pause: it was too long at last to fit this story. At last it was Petrus who spoke; his voice was slow and hoarse, the voice of a woman about to be overtaken by menopause. He was too proud to ask.

"Josephine knew his name. She knew the name of the chicken thief and I'm sure much more besides. I see no other reason for her to have gone away."

"That may be, don Jeremías," Medina said syllable by syllable, watchful of the whip's verticality. "Why *would* she have gone?"

It had been so long since Petrus had laughed that his wide-open, black mouth began first with a long mooing sound and then tapered off into the bleat of a lost calf.

"Why explain, Commissioner? Women are whores. Every one of

them. Worse than us. Mares, even better. Not even real whores. I've known a few I'd take my hat off to, I suppose. They were ladies. A long time ago. But women today are little whores, no better than that. Sad little whores."

"True, don Jeremías," Medina recoiled at the memory of Petrus's señora offering him tea and cake in that very parlor. "Almost all, anyway. Poor things, that's what they're born for. You fight to make a lumberyard. Fight against the whole world. I fight—Saturdays to go to bed drunk, sometimes to find out who the owner of the stolen sheep is. And I need time to paint. Paint the river, paint *you*."

"I bought two of your paintings," Petrus said. "Two or three."

"Yes, you did, don Jeremías, and you paid well for them. But they aren't here in the parlor. They're out in the peons' quarters. That's neither here nor there. You're right, what you were saying. They don't have an ounce of brain to be anything more than what you said they were."

The whip fell, tilted into the man's legs, then lay lengthwise on the floor. Petrus, sitting down, opened his hand:

"What do you say we have a drink, Commissioner?"

When he left, Medina saw one of the animals in the shade, out of the sun, taking a long siesta.

Translated by Andrew Hurley

Adolfo Bioy Casares
(1914–   )

The Argentine Adolfo Bioy Casares was born in Buenos Aires of wealthy parents with large holdings in the dairy industry. In his teens he published a quantity of stories and poems, including at least one book under a pseudonym—all of which he later disavowed. In the early thirties, at the behest of his mother, who wanted a suitable mentor for her gifted son, Bioy was introduced to Borges (some fifteen years his senior) by Victoria de Ocampo. Borges and he began to meet occasionally, and in 1936 they founded a short-lived literary review, *Destiempo*, whose three issues contained some still youthful contributions from Bioy.

Only four years later, however, with the publication of his first novel, *The Invention of Morel* (1940), Bioy's persuasive powers as a highly original fantasist in his own right had clearly emerged. A haunting futuristic parable of love's frustration by space and time, the novel would eventually inspire the screenplay for Alain Resnais's *Last Year at Marienbad* (1962). A month later, an anthology of fantastic literature appeared, edited by Borges, Bioy, and the poet Silvina Ocampo (Victoria's younger sister, who had married Bioy the previous summer). The anthology contained a prologue by Bioy outlining the history and the conventions of the fantastic genre, which complemented Borges's attack on the realistic and psychological novel contained in his prologue to Bioy's novel; and the two prologues together had the effect of a manifesto that would exert a powerful influence on the development of "magic realism" in the Latin American narrative.

In 1942, he and Borges published under the pseudonym of H. Bustos Domecq a parodic collection of detective stories entitled

Six Problems for Don Isidro Parodi, whose detective protagonist solves murders while sitting in his prison cell. Other Domecq titles followed, as well as an anthology of detective stories edited by them with Silvina. In 1945, Bioy published his second novel, *A Plan for Escape,* which gently parodied H. G. Wells's *The Island of Dr. Moreau,* and three years later *The Celestial Plot* (1948), a masterful collection of baroquely plotted stories that deepened his exploration of the fantastic. His and Borges's opposition to Perón during this period included collaboration on "The Monster's Celebration," a savage parody of a Perónist rally grotesquely narrated by an enthralled onlooker, which could only be circulated in manuscript at the time.

In Bioy's subsequent novels and stories, the fantastic elements are more controlled and subdued while the exploration of the complexities of love and the limits of desire gradually deepens. With *The Dream of Heroes* (1954), a man's opportunity to relive his life reverberates with echoes of the myth of Orpheus and Eurydice; while *Asleep in the Sun* (1977) reverses the theme of Beauty and the Beast. Bioy has published two other novels in English: *Diary of the War of the Pig* (1969) and *The Diary of a Photographer* (1988).

The Idol

I have just drunk a cup of coffee. I have the illusion that my mind is clear, and I feel vaguely unwell. My present state is preferable to the dangers that await me when I sleep: the figures that emerge, one from another, as if from an invisible fountain. I pause in rapt contemplation of the infinite whiteness of the Meissen porcelain. The small figures of Horus, the god of libraries, which was sent me from Cairo by my correspondent, the Coptic merchant Paphnuti, projects a definite and severe shadow on the wall. From time to time I hear the antique bronze clock, and I am aware that at three o'clock this morning the three nymphs will appear to the solemn, triple, and joyous melody. I regard the wood of the table, the leather of the chair, the fabric of my clothes, the nails on my fingers. The presence of material objects never seemed as intense to me as it does tonight. I recall enviously that a certain famous novelist used to drink tea and work on the book he was writing whenever he suffered from insomnia. My task, a more personal one, is merely to tell a story; but for me and (perhaps) for one of my readers that story may be of the utmost importance. One beginning seems as good as another; I propose this one:

My professional relationship with Martín Garmendia dates from 1929, when I furnished and decorated his apartment on Bulnes Street. Our mutual friend, Mrs. Riso, suggested me for the job and I believe I completed it satisfactorily. Since that time Mr. Garmendia has honored me with his business and, what is more significant, with his friendship.

How hard I worked in those days! Burdened with heavy lamps,

44

velvets, and figurines I traversed the five hundred yards between his apartment and my house on Alvear Avenue innumerable times. It is not presumptuous to say that the problems presented by the decoration of three or four rooms for Mr. Garmendia would have overwhelmed a less agile taste than my own. For example, there was the problem of the living room. It is a square room, and the window and doors are arranged asymmetrically. Very well, I admit it: in an anxious moment I was afraid that the table, the sofa, the rug, the book collection—like Kant's, composed exclusively of books dedicated by friends and admirers—would never fit in well together. But I must not let myself digress on artistic reminiscences. I am writing as a man now, not as an interior designer. I should merely like to point out that the objects I touch acquire a life, vigor, and perhaps a charm of their own.

A few days after I finished the work, Garmendia came to my house. I did not attend to him at once, but let him wander through the rooms to soothe his spirit with the beauty, less profuse than authentic, of my collections. Then I asked if he wished to make a complaint. He said that he did. I closed my eyes, sharpening my wits to prepare for any reproach. My friend did not speak. Finally I half opened my eyes, and saw that he was indicating a tea set of white, blue, black, and gold porcelain in a showcase. Garmendia had fallen in love with the set, and was complaining that I had never offered it to him. He asked me how much it cost and where it was from. If the first question, for a collector like Garmendia, is unimportant, the second is fundamental. I improvised a price for each piece. I looked at the mark on a cup, searched through my papers, and, not without some agitation, realized that I did not know the origin of the set at that moment. Why should I deny it? I was horrified. The situation was dangerous. In my work such ignorance can be fatal. Under the circumstances I could scarcely be blamed for assuring my friend that his tea set was from Ludwigsburg. I never had an opportunity to correct the error. Garmendia made an exhaustive study of the history of the city, the castle, the porcelain and its distinguishing characteristics; the genealogy of the dukes and kings; the sentimental biography of Fräulein von Grävenitz. For those of us who met at tea time in the dense interior of the apartment on Bulnes Street, the "Ludwigsburg" was not simply a tactile and visual delight; it was also a pretext for our host to relate his pertinent set of anecdotes.

No sooner had some of my kindly acts and time—above all, time—begun to soothe my conscience when a devilish improvisation was my undoing once again. I sold Garmendia three very rare pieces—a teapot, a creamer pitcher, and a sugar bowl—of blanc de chine. I should have described them as fraudulent Te-hua (today those imitations are as much in demand as the entirely improbable originals); I described them irrevocably as Vieux Canton. My secret debt to Garmendia, like a wound, was opened again.

And, therefore, on the last of my periodic trips to Europe in 1930, my desire to acquire objects that could interest Garmendia influenced more than one of my purchases.

The urge to provide my clientele with a continuous injection of beauty sent me to the most famous antique markets of Spain, Belgium, and Holland; then brought me to the Via del Babbuíno in Rome, and the Hotel Drouot in Paris; and led me, finally, to iso-lated places like Gulniac, in Brittany. I arrived there two weeks before the auction sale at the castle. On the advice of a friend I took a room at the pension of Madame Belardeau, a widow who always wore black and flaunted a maternal air. The only other guest was a rheumatic Englishman named Thompson who spent the whole day submerged (probably naked) in a tub of sand which had been placed, for his convenience, in the dining room.

I asked them about the people who lived in the castle. The lady assured me that the last of the Gulniacs (like the libertine in plays, who always arrives at the third act in a wheel chair) had lost his money and his health in orgies. I asked who participated in the orgies. Were they from the town? (She appeared to be insulted.) Or were they from Paris and other places? (She expressed disbe-lief.) For a moment I lost my patience.

"All right," I snapped. "I give up. If you won't talk about the people, tell me about the orgies. What were they like?"

"Diabolical."

"Aha!" I said, half closing my eyes and savoring the unfailing flight of my imagination. "Gulniac is a retired colonial official. I can guess what his atrocious sprees are like. Alone, locked in his room, he gets drunk."

"Gulniac never touches alcohol," the lady assured me. "As for your statement that he was a colonial official, that is too monstrous for words."

"Please don't be angry," I said. "But about those orgies—they must have been quite wild to make Gulniac lose his health."

"His sight, which is more important," she interrupted.

"Is he blind?"

"All the men in his family become blind before they die. It must be a hereditary affliction. There is an anonymous poem from the fifteenth century about the blindness of the Gulniacs. Would you like to hear it?"

She recited it, I wrote it down, I translated it. It not only mentioned blindness: it alluded to the cult of the dog, the frenzy of the rites of initiation, the cruelty of the priestesses (girls who were as fresh and wholesome as the country air). She abounded in anecdotes and long, irrelevant, confused digressions. Until yesterday, I remembered very little of the original; and only this one stanza of the translation:

> Perfect and cruel are your nights,
> Though stars reflect in water blue
> And Heaven's hound still watches you
> With eyes of all his proselytes.

Yesterday, in a dream, I retrieved the original; this is the French version of the stanza I quoted:

> Ah, tu ne vois pas la nuit cruelle
> Qui brille; cet invisible temple
> D'où le céleste chien te contemple
> Avec les yeux morts de ses fidèles.

From the tub Thompson remarked, "I see the old bard did not forget his Shelley, who speaks of 'Heaven's winged hound' in the *Prometheus*."

I asked if it would be possible to visit the castle.

"Visitors will not be tolerated until two or three days before the auction," said the lady.

My room faced a deep and tremulous wood; in the distance I could see the castle tower through the autumnal gold of the elms. I gazed at it, burning with the most impatient curiosity. How could I wait a week, I asked myself, when to wait even for a few minutes was such exquisite torture? And so it happened that one afternoon, after consuming a stimulating *champagne nature* at lunch, I wandered through the wood, and at length came face to face with an insignificant, rust-consumed door. I pulled the bell rope, and the remnants of my courage abandoned me. Lacking the strength to run away, I waited with stoic resignation for the dogs and the insults of the last of the Gulniacs. The door was opened instead by three charming young ladies, one of whom (the other two remained silent and appeared to be her servants) apologized for the disorderly condition of the castle and claimed for herself the honor of being my guide. She led me through halls and underground passages, cellars and towers, showing me some treasures, some beauty, much history. She gave me an animated summary of the background of each foot of architecture and each inch of orna- mentation, and finally brought the tour to a close by serving toast and hot chocolate, which she and her servants had prepared.

Needless to say, such a reception surprised me, for I had been afraid that around each corner, behind every door, the master of the house would be lurking, virulent and autocratic.

Refreshed by the nourishment, I ventured to ask, "And Monsieur Gulniac?"

"He never leaves his room," they replied.

"He is blind, I believe?"

"Yes, almost completely."

I thought that it would be indiscreet to ask for explanations.

At the auction I acquired several curios, and then regretted what I had bought and what I did not buy, as I always do.

At a really favorable price I purchased the enormous sword that Alain Barbetorte used when he killed the Saxon giant. It still in- terrupts the delicate harmony of my rooms, as it waits for an un- likely buyer. I also bought an ancient Celtic idol: a wooden statue not quite twenty inches high of an enthroned god with a dog's head. I suspect that it is a Breton version of Anubis. In the Egyp- tian form the god has a finer head, more like a jackal's. Here it was the head of a coarse watchdog.

But what caused me to select those objects? Why did I look for the documented piece, and reject the *potiche*? Why did I prefer the fallacious charm of history to the genuine charm of form? Why did I, a connoisseur, buy the St. Cyril and refuse the pitcher and washbowl I found in the untidy squalor of a servant's room? Such discoveries—the chairs from Vienna and Las Flores; the purple glass vase, shaped like a hand with a ring on one finger, from Luján; the crockery *mate* cups from Tapalqué—had contributed greatly to my prestige. I was no doubt misled by the search for authenticity, Garmendia's criterion.

What induced me to buy the idol, for example? The corrupt and odious expression I noticed on its face the very first moment I saw it? Its legend?

We followed a dark narrow corridor down to the chamber of the dog. An oblique ray of light from a side window fell directly on the god. Beneath the throne, there was a long stone couch. Behind it, nailed to the wall, were two stone tablets. Two eyes were carved on one, and a door was carved on the other. The god was completely covered with nails. My little guide told me the legends that explained it. According to the best-known legend in Gulniac— the statue is quite famous—each nail represented a soul won for the god. Another version of questionable validity, preferred by certain erudite historians, maintained that an early bishop of Brittany, alarmed by the wide diffusion of the superstition, ordered the idol's body to be covered with nails. That did not seem credible (and my charming guide was of the same opinion). For if the bishop was really sincere, why did he protect the idol with an armor of nail heads instead of simply destroying it outright? Why did he leave its vicious face uncovered? I studied it carefully. Then I understood why the statue stared with that atrocious, vacant expression: it had no eyes.

"They made it without eyes to show that it has no soul," said the girl.

At the auction I also bought a statue of St. Cyril (it had once been the property of Chateaubriand), Charette's autograph, and the manuscript of Hardouin's *Chronologie.*

When I returned to Buenos Aires I allowed Garmendia to be the first to view the things I had acquired during my journey. He was interested in the St. Cyril. I sold him the dog. Following my exact instructions, he placed it in a corner of his living room. Eureka! The dog did not look the least bit awesome by the Aubusson, by the silver candelabra, and by the glass, ebony, and damask of his showcases. What was even more extraordinary, it did not seem to be out of place.

One beautiful morning at the end of August—one of those mornings when the approach of spring is betrayed by a certain warmth in the air, a special vehemence of the verdure, an easing of respiratory congestion—I was arranging the shelf of antique maps (or was it the antique clocks?) when the ringing of the doorbell startled me. Fearing that it was some inopportune buyer, I ran to open the door. A young girl with a suitcase walked confidently into the room. Something about her—the cheap and frowzy clothing, her lean, angular body, and her long, muscular arms— reminded me of the male college student disguised as a woman in a varsity show. But my portrait of Geneviève Estermaria would be quite unfaithful if I did not add that her face was very beautiful. Her hair was black, her skin white, with rosy patches on her cheeks.

The formation of her head, the placement of her eyes, suggested a cat; there was an unexpected vigor in her thick neck; her body had no curves. She was wearing a dress that was extremely green, and long, flat shoes.

The girl looked into my eyes and smiled innocently. Then she asked me in a harsh French accent if I knew who she was. I was still thinking about the maps; I was planning a new arrangement for the Persian miniatures and weighing the advantages and risks of appropriating the screen that belonged to Coromandel, the old boarder in the backroom, and claiming it as one of my latest acquisitions from the Hotel Drouot; and so, quite frankly, the enigma she proposed did not interest me very much. Grasping my flannel cloth firmly, I began to clean the English clock of William Beckford. Geneviève modified her question—I believe she changed it to "Don't you remember me?"—then she put her valise on the floor, and handed me the clocks one by one so I could clean them. We left the shelf in perfect order. When we turned to the Persian miniatures, I learned that my exasperating helper was one of the silent servant girls I had seen during my first visit to the castle of Gulniac.

"It appears," I said with an irony that was eclipsed by my limited knowledge of French, "that you left your enviable gift of silence in Brittany."

She replied that she hoped to find a good home where she could work as a maid. She possessed only a few francs and had placed all her hopes in me.

"I don't know anyone in this country," said Geneviève Estermaria naively.

Silently, with awkward, dangerous hands, with grim determination and a candid and anxious expression, she helped me to put my rooms in order. I admit that I began to worry about her immediate destiny. Although I told myself that her plight was no concern of mine, I was not able to put it out of my mind. I was sure that if I sent her away—even though I made a pretense at the most ridiculous courtesies, such as "Come again soon!" and the like, she would burst into tears. In truth I would be abandoning her in a strange city. It did not occur to me to wonder whether the girl had had ulterior motives in arriving alone, or whether her apparent lack of guile was only a pose.

"I'll see what I can do for you," I said. She looked so disconsolate that I added (against my better judgment), "But for now go upstairs and try not to let any of my clients see you."

"Very well, sir," she replied uncomprehendingly.

"On the second floor there are many empty rooms," I continued. "Stay in one until I call you. Or if you wish," I added, revealing my weakness and my incoherence, "go down to the basement—the kitchen is there—and prepare something for lunch."

I do not recall whether I mentioned that my display occupies a *pavillon de chasse* on Alvear Avenue, a little Louis XV villa faced with imitation stone. My economy is (was) perfect. A cleaning woman—old and painted—would come each morning (she was ill the day Geneviève arrived). I am responsible to no one but myself; it occurred to me that I might have a job for Geneviève, especially if she would be willing to work for her room and board. But would she attain the standard of efficiency I naturally demand? My brief experience with her that morning had unnerved me: she did not distinguish between the size of objects that were smaller than her hand, nor could she tell the difference between the front and the back of the miniatures. With brazen assurance she found whimsical similarities between my face and the head of an amusing Venetian carving of an elephant.

But to return to my house: the kitchen, as I said before, is in the basement, where, in addition to a collection of empty boxes, I keep enough supplies to prepare simple meals in case of emergency. My display is on the first and second floors. On the latter, not far from an antiquated bathroom, there is a small storage room that I use for a bedroom. The top floor, the attic, has servants' quarters; they are vacant, provide no income, and are unfurnished. I sent the girl up to one of those comfortable but empty rooms. Imagine my surprise when I found that she was in the kitchen, when I heard her invite me to sit down at the table, when I consumed a luncheon that was superlative—not for the combination of dishes, but for each one alone, worthy of Foyot and the best years of Paillard. First, there was a memorable golden omelet, baptized with mock pomposity by my capricious *chef-maître d'hotel: omelette à la mère* something-or-other. That was followed by beans and meat with tomato sauce, onion, and pepper. I decided that the banquet should be complete, so I uncorked a *demi-bouteille* of St. Emilion Claret. After my second glass Geneviève seemed infused with a deep inner radiance. By comparison (I reflected) the young ladies of our country are drab, shallow, tiresome. By dessert—crepes suzette—Geneviève and I had become rather good friends (the way you befriend the stray dog that follows you in the street). But I still had a problem to solve: Geneviève's immediate destiny. The girl could not stay with me permanently. She was not suitable as a salesperson, but perhaps she could be my cook— But I must confess I was terrified by the thought of gaining excess weight. One week of Breton cuisine and I would have to appeal to those unpleasant masseurs known as gymnastics and hiking. And so it seemed that I had to find a way to get that girl, that veritable devil, out of my house.

To overcome my feeling of having eaten too much, I went out for a walk. I decided to visit Garmendia, and sample his candied fruits, enjoy a *chartreuse,* and smoke a cigar (his sweets and his liqueurs are on a par with his tobacco). Fortunately I met the concierge as I entered the building. Before it was too late I learned from her turbulent outburst that Garmendia was in bed with influenza. I did not go up to his apartment: I detest annoying anyone who is sick, and I always fear contagion. I also learned that the woman, in spite of her asseverations of good will, would be unable to care for Mr. Garmendia, who had a very high fever, without neglecting her regular work. The hour for great decisions had come. We could not wait for Garmendia to resolve the impasse, I said. That very afternoon I would bring a reliable young lady who would be both a nurse and a servant during his illness. If the concierge wished to tell Mr. Garmendia, she had my permission; but my decision, once made, could not be altered.

Feeling relieved, I walked back to Alvear Avenue with a lighter step. But soon afterward depression overtook me again. It would not be easy to tell Geneviève of my decision. First I would have to lay the groundwork, then wheedle and cajole.

I was turning my key in the lock when Geneviève opened the door unexpectedly. My key ring broke, scattering the keys in every direction. My annoyance gave me the courage to tell her about my plan.

"I have a sick friend," I explained in a French that was more fluent than correct. "I want a reliable person to take care of him."

When she realized what I wanted her to do, Geneviève expressed no objection, no emotion. Singing—her voice was as fresh and spontaneous as a waterfall—she went to get her things and, still singing, came down carrying her straw valise. I escorted her to my friend's apartment building and left her in the hands of the astonished concierge.

Some days later I visited my friend. At six-thirty, Geneviève entered the room adorned with trays, porcelain, and food. In her uniform—the prescribed black dress with starched white cap and apron, the excessively white gloves—she was an animated and lovely woman.

"She has become very popular in the neighborhood," declared Garmendia with mysterious pride. "Even though she knows very little Spanish, she is everyone's friend. And she can hold her own at the market. No one would dare to overcharge her—they respect her too much!"

He added that he would not say one word against Geneviève. During his illness the girl had taken care of him like a mother, and he would always be grateful.

That same afternoon Garmendia gave me his most recent published work, a small book entitled *Mates, Bombillas, Containers for Yerba Mate, Sugar Bowls, and Other Relics from the Days of Mama Inés*. With pride I showed Geneviève the copy he had inscribed to me in his own hand.

"Is that all he has written?" she asked.

"What do you mean—is that all?" I repeated sarcastically. "All that!"

I waved before her astonished eyes the fifteen copies sent by the printer.

Looking distraught, Geneviève finally removed the tea service and one of us, I don't remember whether it was Garmendia or I— remarked on how maddening it would be to fall in love with a girl like her. We were joking about the possibility when Garmendia suddenly recalled a dream he had had the night before.

"It was grotesque," he said, and I would almost swear that he blushed.

He had dreamed that he was madly in love with Geneviève and she refused him.

"I shall give you my hand on one condition," Geneviève had said. In the dream those words connoted surrender, not just the offer of her hand. As for the condition, Garmendia could not remember it.

My work—or more precisely the decoration of a *maison de plaisance* in Glew—took me away from Buenos Aires for a long week. When I returned I found Garmendia tired and nervous.

"I know it's absurd," he exclaimed, "but this woman is destroying me. I dream of her every night. I have foolish, romantic dreams that disgust me when I awake. When I sleep I love her with a chaste and intrepid passion."

"And is Geneviève chaste too?" I asked, burning with the inevitable vulgarity that lies within every man.

"Yes. Perhaps that is why the obsession persists."

"Then you will have to solve your problem during the daytime."

"I prefer to continue with my dreams," he replied solemnly. After a pause he added, "What I am going to tell you is ridiculous. Perhaps you will despise me for it. But these dreams have shattered my peace of mind."

I did not know whether I had heard the whole problem or merely an introduction.

"Perhaps," proceeded Garmendia, "if I do not see her during the daytime, I shall forget her at night. Please don't be offended— I don't mean this as a reproach, but you know about this matter, and I thought you might be able to help me."

I told him I did not understand. Without stopping, he went on, "Would you find another job for Geneviève? I must get her away from here."

Business was not going at all badly, although more than one object I had acquired on my last trip was slow to sell; and my cleaning woman, on the pretext that she had married, no longer worked for me; so I considered the possibility of hiring Geneviève in her place. When I make a decision, I act promptly without deliberation or misgivings. That same evening I went to fetch my little French girl.

I spent the weekend at the beautiful country estate of some friends at Aldo Bozzini. I returned home with a basket filled to overflowing with fresh vegetables, a trophy that the artist, the health faddist, and the perennial nature lover would have viewed with equal envy. My thoughts were of Geneviève, and of how pleased and grateful she would be to prepare those idyllic products of the soil.

But as I was about to cross the threshold of my house, I thought of Garmendia, his delicate health, his aversion to canned food— "devitaminized," as he calls it—the many favors he had done for me and, without further ado, I decided to take my basket to him.

I found him in a state of agitation that verged on anger. My gift, however, caused him to shed his animus. He spoke about his dreams—they had not ceased—and about Geneviève, with some remorse, some nostalgia. He confessed that in each dream his love became more extravagant. In one of the most recent dreams he had given Geneviève a beautiful ruby ring that once belonged to his mother.

Then he told me about the origin of the dreams.

"I was very ill," he explained. "I still had some fever, but was beginning to feel better. Geneviève came in to cheer me up. She told me that the son of the warehouse foreman had also had influenza. To celebrate his recovery, his parents had given him a little shaggy dog. Then I dozed off, and as I slept the dog underwent alarming alterations and I began to fall in love with Geneviève."

"And now?" I asked.

"Now it is horrible," he said, and covered his eyes.

"What do you plan to do?"

"If I only knew—" he said. "Perhaps you should take the dog." He was not referring to the shaggy dog of the foreman's son, but to the idol. "Geneviève's departure has not been enough."

I pondered on my friend's ideas about dreams. What he needed to do, I reflected, was to remove things from his mind, not from his house. And yet I did as he suggested. As I took the idol away, I had an insight. When I returned to Garmendia's living room, I had to admit that the absence of the dog had destroyed the magic harmony of the room. I tried all kinds of capricious arrangements of furniture and bric-a-brac, but the result was always the same: something was lacking. Then I ventured to reveal my plan.

"No more appeasement!" I said with amazing composure. "In the end this feckless policy will get you nowhere. First Geneviève; then the dog; and who knows where it will end? It would be wiser to make a complete change. You need a totally different atmosphere."

I observed Garmendia in silence. His irksome face bore traces of torpor and surprise.

Undismayed, I continued, "In these rooms, a man who has suffered an obsession is trapped like a prisoner. Why, the very atmosphere is obsessive, diabolical, nightmarish."

"What do you suggest?" he asked.

I detected the lack of interest in his tone. It was clear that Garmendia's dream had changed him. He was no longer the trusting, enthusiastic friend I had known in better days, and the change saddened me.

"What do I suggest? Nothing could be simpler. Substitute an ascetic, modern atmosphere for this rococo and *fin de siècle*—in short, sick—one. Now, I happen to have some really sedative paintings by Juan Gris, and perhaps a Braque; I have chairs and, by a stroke of luck, some screens made from designs by Man Ray; and some ceramics decorated with long poems by Tsara and Breton."

My friend looked at me impassively. One maxim I never forgot is that a salesman never gets discouraged.

"To make the change as painless as possible," I added, "I shall accept all these objects on consignment."

Once again I had occasion to congratulate myself on the flair with which I handle my affairs and persuade clients and friends to see things my way.

For Garmendia answered shortly, "As you wish."

I perceived, however, that he seemed unhappy, I might even say utterly disenchanted. The painful truth is that from that moment on, Garmendia was cool, even rude to me.

The delicacy of my reply gave me reason to be proud. "Unless you show a little more enthusiasm, I shall do nothing, absolutely nothing."

As soon as I returned home, I began to assemble the modern furniture. The next day the movers came early. *A tout seigneur, tout honneur:* the poor devils worked like animals. Before long they had removed everything from the apartment on Bulnes Street. Without stopping to rest, they quickly filled the living room with the new pieces, all wide and very comfortable. When the workmen left, the artist took over. With good taste and a hammer I had the truly herculean task of getting order out of that chaos. Scrupulous as usual, I refused to enlist Geneviève's valuable cooperation; who knows what atrocious repercussions her return might have had on Garmendia's dreams.

When I have a job to do, time means nothing to me. I spent a whole week on Bulnes Street. My friend stayed out of sight. There were some fleeting but bitter moments when I felt certain that he was angry and deliberately avoided me.

Meanwhile, Geneviève was weaving the black web of perfidy. She told me that a client, that *rara avis,* had visited my showrooms during my absence. Instead of running to Bulnes Street to find me, or at least selling him something (but since when, *s'il vous plaît,* does Mademoiselle Geneviève understand my price code?), she chatted with him and even arranged, behind my back, to work as a maid at his bachelor apartment. What an unfortunate turn of events! (She told me about it one night when I came home after a hard day's work, expecting to get some desperately needed rest.) I reproached her for her appalling conduct. She assured me that she would do whatever I ordered; she resorted to all kinds of subterfuges and evasions, and tried to change the subject by telling me that a sheepdog had been lost.

"What sheepdog?" I asked.

"The one that lives in the dark garden at the corner of Colonel Diaz Street," she replied quickly.

Alas! My worst fears were soon confirmed. I took my hat, gloves, and walking stick, and hurried to the corner she had mentioned. After peering through the fence into the empty garden, I rang the doorbell. I asked the concierge whether a dog had been lost. He said that no one in the building kept a dog.

Faced with my solitude and my anxiety, I exhausted my body but found no peace for my soul walking through the streets of the section of town that used to be known as Tierra del Fuego.

An even greater disappointment awaited me on my return home. Geneviève had gone out, leaving no explanation. Tormented by anger, depression, and despair, I could imagine her scrubbing floors in the disreputable residence of my unknown client. First I decided to wait up until she returned. It was my melancholy, very transitory, consolation to invent sarcastic innuendoes, to imagine her humiliation and her remorse when I hurled them at her. Then I knew that my complacence was only a deceptive snare that would embroil me in further torments of my own making.

The wait could be a long one, and my nerves were in no condition to stand it, so I undressed and went to bed. That night was atrocious. I should have known better than to try to sleep. I tossed and turned for hours, and finally, in the pallid early morning hours, I found oblivion as sleep engulfed me. I dreamed that I was strolling through the dark garden at the corner of Colonel Diaz Street; I was about to enter the house when I awoke. It was nine o'clock in the morning and I felt rested and refreshed. When my memory became more acute, I had the impression of scarcely having slept at all during the course of that brief dream.

My anxiety of the previous night seemed impossible to explain. I thought about it calmly, as if it were something apart from me and quite amusing; almost as if it were a sort of madness that had been completely cured. Without ascertaining whether Geneviève was at home—my indifference caused me to miss breakfast—I went to Bulnes Street with the pathetic hope of receiving payment in part or in full for the new furniture.

Garmendia received me coldly. The poor man could not conceal his feelings; he was really annoyed. There were moments when I worried about the ceramic vase inscribed with verses by André Breton, which seemed destined to come crashing against my head.

His description of the objects I had arranged in his apartment left me feeling crushed; it is almost a sacrilege to reproduce his words:

"These are the worst examples of foolishness, ineptitude, and dishonesty I have ever seen!"

He proffered other enormities, then interrupted himself, shouting melodramatically, "And, furthermore, I shall never forgive you for having taken Geneviève away from me!"

"I don't understand you," I replied honestly; and at that very moment I began to have doubts about his sanity.

"You understand me perfectly," he declared.

As if I had not heard him, I continued, "If you want the girl back, you can have her. I can't send her this afternoon because she made arrangements—without consulting me, to be sure—to work at another man's apartment. I'll speak to him about it today or tomorrow and—you have my word—there will be no difficulty whatever."

He listened to my noble and persuasive speech with lowered eyes, without encouraging me even once with words or gestures of assent. His cold and bitter reply left me stupefied.

"Allow me," he said, "allow me to say that your word means absolutely nothing."

I left my friend's house forthwith, feeling that our relationship had entered a critical, unpromising phase. Perhaps that change was due to a sudden attack of distrust and parsimony, the chronic afflictions of the rich. To conceal those despicable feelings, he had pretended to be jealous.

It rather frightens me to think about Garmendia's reaction: discarding the confidence he owed to me as a friend, he ascribed my desire to change his décor—the cause of his madness—to pecuniary motives. If I had any reason other than to dispel his obsession, it was simply to exercise my taste and artistic talent at a time when business was virtually paralyzed. But to consider my assistance as a business transaction was quite ridiculous. I have sold very few of the articles he gave me on consignment, and I have not received one cent—and probably never will—for the furnishings in his apartment.

When I came home, I found Geneviève reclining gracefully beside the Celtic idol and conversing affably with a repulsive potbellied individual. He had a long black moustache, a black suit, and black gloves. I realized at once that he was the fellow who wanted her to work for him.

In spite of my agitation I saw (I am sure of this) that the girl was wearing the beautiful ruby ring that had belonged to Garmendia's mother. I am also sure that Geneviève noticed my astonished glance.

I stammered a peremptory demand for explanations, but Geneviève, pretending not to understand, pointed vaguely in the direction of the man and then fled from the room.

With exquisite urbanity I asked him what he wished.

"Well," he said, struggling with respiratory difficulties, "I've—uh—I've come for the young lady, the French girl, who works here—or used to, anyway."

"Do you want me to call her?" I asked.

"No—it's not necessary—or, all right, if you wish," he replied. "I've let my maid go, and I just wanted to find out when this girl would be able to report for work."

I felt as if salt had been sprinkled on an open wound.

"You just wanted to know when Geneviève would be able to report for work? Very well. But there is one difficulty."

The man raised his eyebrows and thrust his enormous face and moustache forward expectantly, expressing a candor that may have been genuine, may have been false, but in any case was decidedly odious.

"Arrangements have already been made," I continued, "for the girl to work at the home of a very close friend of mine."

"Well, then," said the man, "I might as well be going. We have nothing else to discuss."

"Oh, but we do!" I said. "I haven't finished yet! Listen to me carefully: Geneviève is not leaving this house. I don't care about friends or previous arrangements, and I shall not permit anyone to speak to her behind my back."

The man opened his eyes wide, pulled his hat down over his ears, and went out puffing like an antiquated and pompous locomotive.

That little incident must have affected me. At night I dreamed of Geneviève. I would swear that I dreamed of her, although I never actually saw her in my dreams, not once. She appeared to me in symbols: she was the impassioned penumbra of the shadows and the secret meaning of all my actions. I dreamed that I entered the house at the corner of Colonel Díaz Street. But the house was very old and very vast, and I was lost in an interminable succession of drawing rooms filled with portraits and tapestries. Tremulous with relief and gratitude, I found a dark, narrow corridor. I followed it, and in the distance I perceived an oblique shaft of light.

My fear and my disgust were so vehement that they caused me to awaken.

Nothing of note happened the next day. It is true that there was one small episode that revealed Geneviève's unsuspected depths. That alone would be enough to explain my conduct, which certainly needs no justification. My duty is clear: I must see that Geneviève does not get any new victims. Once and for all I must put an end to her hereditary, blind, and stubborn depravity. That is why I shall never let her go.

When she brought my breakfast, I asked her about the ruby ring. She looked down at her hands innocently. The ring was not on her finger. Not to be intimidated by her cunning evasion, I repeated the question. First she denied the existence of any ring; then she admitted having found it in a gutter, puddle, or indefinite location on the street; she said that it was only a cheap piece of costume jewelry; and added that she had lost it at nightfall. My repeated questions were useless: they produced tears, but not confessions. Possibly she was telling the truth—a false blush and a genuine one are almost identical—to unnerve me.

Trembling I descended the staircase, opened the balcony door, and looked out. I have no recollection of having seen anything: neither the sun nor the cars not the people nor the houses nor the trees. The world had died for me. Soon afterward I found myself polishing the nails on the idol with a flannel cloth. The metal was very old, and my halfhearted efforts were to no avail. I was not able to bring out the luster of a single nail; the idol did not lose its ancient and terrifying look.

Last night, with singular candor, I slept again. Inevitably I found myself back in the dark, narrow corridor, not far from the room with the oblique shaft of light. I felt that I should stay away from that room; that I should turn back and, before it was too late, escape; but I also had the intolerable certainty that Geneviève and Garmendia were there. It seemed preferable to die than to live with that doubt, so I took a step forward. From the corridor I could see only the part of the room that was directly opposite the door; but the secret mechanics of dreams let me see what I feared. Garmendia was lying on the stone couch; the girl, wearing a thin white tunic, which in my dream denoted a priestess, was kneeling by the couch, gazing at him ecstatically. There were some nails and a hammer on the floor. With infinite slowness Geneviève took a nail, lifted the hammer, and then I covered my eyes. A moment later she was smiling and saying, "Don't worry," and, as if to reassure me, she indicated two new nails glittering on the idol's body. I felt the urge to escape. The girl recited the long poem of the Gulniacs. As I watched her intently, I experienced something like love. She called to me gaily. Then her words began to change consistency and meaning, until the change was sudden and total, like a captive fish threshing noisily on the surface of the water, when it had been swimming in the quiet depths moments before. That was what woke me: Geneviève, standing by my bed, was repeating some words in a ritualistic fashion and staring at me.

"Garmendia's concierge wishes to see you," she was saying. "Shall I have her come in?"

"Certainly not!" I replied indignantly. "How can I see her now?"

The dream must have impressed me, for I changed my mind immediately.

"Very well," I said. "Show her in, show her in."

I hastily reached for the brilliantine on my night table and restored my unruly hair to a semblance of order.

The woman, escorted by Geneviève, entered my bedroom. I could see that she was willing, even determined, to burst into tears.

"What is the matter now?" I asked with resignation.

"You must come at once," she replied.

"What is the matter?" I insisted.

"Mr. Garmendia is ill, very ill," she screamed, on the verge of hysteria.

"Go back and stay with him," I said. "I'll be right over."

I had a prefiguring of an imminent eruption of words, tears, hiccups. I motioned to Geneviève to show the concierge out.

The woman was waiting at the door when I arrived at Bulnes Street. She clasped her hands, shook her head, and tried to speak.

"Upstairs!" I said briskly. "Come on!"

We went up. The woman opened the door. I stood on the threshold. The apartment appeared to be in total darkness.

"Garmendia," I said. "Garmendia!"

There was no reply. After a brief hesitation I decided to enter the room. I took a step, and shouted, "Garmendia!"

My friend's voice, as if a mortal indifference had drained it of all feeling, spoke softly: "What do you want?"

"Why are you in the dark?" I asked, relieved that he had spoken at last.

I opened the windows.

Garmendia was sitting on a metal chair in that almost abstract gray, white, and yellow room. For some mysterious reason I felt sorry for him.

I held out my hand to touch his shoulder, but something—his strange immobility, the fixity of his glance, which never wavered from an imaginary object in the air—deterred me.

"What is the matter?"

"What difference does it make to you?" he replied. "You have stolen Geneviève. Geneviève has stolen my soul."

"No one has stolen anything," I objected vigorously. "Anyway, this is no time for speeches."

"I am not making speeches," he said. "I am blind."

I waved my hand in front of his eyes. He closed them.

"If you think you're blind," I remarked, "you're crazy!"

Those words, spoken with spontaneous vulgarity, were the last I ever uttered in the presence of my friend. In my attempt at humor I had stumbled onto the exact and atrocious diagnosis. Garmendia was not blind: he thought he was blind because he had gone mad.

I gave some vague instructions to the concierge and, feeling apprehensive, went home. I got through the morning as well as I could. I dusted and arranged showcases, put the rooms in order (removing a desk here, adding a chair there)—mechanical work, more appropriate for a robot than for an artistic man like myself. I ate lunch and then went to my study to smoke the last cigar Garmendia had given me. While I contemplated the melancholy smoke rings, I recalled my dream of the previous night and I had a sudden insight. As if I were obeying a will that was no longer my own, I stood up, I walked. Like a person in a faint who glimpses a light and then begins to regain consciousness, I conceived a hope: the hope that I was mistaken. Terrified, I looked at the tremendous Celtic idol.

I was not mistaken. Two new nails glittered on its body.

"Geneviève! Geneviève!" I shouted.

The girl hurried into the room looking alarmed. At first her blue eyes and her virtuous braids almost convinced me of her innocence. But I overcame the temptation to forget everything that had happened, to believe in her apparent ingenuousness.

"What about these new nails?" I asked.

"I don't know anything about it," she said.

"What do you mean? *I* certainly didn't put them there!"

The expression of alarm disappeared from Geneviève's face.

"Neither did I," she said placidly. She paused, and added, "Remember, you keep the hammer and nails under lock and key!"

That was the truth. I have not yet lost my mind completely, and I do not permit incompetent hands to tamper with nails that are no longer being imported or to touch my old English hammer. At first I was naturally indignant, really angry. Then I realized that if the new nails on the dog had not been put there by Geneviève or by me, there was a difficult problem to be solved. I considered the most implausible explanations—for example, that Geneviève's ghost, the Geneviève dreamed by me and also, alas! by Garmendia, had placed those nails on the idol's body. As I considered that absurd idea, I began to feel drowsy; I leaned back in my comfort- able chair, half-closed my eyes—Then I jumped up, aware of the danger. I walked around the room, trying to stay awake. I felt that the dog was watching me with his awful eyeless face. In desperation I remembered that it was I who had brought him back from Bulnes Street. I realized that I should not make the same mistake Garmen- dia made; the mere removal of the girl and the dog from my house would not save me from them. But was there any hope that I could save myself? When I thought of what had happened to Garmendia, I believed that there was. It seemed impossible that I would have to endure this dreadful fate. But when I remembered my dreams and my inevitable progress toward the chamber of the dog, I was less certain. Until I find a way out of this situation, I thought, until I find whether there is a way out, I must not let myself sleep. That escape would be too atrocious.

I remembered the dreams and perhaps I slept. I was in the dark, narrow corridor, I walked slowly down it. When I was about to enter the chamber, I made an involuntary movement of terror (as if my whole consciousness were not completely submerged in sleep, as if I were a drowning man in a shipwreck reaching up to grasp the part of the ship that was still above water). I awoke. I found myself sitting in my easy-chair, but I did not recall having sat down. I regarded its monstrous leather arms with disgust. I stood up. Instinctively I ran to the center of the room. I felt horrified by all the objects, all the manifestations of the matter that was ambushing me and pursuing me like an infallible hunter. I discovered (or thought I discovered) that to be alive is to flee, in an ephemeral and paradoxical way, from matter; and that the fear that assailed me then was the fear of death.

I would go outside, I would go away, I would walk for many miles. Impetuously, I imagined immediate changes of location. Then I realized the futility of my plan. I would be like a bird that flew away with its cage attached to its back. It would be better simply to stay home quietly, without moving a muscle. Fatigue could be dangerous: it could cause me to sleep.

The evening has slipped by rapidly. I have not slept, but from time to time I have memories that come (I am certain) from a dream. How can I explain that recurrent phenomenon? Do I close my eyes, dream for an instant, and then awaken? But that cannot be, for I have not closed my eyes once all day. If I had, I would remember the moment of awakening; my eyelids would not feel so heavy. But, if I have not been dreaming, where did I see, only a short while ago, the corridor that descends to the chamber of the dog? Where did I see Garmendia's eyes carved on a stone tablet, and where did I see him open a door carved on another tablet beside it? Where did I see Geneviève reclining on a stone couch, calling to me? Where did I kneel down, and where did someone set a condition for me to fulfill, a condition I cannot remember now? And was I awake or dreaming when I saw the man who tried to take Geneviève away from me pacing up and down in front of my house? Was I dreaming or was I awake when I heard, from my balcony, a conversation between that man and Geneviève, at my front door? Was I awake or was I dreaming when I heard Geneviève say good-bye and call, "I'll see you tomorrow"?

If I had not begun to write, my dreams would have led me, inevitably, to depression and madness. Early this morning, when I started to write, I found salvation. There were times when I wrote with genuine pleasure. Near the end I became very drowsy—I suppose that is only too apparent. Now and then I was aroused by my nightmares, or by the bronze clock with its hourly melody and its nymphs and shepherds, or by the sound of Geneviève cleaning in the basement. As if she did not wish to go to bed before her master, she has been working all night long. I can hear her moving about beneath my room. If I did not know it was she, I would swear there was an animal down there. The agitation in the basement is almost continuous. Occasionally I manage to forget it.

Geneviève and her mysterious task do not worry me. I am not afraid. When I reach the end of this page I shall write, very carefully, very firmly, the words *The End;* then, with the relief of a man who returns to his beloved after a painful attempt at separation, I shall submit to the tender, cold, and chaste embrace of my bed, and I shall lapse into a beatific slumber. And what a rest I shall have! My ordeal has led me to the truth at last. A long series of coincidences that can be explained easily—or can be left unexplained, like life, like each one of us—suggested to me a fantastic story in which I am both the victim and the hero.

There is no such story. I shall sleep without fear. Geneviève will not make me blind. Geneviève will not steal my soul. (Is there anything more stupid than the myth of Faust?) It is possible to steal a person's soul only if he has already lost it. Mine, when I am happy, is more than adequate.

Geneviève has just interrupted me. She came into my room and, with singular solicitude, with a gentle reproach, she said that it is morning now, that I must go to bed, that I must rest, that I must sleep.

Translated by Ruth L. C. Simms

Manuel Puig
(1932–1990)

Born in Villegas, an isolated town of the pampas, the Argentine Manuel Puig escaped to the movies. As a child he spent five nights a week watching the Hollywood classics of the thirties and forties, which led to an early command of English. In 1943, a baby brother died, and three years later the young Puig was sent off to secondary school in Buenos Aires because only primary school existed in his hometown. He studied English, French, and Italian—"the languages of the cinema"—and through a school friend became acquainted with the theories of Freud. At the University of Buenos Aires, he switched from architecture to philosophy. Then, after a distasteful stint as a translator while completing his military service, he received a scholarship in 1956 to study film at the Cinecittà in Rome.

While in Italy, Puig worked on several films including *A Farewell to Arms.* He also attempted, unsuccessfully, several film scripts but found the medium too restrictive. One of these attempts—to embody the voice of one of his aunts—led to his first novel, *Betrayed by Rita Hayworth* (1968), which he finished in New York in 1965, while working as an Air France ticket agent at Idlewild.

The novel ran into problems with censorship, first in Spain, where it was a finalist for the Biblioteca Breve Prize, and then in Argentina, where Puig returned in 1967. And when he wrote a second novel, *Heartbreak Tango* (1969), in the form of a magazine serial, the magazine that had originally commissioned it suddenly turned it down. Then Gallimard publishers in France came out with a highly acclaimed French version of *Betrayed,* which motivated major publishers in Argentina to pick up both novels, and they were soon bestsellers.

In 1973, Puig returned to New York after having published *The Buenos Aires Affair,* which confirmed his reputation as a major voice in Latin American fiction. Living now in Greenwich Village, he continued work on his most controversial novel, detailing the explosive relationship between two cellmates in a Buenos Aires prison—an aging homosexual who tells the stories of his favorite films to seduce a young Marxist who wishes to use him politically. The result was the now classic *Kiss of the Spider Woman* (1976), which had an initially problematical publishing career in Europe and the United States and was banned in Argentina and, like the rest of his works, in Cuba.

In 1980, Puig moved to Rio de Janeiro, where he wrote several plays that have had successful runs abroad, including an adaptation of *Kiss.* Then in 1990, after moving with his mother to Cuernavaca, Mexico, he died suddenly of heart failure following a gallbladder operation in Mexico City. His other fictional works include the novels *Pubis Angelical* (1979), *Eternal Curse on the Reader of These Pages* (1980, written in English), *Blood of Requited Love* (1982, written in Portuguese), and *Tropical Night Falling* (1988).

Relative Humidity 95%

His eyes pry open, the edges of his eyelids sticky from dried, viscous secretions, his hand closes and the fist rubs at one eye, the other eye is open, his mouth, a taste in it turned bitter, is open so he can breathe, his nose is blocked, congested, obstructed by secretions dried to the walls of the passages, soft wetness farther inside, his throat clogged with secretions; his eyelids have not stuck together again, his eyes are open now, looking at the window and the beam of sunlight coming in between the two curtains; his eyes, wet along the eyelid, burn inside when the sunlight hits the nerve, an irritated redness in the cornea spreads. His feet are sweaty, between his toes a wettish powdery crust, the toes arch, they greasily rub at each other, his exposed fingers, cold, find cover under the warm sheet, his groin warm and moist where his fingers nestle into the thatch of pubic hair, and his hot testicles are stuck to his thighs by sweat. His right hand throws back the sheet, his right hand grasps the doorknob, his right hand rubs his head, the thin hair tousled about his bald crown, he turns on the cold-water tap, he splashes water on his eyelids inflamed from sleep, the permanent wrinkles of forty-five years, with the cold water he completely washes the sleep out of his eyes, his left hand turns on the hot-water tap, he blows his nose but there are still flecks of stiff mucosity stuck inside, they won't come unstuck, his breathing still partial through his nose, a cold current through his gut, his eyelids lower, all his eyes see is red before him, red shot with reddish brown, "I'm going to convince them if I have to strangle them to do it."

"Everything'll be fine," the white china cups, the circle of the mouth of the cup, the same circle described by the mouths of Greek amphorae sitting in display cases in museums, pictures of them in the margin of the dictionary alongside the definition of the word *amphora,* he pours the coffee into the cup, the rivers of black water from Africa, coppery-black dense water the blood of the Negroes of Africa the homeland of coffee, imported first by Marco Polo, from China, the Negro who serves coffee to the Greek sages pouring it from the amphorae the slaves carry without burning their hands, not needing to use the little square of quilted wool to hold the hot vessels just taken off the three-burnered stove, those little cooking fires of the Indians, striking at flint until they made a spark, then holding a bundle of dry strawy grass to it and the fire starting. Coffee in Europe for the first time brought by the discoverer of America Christopher Columbus, no, he brought the potato and tobacco, coffee from the East, although the first soil coffee grew in must have been African, black reddish-brown, the gleaming rivers of water thick with mud, the rivers' surface of melted steel reflecting the sun, and the blood running through the veins of Negroes dense with nourishment from the flesh of wild beasts, when the wild beasts were killed their roasted flesh making it possible for the Negro to grow like a cane shoot supported by ribs of flexible metal in its spine, their skin and viscera the color of coffee, the plant growing, yielding beans to be ground up, within themselves they hold the particles of river mud because they are planted on its banks, the swollen waters of the river carrying the bones of animals whose calcium gives life to the plants and to the beans of the coffee, the Negroes alert to the barely perceptible rustle of wild beasts as they pass, as he drinks from the white cup the coffee pours strength into his body, waking my husband's brain for his interview with the president of the National Bank of Argentina, "Nothing is lost, all is transformed ... No, seriously, it'll go all right."

"So now you've changed your mind, now you think everything's going to be all right," his legs flex, stretch, and the full weight of his body no longer rests on the kitchen chair, the muscles of his legs touching the floor are flexed, his right hand picks up the cup, his lips stick to the rim of the cup, a slow yellow-white flash shoots through part of his cerebral tissue, his eyelids lower, the tips of his optic nerve see yellow-white before them on the inside of his eyelid and behind on its jagged spurs and peaks, the area to the left that the yellowish light has just now crossed wrinkles electrically, his right hand puts sugar in the coffee, the spoon stirs the contents of the cup, up his trachea, which opens like a funnel when it reaches his throat, there suddenly comes a convulsion, his right hand goes toward the sugarbowl and returns to the cup without the spoon, in his throat a sip of coffee pushes at the bitter remains of phlegm still clinging, in the sugarbowl the spoon with little crystals of coffee-colored sugar clinging to its metal sides, "Didn't you read that article on Henry Ford last night? I asked you to read it last night."

"Be careful not to let some stupid little thing they say to you in the Bank upset you," clouds hang in the sky, the weather in Buenos Aires in the summer dominated by warm winds from the North, a whitish fog, lighter than the air, rising out of the humidity of the river, rising and being dirtied by the greasy soot from the factories sitting in a ring all around the city of Buenos Aires except in the northern section that lies on the banks of the river as wide as the sea and as dirty as a bog and as reddish-brown as the soil at the bottom of the river the same color as its surface at which there is now dissolved fully half of the mud that makes the bottom, but between the houses and the river there runs the northern railroad line, and its engines spew black smoke like the black smoke of the factories, so the capital of the Republic of Argentina lies inside a circle of dense smoke: the color black is not as dirty as the color brown in the white lather of the soap powder, a handful of not totally white powder dissolved in hot water, the more it dissolves the whiter it gets, either soap powder or tiny, tiny flakes, just the slightest tinge of gray, and suddenly the suds erupt at the bottom of the washtub as white as seaspray seen from afar, seen from up close it has sand in it and pieces of seaweed, "I don't know how tough it'll be. What I do know is that when all's said and done a 'mere employee' has a safe salary at least."

"Listen, one of these days I'm going to turn around and give it to you before I catch myself," his right hand closes in a fist, his knuckles touch the sharp-pointed corner of the cellophane wrapper of the package of cigarettes, his left hand holds the morning newspaper.

"Last night you were bitching about the light on the night table when I turned it on to read the article on Henry Ford," the bows have shot arrows straight to the mark, arrows shot from the greenish iris and the black pupil of the eye, in hearts Cupid's arrows are drunk with blood, there is a pail full of poison in which the arrows are dipped before they're shot, "The fucking thieves in this government don't have to go to any bank to ask for anything."

"With the salary you get you were going to have an apartment and a car? and summer vacations, and send your son to the University?" his left foot twined around the chair leg, he presses the tendons of his instep against the edge of one rung, he strains them against the bone THE NEW M.D.S WILL RECEIVE THE ARMBAND OF THE APOSTOLIC ORDER OF DOCTORS OF MEDICINE IN THE AUDITORIUM OF THE COLLEGE OF MEDICINE—DOCTOR EUGENIO CARREÑO DISEASES OF THE DIGESTIVE SYSTEM OFFICE HOURS MONDAY TO FRIDAY 2:00 TO 7:00 PM 1098 SARMIENTO ST. FIRST FLOOR APARTMENT H TELEPHONE 89-9076 BUENOS AIRES—CODILAC ENTERPRISES BUILD AND BE THE OWNER OF YOUR OWN HOUSE TOMORROW WITH A DOWN PAYMENT OF ONLY 3000 PESOS HOME ADMINISTRATION IN THE CENTER OF THE BOOMING NORTHERN AREA ARCHITECTS NARCISO HORACIO BARRINI AND JORGE CHASTEGUI FIRST PRIZE CITY DEVELOPMENT ARCHITECTURE 1955—ATTORNEY EMILIO PETRONI NAMED PRESIDENT OF THE NATIONAL BOARD OF MEATS—MAN OF THE CENTURY BY GEORGE W. LAYS THE LIFE OF HENRY FORD A SMILING FIGURE OF A MAN OF SHORT STATURE IS THE IMAGE THAT SPRINGS TO THE MINDS OF THE WORKERS IN THE FORD PLANT WHEN THE NAME OF THE "BOSS" IS MENTIONED THE BOSS'S CONTAGIOUS SMILE THAT GETS A SMILE OF RECOGNITION IN TURN FROM EVERYBODY FROM THE VICE PRESIDENT OF THE BOARD OF DIRECTORS TO THE NIGHT SHIFT JANITOR SWEEPING UP CIGARETTE BUTTS IN THE REC ROOM NEXT TO THE SHOP his right hand picks up the sealed pack of cigarettes, he runs his fingernail along the cellophane to open it, his right hand returns to its initial position without having split the cellophane, "What's the lazy bum waiting for, to get out of that bed!?"

"I heard him tossing and turning last night, he couldn't get to sleep, the kid's always had trouble getting to sleep, like me, like you," a stain of secretion on the sheet, the awakening of boys between five and eleven years, they open their eyes, they unstick their eyelids, butterflies lightly, slowly clap their vertical wings, which touch but don't stick together, they have no secretions, children's eyelids have to be separated, kids' eyes slightly irritated, rinse them with cold water in the morning, the clean eyes of children, at seven their parents call them, the school bell rings at eight. At five o'clock in the morning in summer, at six in winter, the grass and flowers are wet with the transparent water of dewdrops, all different sizes, no, teenagers are marked by the puberty that begins at twelve, children sleep indoors, gardens sleep outdoors and in the morning they're covered with dew, children sleeping in gardens wake up covered with nothing but dew, indoors they sleep covered with

warm covers, linen sheets and wool blankets with silk borders, a
sudden blast of air as he steps out of the bathroom full of steam,
the bedroom cold, possible drafts, the father is a little wheezy from
cigarettes, children get wheezy in drafts, "The main thing is that
you talk to the manager, be sure it's the manager, don't let yourself
get sent away by some secretary."

"What time're his classes?" his larynx feels warm for a few seconds from the puff of smoke.

"All day, practically. Last night a terrible wind came up. Didn't
you hear me when I got up to close the window?" a wide yellow
secretion the stain on the sheet, the nightmares of teenaged boys,
the eyelashes get all tangled up, stuck together by secretions from
the eye, the father is all stopped up, he smokes two packs a day, the
same secretion from the eye, from the nose, he spits to free his
throat from all the phlegm, the oysters fibrous, repulsive, green,
brown, the purple ones with streaks of coagulated blood the most
repulsive of all, the mold of the dishes that hold the stuff to do
experiments with, the experiments with penicillin, in the bigger
flasks, "Call me the minute you get out of the bank and tell me."

"Today it's going to be even hotter," he inhales the smoke, the
walls of his throat hold it in.

"Once he gets his degree life'll be a lot easier, he won't have
your troubles, for god's sake," a sheet of rolled paper in his hand,
diplomas from ancient Egypt came from papyrus, fleshy-leafed
plants along the banks of the Nile cut into thin strips still moist
with cool sap, not greasy parchment which had to come from cow-
hide or something, papyrus with the faintest shade of green almost
white along the green Nile, a bluish sort of green, the flower reflected in the blue water, the plants grow and look up at the sky
but their drooping branches look at the sky reflected in the river,
which is why it's blue, the vegetable kingdom knows no murder,
animals live by killing one another, though, the red-of-tooth-and-
claw struggle for life, the blow of the tapir's claw rips off the flesh
of the shoat, almost the same species of animal but without the
other's evil, and the fatty meat torn off is cooked, fried under the
African sun, the land of the wise men of Alexandria, a few steps
from the cool rooms of the oldest library in the world, the earth
is stained with animals' blood and fatty grease, there is nothing
purer than papyrus, an architect's degree, a diploma written on a
surface white with the slightest shimmer of green.

"If he doesn't get it, he'll be the one to put the noose around
his own neck," his jawbone goes up and down and his inflamed

eardrums pop, squeezed by the pressure of the wax protecting them.

"You're stopped up from cigarettes, not from a cold," not those lovely jars sitting on the shelves in the grocery store, bottles with labels on them, the names of what they hold written in neat letters on a silvery background—the big jars of grated coconut, as shining and iridescent as amber, jars of soft fine white sugar, of sifted flour for making a child's birthday cake—but rather bigger bottles, like small barrels made of heavy glass, half full of substances for making mold with, for the experiments by the inventor of penicillin, in that documentary, Fleming, they produce a greenish, fibrous growth of mold that fills the dish, not as fibrous on the edges, maybe, as his phlegm, but in the center, the central nucleus, the pit of the mold, it's as dense or even more so than the phlegm, the dirty handkerchiefs covered with mucosity repulsive when you wash them, at seventeen boys have all the secretions of men, "I forgot to order wine and soda when I called the grocery store."

"This early in the morning and I've already started sweating," his thumb and forefinger grind the cigarette butt into the ashtray, mash the fire out.

"Should I open the drapes so there'll be less humidity with the sun, or try to keep out the heat?" the cloud whirling at great speed is a black smear, during a bad dream a teenager still has the soul of a child and since he's asleep he can't take his eyes off the very center of that cloud which at last engulfs him, babies wet their beds, a baby's pee is water barely tinged with impurities, "You're probably going to give him your cold ... Don't pull out that dirty handkerchief in front of the bank manager, and don't wear an undershirt, the humidity makes the weather too hot for it, all the streets are wet and it hasn't even rained."

"Should I carry my umbrella?" the acid gas expelled by his stomach rises through his throat.

"I had something to tell you, but now I've forgotten ... No, forget your umbrella, there's no rain forecast," the bad dreams come once, because of indigestion, when he sleeps, they come night after night, clouds hang over him, the weather conditions of Buenos Aires in the summer are determined by warm winds from the north, "I don't think it's going to rain."

"What were you going to tell me? Try to remember," his fingernails scratch at the cellophane, the printed paper, the silvery paper of the pack of cigarettes.

"I can't remember. Did you read about the delegation they're sending to Europe to unveil the monument to San Martín? Who's paying the expenses? The small businessman, that's who, we are, because the worker and the clerk hardly pay any taxes at all, so you're paying for the trip for those lazy bums, with your hard work."

"The Bank can't just stop helping people that want to work, they have to help me," MINISTRY OF COMMERCE AND INDUSTRY—THE SEC- RETARY OF AGRICULTURAL DEVELOPMENT THROUGH HIS SPOKESMAN GENERAL-SECRETARY ISIDRO L. BALIZAN MADE PUBLIC AT A PRESS CON- FERENCE YESTERDAY A NEW PROGRAM FOR A NEW CONSUMER PRICE SCALE FOR FOOD PRODUCTS THIS INITIATIVE IS IN RESPONSE TO THE NEED FOR INTERNAL CONSUMPTION OF THESE PRODUCTS AS RAW MA- TERIALS FOR NATIONAL INDUSTRIES RATHER THAN EXPORTING THEM AS RAW MATERIALS, USING THE PROCEEDS AS A BASIS FOR INCOME TO THE NATIONAL TREASURY OR AS A SPECIES OF EXCHANGE FOR THE IMPOR- TATION OF STAPLES AND OTHER ESSENTIAL GOODS NOT CURRENTLY ON THE NATIONAL MARKET "We missed the news. When's this kid getting up?"

"I don't believe in this government," the TV news in black and white, grand rooms with high ceilings, gilded plaster moldings that reflect the thousand sparkles on the fringe of little lamps, the fac- eted drops on the great chandeliers spun entirely of crystal illu- minating the wood-paneled walls waxed to a gleam, men in dark suits, their vests framing their stiff starched radiant collars, the stiff collars too reflecting the sparkle of the lamps, and their hair slicked back with gum-arabic dissolved in water and perfume, the various brands of brilliantine, some of them more like oil while some of them solidify, the dry flaccid skin falling into a double chin and the bifocals or trifocals reveal and multiply the little round eye behind them, when the photographers' flashes light up the visual frame, the pinstripes become incandescent lines, the sparkles die in the brighter flame, the fire that touches the bifocals and trifocals and the brilliantined hair, and the stiff collars are choking the fatal word which announces the official and the prices he is about to raise, "I can't imagine what time he went to bed."

"You'd think they'd let somebody directly interested in business talk at one of those press conferences, even if it was just somebody interested in small business." WEATHER OUTLOOK FOR TODAY IN THE CAPITAL AND SURROUNDING AREAS—CLOUDY SKIES WITH A HIGH BE- TWEEN 86 AND 89 DEGREES, RELATIVE HUMIDITY 95% "You see, he's not getting up. When's his exam?"

far, old, floors, short, stretches, long, voices, far off, reach, me, touch, the room, farther, the door ajar, the kitchen, the table is set in the dining room every day, the cups, they speak to me, they yell at me, there's no horizon anymore, the house across the street, the sun high, it's late, in summer it's late anyway, eight-thirty, a theorem, fifty different theorems, seven steps, eight separate steps, segments, are divided, added, they're practically wiped out by square roots, the figure, grows as it's raised, *nth* power, the max, the greatest number, strung out infinitely into more digits, a number grows, it stretches forever, crosses the seas, comes to islands, tropical paradises, the sun strong, the water cool, the ocean green, blue, transparent all the way to the bottom, a child drowns in the mud, near the shore, the river, brown, in the mud, in one day the sun heats the water in the river, at night hot, the moon doesn't cool the river, summer makes the night hotter than the day, garbage, rubbish, tissue paper and wet aluminum foil an empty package of cigarettes sticks to a dead fish that guys out for a day's fishing throw back into the river, the fish you can't eat, a plank in the water as soft as cardboard, a sliver of wood with the point broken off

"He's gone back to sleep," the little Eskimo children in their polar-bear hoods, a perfect frame for their cool, fresh faces, their cheeks round and hot with pink baby blood, hardly any room for their little Chinese eyes.

the widest river in the world, swim across it, the Plata, in a boat, in a boat rowing, muscles red, t-shirt black, the strength of arms as they move the oar pushing the boat forward with no fear of the water, the boat sinks, I swim, another boat comes, I won't get out of its way, the man rowing gets mad, his arm up if I don't say I'm sorry, I don't apologize for swimming, the river is very wide, the widest river in the world, couldn't the guy rowing go around, it's me that's crossing the river, he's crossing it too, he doesn't apologize, he doesn't use the oar to hit me, his hand closes into an iron fist, a big choppy wave and a gust of rainy southeast wind, that boat is overturned too, the oarsman turns back to the bank, he sinks, exhausted, he drowns, in the boat he wasn't carrying any cute little thing in a bikini, she was waiting for him on the other side, nobody can see her so she lies in the sun naked, her bikini is drying in the sun, no one can see her behind the high grass

"There has to be some decent sort of person in the government, if you go to them with some sane proposal they've got to admit you're right, they can't go against the small business, that's the industry that can grow, that can grow into what they need, but you've got to have good aim, you've got to hit the decent sort of person that'll listen to you," the walls of his stomach give off a sharp, acid air that rises to the opening of his esophagus but the muscle that contracts there stops it, the hot gas after it has passed the tight half-occluded muscle of the esophagus snakes upward to the pharynx coated partly by mucous secretions, reaches his olfactory nerves which tremble at the rumble of its arrival, "Then they send some engineer to the plant, some inspector that knows less than any experienced worker there, and my son studies architecture instead of engineering so he can give his father a hand some day."

hand, arm, lathe, hands of steel, a lathe of steel lubricated, the practiced hand, worker, practical, specialized, the houses of Barcelona with their balconies shaped like leaves, cement leaves, plaster vines, the architecture, apartment house, ugly, face, terrific deal, terrific, terror, square box, the balconies in the strange style of Art Nouveau, Gaudí the Spaniard, the photographs of Art Nouveau houses, sepia and white in the magazine, the park full of the mad houses of Gaudí, ugly, a failure, the architecture

"Don't the engineers from Banco Industrial know anything? Are they totally incompetent?"

"All they're looking for is a little money under the table."

"A little or a lot?"

"If this kid gets his degree in architecture and then goes to work for some company for a measly salary, I'll kill him."

"It's the same in every profession—the guy with connections, the guy with social standing gets ahead," intelligence is a spotlight in the night, a shaft of light emerging from the very center of the gray matter into the unknown, "Last night I woke up in the middle of the night and it took me two hours to get back to sleep."

"It must have been your son that woke you up when he came in."

"I told you I didn't hear him."

"What are you getting so red about? You're lying, that's why!"

"Why should I lie to you?"

"You think I don't know when you're lying to me!"

"I have never lied to you."

"You think I'll never find out you're hiding something from me!"

"Why should I be hiding anything from you?"

"Don't take this the wrong way, but we're going to have to tie your son's hands."

"Don't talk so loud, he's sleeping, students need their sleep."

"We're going to have to tie his hands when he goes to bed at night."

the sky dark, a sharp flash of silver fire, the sky cracks in two where the bolt of lightning blazes, a bolt of lightning, my bed in the air, the floor drops, disappears, when the bed begins to fall I can't tell how far I'm going to drop, the great abyss, the precipice, the rocks and boulders hard, stained with bile and drool, below everything is dark, below there flows a thread of freezing water through a bed of empty tin cans, sharp rusty edges

"I'm going to use this meat and make a whole batch of breaded veal cutlets before it goes bad," a devil is in the inferno, a huge belly, his stilts like the legs of a heron, his face creased and wrinkled, his nose like a beak and on his head a few hairs sprouting, his bilious eyes yellow and green, they throw fat onto the fire, a repulsive devil, old, fat, smiles happily at every misery, "Don't talk like that—don't say such nasty things."

"We're going to have to tie his hands up, I'm telling you, because every night I hear the noise he makes with the sheets," on his retina a crack in the paint climbing up the wall, and his eyelids rise, to look at the ceiling, the wires to the light, the conduit that carries them, the electrical tape, the hole the threaded end goes into, into the brass lamp, the electrical tape, the conduit that carries the wires that disappear up into the ceiling, continuing on into the network of wiring covered with reinforced cement, bricks, mortar, plaster, and paint

Translated by Andrew Hurley

TWO

CHILE

Isabel Allende
(1942–   )

The Chilean Isabel Allende was actually born in Lima, Peru, where
her father was serving as a diplomat. After her parents divorced,
the three-year-old Allende was taken back to Santiago, Chile, by her
mother to live with the grandparents. It was a home filled with
books and "spirits," for even after the death of her astrologer-
grandmother, her grandfather continued to summon his wife and
speak to her as a daily presence in the house. Although Allende saw
no more of her father, as a child she spent time with his brother
Salvador Allende Gossens, the ill-fated future president of Chile,
and his three daughters.

When her mother remarried, to another Chilean diplomat, the
young Allende traveled with them to Europe and the Middle East,
returning from a posting in Lebanon when the violence there
intensified. At sixteen, she left school and after several jobs became
a journalist. She went on to work for Chilean television as a host
on talk shows and as a newscaster. At twenty, Allende married and
began to write children's tales.

The bloody military coup that resulted in the death of her uncle,
the first democratically elected Marxist president in the hemisphere,
was the confessed turning point in her life. Forced to face and,
ultimately, to flee a systematically imposed reign of terror under
the Pinochet regime, Allende emigrated with her husband and their
children to Venezuela.

Then in 1981, she received a call from her maternal grandfather
that became the catalyst for her extraordinarily successful first
novel, *The House of the Spirits*. He was approaching his one
hundredth birthday and had decided to die. It was to save his

"spirit" that she began to write to him the interminable letter of recollections that would eventually produce the magical chronicle of the Trueba family, covering three generations of domestic and political turmoil in an unnamed Latin American country. Published a year later, it became an international bestseller, the first by a Latin American woman.

Three years later, *Of Love and Shadows* (1985) appeared—a more overtly political novel addressing through a love story the horrors of the "disappeared," who were taken off by the government authorities to be secretly tortured and murdered, but whose bodies were never returned to the families of the victims. Allende's other works include the novel *Eva Luna* (1987) and *The Stories of Eva Luna* (1991).

Toad's Mouth

Times were very hard in the south. Not in the south of this country, but the south of the world, where the seasons are reversed and winter does not come at Christmastime, as it does in civilized nations, but, as in barbaric lands, in the middle of the year. Stone, sedge, and ice; endless plains that toward Tierra del Fuego break up into a rosary of islands, peaks of a snowy cordillera closing off the distant horizon, and silence that dates from the birth of time, interrupted periodically by the subterranean sigh of glaciers slipping slowly toward the sea. It is a harsh land inhabited by rough men. Since there was nothing there at the beginning of the century the English could carry away, they obtained permits to raise sheep. After a few years the animals had multiplied in such numbers that from a distance they looked like clouds trapped against the ground; they ate all the vegetation and trampled the last altars of the indigenous cultures. This was where Hermelinda earned a living with her games of fantasy.

The large headquarters of Sheepbreeders, Ltd., rose up from the sterile plain like a forgotten cake; it was surrounded by an absurd lawn and defended against the depredations of the climate by the superintendent's wife, who could not resign herself to life outside the heart of the British Empire and continued to dress for solitary dinners with her husband, a phlegmatic gentleman buried beneath his pride in obsolete traditions. The native Spanish-speaking drovers lived in the camp barracks, separated from their English *patrones* by fences of thorny shrubs and wild roses planted in a vain attempt to limit the immensity of the pampas and create for the foreigners the illusion of a gentle English countryside.

Under surveillance of the management's guards, aching with cold without so much as a bowl of hot soup for months, the workers survived in misery, as neglected as the sheep they herded. In the evening, there was always someone who would pick up the guitar and fill the air with sentimental songs. They were so impoverished for love that despite the saltpeter the cook sprinkled over their food to cool their bodily ardor and the fires of memory the drovers lay with their sheep, even with a seal if they could get to the coast and catch one. The seals had large mammae, like a nursing mother's, and if they skinned the still living, warm, palpitating seal, a love-starved man could close his eyes and imagine he was embracing a siren. Even with such obstacles, the workers enjoyed themselves more than their employers, thanks to Hermelinda's illicit games.

Hermelinda was the only young woman in all the land—aside from the English lady who crossed through the rose fence with her shotgun only when in search of hares; even then, all the men could glimpse was a bit of veiled hat amid a cloud of dust and yelping English setters. Hermelinda, in contrast, was a female they could see and count on, one with a heady mixture of blood in her veins and a hearty taste for a good time. She was in the business of solace out of pure and simple vocation; she liked almost all the men in general, and many in particular. She reigned among them like a queen bee. She loved their smell of work and desire, their harsh voices, their unshaven cheeks, their bodies, so vigorous and at the same time so pliable in her hands, their pugnacious natures and naïve hearts. She knew the illusory strength and extreme vulnerability of her clients, but she never took advantage of those weaknesses; on the contrary, she was moved by both. Her rambunctious nature was tempered by traces of maternal tenderness, and night often found her sewing patches on a shirt, stewing a chicken for some sick drover, or writing love letters for distant sweethearts. She made her fortune on a mattress stuffed with raw wool under a leaky zinc roof that moaned like lutes and oboes when the wind blew. Hermelinda's flesh was firm and her skin unblemished; she laughed with gusto and had grit to spare, far more than any terrified ewe or flayed seal could offer. In every embrace, however brief, she proved herself an enthusiastic and playful friend. Word of her firm horse-woman's legs and breasts without a trace of wear had spread across the six hundred kilometers of that wild province, and lovers traveled many miles to spend a while in her company. On Fridays, riders galloped frantically from such far reaches that as they arrived their foaming mounts dropped beneath them. The English *patrones* had outlawed the consumption of alcohol, but Hermelinda had found a way to distill a bootleg liquor that raised the spirits and ruined the liver of her guests. It also served to fuel the lamps at the hour of the entertainment. Bets began after the third round of drinks, when it was impossible for the men to focus their eyes or sharpen their wits.

Hermelinda had conceived a plan to turn a sure profit without cheating anyone. In addition to cards and dice, the men could try their hand at a number of games in which the prize was her person. The losers handed over their money to her, as did those who won, but the winners gained the right to dally briefly in her company, without pretext or preliminary—not because she was unwilling but because she lacked time to give each man special attention. The players in Blind Rooster removed their trousers but kept on their jackets, caps, and sheepskin-lined boots as protection against the antarctic cold whistling through the floorboards. Hermelinda blindfolded them and the chase began. At times they raised such a ruckus that their huffing and guffaws spread through the night beyond the roses to the ears of the impassive English couple who sat sipping a last cup of Ceylon tea before bed, pretending they heard nothing but the caprice of the wind across the pampas. The first man to lay a hand on Hermelinda blessed his good fortune as he trapped her in his arms and crowed a triumphant cock-a-doodle-doo. Swing was another of the games. Hermelinda would sit on a plank strung from the roof. Laughing before the men's hungry gazes, she would flex her legs so all could see she had nothing on beneath the yellow petticoats. The players, in an orderly line, had a single chance to possess her, and anyone who succeeded found himself clasped between the beauty's thighs, swept off his feet in a whirl of petticoats, rocked to his bone marrow, and lifted toward the sky. Very few reached the goal; most rolled to the floor amid the hoots of their companions.

A man could lose a month's pay in fifteen minutes playing the game of Toad's Mouth. Hermelinda would draw a chalk line on the floor and four steps away draw a large circle in which she lay down on her back, knees spread wide, legs golden in the light of the spirit lamps. The dark center of her body would be revealed as open as a fruit, as a merry toad's mouth, while the air in the room grew heavy and hot. The players took a position behind the chalk line and tossed their coins toward the target. Some were expert marksmen, with a hand so steady they could stop a panicked animal running at full speed by slinging two stone bolas between its legs, but Hermelinda had an evasive way of sliding her body, shifting it so that at the last instant the coin missed its mark. Those that landed inside the chalk circle belonged to her. If one chanced to enter the gate of heaven, it won for its owner a sultan's treasure: two hours alone with her behind the curtain in absolute ecstasy, seeking consolation for all past wants and dreams of the pleasures of paradise. They told, the men who had lived those two precious hours, that Hermelinda knew ancient love secrets and could lead a man to the threshold of death and bring him back transformed into a wise man.

Until the day that an Asturian named Pablo appeared, very few had won that pair of wondrous hours, although several had enjoyed similar pleasure—but for half their salary, not a few coins. By then Hermelinda had accumulated a small fortune, but the idea of retiring to a more conventional life had never occurred to her; in fact, she took great pleasure in her work and was proud of the sparks of pleasure she afforded the drovers. This Pablo was a lean man with the bones of a bird and hands of a child, whose physical appearance contradicted his tremendous tenacity. Beside the opulent and jovial Hermelinda he looked like a peevish banty rooster, but anyone who thought he could enjoy a good laugh at El Asturiano's expense was in for a disagreeable surprise. The tiny foreigner tensed like a viper at the first provocation, ready to lash out at anyone who stood in his way, but the row was always settled before it began because Hermelinda's first rule was that no one fought beneath her roof. Once his dignity had been established, Pablo relaxed. He had a determined, rather funereal, expression; he spoke very little and when he did he revealed his European origins. He had left Spain one jump ahead of the police, and he earned his daily bread running contraband through the narrow Andean passes. He was known to be a surly, pugnacious loner who ridiculed the weather, the sheep, and the English. He had no fixed home and he admitted to no loves or obligations, but he was not getting any younger and solitude was seeping into his bones. Sometimes when he awoke at dawn on the icy ground, wrapped in his black Castilian cape and with his saddle for a pillow, every inch of his body ached. The pain was not the pain of stiff muscles but an accumulation of sorrow and neglect. He was tired of living like a lone wolf, but neither was he cut out for domestication. He had come south because he had heard the rumor that at the end of the world there was a woman who could change the way the wind blew, and he wanted to see her with his own eyes. The vast distance and the risks of the road had not dampened his determination, and when finally he found Hermelinda's saloon and had her in arm's reach, he could see she was forged of the same hard metal as he, and he decided that after such a long journey life would not be worth living without her. He settled into a corner of the room to study her and calculate his possibilities.

El Asturiano had guts of steel; even after several glasses of Hermelinda's liquor his eyes were still clear. He refused to remove his clothes for St. Michael's Patrol, or Mandandirun-dirun-dan, or other contests he found frankly infantile, but toward the end of the evening, when it was time for the crowning moment—The Toad—he shook off the fumes of the alcohol and joined the chorus of men around the chalk circle. To him, Hermelinda was as beautiful and wild as a puma. He felt the stirrings of his hunter's instinct, and the undefined pain of the alienation that had tormented him during his journey turned to tingling anticipation. He saw the feet shod in low boots, the woven stockings rolled below the knee, the long bones and tense muscles of those legs of gold in the froth of full petticoats, and he knew that he would have but one opportunity to win. He took his position, planting his feet on the floor and rocking back and forth until he found the true axis of his being; he transfixed Hermelinda with a knifelike gaze, forcing her to abandon her contortionist's tricks. Or that may not have been how it was; it may be that she chose him from among the others to honor with her company. Pablo squinted, exhaled a deep breath, and after a second or two of absolute concentration, tossed his coin. Everyone watched as it formed a perfect arc and entered cleanly in the slot. A salvo of applause and envious whistles celebrated the feat. Nonchalantly, the smuggler hitched up his pants, took three steps forward, seized Hermelinda's hand and pulled her to her feet, prepared to prove in his two hours that she could not do without him. He almost dragged her from the room; the men stood around drinking and checking their watches until the period of the reward had passed, but neither Hermelinda nor the foreigner appeared. Three hours went by, four, the whole night; morning dawned and the bells rang for work, and still the door did not open.

At noon the lovers emerged. Pablo, without a glance for anyone, went outside to saddle his horse, a horse for Hermelinda, and a mule to carry their belongings. Hermelinda was wearing riding pants and jacket, and a canvas bag filled with coins was tied to her waist. There was a new expression in her eyes and a satisfied swish to her memorable rump. Solemnly, they strapped their goods onto the mule, mounted their horses, and set off. Hermelinda made a vague wave of farewell to her desolate admirers, and followed El Asturiano across the barren plains without a backward glance. She never returned.

The dismay occasioned by Hermelinda's departure was so great that to divert the workmen the management of Sheepbreeders, Ltd., installed swings, bought a target for darts and arrows, and had an enormous open-mouth ceramic toad imported from London so the drovers could refine their skill in coin tossing, but before a general indifference, those toys ended up on the superintendent's terrace, where as dusk falls the English still play with them to combat their boredom.

Translated by Margaret Sayers Peden

THREE

BRAZIL

Jorge Amado
(1912–   )

Born on a small cacao plantation in the wilds of southern Bahia,
the Brazilian novelist Jorge Amado is Latin America's most popular
and prolific author. His mother was part Indian, and his father, one
of the legendary "colonels" who tamed the backlands with the
barrel of a rifle. In the great flood of 1914, Amado's family lost
everything, and his parents spent the next three years peddling the
wooden clogs they made in the poorer neighborhoods of Ilheus, the
export capital of cacao. Then in 1917 his father started another
plantation near Sequeiro do Espinho, the disputed territory of the
violent cacao wars that ended with the decade and were later
memorialized in Amado's epic novel *The Violent Land* (1943).

At ten, the author was sent off to a Jesuit boarding school in
Salvador but, two years later, ran off to the backlands, where after
several months an uncle found him. He spent another two years at
boarding school, then at fourteen took a job as a journalist in
Salvador, while living in the popular quarter of the old city. With
the crash of 1929, Amado's father lost most of his holdings but
managed to send Jorge to preparatory school in Rio, where his class
was graduated by edict because of the revolution of 1930 (which
brought Getúlio Vargas to power). The following year the author
published his first work of fiction, an ambiguous but highly praised
novel depicting the restless intellectual uncertainty of his
generation. While attending law school in Rio, he did more writing
than studying but completed his degree. In the meantime, however,
he met and married his first wife and published his first
"proletarian" novel of social protest, *Cacao* (1933), which became a
cause célèbre when confiscated by the police. Within the year his

reputation and popularity were firmly established with publication of *Sweat* (1934), his brutal novel of tenement life in the Salvador slums. Both novels were quickly published abroad, first in Moscow and then in Buenos Aires.

In the late thirties, Amado joined the Brazilian Communist Party after having published a strikingly lyrical series of novels—*Jubiabá* (1935), *Sea of Death* (1936), and *Captains of the Sands* (1937)—set among the wharves and shantytowns of All Saints Bay. Such works, by recasting the popular cadences of the Northeastern balladeers, gave compelling voice to the Afro-Brazilian underclass and their hitherto violently repressed cultural heritage. As a result, Amado was frequently arrested and his books were banned and even burned.

In 1937, he traveled by ship to Mexico, then on to New York, where he met with left wing and communist intellectuals of the period. Four years later he went again into exile, this time to Montevideo and Buenos Aires, where he wrote an incendiary biography of the popular Brazilian revolutionary leader Luís Carlos Prestes, who had been in prison since the failed communist uprising of 1935. Late in 1942, Amado returned to Brazil to join the growing anti-Axis agitation, for which he was promptly arrested. When Vargas fell from power, in 1945, the Brazilian Communist Party was legalized and Amado won a seat in the constituent assembly, where he introduced legislation providing for freedom of religious worship in Brazil.

When the communist party was declared illegal in 1948, Amado was forced into exile with his second wife and their child. They spent two years in Paris, whereupon they were expelled from France (along with other notable Latin American intellectuals) because of the politics of the Cold War. Amado fled with his family to Czechoslovakia. Though he returned to Brazil in 1952, after receiving the Stalin Peace Prize, he remained active in the World Peace Movement he had helped to found. In 1954, he attended the Second Soviet Writers Congress in Moscow and spoke controversially in favor of a loosening of the intellectual strictures of socialist realism.

Then, in 1955, Amado broke with the party and devoted his time completely to writing. Three years later he published the internationally acclaimed *Gabriela, Clove and Cinnamon* (1958), which was quickly followed by his baroquely comic homage to the possibilities of life in the face of death, a brilliant novella entitled *The Two Deaths of Quincas Wateryell* (1959). In the sixties and seventies, he traveled extensively, wrote the whimsically erotic fantasy of *Dona Flor and Her Two Husbands* (1966), and actively opposed the post-1964 military dictatorship by refusing to submit his works to prior censorship.

In 1985, Amado published *Showdown*, a dense novel of almost mythological resonance about the founding of the town of his birth, a work many consider to be his masterpiece. Since then he has divided his time mainly between Bahia and Paris, where he was awarded the Legion of Honor. Amado's other works in translation include: *The Golden Harvest* (1944), *Home Is the Sailor* (1961), *Shepherds of the Night* (1964), *Tent of Miracles* (1969), *Tereza Batista Home from the Wars* (1972), *Tieta* (1977), *Pen Sword Camisole* (1980), and *The War of the Saints: A Tale of Sorcery* (1988).

The Miracle of the Birds

The miracle occurred on a lively market day in Piranhas, a town on the São Francisco River in the state of Alagoas, Brazil. It was witnessed by hundreds of townspeople, running the social gamut from a rich colonel named Jarde Ramalho, who had seen action against Lampião, the Bandit of the Backlands, to dirt farmers in town for the day to sell their manioc flour and fresh-picked corn. An illustrious visitor who was being fêted that day in Piranhas, the widow of our great regional novelist Graciliano Ramos, saw it too; and since Dona Heloisa Ramos is notoriously truthful, her testimony alone should be enough to prove the veracity of my tale.

The protagonist in this affair was Ubaldo Capadócio, known far and wide for his competence in the three trades of lover, minstrel, and composer of popular ballads, which were printed up in leaf-lets and pinned to a clothesline, to be sold in the marketplace. His antagonist was Captain Lindolfo Ezequiel, whose reputation for primitive courage and cruelty was a byword in the state of Alagoas, where men are undeniably men. Exactly what kind of captain he was is unclear, but everyone knew he had earned his stripes by dispatching other men to the graveyard. The two occupations for which he was famous were those of hired killer, which paid well and earned him respect, and husband to Sabô—a position requir-ing uncommon ability, energy, and constant violent threats to the masculine population. For Sabô, if truth be told, respected neither her husband's military rank nor his ugly scowl and the lethal weapon he wore. Sabô flaunted herself in front of all the men and figured in the dreams of every last one of them (including boys

94

under fourteen) whether single, married, engaged, or living with another woman. But the only person brave enough to risk arousing the captain's murderous masculine pride and an unceremonious death from the barrel of a gun was Sabô herself. All the men who were hot for her ground their teeth, tucked their tails between their legs, and turned their eyes away from Sabô the siren.

All but Ubaldo Capadócio. Not because he was reckless or brave as a lion, but out of sheer ignorance of local custom. After all, he was only a stranger passing through in search of readers and a bustling marketplace where he could sell the ballads he had composed (the latest of which, "The Story of the Society Lady Who Fell in Love With a Werewolf," was selling like hotcakes, and deserved to); a party where he could play his concertina and improvise verses; and an inviting bed where he could rest from his labors and snuggle up to a pretty brunette. Whatever his motive, the fact is that he did brave the bully, and what's more he did it in a woman's shortie nightgown; the top of Sabô's pink baby-doll pajamas, to be exact.

Ubaldo Capadócio the minstrel was a heart-breaker and a fine figure of a man: tall, lean, and nimble, with a tousled mop of hair and an easy laugh. A gifted conversationalist in any company, he knew how to season his talk with wit and learning; wherever he found himself an animated circle formed instantly around him. All through the vast back country of Bahia and Sergipe where he worked, worried, and loved, Ubaldo was loved in return and his talents were always in demand. He was showered with invitations to enliven christenings, weddings, and wakes; he had no equal when it came to toasting a bride and bridegroom, or telling stories at a wake that could make a dead man laugh or cry. And that's no idle expression. It really happened and I could round up plenty of live witnesses to prove it. I'll mention just two of them here: master artist Calasans Neto and Florisvaldo Matos, the troubadour of Sergipe. They both saw the deceased Aristóbulo Negritude burst out in a horse laugh, right where he lay dead as a doornail in his coffin, when Ubaldo Capadócio told the story of the beached whale in Maragogipe. I won't ask my friend Carybé the painter to testify because everybody knows he's a liar. The way he tells it, Negritude didn't just laugh, he added a dirty twist to the story as well. But those of us in the know say it was Carybé—no upstanding citizen— who put in the smutty details himself. Aristóbulo may have been a know-it-all but he drew the line at butting in on another man's story; he knew how a proper corpse ought to behave.

It was at shindigs that Ubaldo really shone. Concertina clasped to his breast, husky voice soaked in rum, languorous imploring eyes, fingers sliding sensuously over the keys, with his playing he charmed sighs and promises from young girls, married women, kept women, fallen women, disconsolate widows (consoling widows came naturally to a generous nature like Ubaldo's). Along with the deep sighs and ardent promises there was usually a barrage of threats and curses, but Ubaldo was no coward and just plowed right ahead.

Wanderer though he was, he had a house and home—several houses and homes—in Bahia and Sergipe. Why not, with his good looks and his reputation? So many women and Ubaldo was true to all of them, for his was a faithful, constant heart. He never broke off with a woman (except for Braulia, but Braulia, for heaven's sake ...!), never sent one away. They left of their own accord, loudly claiming they had been used and betrayed, when they found out about all the others—though how abstinence could be expected of a romantic wandering bard away from home for weeks and months at a time I don't know. These abrupt partings were never Capadócio's idea and they always made him unhappy. Whenever a woman left him he felt as if he were losing the only one in the world. However many others there might be, each one was the only one, and if that riddle baffles you then you don't know much about love. What could be the cause of such repeated ingratitude, such unreasoning selfishness, when he, Ubaldo Capadócio, could always be counted on as a breadwinner, a prop, and a mainstay to his women, with more than enough skill and imagination to satisfy them all and to spare?

Some women, in fact, didn't abandon him but took him the way he was. Which explains why, at the time of the miracle in Piranhas, Ubaldo Capadócio, at thirty-two years of age, was maintaining three families on his earnings as a popular poet, balladeer, and musician. What with his concertina and his guitar, his husky voice and his rhymes—rich rhymes or poor, it didn't matter—it was poetry that put food on the table for his three wives, none of them lawfully wedded, and nine children, three of whom were not his.

Two of the households were traditionally constituted families complete with wife and children, while the third had not yet produced any offspring. For Rosecler, the new addition, who was still in the honeymoon stage, it was too early for pregnancy and birth;

Ubaldo spent more on the rings, bracelets, necklaces, and other baubles she loved than on either of the other two; in return Rosecler gave him passionate tenderness, a mixture of honey and pepper.

Ubaldo Capadócio, then, was running over with rhymes and with children, only half a dozen of whom, as we've said, were his by blood: three with Romilda, three with Valdelice. Of the three adopted boys, the eldest came with Romilda when this handsome mulatto woman decided to leave her husband behind his counter in Aracaju and follow the plangent chords of the lonely troubadour's guitar. Yes, lonely and forlorn, because when a man wants a certain woman—when he's so hungry for her he can't get her out of his mind—even if he's playing around with other women day and night he might as well be alone; that one confounded woman is the only companion who can cheer him up and cure him of his lonesome blues. Seeing him brought so low, Romilda softened and bundled up her things, but first she told him she was willing to leave her husband but not her little boy; that she couldn't be separated from him. "He'll be my son," swore Capadócio dramatically with his hand on his heart. He didn't care whether she brought along one child, three children, or four; it was all the same to him, he was so crazy to get Romilda into bed, touch her breasts, stroke her thighs. "Bring your little boy, bring your nephew, bring your whole family if you want to!"

The second boy, named Dante after the poet, was adopted by Capadócio and Valdelice after his mother died, leaving the six-month-old baby with a fierce case of dysentery. Entrusting him to his father was out of the question. Bernardo Sabença, a talented storyteller and improviser who could drink his bar companions under the table, had no aptitude whatever for child-rearing, especially when the child had loose bowels and stank.

As for the third boy, nicknamed Cavy because he shared that rodent's voracious appetite, they knew nothing at all about him—parents, age, name—but had simply picked him up by the side of a back-country road eating clay, which isn't nourishing but tastes pretty good. After a close examination of Cavy's features and ways—fair hair, blue eyes, clever hands that were quick to grasp any object within reach—Valdelice, who was something of an amateur psychologist, concluded that his father must have been a lordly landowner, a "doctor," and that he had inherited his dark complexion from his mother.

For those who want more precise information about Capadócio's family life, I'll just add that he sometimes resided with the fair Romilda in Lagarto in the state of Sergipe, while the Valdelice-Capadócio residence was in Baraúnas Alley, Amargosa, Bahia. Love-hungry young Rosecler lives in Bahia too, in a suburb of a big city, Jequiê. Ubaldo Capadócio kissed his three wives with a cheery "So long, see you soon" (no one but a dead man on the way to his funeral ought to say the word "goodbye") and set off to make his fortune in the famous state of Alagoas, where life is cheap but poetry is prized; where a talented minstrel can reap applause, earn good money, and, if he's brave enough, warm the bed of some fine brunettes.

Ubaldo's expedition into the rugged Alagoan backlands was going splendidly. At parties, fairs, christenings, even a bishop's pastoral mission to Arapiraca, Ubaldo Capadócio turned up with his concertina, his guitar, and a suitcase full of ballads all ready to hang on the line, raking in a fair harvest of coins and breaking hearts right and left. After some time he reached the São Francisco River and made his way along its banks until he came to Piranhas. The scene of our story was famous for the beauty of its setting, for its colonial houses, and for having stood fast against Lampião's band years ago, a feat sung in many a ballad of the time. Yet another source of local pride was the fact that the town sheltered within its unbreached stone walls the aforementioned Captain Lindolfo Ezequiel and his legal wife, Sabô, also aforementioned but clearly deserving more ample reference to her graceful form, her dancing walk, a rear end that was a living legend, the dimples in her cheeks, and the way the hussy bit her lips to make them redder, as if saying, Oh yes, I'd like to, ooh, I wish I could, and so on and so forth. Sabô wasn't a woman at all, she was a temptation of the devil turned loose in Piranhas. But what man was reckless enough to give in? Yes, Piranhas was the home of the brave, the dauntless, the bold—Lampião could have borne witness to that. On the other hand, Lindolfo Ezequiel had already dispatched a fair number of his neighbors to the other world, some at the behest of powerful men, in order to make good money for himself and his free-spending wife, and others on his own hook because he mistrusted their intentions toward the virtuous Sabô. In the mind of her just but jealous husband, Sabô was a snow-white dove.

Our troubadour, Ubaldo Capadócio, had been in trouble over women more than once. He had jumped out of windows, jumped over fences, jumped over walls, streaked through the bushes, burst into other people's houses yelling for help, and plunged headlong into the Paraguassu River. One time a bullet had dusted his jacket but Xangô, his powerful spirit guide, protected him. Actually, since the would-be avenger was a military man and a sharpshooter, Ubaldo was never in much danger of being hit.

As soon as he got to Piranhas he made for Sabô's bed, which also belonged, by right of lawful marriage lines from priest and judge, to Lindolfo Ezequiel. The captain and his artillery happened to be off on a short business trip to a distant town, where a congressman had a little job for him to do. "Coast is clear," poor little Sabô called softly, so anxious to make the most of her chance. Not that Ubaldo hadn't been given fair warning from a fellow versifier, the owner of the pension where he was staying: "Better stay clear, pal, Lindolfo has more than thirty notches on his gun, not counting the first few before he started hiring himself out as a professional." Ubaldo didn't put much stock in what he heard; he knew what braggarts Alagoans are, and besides, to him women were always worth taking risks for.

He crossed Sabô's threshold at nightfall and was seen. He was still there the next morning when the sun was high in the sky; the affectionate girl couldn't get enough of him and as for the balladeer, when he found a partner worthy of his mettle he liked to show off—not just his fire and potency, but all of his refinements and skill. He was no ignoramus when it came to sex; he had frequented five-star establishments, including one where the madam was French, and had learned everything they had to teach. Ubaldo was one hell of a lover.

No one ever knew why Lindolfo Ezequiel doubled back on his tracks and got back to Piranhas when the weekly market was at its height, just when Ubaldo and Sabô were acting out the fast, fond, quintessential farewell, knowing time was getting short but drawing it out because they were weary, lingering tenderly because they already missed each other. And here came the killer waving his blunderbuss, puffing and threatening death preceded by castration in the public square. A curious crowd gathered behind him, the biggest since the Holy Week procession.

When Lindolfo set foot in the doorway Sabô recognized his tread. "That's my husband," she said with a giggle.

Ubaldo reacted instantly, as he always did on these occasions, and glanced swiftly around for something to cover his nakedness. He was no exhibitionist; in public he preferred to be decently dressed. All he could find in his haste was the top half of Sabô's pink baby-doll nightie, which he pulled on over his head. He was so tall the dainty garment didn't even reach his navel. But naked, as slandering tongues have it, he was not. He leaped through the window as the cuckold burst into the room, brandishing his revolver. Sabô, the chaste wife and innocent victim, accused the balladeer of trying to seduce her and rape her. But she had resisted heroically, and now she clamored for vengeance. "Don't worry, baby, I'm gonna tear his balls out and then shoot him in the head. Don't worry none about your reputation."

The two men pounded through the marketplace, the fleeing minstrel in his shortie nightgown, prick in full view and doomed balls swinging like the clapper of a bell. Hot on his heels and armed to the teeth came the captain with a wicked, sharp pig-gelding knife in his hand. Following close behind them was the eager crowd. Worn out from a night of celebration and a morning spent saying goodbye, Ubaldo Capadócio was losing ground. The killer and his knife were gaining on him and he felt a mortal chill in his balls.

Squarely in the middle of their path was the bird market, a whole pile of wooden cages stacked on top of one other, blocking the way. What with his speed and his fear Ubaldo couldn't veer around them fast enough. He crashed right into the wall of cages and the birds, hundreds of them, fluttered free. One minute the air was full of birds—pigeons and thrushes, orioles and cardinals, canaries and lovebirds—and the next they had picked up Ubaldo Capadócio by his flimsy nightgown and flown away with him. Ahead of them, twelve macaws opened a pathway through the clouds, escorting the troubadour as lightly as a verse wafted by a zephyr.

Lindolfo Ezequiel was rooted to the spot in the middle of the square, where he remains to this day. He turned into a magnificent horntree, the biggest horntree in the Northeast, a unique source of raw material out of which artisans fashion combs, rings, drinking cups, and all kinds of other things. Thus the former killer was transformed into an object of real public utility. As for Sabô, she belongs to the whole community now, under the immediate protection of Colonel Jarde Ramalho, who attentively observed both the chase and the miracle.

The birds flew over Alagoas bearing Ubaldo Capadócio, his balls safely intact, on the breeze. When they had crossed the Sergipe state line they set him down in a convent, where the nuns welcomed him courteously and asked him no questions.

Translated by Barbara Merello

Murilo Rubião
(1916–   )

Like Guimarães Rosa, the Brazilian Murilo Rubião was also born in
Minas Gerais, a state known for the almost Scottish reticence of its
inhabitants. And no two writers have shown more reluctance to
publish. At seven, Rubião left the small-town environment that was
to characterize so many of his stories and moved to the state
capital, Belo Horizonte. His was a childhood surrounded by writers
(including his grandfather, father, an uncle, and several cousins)
and nourished by the interminable reading and rereading of fairy
tales, the Scriptures, *Don Quixote,* and *A Thousand and One Nights,* as
well as of his acknowledged master Machado de Assis.

In 1938, he founded with a group of fellow students at the
University of Minas the first of a number of literary reviews he was
to be connected with throughout his career, and the following year
he became editor of the *Folha de Minas* newspaper. By the time he
received his law degree in 1942, Rubião had already begun to
publish the first versions of the peculiar fantasies he was to collect
and recollect over the next three decades, beginning in 1948 with
the title story of *The Ex-Magician and Other Stories.* In 1945, he
attended the First Brazilian Congress of Writers, which called for
an immediate halt to censorship and was instrumental in putting
an end to the Vargas dictatorship. In the fifties he worked as a state
bureaucrat; then from 1956 to 1960 he served as attaché to the
Brazilian embassy in Madrid—four confessedly lonely years in
which he wrote only one story, "Teleco, the Rabbit," and nearly
gave up writing altogether.

Returning to Brazil, and to Minas, he founded the influential
literary supplement of the *Minas Gerais* daily, republished the most

complete version to date of his early stories, and began work on an entirely new collection that would be published in 1974. In this same year, Rubião's early fiction was "rediscovered" and became a bestseller. There are rumors of a third collection of stories, but the few dozen impeccable tales he has allowed to appear in his lifetime have already assured him the place of undisputed master of the fantastic in modern Brazilian literature.

The Ex-Magician from
the Minhota Tavern

Bow down thine ear, O Lord, and
hear me: for I am poor and needy.
Psalms, LXXXVI:1

Nowadays I'm a civil servant, which is not my greatest misfortune.

To be honest, I was not prepared for suffering. Each man, on reaching a certain age, is perfectly equipped to face the avalanche of tedium and bitterness, since from his early childhood he has become accustomed to the vicissitudes of daily life through a gradual process of continual vexation.

This did not happen to me. I was cast into existence without parents, without infancy or adolescence.

I found myself one day, with light gray hair, in the mirror of the Minhota Tavern, a discovery which in no way frightened me, any more than it astonished me to take the owner of the restaurant out of my pocket. He, rather perplexed, asked me how could I have done such a thing.

What could I answer, given my situation, a person who lacked the least explanation for his presence in the world? I said to him that I was tired, that I was born tired and weary.

Without weighing my answer or questioning me any further, he made me an offer of a job, and so I began, from that time on, to entertain the clientele of the establishment with my magical activity.

The man himself, however, failed to appreciate my habit of offering onlookers a variety of free lunches, which I would mysteriously draw forth from the inside of my own jacket. Judging it to be not the best of transactions merely to increase the number of customers—without a corresponding growth in profits—he introduced me to the impresario of the Andalusian Circus Garden, who, when told of my aptitudes, offered to hire me. First, however, he was advised to take certain precautions over my tricks, since I might just decide to distribute free admissions to the performances.

Contrary to the pessimistic expectations of my first employer, my behavior was exemplary. My public engagements not only thrilled multitudes, but brought in fabulous profits for the company owners as well.

Audiences, in general, received me rather coolly, perhaps because I failed to present myself in tails and a top hat. But as soon as I began involuntarily to extract rabbits, snakes, lizards from a hat, spectators tingled with excitement, above all in the last number, when I would cause an alligator to appear from the tips of my fingers. Then, by compressing the animal from both ends, I changed him into an accordion and brought the act to its close by playing the Cochin China National Anthem. Applause would burst forth from all sides, under my remote gaze.

The manager of the circus, observing me from a distance, was exasperated by my indifference to the public's acclaim, especially when it came from the younger children who would show up to clap for me at Sunday matinees. Why be moved, though, if those innocent faces, destined to endure the suffering inflicted upon any man's coming of age, aroused no pity in me, much less any anger, over their having everything I longed for but did not myself possess: birth, and a past.

As I grew more popular, my life became intolerable.

At times, sitting in some café, stubbornly observing the populace filing past on the sidewalks, I would end up pulling doves, gulls, skunks out of my pocket. The people around me, judging my behavior to be intentional, invariably broke into shrill peals of laughter. I would stare at the floor dejectedly, and mutter against the world and birds.

Whenever, absentmindedly, I happened to open my hands, curious objects slid out of them. On a certain occasion I surprised myself by pulling one shape after another out of my sleeve. In the end I was completely surrounded by strange shapes, without any idea of what purpose to attribute to them.

What could I do? I looked all around me, my eyes pleading for some kind of help, in vain, an excruciating state of affairs.

Almost always, if I took out my handkerchief to blow my nose, I astonished those nearby by pulling a whole bedsheet out of my pocket. If I fidgeted with the collar of my coat, a large buzzard would immediately appear. On other occasions, while trying to tie my shoelaces, snakes would slither out of my trousers. Women and children started screaming. Guards came over, bystanders crowding around, a scandal. I would have to report to police headquarters and listen patiently while I was prohibited by the authorities from any further setting loose of serpents on public thoroughfares.

I raised no objection. Timid, I humbly mentioned my condition of magician, reaffirmed my intention not to bother anyone.

I became accustomed, at night, to waking up quite suddenly in the middle of a sound sleep, with a loud bird flapping its wings as it took flight from my ear.

On one of these occasions, completely furious, and resolved never again to practice magic, I cut off my hands. To no purpose. As soon as I moved, they reappeared, fresh and perfect, on the ends of the stump of each arm!

I had to resolve my despair somehow. After weighing the matter carefully, I concluded that only death would put a proper end to my misfortune.

Steadfast in my decision, I took a dozen lions out of my pockets and, crossing my arms, waited for the moment when I would be devoured. They did me no harm. Surrounding me, they sniffed at my clothes and, eyeing the landscape, slunk away.

Next morning they were back again and sat themselves provocatively before me.

"What do you expect from me, stupid animals?" I roared indignantly.

They shook their manes sadly and pleaded with me to make them disappear.

"This world is tremendously tedious," they declared.

I failed to restrain my outright rage. I killed them all, and began to devour them myself. I had hopes of dying the victim of a fatal indigestion.

Misfortune of misfortunes! I suffered an enormous stomachache, and continued to live.

This failure only multiplied my sense of frustration. I left the city limits and went off in search of the mountains. Reaching the highest peak, which dominated the dark abyss, I relinquished my body to space.

I felt no more than a slight sensation of the closeness of death— almost at once I found myself suspended from a parachute. With difficulty, battering myself against rocks, maimed and grimy, I finally returned to the city, where my first step was to acquire a pistol.

At home again and lying on my bed, I raised the weapon to my ear. I pulled the trigger, expecting a loud report and the pain of the bullet tearing through my head.

There was no shot, and no death: the handgun turned into a pencil.

I rolled to the floor, sobbing. I who could create other beings had no means to liberate myself from existence.

An expression I overhead by accident, out on the street one day, brought me renewed hope of a definitive break with life. From a sad man I heard that to be a civil servant was to commit suicide little by little.

I was in no condition to determine which form of suicide was best suited to me: slow or quick. As a result, I took a job in the Department of State.

1930, a bitter year, longer than those that followed the first man-ifestation I had of my existence, back in the mirror at the Minhota Tavern.

I did not die, as I had hoped to. The greater my afflictions were, the greater my misfortune.

While I was a magician, I had had very little to do with people— the stage always kept me at a comfortable distance. Now that I was obliged to have constant contact with my fellow creatures, it was necessary to understand them, and to disguise the repugnance they aroused in me.

The worst of it was that, my duties being rather trivial, I found myself in the position of having to hang around uselessly for hours at a stretch. Idleness led to my resenting the lack of a past. Why was it only me, among all those existing before my very eyes, who had nothing to recall? My days floated in confusion, mixed with a few paltry recollections, the small plus of three years in existence.

Love, which came to me by way of another civil servant, her desk close to mine, distracted me for a time from my worries.

Momentary distraction. My restlessness quickly returned, I strug-gled with uncertainties. How was I to propose to this colleague of mine if I had never made declarations of love, nor had a single amorous experience?

1931 began cheerlessly, with threats of mass dismissals in our department and a refusal by the typist to consider my proposal. Faced with the possibility of being discharged, I tried somehow to look after my own interests. (The job mattered little to me. I was simply afraid of leaving behind a woman by whom I had been rejected, but whose presence slowly became indispensable to me.)

I went to the supervisor of our section and announced that I could not be fired because, after ten years in the department, I now possessed job security.

He stared at me for some time in total silence. Then, frowning at me, he said he was astonished by my cynicism. He would never have expected anyone with only one year of service to have the audacity to claim ten.

To prove to him that my attitude was not frivolous, I rummaged through my pockets for some documents corroborating the authenticity of my claim. Stunned, I managed to pull out only a crumpled piece of paper, the fragment of a poem inspired by the breasts of the typist.

Anxiously, I turned all my pockets inside out, but found nothing more. . . .

I was forced to admit defeat. I had trusted too much in my powers to make magic, which had been nullified by bureaucracy.

Nowadays, without the aforementioned and miraculous gift of wizardry, I am unable to relinquish the very worst of human occupations. I lack the love of my typist companion and the presence of friends, which obliges me to frequent solitary places. I am often caught attempting to remove, from the inside of my clothes with my fingers, little things which no one glimpses anyway, no matter how attentively they gaze.

They think that I'm crazy, chiefly when I toss into the air those tiny objects.

I have the impression that a swallow is about to disengage itself from my fingertips. I sigh aloud, deeply.

Of course, the illusion gives me no comfort. It only serves to intensify my regret not to have created a total magical world.

At certain moments I imagine how marvelous it would be to extract red, blue, white, and green handkerchiefs from my body, fill the night with fireworks, turn my face to the sky and let a rainbow pour forth from my lips, a rainbow that could cover the earth from one extremity to the other. Then the applause from the old men with their white hair, and from gentle children.

Translated by Thomas Colchie

Clarice Lispector
(1925–1977)

Born of Ukranian Jews who emigrated to Brazil when she was two months old, Clarice Lispector has come to be recognized, in the decade following her death, as the greatest modern short-story writer in the Portuguese language. Until she was twelve, her family lived in poverty in the Northeastern state capitals of Maceió and later Recife. Her mother had died in 1934 after a long paralysis resulting from the births of Lispector's two younger sisters.

In 1937, the family moved to Rio de Janeiro, where Lispector decided to become a writer. While completing her secondary schooling there, she had her first story published after having been falsely accused of copying it out of a book. In the forties, she discovered the works of Hermann Hesse and Katherine Mansfield, then attended law school while working as editor for a press agency and afterward as reporter for a Rio daily. In 1943, Lispector married a fellow law student and, a year later, received her degree and published her first novel, *Near to the Wild Heart* (1944).

She spent the next fifteen years living and writing abroad, wherever her husband happened to be posted as diplomat: Italy, Switzerland, England, and the United States. When the marriage ended in 1959, Lispector returned to Rio with her two children and the following year published a singular collection of short stories called *Family Ties*. Each of its eight disquieting tales is a haunting epiphany. The novel *Apple in the Dark,* published in 1961, brought her deserved recognition as a writer of extraordinary stylistic precision and enormous philosophical consequence.

Lispector had a difficult time financially, since she supported herself and her children solely by her writing. Her life was further complicated by her elder son's mental illness and her own chronic insomnia. Lispector died in a public hospital after suffering a year from cancer. Among her other translated works are a collection of short fiction, *The Foreign Legion* (1964), two of her finest novels, *The Passion According to G.H.* (1964) and *The Hour of the Star* (1977), and the posthumous *The Stream of Life* (1978).

Feeling a little tired, with her purchases bulging her new string bag, Anna boarded the tram. She placed the bag on her lap and the tram started off. Settling back in her seat she tried to find a comfortable position, with a sigh of mild satisfaction.

Anna had nice children, she reflected with certainty and pleasure. They were growing up, bathing themselves and misbehaving; they were demanding more and more of her time. The kitchen, after all, was spacious with its old stove that made explosive noises. The heat was oppressive in the apartment, which they were paying off in installments, and the wind, playing against the curtains she had made herself, reminded her that if she wanted to she could pause to wipe her forehead, and contemplate the calm horizon. Like a farmer. She had planted the seeds she held in her hand, no others, but only those. And they were growing into trees. Her brisk conversations with the electricity man were growing, the water filling the tank was growing, her children were growing, the table was growing with food, her husband arriving with the newspapers and smiling with hunger, the irritating singing of the maids resounding through the block. Anna tranquilly put her small, strong hand, her life current to everything. Certain times of the afternoon struck her as being critical. At a certain hour of the afternoon the trees she had planted laughed at her. And when nothing more required her strength, she became anxious. Meanwhile she felt herself more solid than ever, her body become a little thicker, and it was worth seeing the manner in which she cut out blouses for the children, the large scissors snapping into the material. All her vaguely artis-

110

tic aspirations had for some time been channeled into making her days fulfilled and beautiful; with time, her taste for the decorative had developed and supplanted intimate disorder. She seemed to have discovered that everything was capable of being perfected, that each thing could be given a harmonious appearance; life itself could be created by Man.

Deep down, Anna had always found it necessary to feel the firm roots of things. And this is what a home had surprisingly provided. Through tortuous paths, she had achieved a woman's destiny, with the surprise of conforming to it almost as if she had invented that destiny herself. The man whom she had married was a real man, the children she mothered were real children. Her previous youth now seemed alien to her, like one of life's illnesses. She had gradually emerged to discover that life could be lived without happiness: by abolishing it she had found a legion of persons, previously invisible, who lived as one works—with perseverance, persistence, and contentment. What had happened to Anna before possessing a home of her own stood forever beyond her reach: that disturbing exaltation she had often confused with unbearable happiness. In exchange she had created something ultimately comprehensible, the life of an adult. This was what she had wanted and chosen.

Her precautions were now reduced to alertness during the dangerous part of the afternoon, when the house was empty and she was no longer needed; when the sun reached its zenith, and each member of the family went about his separate duties. Looking at the polished furniture, she felt her heart contract a little with fear. But in her life there was no opportunity to cherish her fears—she suppressed them with that same ingenuity she had acquired from domestic struggles. Then she would go out shopping or take things to be mended, unobtrusively looking after her home and her family. When she returned it would already be late afternoon and the children back from school would absorb her attention. Until the evening descended with its quiet excitement. In the morning she would awaken surrounded by her calm domestic duties. She would find the furniture dusty and dirty once more, as if it had returned repentant. As for herself, she mysteriously formed part of the soft, dark roots of the earth. And anonymously she nourished life. It was pleasant like this. This was what she had wanted and chosen.

The tram swayed on its rails and turned into the main road. Suddenly the wind became more humid, announcing not only the passing of the afternoon but the end of that uncertain hour. Anna sighed with relief and a deep sense of acceptance gave her face an air of womanhood.

The tram would drag along and then suddenly jolt to a halt. As far as Humaitá she could relax. Suddenly she saw the man station-ary at the tram stop. The difference between him and others was that he was really stationary. He stood with his hands held out in front of him—blind.

But what else was there about him that made Anna sit up in distrust? Something disquieting was happening. Then she discov-ered what it was: the blind man was chewing gum ... a blind man chewing gum. Anna still had time to reflect for a second that her brothers were coming to dinner—her heart pounding at regular intervals. Leaning forward, she studied the blind man intently, as one observes something incapable of returning our gaze. Relaxed, and with open eyes, he was chewing gum in the failing light. The facial movements of his chewing made him appear to smile then suddenly stop smiling, to smile and stop smiling. Anna stared at him as if he had insulted her. And anyone watching would have received the impression of a woman filled with hatred. She contin-ued to stare at him, leaning more and more forward—until the tram gave a sudden jerk, throwing her unexpectedly backward. The heavy string bag toppled from her lap and landed on the floor. Anna cried out, the conductor gave the signal to stop before realizing what was happening, and the tram came to an abrupt halt. The other passengers looked on in amazement. Too paralyzed to gather up her shopping, Anna sat upright, her face suddenly pale. An expression, long since forgotten, awkwardly reappeared, unexpected and inexplicable. The Negro newsboy smiled as he handed over her bundle. The eggs had broken in their newspaper wrapping. Yellow sticky yolks dripped between the strands of the bag. The blind man had interrupted his chewing and held out his unsteady hands, trying in vain to grasp what had happened. She removed the parcel of eggs from the string bag accompanied by the smiles of the passengers. A second signal from the conductor and the tram moved off with another jerk.

A few moments later people were no longer staring at her. The tram was rattling on the rails and the blind man chewing gum had remained behind forever. But the damage had been done.

The string bag felt rough between her fingers, not soft and fa-miliar as when she had knitted it. The bag had lost its meaning; to find herself on that tram was a broken thread; she did not know what to do with the purchases on her lap. Like some strange music, the world started up again around her. The damage had been done. But why? Had she forgotten that there were blind people? Compassion choked her. Anna's breathing became heavy. Even those things which had existed before the episode were now on the alert, more hostile, and even perishable. The world had once more become a nightmare. Several years fell away, the yellow yolks trickled. Exiled from her own days, it seemed to her that the people in the streets were vulnerable, that they barely maintained their equilibrium on the surface of the darkness—and for a moment they appeared to lack any sense of direction. The perception of an absence of law came so unexpectedly that Anna clutched the seat in front of her, as if she might fall off the tram, as if things might be overturned with the same calm they had possessed when order reigned.

What she called a crisis had come at last. And its sign was the intense pleasure with which she now looked at things, suffering and alarmed. The heat had become more oppressive, everything had gained new power and a stronger voice. In the Rua Voluntários da Pátria, revolution seemed imminent, the grids of the gutters were dry, the air dusty. A blind man chewing gum had plunged the world into a mysterious excitement. In every strong person there was a lack of compassion for the blind man, and their strength terrified her. Beside her sat a woman in blue with an expression which made Anna avert her gaze rapidly. On the pavement a mother shook her little boy. Two lovers held hands smiling.... And the blind man? Anna had lapsed into a mood of compassion which greatly distressed her.

She had skilfully pacified life; she had taken so much care to avoid upheavals. She had cultivated an atmosphere of serene understanding, separating each person from the others. Her clothes were clearly designed to be practical, and she could choose the evening's film from the newspaper—and everything was done in such a manner that each day should smoothly succeed the previous one. And a blind man chewing gum was destroying all this. Through her compassion Anna felt that life was filled to the brim with a sickening nausea.

Only then did she realize that she had passed her stop ages ago. In her weak state everything touched her with alarm. She got off the tram, her legs shaking, and looked around her, clutching the string bag stained with egg. For a moment she was unable to get her bearings. She seemed to have plunged into the middle of the night.

It was a long road, with high yellow walls. Her heart beat with

fear as she tried in vain to recognize her surroundings; while the
life she had discovered continued to pulsate, a gentler, more mysterious wind caressed her face. She stood quietly observing the
wall. At last she recognized it. Advancing a little further alongside
a hedge, she passed through the gates of the botanical garden.

She strolled wearily up the central avenue, between the palm
trees. There was no one in the garden. She put her parcels down
on the ground and sat down on the bench of a side path where
she remained for some time.

The wilderness seemed to calm her, the silence regulating her
breathing and soothing her senses.

From afar she saw the avenue where the evening was round and
clear. But the shadows of the branches covered the side path.

Around her there were tranquil noises, the scent of trees, chance
encounters among the creeping plants. The entire garden fragmented by the ever more fleeting moments of the evening. From
whence came the drowsiness with which she was surrounded? As
if induced by the drone of birds and bees. Everything seemed
strange, much too gentle, much too great.

A gentle, familiar movement startled her and she turned round
rapidly. Nothing appeared to have stirred. But in the central lane
there stood, immobile, an enormous cat. Its fur was soft. With another silent movement, it disappeared.

Agitated, she looked about her. The branches swayed, their shadows wavering on the ground. A sparrow foraged in the soil. And
suddenly, in terror, she imagined that she had fallen into an ambush. In the garden there was a secret activity in progress which
she was beginning to penetrate.

On the trees, the fruits were black and sweet as honey. On the
ground there lay dry fruit stones full of circumvolutions like small
rotted cerebrums. The bench was stained with purple sap. With
gentle persistence the waters murmured. On the tree trunk the
luxurious feelers of parasites fastened themselves. The rawness of
the world was peaceful. The murder was deep. And death was not
what one had imagined.

As well as being imaginary, this was a world to be devoured with
one's teeth, a world of voluminous dahlias and tulips. The trunks
were pervaded by leafy parasites, their embrace soft and clinging.
Like the resistance that precedes surrender, it was fascinating; the
woman felt disgusted, and it was fascinating.

The trees were laden, and the world was so rich that it was rotting. When Anna reflected that there were children and grown

men suffering hunger, the nausea reached her throat as if she were pregnant and abandoned. The moral of the garden was something different. Now that the blind man had guided her to it, she trembled on the threshold of a dark, fascinating world where monstrous water lilies floated. The small flowers scattered on the grass did not appear to be yellow or pink, but the color of inferior gold and scarlet. Their decay was profound, perfumed. But all these oppressive things she watched, her head surrounded by a swarm of insects, sent by some more refined life in the world. The breeze penetrated between the flowers. Anna imagined rather than felt its sweetened scent. The garden was so beautiful that she feared hell.

It was almost night now and everything seemed replete and heavy; a squirrel leapt in the darkness. Under her feet the earth was soft. Anna inhaled its odor with delight. It was both fascinating and repulsive.

But when she remembered the children, before whom she now felt guilty, she straightened up with a cry of pain. She clutched the package, advanced through the dark side path, and reached the avenue. She was almost running, and she saw the garden all around her aloof and impersonal. She shook the locked gates, and went on shaking them, gripping the rough timber. The watchman appeared, alarmed at not having seen her.

Until she reached the entrance of the building, she seemed to be on the brink of disaster. She ran with the string bag to the elevator, her heart beating in her breast—what was happening? Her compassion for the blind man was as fierce as anguish but the world seemed hers, dirty, perishable, hers. She opened the door of her flat. The room was large, square, the polished knobs were shining, the window panes were shining, the lamp shone brightly—what new land was this? And for a moment that wholesome life she had led until today seemed morally crazy. The little boy who came running up to embrace her was a creature with long legs and a face resembling her own. She pressed him firmly to her in anxiety and fear. Trembling, she protected herself. Life was vulnerable. She loved the world, she loved all things created, she loved with loathing. In the same way as she had always been fascinated by oysters, with that vague sentiment of revulsion which the approach of truth provoked, admonishing her. She embraced her son, almost hurting him. Almost as if she knew of some evil—the blind man or the beautiful botanical garden—she was clinging to him, to him whom she loved above all things. She had been touched by the demon of faith.

"Life is horrible," she said to him in a low voice, as if famished. What would she do if she answered the blind man's call? She would go alone.... There were poor and rich places that needed her. She needed them. "I am afraid," she said. She felt the delicate ribs of the child between her arms, she heard his frightened weeping.

"Mummy," the child called. She held him away from her; she studied his face and her heart shrank.

"Don't let Mummy forget you," she said. No sooner had the child felt her embrace weaken than he escaped and ran to the door of the room, from where he watched her more safely. It was the worst look that she had ever received. The blood rose hot to her cheeks.

She sank into a chair, with her fingers still clasping the string bag. What was she ashamed of? There was no way of escaping. The very crust of the days she had forged had broken and the water was escaping. She stood before the oysters. And there was no way of averting her gaze. What was she ashamed of? Certainly it was no longer pity, it was more than pity: her heart had filled with the worst will to live.

She no longer knew if she was on the side of the blind man or of the thick plants. The man little by little had moved away, and in her torment she appeared to have passed over to the side of those who had injured his eyes. The botanical garden, tranquil and high, had been a revelation. With horror, she discovered that she belonged to the strong part of the world, and what name should she give to her fierce compassion? Would she be obliged to kiss the leper, since she would never be just a sister? "A blind man has drawn me to the worst of myself," she thought, amazed. She felt herself banished because no pauper would drink water from her burning hands. Ah! It was easier to be a saint than a person! Good heavens, then was it not real, that pity which had fathomed the deepest waters in her heart? But it was the compassion of a lion.

Humiliated, she knew that the blind man would prefer a poorer love. And, trembling, she also knew why. The life of the botanical garden summoned her as a werewolf is summoned by the moonlight. "Oh! but she loved the blind man," she thought with tears in her eyes. Meanwhile it was not with this sentiment that one would go to church. "I am frightened," she whispered alone in the room. She got up and went to the kitchen to help the maid prepare dinner.

But life made her shiver like the cold of winter. She heard the school bell pealing, distant and constant. The small horror of the dust gathering in threads around the bottom of the stove, where she had discovered a small spider. Lifting a vase to change the water—there was the horror of the flower submitting itself, languid and loathsome, to her hands. The same secret activity was going on here in the kitchen. Near the waste bin, she crushed an ant with her foot. The small murder of the ant. Its minute body trembled. Drops of water fell on the stagnant water in the pool.

The summer beetles. The horror of those expressionless beetles. All around there was a silent, slow, insistent life. Horror upon horror. She went from one side of the kitchen to the other, cutting the steaks, mixing the cream. Circling around her head, around the light, the flies of a warm summer's evening. A night in which compassion was as crude as false love. Sweat trickled between her breasts. Faith broke her; the heat of the oven burned in her eyes.

Then her husband arrived, followed by her brothers and their wives, and her brothers' children.

They dined with all the windows open, on the ninth floor. An airplane shuddered menacingly in the heat of the sky. Although she had used few eggs, the dinner was good. The children stayed up, playing on the carpet with their cousins. It was summer and it would be useless to force them to go to sleep. Anna was a little pale and laughed gently with the others.

After dinner, the first cool breeze finally entered the room. The family was seated round the table, tired after their day, happy in the absence of any discord, eager not to find fault. They laughed at everything, with warmth and humanity. The children grew up admirably around them. Anna took the moment like a butterfly, between her fingers before it might escape forever.

Later, when they had all left and the children were in bed, she was just a woman looking out of the window. The city was asleep and warm. Would the experience unleashed by the blind man fill her days? How many years would it take before she once more grew old? The slightest movement on her part and she would trample one of her children. But with the ill-will of a lover, she seemed to accept that the fly would emerge from the flower, and the giant water lilies would float in the darkness of the lake. The blind man was hanging among the fruits of the botanical garden.

What if that were the stove exploding with fire spreading through the house, she thought to herself as she ran to the kitchen where she found her husband in front of the spilt coffee.

"What happened?" she cried, shaking from head to foot. He was taken aback by his wife's alarm. And suddenly understanding, he laughed.

"It was nothing," he said, "I am just a clumsy fellow." He looked tired, with dark circles under his eyes.

But, confronted by the strange expression on Anna's face, he studied her more closely. Then he drew her to him in a sudden caress.

"I don't want anything ever to happen to you!" she said.

"You can't prevent the stove from having its little explosions," he replied, smiling. She remained limp in his arms. This afternoon something tranquil had exploded, and in the house everything struck a tragicomic note.

"It's time to go to bed," he said, "it's late." In a gesture which was not his, but which seemed natural, he held his wife's hand, taking her with him, without looking back, removing her from the danger of living.

The giddiness of compassion had spent itself. And if she had crossed love and its hell, she was now combing her hair before the mirror, without any world for the moment in her heart. Before getting into bed, as if she was snuffing a candle, she blew out that day's tiny flame.

Translated by Giovanni Pontiero

Joaquim Maria Machado de Assis
(1839–1908)

Machado de Assis was the Brazilian son of a mulatto housepainter and a Portuguese washerwoman from the Azores, tenants on the property of an influential senator's widow in Rio de Janeiro. The estate overlooked the bay of a still tiny, rather squalid capital city of mostly unpaved streets. Machado was a frail, epileptic child but was favored by the widow, who allowed him the run of the villa and saw to his early education. When his younger sister and mother died, his father remarried. His mulatta stepmother continued his education, and the couple managed to send the boy to public primary school for a time.

After the death of his father, in 1851, stepmother and son moved to a different neighborhood, allowing her to work as a baker in a small secondary school where Machado seems to have furthered his studies at least informally. At the same time the boy sold sweets to supplement his stepmother's income. In 1855, he published his first poem and the following year took a job as an apprentice typographer at the National Printing House. Three years later he was working as a cashier for a publishing house whose bookstore served as the gathering place for the Carioca intelligentsia of the period.

Over the next decade, Machado collaborated with several leading newspapers, writing poetry and fiction in a romantic vein and reviewing for the theater. In 1869, the year he published his first book of short stories, he married Carolina Augusta Xavier de Novais, the sister of a Portuguese poet and close friend of Machado's. She was to play a decisive role in the author's literary development by leading him to the Portuguese classics and subsequently to the English authors who would help him shed the romanticism of his early novels.

In 1873, the year after publication of his first novel, Machado obtained an appointment in the ministry of agriculture, initiating the lifelong bureaucratic career that brought him economic security for his writing. Three highly successful novels followed, each typifying the morals and intrigues of upper-class society: *The Hand and the Glove* (1874), *Helena* (1876), and *Iaiá Garcia* (1878).

At thirty-nine years of age, although in chronic ill-health (his epilepsy had returned; he suffered intestinal disorders and his eyesight was failing), Machado seemed the paradigm of the happily married, much appreciated, literary bureaucrat. But it was not merely his physical health that was declining; he was undergoing an intellectual crisis of equal gravity. Though each succeeding novel was technically more proficient, there was a disturbing lack of artistic profundity to the novel of manners that increasingly troubled Machado. At the same time, in his 1878 review of *Cousin Basílio* by the noted Portuguese novelist Eça de Queirós, he was equally dismissive of what he considered to be the cul-de-sac of European naturalism, or what he termed the "servile photographic reproduction of the petty and the ignoble." By the end of the year, this general malaise had forced him to take a three-month leave of absence from his job in order to retire with his wife to the country suburb of Friburgo. While he convalesced there, his wife read to him from Shakespeare, Stendhal, and Sterne, the effect of which was to transform his conception of the novel.

When the couple finally returned to Rio de Janeiro, Machado began work on the first of his major novels, *Epitaph of a Small Winner,* which he published serially in 1880. With this astonishing "memoir" composed from beyond the grave by a "deceased" Bras Cubas, the omniscient author of the early novels is subjectively engulfed by the delirious ruminations of his protagonist narrator, while time and space recede into the ambiguous zones of the psyche and irony provides the comic acid for dissolving the moral conventions of both society and the novel. In the works that followed, especially *The Psychiatrist* (1881), *The Heritage of Quincas Borba (Philosopher or Dog?)* (1891), and *Dom Casmurro* (1899), the genius of Machado mined (and undermined) the realistic novel in as ambiguous, complex, and enduring a fashion as that of his North American contemporary Henry James. Both were to have a decisive influence on the development of the modern Latin American narrative. Some of Machado's finest short stories have been collected in two volumes in English translation: *The Psychiatrist and Other Stories* and *The Devil's Church and Other Stories.* Other translations include the novels *Esau and Jacob* (1904) and *Counselor Ayres' Memoir* (1908).

The Psychiatrist

I. How Itaguai Acquired a Madhouse

The chronicles of Itaguai related that in remote times a certain physician of noble birth, Simão Bacamarte, lived there and that he was one of the greatest doctors in all Brazil, Portugal, and the Spains. He had studied for many years in both Padua and Coimbra. When, at the age of thirty-four, he announced his decision to return to Brazil and his home town of Itaguai, the King of Portugal tried to dissuade him; he offered Bacamarte his choice between the Presidency of Coimbra University and the office of Chief Expediter of Government Affairs. The doctor politely declined.

"Science," he told His Majesty, "is my only office; Itaguai, my universe."

He took up residence there and dedicated himself to the theory and practice of medicine. He alternated therapy with study and research; he demonstrated theorems with poultices.

In his fortieth year Bacamarte married the widow of a circuit judge. Her name was Dona Evarista da Costa e Mascarenhas, and she was neither beautiful nor charming. One of his uncles, an outspoken man, asked him why he had not selected a more attractive woman. The doctor replied that Dona Evarista enjoyed perfect digestion, excellent eyesight, and normal blood pressure; she had had no serious illnesses and her urinalysis was negative. It was likely she would give him healthy, robust children. If, in addition to her physiological accomplishments, Dona Evarista possessed a face composed of features neither individually pretty nor mutually compatible, he thanked God for it, for he would not be tempted to sacrifice his scientific pursuits to the contemplation of his wife's attractions.

But Dona Evarista failed to satisfy her husband's expectations. She produced no robust children and, for that matter, no puny ones either. The scientific temperament is by nature patient; Bacamarte waited three, four, five years. At the end of this period he began an exhaustive study of sterility. He reread the works of all the authorities (including the Arabian), sent inquiries to the Italian and German universities, and finally recommended a special diet. But Dona Evarista, nourished almost exclusively on succulent Itaguai pork, paid no heed; and to this lack of wifely submissiveness—understandable but regrettable—we owe the total extinction of the Bacamartian dynasty.

The pursuit of science is sometimes itself therapeutic. Dr. Bacamarte cured himself of his disappointment by plunging even deeper into his work. It was at this time that one of the byways of medicine attracted his attention: psychopathology. The entire colony and, for that matter, the kingdom itself could not boast one authority on the subject. It was a field, indeed, in which little responsible work had been done anywhere in the world. Simão Bacamarte saw an opportunity for Lusitanian and, more specifically, Brazilian science to cover itself with "imperishable laurels"—an expression he himself used, but only in a moment of ecstasy and within the confines of his home; to the outside world he was always modest and restrained, as befits a man of learning.

"The health of the soul!" he exclaimed. "The loftiest possible goal for a doctor."

"For a great doctor like yourself, yes." This emendation came from Crispim Soares, the town druggist and one of Bacamarte's most intimate friends.

The chroniclers chide the Itaguai Town Council for its neglect of the mentally ill. Violent madmen were locked up at home; peaceable lunatics were simply left at large; and none, violent or peaceable, received care of any sort. Simão Bacamarte proposed to change all this. He decided to build an asylum and he asked the Council for authority to receive and treat all the mentally ill of Itaguai and the surrounding area. He would be paid by the patient's family or, if the family was very poor, by the Council. The proposal aroused excitement and curiosity throughout the town. There was considerable opposition, for it is always difficult to uproot the established way of doing things, however absurd or evil it may be. The idea of having madmen live together in the same house seemed itself to be a symptom of madness, as many intimated even to the doctor's wife.

"Look, Dona Evarista," said Father Lopes, the local vicar, "see if you can't get your husband to take a little holiday. In Rio de Janeiro, maybe. All this intensive study, a man can take just so much of it and then his mind . . ."

Dona Evarista was terrified. She went to her husband and said that she had a consuming desire to take a trip with him to Rio de Janeiro. There, she said, she would eat whatever he thought necessary for the attainment of a certain objective. But the astute doctor immediately perceived what was on his wife's mind and replied that she need have no fear. He then went to the town hall, where the Council was debating his proposal, which he supported with such eloquence that it was approved without amendment on the first ballot. The Council also adopted a tax designed to pay for the lodging, sustenance, and treatment of the indigent mad. This involved a bit of a problem, for everything in Itaguai was already being taxed. After considerable study the Council authorized the use of two plumes on the horses drawing a funeral coach. Anyone wishing to take advantage of this privilege would pay a tax of a stated amount for each hour from the time of death to the termination of the rites at the grave. The town clerk was asked to determine the probable revenue from the new tax, but he got lost in arithmetical calculations, and one of the Councilmen, who was opposed to the doctor's undertaking, suggested that the clerk be relieved of a useless task.

"The calculations are unnecessary," he said, "because Dr. Bacamarte's project will never be executed. Who ever heard of putting a lot of crazy people together in one house?"

But the worthy Councilman was wrong. Bacamarte built his madhouse on New Street, the finest thoroughfare in Itaguai. The building had a courtyard in the center and two hundred cubicles, each with one window. The doctor, an ardent student of Arabian lore, found a passage in the Koran in which Mohammed declared that the insane were holy, for Allah had deprived them of their judgment in order to keep them from sinning. Bacamarte found the idea at once beautiful and profound, and he had the passage engraved on the façade of the house. But he feared that this might offend the Vicar and, through him, the Bishop. Accordingly, he attributed the quotation to Benedict VIII.

The asylum was called the Green House, for its windows were

the first of that color ever seen in Itaguai. The formal opening was celebrated magnificently. People came from the entire region, some even from Rio de Janeiro, to witness the ceremonies, which lasted seven days. Some patients had already been admitted, and their relatives took advantage of this opportunity to observe the paternal care and Christian charity with which they were treated. Dona Evarista, delighted by her husband's glory, covered herself with silks, jewels, and flowers. She was a real queen during those memorable days. Everyone came to visit her two or three times. People not only paid court to her but praised her, for—and this fact does great honor to the society of the time—they thought of Dona Evarista in terms of the lofty spirit and prestige of her husband; they envied her, to be sure, but with the noble and blessed envy of admiration.

II.   A Torrent of Madmen

Three days later, talking in an expansive mood with the druggist Crispim Soares, the psychiatrist revealed his inmost thoughts.

"Charity, Soares, definitely enters into my method. It is the seasoning in the recipe, for thus I interpret the words of St. Paul to the Corinthians: 'Though I understand all mysteries and all knowledge ... and have not charity, I am nothing.' But the main thing in my work at the Green House is to study insanity in depth, to learn its various gradations, to classify the various cases, and finally to discover the cause of the phenomenon and its remedy. This is my heart's desire. I believe that in this way I can render a valuable service to humanity."

"A great service," said Crispim Soares.

"Without this asylum," continued the psychiatrist, "I might conceivably accomplish a little. But it provides far greater scope and opportunity for my studies than I would otherwise have."

"Far greater," agreed the druggist.

And he was right. From all the towns and villages in the vicinity came the violent, the depressed, the monomaniacal—the mentally ill of every type and variety. At the end of four months the Green House was a little community in itself. A gallery with thirty-seven more cubicles had to be added. Father Lopes confessed that he had not imagined there were so many madmen in the world nor that such strange cases of madness existed. One of the patients, a coarse, ignorant young man, gave a speech every day after lunch.

It was an academic discourse, with metaphors, antitheses, and apostrophes, ornamented with Greek words and quotations from Cicero, Apuleius, and Tertullian. The Vicar could hardly believe his ears. What, a fellow he had seen only three months ago hanging around street corners!

"Quite so," replied the psychiatrist. "But Your Reverence has observed for himself. This happens every day."

"The only explanation I can think of," said the priest, "is the confusion of languages on the Tower of Babel. They were so completely mixed together that now, probably, when a man loses his reason, he easily slips from one into another."

"That may well be the divine explanation," agreed the psychiatrist after a moment's reflection, "but I'm looking for a purely scientific, human explanation—and I believe there is one."

"Maybe so, but I really can't imagine what it could be."

Several of the patients had been driven mad by love. One of these spent all his time wandering through the building and courtyard in search of his wife, whom he had killed in a fit of jealousy that marked the beginning of his insanity. Another thought he was the morning star. He had repeatedly proposed marriage to a certain young lady, and she had continually put him off. He knew why: she thought him dreadfully dull and was waiting to see if she could catch a more interesting husband. So he became a brilliant star, standing with feet and arms outspread like rays. He would remain in this position for hours, waiting to be supplanted by the rising sun.

There were some noteworthy cases of megalomania. One patient, the son of a cheap tailor, invented a genealogy in which he traced his ancestry back to members of royalty and, through them, ultimately to Jehovah. He would recite the entire list of his male progenitors, with a "begat" to link each father and son. Then he would slap his forehead, snap his fingers, and say it all over again. Another patient had a somewhat similar idea but developed it with more rigorous logic. Beginning with the proposition that he was a child of God, which even the Vicar would not have denied, he reasoned that, as the species of the child is the same as that of the parent, he himself must be a god. This conclusion, derived from two irrefutable premises—one Biblical, the other scientific—placed him far above the lunatics who identified themselves with Caesar, Alexander, or other mere mortals.

More remarkable even than the manias and delusions of the madmen was the patience of the psychiatrist. He began by engaging two administrative assistants—an idea that he accepted from Crispim Soares along with the druggist's two nephews. He gave these young men the task of enforcing the rules and regulations that the Town Council had approved for the asylum. They also kept the records and were in charge of the distribution of food and clothing. Thus, the doctor was free to devote all his time to psychiatry.

"The Green House," he told the Vicar, "now has its temporal government and its spiritual government."*

Father Lopes laughed. "What a delightful novelty," he said, "to find a society in which the spiritual dominates."

Relieved of administrative burdens, Dr. Bacamarte began an exhaustive study of each patient: his personal and family history, his habits, his likes and dislikes, his hobbies, his attitudes toward others, and so on. He also spent long hours studying, inventing, and experimenting with psychotherapeutic methods. He slept little and ate little; and while he ate he was still working, for at the dinner table he would read an old text or ponder a difficult problem. Often he sat through an entire dinner without saying a word to Dona Evarista.

III.   God Knows What He Is Doing

By the end of two months the psychiatrist's wife was the most wretched of women. She did not reproach her husband but suffered in silence. She declined into a state of deep melancholy, became thin and yellowish, ate little, and sighed continually. One day, at dinner, he asked what was wrong with her. She sadly replied that it was nothing. Then she ventured for the first time to complain a little, saying she considered herself as much a widow now as before she married him.

"Who would ever have thought that a bunch of lunatics . . ."

She did not complete the sentence. Or, rather, she completed it by raising her eyes to the ceiling. Dona Evarista's eyes were her most attractive feature—large, black, and bathed in a vaporous light like the dawn. She had used them in much the same way when trying to get Simão Bacamarte to propose. Now she was brandishing her weapon again, this time for the apparent purpose of cutting science's throat. But the psychiatrist was not perturbed. His

*A play on words, for *espiritual* means both "spiritual" and "pertaining to the mind."

eyes remained steady, calm, enduring. No wrinkle disturbed his brow, as serene as the waters of Botafogo Bay. Perhaps a slight smile played on his lips as he said:

"You may go to Rio de Janeiro."

Dona Evarista felt as if the floor had vanished and she were floating on air. She had never been to Rio, which, although hardly a shadow of what it is today, was, by comparison with Itaguai, a great and fascinating metropolis. Ever since childhood she had dreamed of going there. She longed for Rio as a Hebrew in the captivity must have longed for Jerusalem, but with her husband settled so definitively in Itaguai she had lost hope. And now, of a sudden, he was permitting her to realize her dream. Dona Evarista could not hide her elation. Simão Bacamarte took her by the hand and smiled in a manner at once conjugal and philosophical.

"How strange is the therapy of the soul!" he thought. "This lady is wasting away because she thinks I do not love her. I give her Rio de Janeiro and she is well again." And he made a note of the phenomenon.

A sudden misgiving pierced Dona Evarista's heart. She concealed her anxiety, however, and merely told her husband that, if he did not go, neither would she, for of course she could not travel alone.

"Your aunt will go with you," replied the psychiatrist.

It should be noted that this expedient had occurred to Dona Evarista. She had not suggested it, for it would impose great expense on her husband. Besides, it was better for the suggestion to come from him.

"Oh, but the money it will cost!" she sighed.

"It doesn't matter," he replied. "Have you any idea of our income?"

He brought her the books of account. Dona Evarista, although impressed by the quantity of the figures, was not quite sure what they signified, so her husband took her to the chest where the money was kept.

Good heavens! There were mountains of gold, thousands upon thousands of cruzados and doubloons. A fortune! While she was drinking it in with her black eyes, the psychiatrist placed his mouth close to her and whispered mischievously:

"Who would ever have thought that a bunch of lunatics ..."

Dona Evarista understood, smiled, and replied with infinite resignation:

"God knows what he is doing."

Three months later she left for Rio in the company of her aunt,
the druggist's wife, one of the druggist's cousins, a priest whom
Bacamarte had known in Lisbon and who happened to be in Itaguai, four maidservants, and five or six male attendants. A small
crowd had come to see them off. The farewells were sad for everyone but the psychiatrist, for he was troubled by nothing outside
the realm of science. Even Dona Evarista's tears, sincere and abundant as they were, did not affect him. If anything concerned him
on that occasion, if he cast a restless and police-like eye over the
crowd, it was only because he suspected the presence of one or
two candidates for commitment to the Green House.

After the departure the druggist and the psychiatrist mounted
their horses and rode homeward. Crispim Soares stared at the road,
between the ears of his roan. Simão Bacamarte swept the horizon
with his eyes, surveyed the distant mountains, and let his horse
find the way home. Perfect symbols of the common man and of
the genius! One fixes his gaze upon the present with all its tears
and privations; the other looks beyond to the glorious dawns of a
future that he himself will shape.

IV. A New Theory

As his horse jogged along, a new and daring hypothesis occurred
to Simão Bacamarte. It was so daring, indeed, that, if substantiated,
it would revolutionize the bases of psychopathology. During the
next few days he mulled it over. Then, in his spare time, he began
to go from house to house, talking with the townspeople about a
thousand and one things and punctuating the conversations with
a penetrating look that terrified even the bravest.

One morning, after this had been going on for about three
weeks, Crispim Soares received a message that the psychiatrist
wished to see him.

"He says it's important," added the messenger.

The druggist turned pale. Something must have happened to his
wife! The chroniclers of Itaguai, it should be noted, dwell upon
Crispim's love for his Cesaria and point out that they had never
been separated in their thirty years of marriage. Only against this
background can one explain the monologue, often overheard by
the servants, with which the druggist reviled himself: "You miss
your wife, do you? You're going crazy without her? It serves you
right! Always truckling to Dr. Bacamarte! Who told you to let Ces-

aria go traveling? Dr. Bacamarte, that's who. Anything he says, you
say amen. So now see what you get for it, you vile, miserable, grov-
eling little lackey! Lickspittle! Flunky!" And he added many other
ugly names that a man ought not call his enemies, much less himself. The effect of the message on him, in this state of mind, can
be readily imagined. He dropped the drugs he had been mixing
and fairly flew to the Green House. Simão Bacamarte greeted him
joyfully, but he wore his joy as a wise man should—buttoned up
to the neck with circumspection.

"I am very happy," he said.

"Some news of our wives?" asked the druggist in a tremulous
voice.

The psychiatrist made a magnificent gesture and replied:

"It is something much more important—a scientific experiment.
I say 'experiment,' for I do not yet venture to affirm the correctness
of my theory. Indeed, this is the very nature of science, Soares:
unending inquiry. But, although only an experiment as yet, it may
change the face of the earth. Till now, madness has been thought
a small island in an ocean of sanity. I am beginning to suspect that
it is not an island at all but a continent."

He fell silent for a while, enjoying the druggist's amazement.
Then he explained his theory at length. The number of persons
suffering from insanity, he believed, was far greater than commonly supposed; and he developed this idea with an abundance
of reasons, texts, and examples. He found many of these examples
in Itaguai, but he recognized the fallacy of confining his data to
one time and place and he therefore resorted to history. He
pointed in particular to certain historical celebrities: Socrates, who
thought he had a personal demon; Pascal, who sewed a report of
a hallucination into the lining of his coat; Mohammed, Caracalla,
Domitian, Caligula, and others. The druggist's surprise at Bacamarte's mingling of the vicious and the merely ridiculous moved
the psychiatrist to explain that these apparently inconsistent attributes were really different aspects of the same thing.

"The grotesque, my friend, is simply ferocity in disguise."

"Clever, very clever!" exclaimed Crispim Soares.

As for the basic idea of enlarging the realm of insanity, the druggist found it a little far-fetched; but modesty, his chief virtue, kept
him from stating his opinion. Instead, he expressed a noble enthusiasm. He declared the idea sublime and added that it was "something for the noisemaker." This expression requires explanation.
Like the other towns, villages, and settlements in the colony at that

time, Itaguai had no newspaper. It used two media for the publication of news: hand-written posters nailed to the doors of the town hall and of the main church, and the noisemaker.

This is how the latter medium worked: a man was hired for one or more days to go through the streets rattling a noisemaker. A crowd would gather and the man would announce whatever he had been paid to announce: a cure for malaria, a gift to the Church, some farm land for sale, and the like. He might even be engaged to read a sonnet to the people. The system continually disturbed the peace of the community, but it survived a long time because of its almost miraculous effectiveness. Incredible as it may seem, the noisemaker actually enabled merchants to sell inferior goods at superior prices and third-rate authors to pass as geniuses. Yes, indeed, not all the institutions of the old regime deserve our century's contempt.

"No, I won't announce my theory to the public," replied the psychiatrist. "I'll do something better: I'll act on it."

The druggist agreed that it might be best to begin that way. "There'll be plenty of time for the noisemaker afterwards," he concluded.

But Simão Bacamarte was not listening. He seemed lost in meditation. When he finally spoke, it was with great deliberation.

"Think of humanity," he said, "as a great oyster shell. Our first task, Soares, is to extract the pearl—that is, reason. In other words, we must determine the nature and boundaries of reason. Madness is simply all that lies beyond those limits. But what is reason if not the equilibrium of the mental faculties? An individual, therefore, who lacks this equilibrium in any particular is, to that extent, insane."

Father Lopes, to whom he also confided his theory, replied that he was not quite sure he understood it but that it sounded a little dangerous and, in any case, would involve more work than one doctor could possibly handle.

"Under the present definition of insanity, which has always been accepted," he added, "the fence around the area is perfectly clear and satisfactory. Why not stay within it?"

The vague suggestion of a smile played on the fine and discreet lips of the psychiatrist, a smile in which disdain blended with pity. But he said nothing. Science merely extended its hand to theology—with such assurance that theology was undecided whether to believe in itself or in science. Itaguai and the entire world were on the brink of a revolution.

V. The Terror

Four days later the population of Itaguai was dismayed to hear that a certain Mr. Costa had been committed to the Green House.

"Impossible!"

"What do you mean impossible! They took him away this morning."

Costa was one of the most highly esteemed citizens of Itaguai. He had inherited 400,000 cruzados in the good coin of King João V. As his uncle said in the will, the interest on this capital would have been enough to support him "till the end of the world." But as soon as he received the inheritance he began to make loans to people without interest: a thousand cruzados to one, two thousand to another, three hundred to another, eight hundred to another, until, at the end of five years, there was nothing left. If poverty had come to him all at once, the shock to the good people of Itaguai would have been enormous. But it came gradually. He went from opulence to wealth, from wealth to comfort, from comfort to indigence, and from indigence to poverty. People who, five years earlier, had always doffed their hats and bowed deeply to him as soon as they saw him a block away, now clapped him on the shoulder, flicked him on the nose, and made coarse remarks. But Costa remained affable, smiling, sublimely resigned. He was untroubled even by the fact that the least courteous were the very ones who owed him money; on the contrary, he seemed to greet them with especial pleasure.

Once, when one of these eternal debtors jeered at him and Costa merely smiled, someone said to him: "You're nice to this fellow because you still hope you can get him to pay what he owes you." Costa did not hesitate an instant. He went to the debtor and forgave the debt. "Sure," said the man who had made the unkind remark, "Costa canceled the debt because he knew he couldn't collect it anyway." Costa was no fool; he had anticipated this reaction. Inventive and jealous of his honor, he found a way two hours later to prove the slur unmerited: he took a few coins and loaned them to the same debtor.

"Now I hope . . . ," he thought.

This act of Costa's convinced the credulous and incredulous alike. Thereafter no one doubted the nobility of spirit of that worthy citizen. All the needy, no matter how timid, came in their patched cloaks and knocked on his door. The words of the man who had impugned his motive continued, however, to gnaw like

worms at his soul. But this also ended, for three months later the
man asked him for one hundred and twenty cruzados, promising
to repay it in two days. This was all that remained of the inheritance, but Costa made the loan immediately, without hesitation or
interest. It was a means of noble redress for the stain on his honor.
In time the debt might have been paid; unfortunately, Costa could
not wait, for five months later he was committed to the Green
House.

The consternation in Itaguai, when the matter became known,
can readily be imagined. No one spoke of anything else. Some said
that Costa had gone mad during lunch, other said it had happened
early in the morning. They told of the mental attacks he had suffered, described by some as violent and frightening, by others as
mild and even amusing. Many people hurried to the Green House.
There they found poor Costa calm if somewhat surprised, speaking
with great lucidity and asking why he had been brought there.
Some went and talked with the psychiatrist. Bacamarte approved
of their esteem and compassion for the patient, but he explained
that science was science and that he could not permit a madman
to remain at large. The last person to intercede (for, after what I
am about to relate, no one dared go to see the dreadful psychiatrist) was a lady cousin of the patient. The doctor told her that
Costa must certainly be insane, for otherwise he would not have
thrown away all the money that . . .

"No! Now there you are wrong!" interrupted the good woman
energetically. "He was not to blame for what he did."

"No?"

"No, Doctor. I'll tell you exactly what happened. My uncle was
not ordinarily a bad man, but when he became angry he was so
fierce that he would not even take off his hat to a religious procession. Well, one day, a short time before he died, he discovered
that a slave had stolen an ox from him. His face became as red as
a pepper; he shook from head to foot; he foamed at the mouth.
Then an ugly, shaggy-haired man came up to him and asked for a
drink of water. My uncle (may God show him the light!) told the
man to go drink in the river—or in hell, for all he cared. The man
glared at him, raised his hand threateningly, and uttered this curse:
'Your money will not last more than seven years and a day, as
surely as this is the star of David!' And he showed a star of David
tattooed on his arm. That was the cause of it all, Doctor—the hex
put on the money by that evil man."

Bacamarte's eyes pierced the poor woman like daggers. When

she had finished, he extended his hand as courteously as if she had been the wife of the Viceroy and invited her to go and talk with her cousin. The miserable woman believed him. He took her to the Green House and locked her up in the ward for those suffering from delusions or hallucinations.

When this duplicity on the part of the illustrious Bacamarte became known, the townspeople were terrified. No one could believe that, for no reason at all, the psychiatrist would lock up a perfectly sane woman whose only offense had been to intercede on behalf of an unfortunate relative. The case was gossiped about on street corners and in barber shops. Within a short time it developed into a full-scale novel, with amorous overtures by the psychiatrist to Costa's cousin, Costa's indignation, the cousin's scorn, and finally the psychiatrist's vengeance on them both. It was all very obvious. But did not the doctor's austerity and his life of devotion to science give the lie to such a story? Not at all! This was merely a cloak by which he concealed his treachery. And one of the more credulous of the townspeople even whispered that he knew certain other things—he would not say what, for he lacked complete proof—but he knew they were true, he could almost swear to them.

"You who are his intimate friend," they asked the druggist, "can't you tell us what's going on, what happened, what reason ...?"

Crispim Soares was delighted. This questioning by his puzzled friends, and by the uneasy and curious in general, amounted to public recognition of his importance. There was no doubt about it, the entire population knew that he, Crispim the druggist, was the psychiatrist's confidant, the great man's collaborator. That is why they all came running to the pharmacy. All this could be read in the druggist's jocund expression and discreet smile—and in his silence, for he made no reply. One, two, perhaps three dry monosyllables at the most, cloaked in a loyal, constant half-smile and full of scientific mysteries which he could reveal to no human being without danger and dishonor.

"There's something very strange going on," thought the townspeople.

But one of them merely shrugged his shoulders and went on his way. He had more important interests. He had just built a magnificent house, with a garden that was a masterpiece of art and taste. His furniture, imported from Hungary and Holland, was visible from the street, for the windows were always open. This man, who had become rich in the manufacture of packsaddles, had always dreamed of owning a sumptuous house, an elaborate garden, and rare furniture. Now he had acquired all these things and, in semi-retirement, was devoting most of his time to the enjoyment of them. His house was undoubtedly the finest in Itaguai, more grandiose than the Green House, nobler than the town hall. There was wailing and gnashing of teeth among Itaguai's social elite whenever they heard it praised or even mentioned—indeed, when they even thought about it. Owned by a mere manufacturer of packsaddles, good God!

"There he is, staring at his own house," the passers-by would say. For it was his custom to station himself every morning in the middle of his garden and gaze lovingly at the house. He would keep this up for a good hour, until called in to lunch.

Although his neighbors always greeted him respectfully enough, they would laugh behind his back. One of them observed that Mateus could make a lot more money manufacturing packsaddles to put on himself—a somewhat unintelligible remark, which nevertheless sent the listeners into ecstasies of laughter.

Every afternoon, when the families went out for their after dinner walks (people dined early in those days), Mateus would station himself at the center window, elegantly clothed in white against a dark background. He would remain there in a majestic pose for three or four hours, until it was dark. One may reasonably infer an intention on Mateus's part to be admired and envied, although he confessed no such purpose to anyone, not even to Father Lopes. His good friend the druggist nevertheless drew the inference and communicated it to Bacamarte. The psychiatrist suggested that, as the saddler's house was of stone, he might have been suffering from petrophilia, an illness that the doctor had discovered and had been studying for some time. This continual gazing at the house . . .

"No, Doctor," interrupted Crispim Soares vigorously.

"No?"

"Pardon me, but perhaps you don't know . . ." And he told the psychiatrist what the saddler did every afternoon.

Simão Bacamarte's eyes lighted up with scientific voluptuousness. He questioned Crispim at some length, and the answers he received were apparently satisfactory, even pleasant, to him. But there was no suggestion of a sinister intent in the psychiatrist's face or manner—quite the contrary—as he asked the druggist's arm for a little stroll in the afternoon sun. It was the first time he had bestowed this honor on his confidant. Crispim, stunned and trembling, accepted the invitation. Just then, two or three people came to see the doctor. Crispim silently consigned them to all the devils. They were delaying the walk; Bacamarte might even take it into his head to invite one of them in Crispim's stead. What impatience! What anxiety! Finally the visitors left and the two men set out on their walk. The psychiatrist chose the direction of Mateus's house. He strolled by the window five or six times, slowly, stopping now and then and observing the saddler's physical attitude and facial expression. Poor Mateus noticed only that he was an object of the curiosity or admiration of the most important figure in Itaguai. He intensified the nobility of his expression, the stateliness of his pose. . . . Alas! he was merely helping to condemn himself. The next day he was committed.

"The Green House is a private prison," said an unsuccessful doctor.

Never had an opinion caught on and spread so rapidly. "A private prison"—the words were repeated from one end of Itaguai to the other. Fearfully, to be sure, for during the week following the Mateus episode twenty-odd persons, including two or three of the town's prominent citizens, had been committed to the Green House. The psychiatrist said that only the mentally ill were admitted, but few believed him. Then came the popular explanations of the matter: revenge, greed, a punishment from God, a monomania afflicting the doctor himself, a secret plan on the part of Rio de Janeiro to destroy the budding prosperity of Itaguai and ultimately to impoverish this rival municipality, and a thousand other products of the public imagination.

At this time the party of travelers returned from their visit of several weeks to Rio de Janeiro. The psychiatrist, the druggist, Father Lopes, the Councilmen, and several other officials went to greet them. The moment when Dona Evarista laid eyes again on her husband is regarded by the chronicles of the time as one of the most sublime instants in the moral history of man, because of the contrast between these two extreme (although both commendable) natures. Dona Evarista uttered a cry, stammered a word or two, and threw herself at her husband in a way that suggested at once the fierceness of a wildcat and the gentle affection of a dove. Not so the noble Bacamarte. With diagnostic objectivity, without disturbing for a moment his scientific austerity, he extended his arms to the lady, who fell into them and fainted. The incident was brief; two minutes later Dona Evarista's friends were greeting her and the homeward procession began.

The psychiatrist's wife was Itaguai's great hope. Everyone

counted on her to alleviate the scourge. Hence the public accla-
mation, the crowds in the streets, the pennants, and the flowers in
the windows. The eminent Bacamarte, having entrusted her to the
arm of Father Lopes, walked contemplatively with measured step.
Dona Evarista, on the contrary, turned her head animatedly from
side to side, observing with curiosity the unexpectedly warm reception. The priest asked about Rio de Janeiro, which he had not seen
since the previous viceroyalty, and Dona Evarista replied that it
was the most beautiful sight there could possibly be in the entire
world. The Public Gardens, now completed, were a paradise in
which she had often strolled—and the Street of Beautiful Nights,
the Fountain of Ducks . . . Ah! the Fountain of Ducks. There really
were ducks there, made of metal and spouting water through their
mouths. A gorgeous thing. The priest said that Rio de Janeiro had
been lovely even in his time there and must be much lovelier now.
Small wonder, for it was so much larger than Itaguai and was,
moreover, the capital. . . . But one could not call Itaguai ugly; it
had some beautiful buildings, such as Mateus's mansion, the Green
House . . .

"And apropos the Green House," said Father Lopes, gliding
skillfully into the subject, "you will find it full of patients."

"Really?"

"Yes. Mateus is there. . . ."

"The saddler?"

"Costa is there too. So is Costa's cousin, and So-and-so, and
What's-his-name, and . . ."

"All insane?"

"Apparently," replied the priest.

"But how? Why?"

Father Lopes drew down the corners of his mouth as if to say
that he did not know or did not wish to tell what he knew—a vague
reply, which could not be repeated to anyone. Dona Evarista found
it strange indeed that all those people should have gone mad. It
might easily happen to one or another—but to *all* of them? Yet
she could hardly doubt the fact. Her husband was a learned man,
a scientist; he would not commit anyone to the Green House without clear proof of insanity.

The priest punctuated her observations with an intermittent
"undoubtedly . . . undoubtedly . . ."

A few hours later about fifty guests were seated at Simão Bacamarte's table for the homecoming dinner. Dona Evarista was the
obligatory subject of toasts, speeches, and verses, all of them highly

metaphorical. She was the wife of the new Hippocrates, the muse of science, an angel, the dawn, charity, consolation, life itself. Her eyes were two stars, according to Crispim Soares, and two suns, by a Councilman's less modest figure. The psychiatrist found all this a bit tiresome but showed no signs of impatience. He merely leaned toward his wife and told her that such flights of fancy, although permissible in rhetoric, were unsubstantiated in fact. Dona Evarista tried to accept this opinion; but, even if she discounted three fourths of the flattery, there was enough left to inflate her considerably. One of the orators, for example—Martim Brito, twenty-five, a pretentious fop, much addicted to women—declaimed that the birth of Dona Evarista had come about in this manner: "After God gave the universe to man and to woman, who are the diamond and the pearl of the divine crown" (and the orator dragged this phrase triumphantly from one end of the table to the other), "God decided to outdo God and so he created Dona Evarista."

The psychiatrist's wife lowered her eyes with exemplary modesty. Two other ladies, who thought Martim Brito's expression of adulation excessive and audacious, turned to observe its effect on Dona Evarista's husband. They found his face clouded with misgivings, threats, and possibly blood. The provocation was great indeed, thought the two ladies. They prayed God to prevent any tragic occurrence—or, better yet, to postpone it until the next day. The more charitable of the two admitted (to herself) that Dona Evarista was above suspicion, for she was so very unattractive. And yet not all tastes were alike. Maybe some men ... This idea caused her to tremble again, although less violently than before; less violently, for the psychiatrist was now smiling at Martim Brito.

When everyone had risen from the table, Bacamarte walked over to him and complimented him on his eulogy of Dona Evarista. He said it was a brilliant improvisation, full of magnificent figures of speech. Had Brito himself originated the thought about Dona Evarista's birth or had he taken it from something he had read? No, it was entirely original; it had come to him as he was speaking and he had considered it suitable for use as a rhetorical climax. As a matter of fact, he always leaned toward the bold and daring rather than the tender or jocose. He favored the epic style. Once, for example, he had composed an ode on the fall of the Marquis of Pombal in which he had said that "the foul dragon of Nihility is crushed in the vengeful claws of the All." And he had invented many other powerful figures of speech. He liked sublime concepts, great and noble images. . . .

"Poor fellow!" though the psychiatrist. "He's probably suffering from a cerebral lesion. Not a very serious case but worthy of study."

Three days later Dona Evarista learned, to her amazement, that Martim Brito was now living at the Green House. A young man with such beautiful thoughts! The two other ladies attributed his commitment to jealousy on the part of the psychiatrist, for the young man's words had been provocatively bold.

Jealousy? But how, then, can one explain the commitment a short time afterwards of persons of whom the doctor could not possibly have been jealous: innocuous, fun-loving Chico, Fabrício the notary, and many others. The terror grew in intensity. One no longer knew who was sane and who was insane. When their husbands went out in the street, the women of Itaguai lit candles to Our Lady. And some of the men hired bodyguards to go around with them.

Everyone who could possibly get out of town, did so. One of the fugitives, however, was seized just as he was leaving. He was Gil Bernardes, a friendly, polite young man; so polite, indeed, that he never said hello to anyone without doffing his hat and bowing to the ground. In the street he would sometimes run forty yards to shake the hand of a gentleman or lady—or even of a child, such as the Circuit Judge's little boy. He had a special talent for affability. He owed his acceptance by society not only to his personal charm but also to the noble tenacity with which he withstood any number of refusals, rejections, cold shoulders, and the like, without becoming discouraged. And, once he gained entry to a house, he never left it—nor did its occupants wish him to leave, for he was a delightful guest. Despite his popularity and the self-confidence it engendered, Gil Bernardes turned pale when he heard one day that the psychiatrist was watching him. The following morning he started to leave town but was apprehended and taken to the Green House.

"This must not be permitted to continue."

"Down with tyranny!"

"Despot! Outlaw! Goliath!"

At first such things were said softly and indoors. Later they were shouted in the streets. Rebellion was raising its ugly head. The thought of a petition to the government for the arrest and deportation of Simão Bacamarte occurred to many people even before Porfírio, with eloquent gestures of indignation, expounded it in his barber shop. Let it be noted—and this is one of the finest pages of a somber history—that as soon as the population of the Green

House began to grow so rapidly, Porfírio's profits also increased, for many of his customers now asked to be bled; but private interests, said the barber, have to yield to the public welfare. "The tyrant must be overthrown!" So great was his dedication to the cause that he uttered this cry shortly after he heard of the commitment of a man named Coelho who was bringing a lawsuit against him.

"How can anyone call Coelho crazy?" shouted Porfírio.

And no one answered. Everybody said he was perfectly sane. The legal action against the barber, involving some real estate, grew not out of hatred or spite but out of the obscure wording of a deed. Coelho had an excellent reputation. A few individuals, to be sure, avoided him; as soon as they saw him approaching in the distance they ran around corners, ducked into stores. The fact is, he loved conversation—long conversation, drunk down in large draughts. Consequently he was almost never alone. He preferred those who also liked to talk, but he would compromise, if necessary, for a unilateral conversation with the more taciturn. Whenever Father Lopes, who disliked Coelho, saw him taking his leave of someone, he quoted Dante, with a minor change of his own:

> "La bocca sollevò dal fiero pasto
> Quel seccatore . . ."*

But the priest's remark did not affect the general esteem in which Coelho was held, for some attributed the remark to mere personal animosity and others thought it was a prayer in Latin.

VI.   The Rebellion

About thirty people allied themselves with the barber. They prepared a formal complaint and took it to the Town Council, which rejected it on the ground that scientific research must be hampered neither by hostile legislation nor by the misconceptions and prejudices of the mob.

"My advice to you," said the President of the Council, "is to disband and go back to work."

The group could hardly contain its anger. The barber declared

---

*"The pest raised his mouth from his savage repast." Father Lopes substituted *seccatore,* "pest," for Dante's *peccator,* "sinner." Count Ugolino, the sinner, was gnawing the head of another sinner. *Inferno,* Canto XXXIII.

that the people would march to the Green House and destroy it;
that Itaguai must no longer be used as a corpse for dissection in
the experiments of a medical despot; that several esteemed and
even distinguished individuals, not to mention many humble and
estimable persons, lay confined in the cubicles of the Green House;
that the psychiatrist was clearly motivated by greed, for his com-
pensation varied directly with the number of alleged madmen in
his care—

"That's not true," interrupted the President.

"Not true?"

"About two weeks ago we received a communication from the
illustrious doctor in which he stated that, in view of the great value,
to him as a scientist, of his observations and experiments, he would
no longer accept payment from the Council or from the patients'
families."

In view of this noble act of self-denial, how could the rebels
persist in their attitude? The psychiatrist might, indeed, make mis-
takes, but obviously he was not motivated by any interest alien to
science; and to establish error on his part, something more would
be needed than disorderly crowds in the street. So spoke the President, and the entire Council applauded.

The barber meditated for a few moments and then declared that
he was invested with a public mandate; he would give Itaguai no
peace until the final destruction of the Green House, "that Bastille
of human reason"—an expression he had heard a local poet use
and which he now repeated with great vigor. Having spoken, he
gave his cohorts a signal and led them out.

The Council was faced with an emergency. It must, at all costs,
prevent rebellion and bloodshed. To make matters worse, one of
the Councilmen who had supported the President was so impressed by the figure of speech, "Bastille of the human reason,"
that he changed his mind. He advocated adoption of a measure to
liquidate the Green House. After the President had expressed his
amazement and indignation, the dissenter observed:

"I know nothing about science, but if so many men whom we
considered sane are locked up as madmen, how do we know that
the real madman is not the psychiatrist himself?"

This Councilman, a highly articulate fellow named Sebastião
Freitas, spoke at some length. He presented the case against the
Green House with restraint but with firm conviction. His colleagues were dumbfounded. The President begged him at least to
help preserve law and order by not expressing his opinions in the

street, where they might give body and soul to what was so far merely a whirlwind of uncoordinated atoms. This figure of speech counterbalanced to some extent the one about the Bastille. Sebastião Freitas promised to take no action for the present but reserved the right to seek the elimination of the Green House by legal means. And he murmured to himself lovingly: "That Bastille of the human reason!"

Nevertheless, the crowd grew. Not thirty but three hundred now followed the barber, whose nickname ought to be mentioned at this point because it gave the rebellion its name: he was called Stewed Corn, and the movement was therefore known as the Revolt of the Stewed Corners. Storming through the streets toward the Green House, they might well have been compared to the mob that stormed the Bastille, with due allowance, of course, for the difference between Paris and Itaguai.

A young child attached to the household ran in from the street and told Dona Evarista the news. The psychiatrist's wife was trying on a silk dress (one of the thirty-seven she had bought in Rio).

"It's probably just a bunch of drunks," she said as she changed the location of a pin. "Benedita, is the hem all right?"

"Yes, ma'am," replied the slave, who was squatting on the floor, "it looks fine. Just turn a little bit. Like that. It's perfect, ma'am."

"They're not a bunch of drunks, Dona Evarista," said the child in fear. "They're shouting: 'Death to Dr. Bacamarte the tyrant.'"

"Be quiet! Benedita, look over here on the left side. Don't you think the seam is a little crooked? We'll have to rip it and sew it again. Try to make it nice and even this time."

"Death to Dr. Bacamarte! Death to the tyrant!" howled three hundred voices in the street.

The blood left Dona Evarista's face. She stood there like a statue, petrified with terror. The slave ran instinctively to the back door. The child, whom Dona Evarista had refused to believe, enjoyed a moment of unexpressed but profound satisfaction.

"Death to the psychiatrist!" shouted the voices, now closer than before.

Dona Evarista, although an easy prey to emotions of pleasure, was reasonably steadfast in adversity. She did not faint. She ran to the inside room where her husband was studying. At the moment of her precipitate entrance, the doctor was examining a passage in Averroës. His eyes, blind to external reality but highly perceptive in the realm of the inner life, rose from the book to the ceiling and returned to the book. Twice, Dona Evarista called him loudly by name without his paying her the least attention. The third time, he heard and asked what was troubling her.

"Can't you hear the shouting?"

The psychiatrist listened. The shouts were coming closer and closer, threatening, terrifying. He understood. Rising from the armchair, he shut the book and, with firm, calm step, walked over to the bookcase and put the volume back in its place. The insertion of the volume caused the books on either side of it to be slightly out of line. Simão Bacamarte carefully straightened them. Then he asked his wife to go to her room.

"No, no," begged his worthy helpmeet. "I want to die at your side where I belong."

Simão Bacamarte insisted that she go. He assured her that it was not a matter of life and death and told her that, even if it were, it would be her duty to remain alive. The unhappy lady bowed her head, tearful and obedient.

"Down with the Green House!" shouted the Stewed Corners.

The psychiatrist went out on the front balcony and faced the rebel mob, whose three hundred heads were radiant with civism and somber with fury. When they saw him they shouted: "Die! Die!" Simão Bacamarte indicated that he wished to speak, but they only shouted the louder. Then the barber waved his hat as a signal to his followers to be silent and told the psychiatrist that he might speak, provided his words did not abuse the patience of the people.

"I shall say little and, if possible, nothing at all. It depends on what it is that you have come to request."

"We aren't requesting anything," replied the barber, trembling with rage. "We are demanding that the Green House be destroyed or at least that all the prisoners in it be freed."

"I don't understand."

"You understand all right, tyrant. We want you to release the victims of your hatred, your whims, your greed. . . ."

The psychiatrist smiled, but the smile of this great man was not perceptible to the eyes of the multitude: it was a slight contraction of two or three muscles, nothing more.

"Gentlemen," he said, "science is a serious thing and it must be treated seriously. For my professional decisions I account to no one but God and the authorities in my special field. If you wish to suggest changes in the administration of the Green House, I am ready to listen to you; but if you wish me to be untrue to myself, further talk would be futile. I could invite you to appoint a committee to come and study the way I treat the madmen who have been committed to my care, but I shall not, for to do so would be to account to you for my methods and this I shall never do to a group of rebels or, for that matter, to laymen of any description."

So spoke the psychiatrist, and the people were astounded at his words. Obviously they had not expected such imperturbability and such resoluteness. Their amazement was even greater when the psychiatrist bowed gravely to them, turned his back, and walked slowly back into the house. The barber soon regained his self-possession and, waving his hat, urged the mob to demolish the Green House. The voices that took up the cry were few and weak. At this decisive moment the barber felt a surging ambition to rule. If he succeeded in overthrowing the psychiatrist and destroying the Green House, he might well take over the Town Council, dominate the other municipal authorities, and make himself the master of Itaguai. For some years now he had striven to have his name included in the ballots from which the Councilmen were selected by lot, but his petitions were denied because his position in society was considered incompatible with such a responsibility. It was a case of now or never. Besides, he had carried the street riot to such a point that defeat would mean prison and perhaps banishment or even the scaffold. Unfortunately, the psychiatrist's reply had taken most of the steam out of the Stewed Corners. When the barber perceived this, he felt like shouting: "Wretches! Cowards!" But he contained himself and merely said:

"My friends, let us fight to the end! The salvation of Itaguai is in your worthy and heroic hands. Let us destroy the foul prison that confines or threatens your children and parents, your mothers and sisters, your relatives and friends, and you yourselves. Do you want to be thrown into a dungeon and starved on bread and water or maybe whipped to death?"

The mob bestirred itself, murmured, shouted, and gathered around the barber. The revolt was emerging from its stupor and threatening to demolish the Green House.

"Come on!" shouted Porfírio, waving his hat.

"Come on!" echoed his followers.

At that moment a corps of dragoons turned the corner and came marching toward the mob.

VII. The Unexpected

The mob appeared stupefied by the arrival of the dragoons; the Stewed Corners could hardly believe that the force of the law was being exerted against them. The dragoons halted and their captain ordered the crowd to disperse. Some of the rebels felt inclined to obey, but others rallied around the barber, who boldly replied to the captain:

"We shall not disperse. If you wish, you may take our lives, but nothing else: we will not yield our honor or our rights, for on them depends the salvation of Itaguai."

Nothing could have been more imprudent or more natural than this reply. It reflected the ecstasy inspired by great crises. Perhaps it reflected also an excess of confidence in the captain's forbearance, a confidence soon dispelled by the captain's order to charge. What followed is indescribable. The mob howled its fury. Some managed to escape by climbing into windows or running down the street, but the majority, inspired by the barber's words, snorted with anger and stood their ground. The defeat of the Stewed Corners appeared imminent, when suddenly one third of the dragoons, for reasons not set forth in the chronicles, went over to the side of the rebels. This unexpected reënforcement naturally heartened the Stewed Corners and discouraged the ranks of legality. The loyal soldiers refused to attack their comrades and, one by one, joined them, with the result that in a few minutes the entire aspect of the struggle had changed. The captain, defended by only a handful of his men against a compact mass of rebels and soldiers, gave up and surrendered his sword to the barber.

The triumphant rebels did not lose an instant. They carried the wounded into the nearest houses and headed for the town hall. The people and the troops fraternized. They shouted *vivas* for the King, the Viceroy, Itaguai, and "our great leader, Porfírio." The barber marched at their head, wielding the sword as dexterously as if it had been merely an unusually long razor. Victory hovered like a halo above him, and the dignity of government informed his every movement.

The Councilmen, watching from the windows, thought that the troops had captured the Stewed Corners. The Council formally resolved to send a petition to the Viceroy asking him to give an extra month's pay to the dragoons, "whose high devotion to duty has saved Itaguai from the chaos of rebellion and mob rule." This phrase was proposed by Sebastião Freitas, whose defense of the rebels had so scandalized his colleagues. But the legislators were soon disillusioned. They could now clearly hear the *vivas* for the barber and the shouts of "death to the Councilmen" and "death to the psychiatrist." The President held his head high and said: "Whatever may be our fate, let us never forget that we are the servants of His Majesty and of the people of Itaguai." Sebastião suggested that perhaps they could best serve the Crown and the town by sneaking out the back door and going to the Circuit Judge's office for advice and help, but all the other members of the Council rejected this suggestion.

A few seconds later the barber and some of his lieutenants entered the chamber and told the Town Council that it had been deposed. The Councilmen surrendered and were put in jail. The the barber's friends urged him to assume the dictatorship of Itaguai in the name of His Majesty. Porfírio accepted this responsibility, although, as he told them, he was fully aware of its weight and of the thorny problems it entailed. He said also that he would be unable to rule without their coöperation, which they promptly promised him. The barber then went to the window and told the people what had happened; they shouted their approval. He chose the title, "Town Protector in the Name of His Majesty and of the People." He immediately issued several important orders, official communications from the new government, a detailed statement to the Viceroy with many protestations of obedience to His Majesty, and finally the following short but forceful proclamation to the people:

> Fellow Itaguaians:
> A corrupt and irresponsible Town Council was conspiring ignominiously against His Majesty and against the people. Public opinion had condemned it, and now a handful of citizens, with the help of His Majesty's brave dragoons, have dissolved it. By unanimous consent I am empowered to rule until His Majesty chooses to take formal action in the premises. Itaguaians, I ask only for your trust and for your help in restoring peace and the public funds, recklessly squandered by the Council. You may count on me to make every personal sacrifice for the common good, and you may rest assured that we shall have the full support of the Crown.
>
> Porfírio Caetano das Neves
> Town Protector in the Name of His Majesty and of the People

Everyone remarked that the proclamation said nothing whatever about the Green House, and some considered this ominous. The danger seemed all the greater when, in the midst of the important changes that were taking place, the psychiatrist committed to the Green House some seven or eight new patients, including a relative of the Protector. Everybody erroneously interpreted Bacamarte's action as a challenge to the barber and thought it likely that within twenty-four hours the terrible prison would be destroyed and the psychiatrist would be in chains.

The day ended happily. While the crier with the noisemaker went from corner to corner reading the proclamation, the people walked about the streets and swore they would be willing to die for the Protector. There were very few shouts of opposition to the Green House, for the people were confident that the government would soon liquidate it. Porfírio declared the day an official holiday and, to promote an alliance between the temporal power and the spiritual power, he asked Father Lopes to celebrate the occasion with a Te Deum. The Vicar issued a public refusal.

"May I at least assume," asked the barber with a threatening frown, "that you will not ally yourself with the enemies of the government?"

"How can I ally myself with your enemies," replied Father Lopes (if one can call it a reply), "when you have no enemies? You say in your proclamation that you are ruling by unanimous consent."

The barber could not help smiling. He really had almost no opposition. Apart from the captain of dragoons, the Council, and some of the town bigwigs, everybody acclaimed him; and even the bigwigs did not actually oppose him. Indeed, the people blessed the name of the man who would finally free Itaguai from the Green House and from the terrible Simão Bacamarte.

VIII.   The Druggist's Dilemma

The next day Porfírio and two of his aides-de-camp left the government palace (the new name of the town hall) and set out for the residence of Simão Bacamarte. The barber knew that it would have been more fitting for him to have ordered Bacamarte to come to the palace, but he was afaid the psychiatrist would refuse and so he decided to exercise forbearance in the use of his powers.

Crispim Soares was in bed at the time. The druggist was undergoing continual mental torture these days. His intimacy with Si-

mão Bacamarte called him to the doctor's defense, and Porfírio's
victory called him to the barber's side. This victory, together with
the intensity of the hatred for Bacamarte, made it unprofitable and
perhaps dangerous for Crispim to continue to associate with the
doctor. But the druggist's wife, a masculine woman who was very
close to Dona Evarista, told him that he owed the psychiatrist an
obligation of loyalty. The dilemma appeared insoluble, so Crispim
avoided it by the only means he could devise: he said he was sick,
and went to bed.

The next day his wife told him that Porfírio and some other
men were headed for Simão Bacamarte's house.

"They're going to arrest him," thought the druggist.

One idea led to another. He imagined that their next step would
be to arrest him, Crispim Soares, as an accessory. The therapeutic
effect of this thought was remarkable. The druggist jumped out of
bed and, despite his wife's protests, dressed and went out. The
chroniclers all agree that Mrs. Soares found great comfort in the
nobility of her husband, who, she assumed, was going to the defense of his friend, and they note with perspicacity the immense
power of a thought, even if untrue; for the druggist walked not to
the house of the psychiatrist but straight to the government palace.
When he got there he expressed disappointment that the barber
was out; he had wanted to assure him of his loyalty and support.
Indeed, he had intended to do this the day before but had been
prevented by illness—an illness that he now evidenced by a forced
cough. The high officials to whom he spoke knew of his intimacy
with the psychiatrist and therefore appreciated the significance of
this declaration of loyalty. They treated the druggist with the greatest respect. They told him that the Protector had gone to the Green
House on important business but would soon return. They offered
him a chair, refreshments, and flattery. They told him that the
cause of the illustrious Porfírio was the cause of every true pa-
triot—a proposition with which Crispim Soares heartily agreed and
which he proposed to affirm in a vigorous communication to the
Viceroy.

IX.   Two Beautiful Cases

The psychiatrist received the barber immediately. He told him
that he had no means of resistance and was therefore prepared to

submit to the new government. He asked only that they not force him to be present at the destruction of the Green House.

"The doctor is under a misapprehension," said Porfírio after a pause. "We are not vandals. Rightly or wrongly, everybody thinks that most of the people locked up here are perfectly sane. But the government recognizes that the question is purely scientific and that scientific issues cannot be resolved by legislation. Moreover, the Green House is now an established municipal institution. We must therefore find a compromise that will both permit its continued operation and placate the public."

The psychiatrist could not conceal his amazement. He confessed that he had expected not only destruction of the Green House but also his own arrest and banishment. The last thing in the world he would have expected was—

"That is because you don't appreciate the grave responsibility of government," interrupted the barber. "The people, in their blindness, may feel righteous indignation about something that they do not understand; they have a right, then, to ask the government to act along certain lines. The government, however, must remember its duty to promote the public interest, whether or not this interest is in full accord with the demands made by the public itself. The revolution, which yesterday overthrew a corrupt and despicable Town Council, screams for destruction of the Green House. But the government must remain calm and objective. It knows that elimination of the Green House would not eliminate insanity. It knows that the mentally ill must receive treatment. It knows also that it cannot itself provide this treatment and that it even lacks the ability to distinguish the sane from the insane. These are matters for science, not for politics. They are matters requiring the sort of delicate, trained judgment that you, not we, are fitted to exercise. All I ask is that you help me give some degree of satisfaction to the people of Itaguai. If you and the government present a united front and propose a compromise of some sort, the people will accept it. Let me suggest, unless you have something better to propose, that we free those patients who are practically cured and those whose illnesses are relatively mild. In this way we can show how benign and generous we are without seriously handicapping your work."

Simão Bacamarte remained silent for about three minutes and then asked: "How many casualties were there in the fighting yesterday?"

The barber thought the question a little odd, but quickly replied that eleven had been killed and twenty-five wounded.

"Eleven dead, twenty-five wounded," repeated the psychiatrist two or three times.

Then he said that he did not like the barber's suggestion and that he would try to devise a better compromise, which he would communicate to the government within a few days. He asked a number of questions about the events of the day before: the attack by the dragoons, the defense, the change of sides by the dragoons, the Council's resistance, and so on. The barber replied in detail, with emphasis on the discredit into which the Council had fallen. He admitted that the government did not yet have the support of the most important men in the community and added that the psychiatrist might be very helpful in this connection. The government would be pleased, indeed, if it could count among its friends the loftiest spirit in Itaguai and, doubtless, in the entire kingdom. Nothing that the barber said, however, changed the expression on the doctor's austere face. Bacamarte evidenced neither vanity nor modesty; he listened in silence, as impassive as a stone god.

"Eleven dead, twenty-five wounded," repeated the psychiatrist after the visitors had left. "Two beautiful cases. This barber shows unmistakable symptoms of psychopathic duplicity. As for proof of the insanity of the people who acclaim him, what more could one ask than the fact that eleven were killed and twenty-five wounded? Two beautiful cases!"

"Long live our glorious Protector!" shouted thirty-odd people who had been awaiting the barber in front of the house.

The psychiatrist went to the window and heard part of the barber's speech:

". . . for my main concern, day and night, is to execute faithfully the will of the people. Trust in me and you will not be disappointed. I ask of you only one thing: be peaceful, maintain order. For order, my friends, is the foundation on which government must rest."

"Long live Porfírio!" shouted the people, waving their hats.

"Two beautiful cases," murmured the psychiatrist.

X.   The Restoration

Within a week there were fifty additional patients in the Green House, all of them strong supporters of the new government. The people felt outraged. The government was stunned; it did not know how to react. João Pina, another barber, said openly that Porfírio had "sold his birthright to Simão Bacamarte for a pot of gold"—a phrase that attracted some of the more indignant citizens to Pina's side. Porfírio, seeing his competitor at the head of a potential insurrection, knew that he would be overthrown if he did not immediately change his course. He therefore issued two decrees, one abolishing the Green House and the other banishing the psychiatrist from Itaguai.

João Pina, however, explained clearly and eloquently that these decrees were a hoax, a mere face-saving gesture. Two hours later Porfírio was deposed and João Pina assumed the heavy burden of government. Pina found copies of the proclamation to the people, the explanatory statement to the Viceroy, and other documents issued by his predecessor. He had new originals made and sent them out over his own name and signature. The chronicles note that the wording of the new documents was a little different. For example, where the other barber had spoken of "a corrupt and irresponsible Town Council," João Pina spoke of "a body contaminated by French doctrines wholly contrary to the sacrosanct interests of His Majesty."

The new dictator barely had time to dispatch the documents when a military force sent by the Viceroy entered the town and restored order. At the psychiatrist's request, the troops immediately handed over to him Porfírio and some fifty other persons, and promised to deliver seventeen more of the barber's followers as soon as they had sufficiently recovered from their wounds.

This period in the crisis of Itaguai represents the culmination of Simão Bacamarte's influence. He got whatever he wanted. For example, the Town Council, now reëstablished, promptly consented to have Sebastião Freitas committed to the asylum. The psychiatrist had requested this in view of the extraordinary inconsistency of the Councilman's opinions, which Bacamarte considered a clear sign of mental illness. Subsequently the same thing happened to Crispim Soares. When the psychiatrist learned that his close friend and staunch supporter had suddenly gone over to the side of the Stewed Corners, he ordered him to be seized and taken to the Green House. The druggist did not deny his switch of allegiance but explained that he had been motivated by an overwhelming fear of the new government. Simão Bacamarte accepted the explanation as true; he pointed out, however, that fear is a common symptom of mental abnormality.

Perhaps the most striking proof of the psychiatrist's influence was the docility with which the Town Council surrendered to him its own President. This worthy official had declared that the affront to the Council could be washed away only by the blood of the Stewed Corners. Bacamarte learned of this through the Secretary of the Council, who repeated the President's words with immense enthusiasm. The psychiatrist first committed the Secretary to the Green House and then proceeded to the town hall. He told the Council that its President was suffering from hemoferal mania, an illness that he planned to study in depth, with, he hoped, immense benefit to the world. The Council hesitated for a moment and then acquiesced.

From that day on, the population of the asylum increased even more rapidly than before. A person could not utter the most commonplace lie, even a lie that clearly benefited him, without being immediately committed to the Green House. Scandalmongers, dandies, people who spent hours at puzzles, people who habitually inquired into the private lives of others, officials puffed up with authority—the psychiatrist's agents brought them all in. He spared sweethearts but not flirts, for he maintained that the former obeyed a healthful impulse, but that the latter yielded to a morbid desire for conquest. He discriminated against neither the avaricious nor the prodigal: both were committed to the asylum; this led people to say that the psychiatrist's concept of madness included practically everybody.

Some of the chroniclers express doubts about Simão Bacamarte's integrity. They note that, at his instigation, the Town Council authorized all persons who boasted of noble blood to wear a silver ring on the thumb of the left hand. These chroniclers point out that, as a consequence of the ordinance, a jeweler who was a close friend of Bacamarte became rich. Another consequence, however, was the commitment of the ring-wearers to the Green House; and the treatment of these unfortunate people, rather than the enrichment of his friend, may well have been the objective of the illustrious physician. Nobody was sure what conduct on the part of the ring-wearers had betrayed their illness. Some thought it was their tendency to gesticulate a great deal, especially with the left hand, no matter where they were—at home, in the street, even in church. Everybody knows that madmen gesticulate a great deal.

"Where will this man stop?" said the important people of the town. "Ah, if only we had supported the Stewed Corners!"

One day, when preparations were being made for a ball to be

held that evening in the town hall, Itaguai was shocked to hear that Simão Bacamarte had sent his own wife to the asylum. At first everyone thought it was a gag of some sort. But it was the absolute truth. Dona Evarista had been committed at two o'clock in the morning.

"I had long suspected that she was a sick woman," said the psy-chiatrist in response to a question from Father Lopes. "Her mod-eration in all other matters was hard to reconcile with her mania for silks, velvets, laces, and jewelry, a mania that began immediately after her return from Rio de Janeiro. It was then that I started to observe her closely. Her conversation was always about these ob-jects. If I talked to her about the royal courts of earlier times, she wanted to know what kind of clothes the women wore. If a lady visited her while I was out, the first thing my wife told me, even before mentioning the purpose of the visit, was how the woman was dressed and which jewels or articles of clothing were pretty and which were ugly. Once (I think Your Reverence will remember this) she said she was going to make a new dress every year for Our Lady of the Mother Church. All these symptoms indicated a serious condition. Tonight, however, the full gravity of her illness became manifest. She had selected the entire outfit she would wear to the ball and had it all fixed and ready. All except one thing: she couldn't decide between a garnet necklace and a sapphire neck-lace. The day before yesterday she asked me which she should wear. I told her it didn't matter, that they both were very becoming. Yesterday at lunch she repeated the question. After dinner she was silent and pensive. I asked her what was the matter. 'I want to wear my beautiful garnet necklace, but my sapphire one is so lovely.' 'Then wear the sapphire necklace.' 'But then I can't wear the garnet necklace.' In the middle of the night, about half-past one, I awoke. She was not in bed. I got up and went to the dressing-room. There she sat with the two necklaces, in front of the mirror, trying on first one and then the other. An obvious case of dementia. I had her put away immediately."

Father Lopes said nothing. The explanation did not wholly sat-isfy him. Perceiving this, the psychiatrist told him that the specific illness of Dona Evarista was vestimania; it was by no means incur-able.

"I hope to have her well within two weeks and, in any event, I expect to learn a great deal from the study of her case," said the psychiatrist in conclusion.

This personal sacrifice greatly enhanced the public image of the illustrious doctor. Suspicion, distrust, accusations were all negated by the commitment of his own wife whom he loved with all his heart. No one could ever again charge him with motives other than those of science itself. He was beyond doubt a man of integrity and profound objectivity, a combination of Cato and Hippocrates.

XI. Release and Joy

And now let the reader share with the people of Itaguai their amazement on learning one day that the madmen of the Green House had been released.

"All of them?"

"All of them."

"Impossible. Some, maybe. But all?"

"All. He said so himself in a communiqué that he sent today to the Town Council."

The psychiatrist informed the Council, first, that he had checked the statistics and had found that four-fifths of the population of Itaguai was in the Green House; second, that this disproportionately large number of patients had led him to reëxamine his fundamental theory of mental illness, a theory that classified as sick all people who were mentally unbalanced; third, that as a consequence of this reëxamination in the light of the statistics, he had concluded not only that his theory was unsound but also that the exactly contrary doctrine was true—that is, that normality lay in a lack of equilibrium and that the abnormal, the really sick, were the well balanced, the thoroughly rational; fourth, that in view of the foregoing he would release the persons now confined and would commit to the Green House all persons found to be mentally ill under the new theory; fifth, that he would continue to devote himself to the pursuit of scientific truth and trusted that the Council would continue to give him its support; and sixth, that he would give back the funds he had received for the board and lodging of the patients, less the amounts already expended, which could be verified by examination of his records and accounts.

The amazement of Itaguai was no greater than the joy of the relatives and friends of the former patients. Dinners, dances, Chinese lanterns, music, everything to celebrate the happy occasion. I shall not describe the festivities, for they are merely peripheral to this history; suffice it to say that they were elaborate, long, and memorable.

In the midst of all this rejoicing, nobody noticed the last part of the fourth item in the psychiatrist's communiqué.

XII.   The Last Part of the Fourth Item

The lanterns were taken down, the ex-patients resumed their former lives, everything appeared normal. Councilman Freitas and the President returned to their accustomed places, and the Council governed Itaguai without external interference. Porfírio the barber had "experienced everything," as the poet said of Napoleon; indeed, Porfírio had experienced more than Napoleon, for Napoleon was never committed to the Green House. The barber now found the obscure security of his trade preferable to the brilliant calamities of power. He was tried for his crimes and convicted, but the people begged His Majesty to pardon their ex-Protector, and His Majesty did so. The authorities decided not to prosecute João Pina, for he had overthrown an unlawful ruler. The chroniclers maintain that Pina's absolution inspired our adage:

> A judge will never throw the book
> At crook who steals from other crook.

An immoral adage, but immensely useful.

There were no more complaints against the psychiatrist. There was not even resentment for his past acts. Indeed, the former patients were grateful because he had declared them sane; they gave a ball in his honor. The chroniclers relate that Dona Evarista decided at first to leave her husband but changed her mind when she contemplated the emptiness of a life without him. Her devotion to this high-minded man overcame her wounded vanity, and they lived together more happily than ever before.

On the basis of the new psychiatric doctrine set forth in the communiqué, Crispim Soares concluded that his prudence in allying himself with the revolution had been a manifestation of mental health. He was deeply touched by Bacamarte's magnanimity: the psychiatrist had extended his hand to his old friend upon releasing him from the Green House.

"A great man," said the druggist to his wife.

We need not specifically note the release of Costa, Coelho, and the other patients named in this history. Each was now free to resume his previous way of life. Martim Brito, for example, who had been committed because of a speech in excessive praise of Dona Evarista, now made another in honor of the doctor, "whose exalted genius lifted its wings and flew far above the common herd until it rivaled the sun in altitude and in brilliance."

"Thank you," said the psychiatrist. "Obviously I was right to set you free."

Meanwhile, the Town Council passed, without debate, an ordinance to take care of the last part of the fourth item in Bacamarte's communiqué. The ordinance authorized the psychiatrist to commit to the Green House all persons whom he found to be mentally well balanced. But, remembering its painful experience in connection with public reaction to the asylum, the Council added a proviso in which it stated that, since the purpose of the ordinance was to provide an opportunity for the doctor to test his new theory, the authorization would remain in effect for only one year, and the Council reserved the right to close the asylum at any time if the maintenance of public order so required.

Sebastião Freitas proposed an amendment to the effect that under no circumstances were members of the Council to be committed to the Green House. The amendment was adopted almost unanimously. The only dissenting vote was cast by Councilman Galvão. He argued that, in authorizing a scientific experiment on the people of Itaguai, the Council would itself be unscientific if it exempted its members or any other segment of the population from subjection to the experiment. "Our public office," he said, "does not exclude us from the human race." But he was shouted down.

Simão Bacamarte accepted the ordinance with all its restrictions. As for the exemption of the Councilmen, he declared that they were in no danger whatever of being committed, for their votes in favor of the amendment showed clearly that they were mentally unbalanced. He asked only that Galvão be delivered to him, for this Councilman had exhibited exceptional mental equilibrium, not only in his objection to the amendment but even more in the calm that he had maintained in the face of unreasonable opposition and abuse on the part of his colleagues. The Council immediately granted the request.

Under the new theory a few acts or statements by a person could not establish his abnormality: a long examination and a thorough study of his history were necessary. Father Lopes, for example, was not taken to the Green House until thirty days after the passage of the ordinance. In the case of the druggist's wife fifty days of study

were required. Crispim Soares raged about the streets, telling everybody that he would tear the tyrant's ears off. One of the men
to whom he spoke—a fellow who, as everyone knew, had an aversion for Bacamarte—ran and warned the psychiatrist. Bacamarte
thanked him warmly and locked him up in recognition of his rec-
titude and his good will even toward someone he disliked, signs of
perfect mental equilibrium.

"This is a very unusual case," said the doctor to Dona Evarista.

By the time Crispim Soares arrived at the psychiatrist's house,
sorrow had overcome his anger. He did not tear Bacamarte's ears
off. The psychiatrist tried to comfort his old friend. He told him
that his wife might be suffering from a cerebral lesion, that there
was a fair chance of recovery, and that meanwhile he must of
course keep her confined. The psychiatrist considered it desirable,
however, for Soares to spend a good deal of time with her, for the
druggist's guile and intellectual dishonesty might help to overcome
the moral superiority that the doctor found in his patient.

"There is no reason," he said, "why you and your wife should
not eat lunch and dinner together every day at the Green House.
You may even stay with her at night."

Simão Bacamarte's words placed the druggist in a new dilemma.
He wanted to be with his wife, but at the same time he dreaded
returning to the Green House. He remained undecided for several
minutes. Then Dona Evarista released him from the dilemma: she
promised to visit his wife frequently and to bear messages between
the two. Crispim Soares kissed her hands in gratitude. His pusil-
lanimous egoism struck the psychiatrist as almost sublime.

Although it took Bacamarte almost half a year to find eighteen
patients for the Green House, he did not relax his efforts to discover the insane. He went from street to street, from house to
house, observing, inquiring, taking notes. And when he committed
someone to the asylum, it was with the same sense of accomplish-
ment with which he had formerly committed dozens at a time. This
very disproportion confirmed his new theory. At last the truth
about mental illness was definitely known. One day Bacamarte
committed the Circuit Judge to the Green House, after weeks of
detailed study of the man's acts and thorough interrogation of his
friends, who included all the important people of Itaguai.

More than once the psychiatrist was on the point of sending
someone to the Green House, only to discover a serious shortcom-
ing at the last moment. In the case of the lawyer Salustiano, for
example, he thought he had found so perfect a combination of

intellectual and moral qualities that it would be dangerous to leave the man at large. He told one of his agents to bring the man in, but the agent, who had known many lawyers, suspected that he might really be sane and persuaded Bacamarte to authorize a little experiment. The agent had a close friend who was charged with having falsified a will. He advised this friend to engage Salustiano as his lawyer.

"Do you really think he'll take the case?"

"Sure he will. Confess everything to him. He'll get you off."

The agent's friend went to the lawyer, admitted that he had falsified the will, and begged him to accept the case. Salustiano did not turn the man away. He studied the charges and supporting evidence. In court he argued at great length, proving conclusively that the will was genuine. After a verdict of acquittal the defendant received the estate under the terms of the will. To this experiment both he and the learned counselor owed their freedom.

Very little escapes the comprehension of a man of genuine insight. For some time Simão Bacamarte had noted the wisdom, patience, and dedication of the agent who devised the experiment. Consequently he determined to commit him to the Green House, in which he gave him one of the choicest cubicles.

The patients were segregated into classes. In one gallery lived only those whose outstanding moral quality was modesty. The notably tolerant occupied another gallery, and still others were set aside for the truthful, the guileless, the loyal, the magnanimous, the wise. Naturally, the friends and relatives of the madmen railed against the new theory. Some even tried to persuade the Town Council to cancel the authorization it had given Bacamarte. The Councilmen, however, remembered with bitterness the word of their former colleague Galvão; they did not wish to see him back in their midst, and so they refused. Simão Bacamarte sent a message to the Council, not thanking it but congratulating it on this act of personal spite.

Some of the important people of Itaguai then went secretly to the barber Porfírio. They promised to support him with men, money, and influence if he would lead another movement against the psychiatrist and the Town Council. He replied that ambition had once led him to violent transgression of the law but that he now recognized the folly of such conduct; that the Council, in its wisdom, had authorized the psychiatrist to conduct his new experiment for a year; that anybody who objected should wait till the end of the year and then, if the Council insisted on renewing the authorization, should petition the Viceroy; that he would not rec-ommend recourse again to a method that had done no good and had caused several deaths and other casualties, which would be an eternal burden on his conscience.

The psychiatrist listened with immense interest when one of his secret agents told him what Porfírio had said. Two days later the barber was locked up in the Green House. "You're damned if you do and you're damned if you don't," observed the new patient.

At the end of the year allowed for verification of the new theory, the Town Council authorized the psychiatrist to continue his work for another six months in order to experiment with methods of therapy. The result of this additional experimentation is so signif-icant that it merits ten chapters, but I shall content myself with one. It will provide the reader with an inspiring example of sci-entific objectivity and selflessness.

XIII. Plus Ultra

However diligent and perceptive he may have been in the dis-covery of madmen, Simão Bacamarte outdid himself when he un-dertook to cure them. All the chroniclers agree that he brought about the most amazing recoveries.

It is indeed hard to imagine a more rational system of therapy. Having divided the patients into classes according to their predom-inant moral qualities, the doctor now proceeded to break down those qualities. He applied a remedy in each case to inculcate ex-actly the opposite characteristic, selecting the specific medicine and dose best suited to the patient's age, personality, and social position.

The cases of modesty may serve as examples. In some, a wig, a fine coat, or a cane would suffice to restore reason to the madman. In more difficult cases the psychiatrist resorted to diamonds, hon-orary degrees, and the like. The illness of one modest lunatic, a poet, resisted every sort of therapy. Bacamarte had almost given up, when an idea occurred to him: he would have the crier with the noisemaker proclaim the patient to be as great as Garção or Pindar.

"It was like a miracle," said the poet's mother to one of her friends. "My boy is entirely well now. A miracle . . ."

Another patient, also in the modest class, seemed incurable. The specific remedy used for the poet would not work, for this patient was not a writer; indeed, he could barely sign his name. But Dr. Bacamarte proved equal to the challenge. He decided to have the patient made Secretary to the Itaguai branch of the Royal Academy. The Secretary and the President of each branch were appointed by the Crown. They enjoyed the privileges of being addressed as Excellency and of wearing a gold medallion. The government at Lisbon refused Bacamarte's request at first; but after the psychiatrist explained that he did not ask the appointment as a real honor for his patient but merely as a therapeutic device to cure a difficult case, and after the Minister of Overseas Possessions (a cousin of the patient) intervened, the government finally granted the request. The consequent cure was hailed as another miracle.

"Wonderful, really wonderful!" said everybody upon seeing the healthy, prideful expression on the faces of the two ex-madmen.

Bacamarte's method was ultimately successful in every case, although in a few the patient's dominant quality proved impregnable. In these cases the psychiatrist won out by attacking at another point, like a good military strategist.

By the end of five months all the patients had been cured. The Green House was empty. Councilman Galvão, so cruelly afflicted with fairness and moderation, had the good fortune to lose an uncle; I say good fortune, for the uncle's will was ambiguous and Galvão obtained a favorable interpretation of it by bribing two judges. With customary integrity, the doctor admitted that the cure had been effected not by him but by nature's *vis medicatrix*. It was quite otherwise in the case of Father Lopes. Bacamarte knew that the priest was utterly ignorant of Greek, and therefore asked him to make a critical analysis of the Septuagint. Father Lopes accepted the task. In two months he had written a book on the subject and was released from the Green House. As for the druggist's wife, she remained there only a short time.

"Why doesn't Crispim come to visit me?" she asked every day.

They gave her various answers and finally told her the plain truth. The worthy matron could not contain her shame and indignation. Her explosions of wrath included such expression as "rat," "coward," and "he even cheats on prescriptions." Simão Bacamarte remarked that, whether or not these characterizations of her husband were true, they clearly established the lady's return to sanity. He promptly released her.

If you think the psychiatrist was radiant with happiness on seeing the last guest leave the Green House, you apparently do not yet understand the man. *Plus ultra* was his motto. For him the discovery of the true theory of mental illness was not enough, nor was the establishment in Itaguai of the reign of reason with the total elimination of psychological abnormality. *Plus ultra!* Something told him that his new theory bore within itself a better, newer theory.

"Let us see," he said to himself, "if I can discover the ultimate, underlying truth."

He paced the length of the immense room, past bookcase after bookcase—the largest library in His Majesty's overseas possessions. A gold-embroidered, damask dressing-gown (a gift from a university) enveloped the regal and austere body of the illustrious physician. The extensive top of his head, which the incessant cogitations of the scientist had rendered bald, was covered by a wig. His feet, neither dainty nor gross but perfectly proportioned to his body, were encased in a pair of ordinary shoes with plain brass buckles. Note the distinction: only those elements that bore some relationship to his work as a scientist were in any sense luxurious; the rest was simple and temperate.

And so the psychiatrist walked up and down his vast library, lost in thought, alien to everything but the dark problem of psychopathology. Suddenly he stopped. Standing before a window, with his left elbow resting on his open right hand and his chin on his closed left hand, he asked himself:

"Were they all really insane? Did I really cure them? Or is not mental imbalance so natural and inherent that it was bound to assert itself with or without my help?"

He soon arrived at this conclusion: the apparently well-balanced minds that he had just "cured" had really been unbalanced all the time, just like the obviously sane minds of the rest of the people. Their apparent illness was superficial and transient.

The psychiatrist contemplated his new doctrine with mixed feelings. He was happy because, after such long study, experimentation, and struggle, he could at last affirm the ultimate truth: there never were and never would be any madmen in Itaguai or anywhere else. But he was unhappy because a doubt assailed him. In the field of psychiatry a generalization so broad, so absolute, was almost inevitably erroneous. If he could find just one undeniably well balanced, virtuous, insane man, the new theory would be acceptable—not as an absolute, exceptionless principle, which was inadmissible, but as a general rule applicable to all but the most extraordinary cases.

According to the chroniclers, this difficulty constituted the most dreadful of the spiritual tempests through which the courageous Bacamarte passed in the course of his stormy professional life. But tempests terrify only the weak. After twenty minutes a gentle but radiant dawn dispelled the darkness from the face of the psychiatrist.

"Of course. That's it, of course."

What Simão Bacamarte meant was that he had found in himself the perfect, undeniable case of insanity. He possessed wisdom, patience, tolerance, truthfulness, loyalty, and moral fortitude—all the qualities that go to make an utter madman.

But then he questioned his own self-observation. Surely he must be imperfect in some way. To ascertain the truth about himself he convoked a gathering of his friends and questioned them. He begged them to answer with absolute frankness. They all agreed that he had not been mistaken.

"No defects?"

"None at all," they replied in chorus.

"No vices?"

"None."

"Perfect in every respect?"

"In every respect."

"No, impossible!" cried the psychiatrist. "I cannot believe that I am so far superior to my fellow men. You are letting yourselves be influenced by your affection for me."

His friends insisted. The psychiatrist hesitated, but Father Lopes made it difficult for him not to accept their judgment.

"Do you know why you are reluctant to recognize in yourself the lofty qualities which we all see so clearly?" said the priest. "It is because you have an additional quality that enhances all the others: modesty."

Simão Bacamarte bowed his head. He was both sad and happy, but more happy than sad. He immediately committed himself to the Green House. His wife and his friends begged him not to. They told him he was perfectly sane. They wept, they pleaded. All in vain.

"This is a matter of science, of a new doctrine," he said, "and I am the first instance of its application. I embody both theory and practice."

"Simão! Simão, my love!" cried his wife. Her face was bathed in tears.

But the doctor, his eyes alight with scientific conviction, gently pushed her away. He entered the Green House, shut the door be-

hind him, and set about the business of curing himself. The chroniclers state, however, that he died seventeen months later as insane
as ever. Some even venture the opinion that he was the only madman (in the vulgar or non-Bacamartian sense) ever committed to
the asylum. But this opinion should not be taken seriously. It was
based on remarks attributed to Father Lopes—doubtless erroneously, for, as everybody knew, the priest liked and admired the
psychiatrist. In any case, the people of Itaguai buried the mortal
remains of Simão Bacamarte with great pomp and solemnity.

Translated by William L. Grossman

Moacyr Scliar
(1937–   )

Born of the descendants of Russian Jews who settled in the southern state of Rio Grande do Sul at the turn of the century, the Brazilian Moacyr Scliar graduated from the Faculty of Medicine in Porto Alegre and published his first collection of short stories in the same year (1962). Like his immigrant ancestors, Scliar's characters "soon found that their God had to share His authority with other Gods who were there in Brazil first," resulting in a paradoxical fiction of compelling ambiguity.

Scliar began working in the public health sector while continuing to write. In 1968, he published a prize-winning collection of twenty-four telegraphically short comic tales entitled *The Carnival of the Animals,* which immediately secured his critical reputation. Five years later he published his first novel, *The One-Man Army.* But it was the appearance of *The Centaur in the Garden* (1980), a dazzlingly tragicomic life of a man who attempts to lead a normal bourgeois existence despite the fact that he is a centaur *and* a Jew, that won him an international reputation.

Now in his mid-fifties, Scliar has produced to date a remarkable twenty works of fiction, including the novels *The Gods of Raquel* (1975), *The Volunteers* (1979), *Max and the Cats* (1981), and *The Strange Nation of Rafael Mendes* (1983), as well as the story collections *The Ballad of the False Messiah* (1986) and *Van Gogh's Ear,* which won the Cuban Casa de las Américas prize in 1989. Though he has officially retired from the position of Director of Public Health for the state of Rio Grande do Sul, Scliar continues service on a voluntary basis. He also writes a weekly column for a Porto Alegre newspaper.

The Plagues

The Waters Are Turned to Blood

Our life was regulated by a seemingly eternal and immutable cycle. Periodically, the waters of the great river would rise, inundating the fields almost as far as our house; afterward they would recede, leaving a coat of fertile slime upon the soil. It was then the planting season. We would plow the land, sow the wheat, and months later, the golden spikes would be swaying in the sun.

And then came the harvest season, and the harvest festival, and again the floods. Year after year.

We were happy. Occasionally we had problems: an illness in the family, or a quarrel, but by and large, we were happy, if happy is the right adjective to qualify a life without major worries or fears. Of course, we were poor; there were many things that we did not have. But what we lacked did not seem important to us.

There were six of us in the small house: my parents, my two brothers, my sister, and I. All of us devoted ourselves to our agricultural tasks. Later I was to learn the craft of writing; it was my father's wish; I think that he wanted me to tell this story, so here it is.

One afternoon we happened to be strolling, as was our wont, along the riverbank when my sister noticed something strange. Look at the color of the water, she said. I looked and at first I saw nothing unusual. The water was muddy, for our river was not one of those mountain brooks with crystalline waters that run friskily amid the stones; it was a mighty watercourse that came from far away, flowing sluggishly, and dragging with it the soil of the banks (but what did we care? It was not our soil); a huge animal, quiet but powerful, this river, which had over the centuries gained the right to its wide bed. It was by no means a beautiful river; but then we did not want it to beautify the landscape—we wanted it to integrate itself into the cycle of our lives, of our work, and in this respect, it fit the bill. There was no need for us to contemplate it in ecstasy. Our secret gratitude was enough.

But there was indeed something strange. The color of the waters tended toward red rather than toward the usual ocher. Red? It had no part in our lives. There was nothing red around us; no red flowers, for instance. As a matter of fact, flowers were something we never planted. We could not allow ourselves such indulgences. On the other hand, it is true that sometimes at sunset, the sky was painted in various colors, scarlet being one of them. But by that time we were already back home. We went to bed early.

My sister (one day she might be acknowledged as an exponent of the new scientific spirit) halted. Surprised, the rest of us halted too. Then leaving us behind, leaving behind the familiar group, her own family, the flesh of her flesh, the blood of her blood (attention, here: the blood of her blood)—she moved forward, as vivacious as ever, and entered the river. She stooped down to pick up something, which she then examined attentively before bringing it to us.

"What is it?" asked Father, and I noticed the furrow in his brow; a furrow that rarely appeared but when it did, it was an ominous sign, as were certain black birds that sometimes would flutter over the region, invariably heralding the death of one of our rare neighbors.

"Don't you people know what it is?" replied my sister, with that superior smile of hers that so irritated Mother: This girl thinks she knows everything, but she still hasn't found a way of freeing us from poverty. "It's a clot. A blood clot."

Strange: a blood clot floating on the waters of our river. Father, who always felt that he was under an obligation to provide an explanation (logical, if at all possible) for everything, suggested that it might be the blood of an animal that had perhaps been immolated in the river. There are superstitious people, he assured us, who resort to such practices to control nature, hoping to harmonize the flux and reflux of the river with the planting season. Sheer nonsense, explicable in terms of the eternal warped notions of human beings.

Yes—but what about the coloring of the water? About this, he did not say anything, and neither did we ask.

We returned home. My sister and I were walking side by side, in silence. Then all of a sudden: Father is wrong, she said, and I was seized with fear. A daughter talking like this about her father? A girl who, strictly speaking, should stay home to help her mother, and who only came to the fields as a special privilege accorded to her by the head of the family? But unaware of my perturbation, she went on: With one of those gadgets capable of magnifying the size of things enormously, she said, we would see corpuscles of various sizes. Some are reddish, and they can color a liquid; others are whitish.

"In other words," she concluded, staring at me fixedly, "the river has been turned to blood."

Blood! Yes, it was blood and I had known it all along. Except that, unlike her, I had not had the nerve to utter the word, far less say it with such confidence and ease. Blood!

Father either had not heard or pretended that he had not. But on the following days, even he had to admit that there was in fact a transformation. The river that flowed before us was a river of blood. And there was no possible explanation for this fact. Not even from the veins of all the animals in the world, slaughtered simultaneously, could such a torrent gush out. We were confronting an extraordinary and terrifying phenomenon. Mother wept day and night, convinced that the end was near.

My older brother, a practical-minded lad (and perhaps for this reason, Father's favorite), thought that we could take advantage of the situation by selling the blood to foreign armies, for as everybody knows, hemorrhage was a common cause of death among badly wounded soldiers. However, this was not going to be possible: Even in the waters of the river, and at the slightest manipulation or turbulation, the blood immediately cohered in clots. Of a colossal size. Every so often, we saw monkeys perched on them.

Father did not let himself become discouraged. He lost no time in trying to find a solution to the problem. Before long, he discovered that he could get clear water by digging wells along the bank of the river; it seemed that the sand of the bank filtered out the blood (all of the blood? Even those elementary particles that my sister had been talking about? I didn't dare to ask her. Neither did she say anything about this matter. The particles in question were added to the list of embarrassing matters, never verbalized, that exist in every family, to a greater or lesser extent. Unuttered words haunt homes like specters, especially on stifling nights when people, their eyes wide open, unable to sleep, look fixedly at the same point in the ceiling. At the very same place where, in the attic, a skeleton remains unburied).

We built a cistern. Day and night, without stopping, we would pour ewers of water into it. And thus we had enough water to drink, to cook, to irrigate the crops until one day the waters of the river began to clear up. The blood clots disappeared. Apparently, things were getting back to normal. We've won, Father shouted as Mother wept for joy.

The Frogs

As it turned out, Father's exultation was premature. One day, a frog appeared in our kitchen. Frogs were not a rare sight in the region, and that one was an absolutely ordinary frog, of a size and appearance normal in such batrachians. It was surprising, though, that it had ventured this far; however, the fact merited only a good-humored remark on the part of Father. On that same day we came upon several other frogs in the cultivated fields; and down by the river there were dozens of them croaking endlessly. This was now rather intriguing but, as Father stated, still within the normal limits, considering that wide variations are not unusual in natural phenomena.

Still, it was an awful lot of frogs ... And on the following days their number increased even more. The situation was becoming unpleasant. It was impossible to walk without trampling on frogs; at mealtimes, we had to remove them from the table so that we could eat; and at night, we found them in our cots.

But even so, we did not lose our sense of humor. My younger brother even adopted one of the batrachians as a pet. For several days, he took the little frog with him everywhere he went; he would feed it flies and rock it to sleep. One night the frog ran away; it was impossible to tell it apart from the thousands, millions of other frogs that were now leaping here, there, and everywhere. Father would laugh at the boy's distress, but Mother was not amused: removing so many frogs from the house was getting to be quite a chore.

My older brother was already thinking of turning the situation to our advantage. There are people that eat frogs, he assured us. The meat has a delicate flavor, it's like chicken.

"Of course, we can use only the thighs, but if we wash them quickly in cold water; if we steep them in a marinade of wine with nutmeg and pepper; if we soak them in milk; if we coat them with flour; if we fry them in butter; and finally, if we arrange them on a platter, we'll have, I'm sure, a delicious dish. Actually, it's just a matter of promoting the recipes skillfully and of marketing the product properly in order to overcome a natural, but inexplicable, repugnance on the part of the public."

It seemed like a good plan, but it was impossible to carry it out. The entire region was having an invasion of frogs; people did not want to hear about the batrachians, much less eat them. Finally, Father became irritated. This is all the government's doings, he said, the politicians don't care a hoot about us, they only think of the farmers when it's time for them to collect taxes from us.

As if in reply to Father's complaints, on the following day a representative from the government showed up. We knew him: He used to be a neighbor of ours, a man nicknamed the Gimp because of a defect in one of his legs. Being unable to work, this man devoted himself to witchcraft. True, without much success, but since he had influential connections, he had obtained a high-ranking post in the central administration of the government. And now he had been sent down our way to find out about the situation.

We followed him as he plodded painfully alongside the river, at times tripping over the batrachians heaped on the sand. So many frogs, he kept exclaiming, amazed, so many frogs!

"Well?" asked Father, impatient, at the end of the inspection. "Can anything be done about it?"

"Certainly." He smiled. "Just as they appeared, they can disappear."

"And what made them appear?" Father persisted.

"Don't you know?" he asked, surprised. "It's a curse. Put on us by the workers who are erecting the monuments. They are outraged; and they say that their god is punishing us. Us, the powerful! Such gall they have!"

Father was perplexed. He never invoked the deities, for he thought that doing so would be unfair. He believed that human beings had to survive by means of their own strength, without the help of mysterious entities. Besides: we, powerful? We who always toiled arduously, we who never exploited anybody? Perplexed and outraged, Father stood there. The wizard promised that the frogs would be eradicated within a short period of time, a promise that pacified Father somewhat, but left my kid brother disconsolate.

Bursting into tears, he asked the man to spare his pet frog, wherever it was. The man promised to take his request into consideration. He did not.

Mosquitoes, Flies

The frogs disappeared, but a few days after they were gone, clouds of mosquitoes invaded the region, attacking us fiercely. We could not work, we could not sleep; the mosquitoes gave us no respite. My sister put forth the hypothesis of an environmental disequilibrium (the frogs, she said, had devoured the mosquitoes; after the killing of the batrachians, the insects began to proliferate), and my older brother was thinking of marketing an insect repellent made from cow dung—but Father was sick and tired of explanations and daring projects. He kept killing the mosquitoes with his big hands:

"I'll show this god! I'll show him!"

It was all in vain. When the mosquitoes finally disappeared, the flies came—huge gadflies that buzzed incessantly around us. They did not sting us, but they tormented us just as much as the mosquitoes had.

"Why don't they let them go?" Mother would ask, anguished. She was referring to those people that were building the monuments. We, the children, thought that letting them go would be a logical arrangement, but Father was becoming increasingly more indignant. No, he did not want them to go; he did not even know them, but he wanted them to stay; now he wanted them to stay.

"To see how far this god of theirs will go. Just to see how far he'll go. Blood, frogs, mosquitoes, flies, I want to see how far he'll go," he would say while furiously milking the cows (we had two), which kept tossing their tails in a vain attempt to protect themselves from the pertinacious gadflies.

Pestilence

One morning one of the cows was found dead. This time Mother lost her patience. She started to scream at her husband, accusing him of having mistreated the animal, thus causing its death. Father said nothing. He was staring fixedly at his own arm, where he saw the first in a series of

Tumors

Could there be a link between the man's gaze and the tumor? Could the intense emotion of that fixed stare, in which hatred and defiance, bitterness and even irony were blended together (in variable proportions depending on the particular moment), have induced a pathological process in the integument of this man, a process that initially manifested itself as a painful bump, which soon turned into a fetid ulcer? My sister did not have an answer to this question; neither she nor anyone else. As for Father, he remained silent. Even when the lesions spread all over his body, even when they began to appear in his wife and children, he still said nothing. Clamping his jaws shut, he would set to work with a vengeance, plowing and sowing and pulling out the weeds with fury. In spite of everything, the wheat was going to thrive; in spite of everything, there was going to be a bumper crop. Or so we hoped until we were struck by

Hail

It happened unexpectedly: one afternoon, heavy clouds obscured the sun, the wind began to blow—and all of a sudden, we were pelted with pebbles of ice, some as big as a clenched fist. Part of the wheat field was destroyed. Father, immobile, his expression somber, seemed bewildered by this disaster. For how much longer, my sister heard him say, for how much longer? And, we had to admit, even an expert weather forecaster would be unable to provide a satisfactory answer to this question. Moreover, the next plague had nothing to do with meteorology. Soon we would be confronting the

Grasshoppers!

The days go by, and one afternoon we are all sitting in front of our house, when a neighbor comes running to us. Gasping for breath, he breaks the news to us: The grasshoppers are coming. An immense cloud, driven by the strong wind that is blowing from the south. Yet another plague!

Father rises to his feet. On his face, an expression of determination:

"That's enough! That's now enough!"

We're going to put up a fight, he decides. With every power we have, we're going to fight the designs of this god whom we don't know, whom we don't worship, and who has been using us for his own obscure purposes. Who is this god, after all? Father cries out, and his voice echoes in the distance. With no reply.

He devises a plan of action. About gods, he knows nothing; but he does know all there is to know about grasshoppers. Voracious insects that can finish off what is left of the wheat field in no time flat. We've got to prevent them from alighting. How? By making noise, says Father. An awful lot of noise, without any letup. The noise will frighten the grasshoppers away. The noise will save us from this evil.

At dawn on the following day we position ourselves on the edge of the cultivated field. In single file, immobile, facing south: Mother, the firstborn, myself, my sister, the baby of the family. Each of us holding a bowl (five altogether: all we've got) and a stone. We stand there, immobile; only the wind ruffles our hair. How do I know this? Well, it's true that the wind is ruffling their hair: my siblings', my mother's, my father's; but I can't see the wind ruffling mine, no, this I can't. I do feel something on my scalp, though: it could be the wind ruffling my hair; but it could be an error of judgment, for my hair is cut short, much shorter than theirs (I like to wear it closely cropped) and it is stiff: of course, it is badly in need of a wash. It could be an error of judgment caused by my desire to have the wind ruffle my hair the way it is ruffling theirs. Or it could be my anxiety ... In short, I have been seized by doubt, and I believe (inasmuch as it is possible for a skeptic to believe) that this doubt will never relinquish its hold on me. God has succeeded in carrying out his designs.

Father, his forehead creased, reviews his small army. He counts on us; or he imagines that he can count on us, that we are with him. Are we? Speaking for my myself: I am. But am I really? Entirely? Completely? But what about these indefinable feelings? And what about these harrowing doubts? God now dwells in me. Inside me he will grow, and he will prosper, and he will triumph. I am lost. We are lost.

We look southward. Southward and upward. Father is now standing by my side. I can only look at him sideways; I can't look him in the eye, but I can guess the multiple components present in his gaze: Hatred. Bitterness. Disbelief. Mockery. Helplessness.

"Why?" is a question, among many others, held within this gaze. A mute, agonized question.

All of a sudden, a dry rustling. My hair, I can feel it (or I think I can), stands on end. Anxious, I scan the horizon; there, a dark cloud begins to emerge: Thin and small at first, it soon grows bigger and denser. It's the grasshoppers. Carried by the warm wind.

It takes them but a few minutes to get to where we stand. A nightmare, those billions of insects buzzing around us.

"Noise!" Father shouts out, but his voice is muffled by the frightful drone of the grasshoppers. "Noise!"

So noise is what we make, banging away on our bowls as if possessed. But it is in vain: the cloud of grasshoppers has already alighted, and the ground is covered with a moving mass.

"The wheat field!" shouts Father. We run there, and with our hands and feet we try to remove the creatures. Before long, however, we give up; the entire field of wheat, or what was left of it after the hail, has already been devoured—spikes, leaves, stems, everything. The baby of the family, amused, laughs and claps his hands; in his innocence, he thinks that it is all a game. Pipe down, bellows my older brother, and bug off. Let him have some fun, shouts Mother amid the infernal noise of the grasshoppers. He's a child, he's innocent. And at least one of us is not suffering. My brother, full of distrust (such is the consequence of this calamity: a son, and the eldest one too, begins to distrust his own mother), makes no reply. He continues to bang on his bowl, already badly battered.

My sister picks up one of the insects, and proceeds to examine it, oblivious to what is happening around her.

"Yes," she murmurs, "they're grasshoppers all right. But . . ."

"But what?" I yell, impatient. "What new discovery have you made? Is it of any significance?"

My sister shakes her head.

"I don't know. They do look odd to me, these creatures."

Father draws closer. Ashen-faced, he looks at us. He shivers as if he had a fever, his teeth chatter. He asks my sister something; she doesn't understand. He repeats his question: He wants to know if grasshoppers are edible. Alarmed, my sister and I exchange glances—could it be that this latest tragedy has made him lose his mind? But she is not one to lose her sangfroid in a situation like this: Yes, she replies warily, there are people in the South who eat grasshoppers.

Father then scoops up a handful of grasshoppers, and begins to devour them. He exhorts us to do the same: Eat, eat while they still have our wheat inside them. We avert our eyes from this scene. Father starts vomiting: Let's take him home, says my older brother in an imperative tone of voice. The voice of someone taking control: A father that quails before grasshoppers, a father that vomits (albeit after ingesting the insects) is not worthy of trust. He cannot head a family. Following our brother, we march toward our house. The baby of the family is quiet, strangely quiet. He is, as later I will deduce, the bearer of one of those secret premonitions that sometimes befall young children, enabling them to foresee, several days in advance, the

Death of the Firstborn

During the days when Father, delirious from a high fever, was confined to bed, my older brother took charge of the family. He would milk the only cow we had left and distribute the milk among us while expounding on his plans: He intended to bury the dead grasshoppers, and in this way fertilize the soil; later he was going to install a watermill to grind the wheat and then export the flour thus produced to faroff regions. And he was counting on us to help him carry out this intensive program of work.

In the meantime, Father recovered from his illness. He resumed his place at the head of the table (even though there was no food to eat); and again he was ordering us around in his booming, authoritative voice. Which my older brother could not accept. He simply could not reconcile himself to the situation. Stubbornly, he refused to obey; one day, in the presence of the whole family, Father cursed him. Affronted, my brother demanded a retraction. And since Father would not comply with his demand, he left the room, slamming the door behind him. On the following day a messenger arrived with the news: All the firstborn were doomed. The Angel of Death would soon be passing through in order to smite them with his sword. All of us happened to be at the table at the time; the reaction of my older brother was astonishing. Atremble, he rose to his feet, his eyes bulging:

"Why me? Why me, when I've always helped around the house, when I've always looked after my brothers and sister? Why should I die? Is it fair? Tell me: is it fair?"

The baby of the family was laughing, thinking it was all in fun (and in fact, my older brother was always very playful with him).

Father remained quiet and motionless; as for my sister and me, we averted our eyes. My older brother then ran into Mother's arms, and bursting into tears, he cried convulsively for ... how long? I don't know. I didn't pay much attention to the passage of time then, to the days that kept flowing slowly and heavily like the logs that drifted down the river. But he must have cried for a long time. Suddenly he raised his head and stared at us in a challenging way. I'm not going to surrender, he said. I'm not going to die without putting up a fight. Then he opened the door and left the house. He was eighteen years old.

He did not return home that day; nor did he return on the following day. Had he run away? Had he been struck by the Angel of Death, like a leaping deer felled by a spear? Our fears did not materialize: he returned at nightfall, exhausted but seething with excitement. He had, he announced, something of great importance to impart: He had discovered a way of evading sure death.

"Yes, the Angel of Death will smite every firstborn child. But he will pass over the houses whose doorways are marked with the blood of an animal killed as a sacrifice."

We stood looking at him. The baby of the family, very astounded. My sister and I, rather astounded. Father and Mother—well, I don't know; if they were astounded, they did not manifest their astonishment. But regardless of the degree of individual astonishment, we all stood there motionless, our eyes fixed on him.

"But can't you understand?" he shouted. "I'm safe. Practically safe!"

Practically: It was what he said. Later on I even checked with my sister, who confirmed: yes, he did say *practically safe.* And ever since that moment I have been wondering if it could have been the word *practically*—which at the time struck me as rather unusual, even strange and suspicious, a word tinged with malignity (the subsequent events were to confirm this unfavorable impression; only recently, after I became more familiar with words and certain facts of life, have I been able to accept, although with some nervousness, the adverb. *Practically!* I shudder)—I have been wondering, as I was saying, if it could have been this word, so odd, to say the least, if not sinister, as I have said earlier—if it could have been this word, this *practically*, that precipitated everything: because, all of a sudden, he ran up to my father, grabbed him by the shoulders, and started to shake him (he was strong, this lad, except that his strength was of no help to him):

"I'm safe, Father! All you have to do is to sacrifice an animal.

Kill the cow. Collect the blood in a pail, then pour the blood over our door. Use plenty of blood, all of it, so that the Angel of Death will have no doubt about it; so that he will pass over our house; so that he will go away; so that he will spare me!"

They stood gazing at each other at that moment. What kind of a gaze it was (the son's, the father's), I had no way of knowing. They were standing in profile to me. I could see their noses, their compressed lips; but I could not see their eyes. If I were endowed with an unusual imagination, I could have made their gaze visible (in the form, say, of luminous rays varying in color and intensity), but even so, how to interpret the expression in their eyes? And what is more—in the perfect superposition of the luminous radiations, how to tell the look of the father from the look of the son? How to fit the expression in their eyes into the complex classification of feelings and emotions devised by human beings, especially when at the time I was far from being familiar with such classification? Even if I had been face to face with my father and my brother, I don't think I would have been able to describe the expression in their eyes adequately. Actually, I don't even know if they were in fact looking at each other. They were standing face to face; but one of them, the older man or the younger man, could have been watching the south, could have been watching the north, could have been watching the spot from where the Angel of Death would supposedly come. But who would be capable of identifying the components of such a look? Or to put it in a different way: How does a person wait for death (in general)? How does a person wait for death, when it is his own death? How does a person wait for death, when it is the death of his firstborn? A father looking at a son who is about to die, a son looking at a father who will die later—who is capable of describing such a gaze? Such are the dilemmas that appear in times of plagues.

The firstborn loosened his grip, and his arms fell to his sides, helpless. You are not going to kill the cow, he mumbled. Yes, it was more than a supposition, it was an assertion, but what the hell did he mean? That we were unwilling to save his life? That we should not kill the cow, now our only source of nourishment? That he loved the cow, whose milk he had drunk ever since he was a child? In short, what was he talking about?

We never knew. Without a sigh, he collapsed heavily to the floor. Father still tried to catch him in his fall, but he simply could not hold him: He was too frail. Nobody had ever obtained proper nourishment from grasshoppers.

We buried our brother on the following morning. As we learned later, he was not the only firstborn that was buried that day. But— it was the last of the plagues to afflict us. Since then, no god has bothered us; at least not significantly; now and then there has been a crop failure, or a minor disaster, but nothing serious. Nothing serious. One could say the following (and it is not one of the most pompous statements that a person can use to end a narrative): Life follows its course in a seemingly eternal cycle.

Translated by Eloah F. Giacomelli

João Guimarães Rosa
(1908–1967)

Juan Rulfo spoke of him as "the greatest author to have emerged from the Americas in our century." The Brazilian author of five monumental works (and two posthumous collections) that seem to defy translation, João Guimarães Rosa is slowly but inevitably finding his rightful place in world literature. The process is wholly consistent with his career as a writer.

Guimarães Rosa was born in Cordisburgo, a small ranch town in the interior of the state of Minas Gerais, appropriately enough in the year of the death of Machado de Assis. At ten, he was sent to boarding school in the state capital, Belo Horizonte, with a curiosity for languages that had led him to acquire a reading knowledge of French and the rudiments of Latin and Greek. He would go on to master these along with Russian, German, English, and Japanese, and would eventually work with his translators on the Italian, French, English, and German translations of his works. Like Joyce in English, Rosa would finally come full circle and reinvent his own Brazilian Portuguese language.

Though Rosa made his literary debut by publishing a short story (never reprinted) in 1929, not until 1946 would he publish his first book, a baroquely fashioned cycle of nine interrelated tales set in the rustic interior of his home state, entitled *Sagarana (rana,* Tupi for "in the manner of"; and *saga,* Old Norse for "epic tale"). In the long interim he took a degree in medicine, married, and set up an itinerant rural medical practice that involved traveling on horse-back about the vicinity of Itaúna in the backlands southwest of the state capital. He also studied philosophy, religion, and the natural sciences (especially botany, biology, and zoology), elements

177

that would inform the cosmic dimensions of his literary
undertakings.

In 1936, Rosa was awarded an important national prize for
Magma, a collection of poetry he was never to publish. Then, in
1938, he began his diplomatic career as counsular attaché in
Hamburg, only to be interned in Baden-Baden by the Nazis four
years later, when the dictator Vargas reluctantly broke Brazilian
diplomatic relations with Germany. Rosa was eventually permitted
to return to Rio, with his second wife, in exchange for some
German diplomats.

After the war he continued his diplomatic service by representing
Brazil at the Paris Peace Conference, and then from 1948 to 1951
he served there as embassy counselor to France. The following year,
Rosa took a long trip on horseback with a number of cowboys
throughout the backlands of Minas Gerais, keeping detailed notes
for the literary works that followed. Finally, in 1956, after twelve
years of silence he published (in January) a 750-page cycle of
novellas entitled *Corpo de Baile* ("Corps de Ballet") and (in May) his
monumental novel *Grande Sertao: Veredas.* Translated into English as
The Devil to Pay in the Backlands, Rosa's novel, whose point of
departure is the Faustian myth of a pact with the Devil, takes the
form of a long, hypnotic monologue narrated by a strangely
mystical Riobaldo Tatarana, who finds himself caught between God
and Satan while wrestling with the male and female polarities of his
own psyche.

Though promoted to diplomat in 1962, he preferred to remain in
his native Brazil as head of the Department of Boundaries. In the
same year he published a second book of stories, translated as *The
Third Bank of the River and Other Stories.* In 1963, he was elected to
the Brazilian Academy of Letters but, because of a premonition,
persistently avoided taking his official chair for four years. He did
so on November 16, 1967, and in his speech bid a strange farewell
to his colleagues. He died of a heart attack three days later.
Brazilian fiction has yet to recover from the loss of its first and
greatest metaphysical writer.

The Third Bank
of the River

My father was a dutiful, orderly, straightforward man. And according to several reliable people of whom I inquired, he had had these qualities since adolescence or even childhood. By my own recollection, he was neither jollier nor more melancholy than the other men we knew. Maybe a little quieter. It was Mother, not Father, who ruled the house. She scolded us daily—my sister, my brother, and me. But it happened one day that Father ordered a boat.

He was very serious about it. It was to be made specially for him, of mimosa wood. It was to be sturdy enough to last twenty or thirty years and just large enough for one person. Mother carried on plenty about it. Was her husband going to become a fisherman all of a sudden? Or a hunter? Father said nothing. Our house was less than a mile from the river, which around there was deep, quiet, and so wide you couldn't see across it.

I can never forget the day the rowboat was delivered. Father showed no joy or other emotion. He just put on his hat as he always did and said good-by to us. He took along no food or bundle of any sort. We expected Mother to rant and rave, but she didn't. She looked very pale and bit her lip, but all she said was: "If you go away, stay away. Don't ever come back!"

Father made no reply. He looked gently at me and motioned me to walk along with him. I feared Mother's wrath, yet I eagerly obeyed. We headed toward the river together. I felt bold and exhilarated, so much so that I said: "Father, will you take me with you in your boat?"

He just looked at me, gave me his blessing, and by a gesture, told me to go back. I made as if to do so but, when his back was turned, I ducked behind some bushes to watch him. Father got into the boat and rowed away. Its shadow slid across the water like a crocodile, long and quiet.

Father did not come back. Nor did he go anywhere, really. He just rowed and floated across and around, out there in the river. Everyone was appalled. What had never happened, what could not possibly happen, was happening. Our relatives, neighbors, and friends came over to discuss the phenomenon.

Mother was ashamed. She said little and conducted herself with great composure. As a consequence, almost everyone thought (though no one said it) that Father had gone insane. A few, however, suggested that Father might be fulfilling a promise he had made to God or to a saint, or that he might have some horrible disease, maybe leprosy, and that he left for the sake of the family, at the same time wishing to remain fairly near them.

Travelers along the river and people living near the bank on one side or the other reported that Father never put foot on land, by day or night. He just moved about on the river, solitary, aimless, like a derelict. Mother and our relatives agreed that the food which he had doubtless hidden in the boat would soon give out and that then he would either leave the river and travel off somewhere (which would be at least a little more respectable) or he would repent and come home.

How far from the truth they were! Father had a secret source of provisions: me. Every day I stole food and brought it to him. The first night after he left, we all lit fires on the shore and prayed and called to him. I was deeply distressed and felt a need to do something more. The following day I went down to the river with a loaf of corn bread, a bunch of bananas, and some bricks of raw brown sugar. I waited impatiently a long, long hour. Then I saw the boat, far off, alone, gliding almost imperceptibly on the smoothness of the river. Father was sitting in the bottom of the boat. He saw me but he did not row toward me or make any gesture. I showed him the food and then I placed it in a hollow rock on the river bank; it was safe there from animals, rain, and dew. I did this day after day, on and on and on. Later I learned, to my surprise, that Mother knew what I was doing and left food around where I could easily steal it. She had a lot of feelings she didn't show.

Mother sent for her brother to come and help on the farm and in business matters. She had the schoolteacher come and tutor us children at home because of the time we had lost. One day, at her request, the priest put on his vestments, went down to the shore, and tried to exorcise the devils that had got into my father. He shouted that Father had a duty to cease his unholy obstinacy. Another day she arranged to have two soldiers come and try to frighten him. All to no avail. My father went by in the distance, sometimes so far away he could barely be seen. He never replied to anyone and no one ever got close to him. When some newspapermen came in a launch to take his picture, Father headed his boat to the other side of the river and into the marshes, which he knew like the palm of his hand but in which other people quickly got lost. There in his private maze, which extended for miles, with heavy foliage overhead and rushes on all sides, he was safe.

We had to get accustomed to the idea of Father's being out on the river. We had to but we couldn't, we never could. I think I was the only one who understood to some degree what our father wanted and what he did not want. The thing I could not understand at all was how he stood the hardship. Day and night, in sun and rain, in heat and in the terrible midyear cold spells, with his old hat on his head and very little other clothing, week after week, month after month, year after year, unheedful of the waste and emptiness in which his life was slipping by. He never set foot on earth or grass, on isle or mainland shore. No doubt he sometimes tied up the boat at a secret place, perhaps at the tip of some island, to get a little sleep. He never lit a fire or even struck a match and he had no flashlight. He took only a small part of the food that I left in the hollow rock—not enough, it seemed to me, for survival. What could his state of health have been? How about the continual drain on his energy, pulling and pushing the oars to control the boat? And how did he survive the annual floods, when the river rose and swept along with it all sorts of dangerous objects— branches of trees, dead bodies of animals—that might suddenly crash against his little boat?

He never talked to a living soul. And we never talked about him. We just thought. No, we could never put our father out of mind. If for a short time we seemed to, it was just a lull from which we would be sharply awakened by the realization of his frightening situation.

My sister got married, but Mother didn't want a wedding party. It would have been a sad affair, for we thought of him every time we ate some especially tasty food. Just as we thought of him in our cozy beds on a cold, stormy night—out there, alone and unprotected, trying to bail out the boat with only his hands and a gourd.

Now and then someone would say that I was getting to look more and more like my father. But I knew that by then his hair and beard must have been shaggy and his nails long. I pictured him thin and sickly, black with hair and sunburn, and almost naked despite the articles of clothing I occasionally left for him.

He didn't seem to care about us at all. But I felt affection and respect for him, and, whenever they praised me because I had done something good, I said: "My father taught me to act that way."

It wasn't exactly accurate but it was a truthful sort of lie. As I said, Father didn't seem to care about us. But then why did he stay around here? Why didn't he go up the river or down the river, beyond the possibility of seeing us or being seen by us? He alone knew the answer.

My sister had a baby boy. She insisted on showing Father his grandson. One beautiful day we all went down to the riverbank, my sister in her white wedding dress, and she lifted the baby high. Her husband held a parasol above them. We shouted to Father and waited. He did not appear. My sister cried; we all cried in each other's arms.

My sister and her husband moved far away. My brother went to live in a city. Times changed, with their usual imperceptible rapidity. Mother finally moved too; she was old and went to live with her daughter. I remained behind, a leftover. I could never think of marrying. I just stayed there with the impedimenta of my life. Father, wandering alone and forlorn on the river, needed me. I knew he needed me, although he never even told me why he was doing it. When I put the question to people bluntly and insistently, all they told me was that they heard that Father had explained it to the man who made the boat. But now this man was dead and nobody knew or remembered anything. There was just some foolish talk, when the rains were especially severe and persistent, that my father was wise like Noah and had the boat built in anticipation of a new flood; I dimly remember people saying this. In any case, I would not condemn my father for what he was doing. My hair was beginning to turn gray.

I have only sad things to say. What bad had I done, what was my great guilt? My father always away and his absence always with me. And the river, always the river, perpetually renewing itself. The river, always. I was beginning to suffer from old age, in which life is just a sort of lingering. I had attacks of illness and of anxiety. I had a nagging rheumatism. And he? Why, why was he doing it? He must have been suffering terribly. He was so old. One day, in his failing strength, he might let the boat capsize; or he might let the current carry it downstream, on and on, until it plunged over the waterfall to the boiling turmoil below. It pressed upon my heart. He was out there and I was forever robbed of my peace. I am guilty of I know not what, and my pain is an open wound inside me. Perhaps I would know—if things were different. I began to guess what was wrong.

Out with it! Had I gone crazy? No, in our house that word was never spoken, never through all the years. No one called anybody crazy, for nobody is crazy. Or maybe everybody. All I did was go there and wave a handkerchief so he would be more likely to see me. I was in complete command of myself. I waited. Finally he appeared in the distance, there, then over there, a vague shape sitting in the back of the boat. I called to him several times. And I said what I was so eager to say, to state formally and under oath. I said it as loud as I could:

"Father, you have been out there long enough. You are old. . . . Come back, you don't have to do it anymore. . . . Come back and I'll go instead. Right now, if you want. Any time. I'll get into the boat. I'll take your place."

And when I had said this my heart beat more firmly.

He heard me. He stood up. He maneuvered with his oars and headed the boat toward me. He had accepted my offer. And suddenly I trembled, down deep. For he had raised his arm and waved—the first time in so many, so many years. And I couldn't . . . In terror, my hair on end, I ran, I fled madly. For he seemed to come from another world. And I'm begging forgiveness, begging, begging.

I experienced the dreadful sense of cold that comes from deadly fear, and I became ill. Nobody ever saw or heard about him again. Am I a man, after such a failure? I am what never should have been. I am what must be silent. I know it is too late. I must stay in the deserts and unmarked plains of my life, and I fear I shall shorten it. But when death comes I want them to take me and put me in a little boat in this perpetual water between the long shores; and I, down the river, lost in the river, inside the river . . . the river . . .

Translated by William L. Grossman

João Ubaldo Ribeiro
(1941-   )

The Brazilian João Ubaldo Ribeiro was born in Itaparica, an island off the coast of Salvador, Bahia. His parents, both lawyers, soon settled in the neighboring state of Sergipe, where the family stayed until Ribeiro was eleven. He mastered Latin and Greek as a child and picked up American English from the children of vacationing diplomats.

At law school in Salvador, Ribeiro was active in the political and cultural milieu of a brilliant Bahian generation that included the musicians Gilberto Gil and Caetano Veloso, the painter Calasans Neto, and the film director Glauber Rocha. Ribeiro went on to take an M.A. in public administration at the University of Southern California in Los Angeles, while minoring in political science.

He began work as a journalist and teacher once he returned to Salvador, but soon turned to writing, he confesses, "in order to have more time for fishing." At twenty-one he had already written his first novel—a politically daring, sexually charged portrait of his generation—which was published three years later, after the bloody military coup it in some ways had portended. In 1971, Ribeiro published the violent "tale of virtue," *Sergeant Getúlio,* that placed him in the forefront of Brazilian fiction and, through his own masterful English translation (published in 1978), won him an international reputation.

Over the next decade Ribeiro completed a third novel, as well as two collections of shorter fiction that opened a comic vein in his writing. In the meantime he adapted a number of fictional works for film and television, including *Sergeant Getúlio* and a novel by Jorge Amado. He went on to spend a year in Portugal (1980–81) on a Gulbenkian Foundation grant, then returned to Brazil to work on a vast family saga spanning four hundred years of Brazilian history.

Closer to Melville and Rabelais than to García Márquez or "magic realism," *An Invincible Memory* (1984) takes as its point of departure the "Soul's Perch" above All Saints Bay, home of the reincarnated spirits of cannibals and captains, slaves and barons who thread their way through a baroque range of subplots and subject matter covering everything from the mating of whales to the making of the Brazilian nation. His English version, published in 1989, confirmed his reputation as a writer quite as comfortable with the comic resonance of the language as is Cabrera Infante. That same year, in Brazil, Ribeiro published *The Smile of the Lizard,* a dark homage to Wells's *The Island of Doctor Moreau,* fraught with the scientific and spiritual implications of modern biogenetic engineering.

It Was a Different Day
____When They Killed the Pig

When they killed the pig it was a different day because long before everyone knew that this was the day they were going to kill the pig. It was known even many days beforehand, although one could never be really sure, because the grownups spoke about the pig in a vague and imprecise manner. In fact, the day they killed the pig happened for the first time in a never well remembered way. One day, for the first time, it seemed everybody woke up early. And the older people knew that this was the day for killing the pig, and it was usually what they talked about as they prepared clay bowls and stretched cords for sausages and told stories of past pigs, the best pigs this land had ever seen, the best in town. So those older people could say with simpleness: Today is the day they are going to kill the pig. A simpleness which contrasted with the eyes of the younger children, whose first thought as they left their beds was whether they were still on vacation or not, or whether it was Sunday or not; for those boys and girls, when they noticed the same inexperience in the eyes of another their age, passed along the information almost breathlessly and glanced sideways as if they were conspiring. Today they are going to kill the pig. And maybe it was one of those subjects that deserved a glare from the grownups when harped upon, one of those secret subjects that made the room fall silent and provoked unknown gestures in the older people if a child entered the room. But the day for killing the pig was always a sunny day, and for some reason on that day the children were left freer than usual. Then, as time passed, the children would wake up already knowing that the pig was going to be killed, and maybe if they were lucky they might be able to tell a younger brother or a girl who lived nearby that the pig was going to be killed, so they could feel wonderment and curiosity in the other and could thus display wisdom and attractions. Also, if the only answer given the children to whom it was not yet permitted to take part in the death of the pig, when they asked what was the meaning of those strident wails they had never heard before, was just, "It's the pig, little one, it's the pig, child," and if the sight of the pig being slain was denied to them, at least they could see the man who was going to kill the pig and many times they gathered enough courage to ask, are you the one who is going to kill the pig? And more often than not he would answer, smiling like somebody who was not going to kill the pig: I am, yes. If the murderer of the pig was a stranger, then it was best to keep a certain distance from him who brought death with a smile, and if some of the children went as far as to talk to him, they would never go alone nor lose sight of the better known and more trusted older people. But there were some children whose pig killers were their own fathers, and so, on those sunny mornings when the sun rose differently and things would never again be the same, the father was the most different thing of them all. Being the father, he could not but be a reason for pride, but it was strange to be in fear of one's own pride, and this made the children's hearts rush and their eyes follow their mothers everywhere, because the mothers did not kill pigs. There were also things to unriddle, since the father spoke, or if it was another adult who spoke he showed his look of approval so familiar to everyone, about the animals and the affection he held for them, and told of the suffering of a cow whose calf had got stuck as it tried to be born. For Aloísio and all his brothers and sisters, the moment was always to be remembered when their father took all of them to see the red sow Noca, and said to them this sow Noca was the miracle of nature. And they all remained looking at the sow Noca suckling her many little pigs, and some of them never ceased to go back there to admire her thick blubbers unfolding over the burrowing snouts of all those little pigs, some more concerned with how the little pigs grew, the others only contemplating the sow and wishing for her to talk and trying to guess her thoughts. Aloísio, this day in which he even mistook the light of the moon that came down through a glass shingle for the light of the sun and almost had a fever from wanting so much to leave his bed, was told that the pig to be killed was the sow Noca herself, but did not dare ask the father why he was going to do that, not so much because he was afraid the father would be angry, although he would not explain anything either, but because he did not want to appear to be a boy who did not understand things and did not want people to say then that they would no longer allow him to see the killing of the pig. He imagined that maybe the reason why the sow Noca had never given an answer to the things he had said to her every once in a while, even when they were all by themselves and with guarantees of secrecy, was that she knew that one day he would betray her and would be watching her execution in all coldness, learning in that operation the manner in which he would kill his own pigs in the future. For, since he was a man, his wife would surely expect him to know how to kill the pigs he raised or fattened, so she could also have her days for killing the pig, like her mother before her and the mother of her mother and all the other mothers, this being the way the world is organized. But he spoke nothing of what he felt, and he was also ashamed to ask what time they were going to kill the sow, so he began to shadow his father wherever he went. He then saw that if the father could not now avoid having another presence, killing the pig was not something to occupy him more than the time necessary to do the killing. Because the father had time to go out of the house, already carrying the pig-killing knife on his belt, and to walk to the store to buy cigarettes, and to write in his blue-covered notebook. And the mother, without conferring with the father, gave orders for the sow Noca to be taken to the place of death, and remained arranging vinegars, bowls, lemons and all the seasoning she used to pile up on a corner of the stove, on top of the place where the firewood was kept, a smell of feasting already in the air, and it could even be that relatives would come visiting, with their faces that changed from year to year and their slight strangeness, especially on account of how familiar one had to be with them as a matter of obligation. The housemaids and the neighbor women and the persons who went in and out of the kitchen and the pantry talked more than usual and also much louder. Aloísio became impatient from watching the father write in the blue notebook, even more so because before each line or word he wagged his pen in airy scrolls without writing anything, and he had the sensation the father was going to die, so he went out to see how they caught the sow Noca and took her to the wooden block where they would tie her, and ignoring her cries would turn her into sausages and pork loins and meats. No, he would never forget the day, he did not know how long ago, when his brother Honório, who was now in

the seminary and wrote letters the mother would read at night
crying and shaking her head, had looked to him so wise and worldly
as he told him, as if making a remark on something trivial, that
they were going to kill the pig Leleu and would let Honório watch,
but would not let Aloísio, and of course Leonor, watch. Now Aloísio could not resist it, and when he saw Leonor leaning against
one of the pillars of the porch and remembered she would still be
likely to ask what were those cries as they started to kill the sow
Noca, he walked forward pretending not to have seen her, stopped,
and as though he was doing his sister a great favor, spoke in her
ear: Today we are going to kill the sow Noca. And he even felt
more pleasure than he had expected, to see that her face paled
and she began to cry. At that moment, he thought he had been
revenged a little for all the times she had had an advantage over
him because the father always wore a different look when he came
home and put her in his lap, and he had never been picked up
that way and now only the mother would put him in her lap, but
very few times. Maybe the father would now be drawn there by her
weeping and would scold him, but Aloísio felt an odd confidence
as he had never felt before, and anticipating any questions the
father might ask, he pointed at his sister with his thumb, and said:
She is crying because we are going to kill the sow Noca, can you
imagine? Now why did you tell her, the father said, but without
showing annoyance, and started to stroke her head. If it was me,
Aloísio thought, people would laugh. But he got over that quickly,
because he remembered that his sister was a woman and women
cried a lot, and besides she was not going to see the death of the
sow. Indeed, when he was already near the wooden block, and the
tree, once so familiar, gave out a loaded shade full of things not
known, and all objects were now sinister, the father propped his
right boot on a root to tighten the straps a little more and made a
low-pitched comment which brought warmth to Aloísio's face, and
he wanted very, very much to be a man, he wanted nobody to be
ever, ever able to say that he had not been a man even if only for
an instant. Women are like that, the father said almost whispering,
with the same amused chuckle he would have when he was talking
in a low voice to his friends, and Aloísio, his face on fire, nodded
and managed to say, speaking with as deep a voice as he could,
"That's right, that's right." Then the father finished tying his boot,
put his hand on Aloísio's shoulder, and they marched together
toward the block, and Aloísio remembered he was also wearing
boots and they were new. The sow Noca was tied down and whin-

ing, knowing very well what was going to happen. Aloísio decided
he would not turn his eyes away nor would he show emotion, but
he could not keep himself from feeling an immense fear when,
after all the preparations and rites he had never imagined, he saw
the father surmount the loins of the great sow and, with a face
even more distant than when he talked about life to the mother,
raise the knife. The sow began to be killed, and all around Aloísio's
eyes there seemed to be a dark wheel and one could only see the
middle of this wheel, where the sow Noca lay being killed. In the
very beginning, less blood came out than he had expected, but
soon everything turned into a red, spattering ball and shouts and
imprecations from the men, and brisk motions among troughs,
cloths and bowls, and the sow tumbled down with a thump. Aloísio,
his breath arrested, was not even able to notice the moment they
started demolishing the sow Noca as though they were demolishing
a house, and was only aware of feeling sick, and he did not know
there existed so many black and gray and white and red and limp
and throbbing and slippery things inside a pig and that many of
those things gave out a hideous smell and the father's hands were
covered with blood, with bits of those things and with that slime
up to his elbows. Neither did he know that they would use saws
and hatchets, and he tightened his jaw very hard as he looked at
the men sawing the sow's hindquarters on top of the block and
filling the bowls with all those things. Those there, the father said
as they were getting ready to head back to the house, are the bowels, which we are going to clean, which we are going to make sausage skins out of. He nodded yes and hoped the father had not
noticed he had closed his eyes and had glanced only furtively at
the bowl filled with blue, stenchy snakes. Without touching him
because his hands were dirty, the father made a gesture with his
chin and they went back to the house, and although Aloísio knew
he had behaved in the most correct way, he was ashamed to be
feeling sick and could not even remember well what had happened. He saw that his boots had been sprinkled with the blood
of the sow Noca, and almost retched. He imagined that as soon as
he went in the house he would go to the bathroom, but he did not
want to run, so no one would take notice of anything. And then,
while time dragged itself on like a snail, they went in the house
and stopped in front of the mother, but fortunately the father was
in a hurry to wash himself and the mother had to go about her
chores in the kitchen, and also fortunately the father preferred to
wash at the backyard spigot, instead of in the bathroom. He had

never known one could sweat so much, while he scrubbed the stains, real and imaginary, from his vomit spewed all over the bathroom because he had hardly been able to close the door when his cheeks were filled up and before he could bend over the toilet, he exploded as if he were going to turn inside out. But he managed to relieve himself anyway and was patient enough to clean all the mess he had made and to still wash his face twice, one time for the vomit, the other time for the sweat. Looking in the mirror to study the expression he wanted to have as he left to participate in the comments about the sow, he opened the door and came out and was happy to see that neither the father nor the mother was on the porch, where it was perfectly natural for him to stay, looking ahead and enjoying the breeze, after all he had seen his first pig. He was still secretly bothered by what had happened, but was confident that the next time it would not be like this, although he did not think now that he would have the courage to go near the block again. But people grow up, Aloísio thought, trying to imagine whether he would grow a moustache when he grew up, and then, through a crack between the doors that opened onto the porch, he saw that the father was talking contentedly to the mother, rubbing a towel behind his ears. He guessed they were going to talk about him, came close to the door, put his ear against the small opening and listened to the father telling the mother—and he was sure of the way the father was smiling—how Aloísio had behaved fine during the sow's dying. He is a man, the father said with admiration, and Aloísio felt his eyes wet, and pride with sickness again, and pulled back to the porch, not knowing what it was that he had. Maybe this is the reason why when he now sees the family gathered together on sunny holidays or when he wakes up among the noises of his children, and grandchildren and parents and grandparents and all relatives, when he sits in a quiet corner and looks at all this, his chest feels heavy and he has the impression that if someone speaks to him, he will begin to cry without ever again being able to stop.

Translated by the author

Lygia Fagundes Telles
(1924–   )

Because her father was a state attorney, the Brazilian Lygia
Fagundes Telles spent much of her childhood moving from town to
town throughout the state of São Paulo. She attributes the eerie,
dislocated ambience of many of her stories to these early
wanderings, as well as to a nursemaid with a penchant for bedtime
tales of witches, goblins, enchanted forests, werewolves, and
headless horsemen. At an early age, Telles developed a habit of
retelling such stories to her playmates, keeping notebooks on the
characters and events to remember them properly and also to
domesticate some of the terrors her gifted nanny had inspired.

She published her first stories in her teens and went on to earn
degrees in law (1945) and in physical education (this to placate her
mother's fears that "such a skinny daughter" could only be a
candidate for tuberculosis). During these student years, Telles
collaborated on the literary journals of the University of São Paulo
and played an active role in the law faculty's opposition to the
Vargas dictatorship. In 1949, she published her first important
collection of stories; she married and eventually had a son.

Her first novel, *The Marble Dance*, appeared in 1955, and its
French translation four years later inspired a literary friendship
with Simone de Beauvoir. In fact, Telles's work is closer to the
psychological precision of the French writers of the forties and
fifties—with an occasional British touch of the *uncanny*—than to the
regionalism and naturalism of her Brazilian contemporaries. And
her mastery of descriptive detail and subjective intimacies has led
some critics abroad to liken her to Colette.

In 1969, she received the Cannes Prix International des Femmes

192

for her short story "Before the Green Masquerade." Recent works include the collection of short stories entitled *Tigrela* (1976) and two novels: *The Girl in the Photograph* (1973) and her gothic masterpiece *Naked Hours* (1990). Telles has worked as an attorney in numerous professional and public service capacities including, most recently, president of the Brazilian Cinematheque, founded by her second husband, the late author and film critic Paulo Emílio Salles Gomes.

The Corset

Everything was harmonious, solid, genuine. At first. The women, particularly the dead women in the photo album, were marvelous; the men, even more marvelous, ah, it would have been hard to find a more perfect family. *Our family,* my grandmother used to say in her beautiful contralto voice. *In our family,* she would stress, casting a complacent look around her, pitying those who were not part of our clan. A little orphan girl like me would have been the most ungrateful of orphans if she didn't thank God every night for having been born in the bosom of a family like ours.

There was no fear. At first. And why should there be fear? The neighbor's house might have been built upon sand but ours was founded upon a *very solid* rock, Grandmother emphasized, she loved Biblical allusions. Let the rains, the winds ... One of my earliest memories regarding myself is of a little girl in a blue smock installed on the velvet floor cushion in the sitting room, which smelled vaguely of altars. Next to me, Grandmother with her knitting. She always carried a bag, where she kept everything: keys, eyeglasses, money, medicine, needles ... It was a huge house, with endless rooms and corridors. Storing everything in the bag saved her a long walk back to her room to get the small pair of scissors. After scheduling the household chores for the day and locking the pantry carefully behind her, she would go to the living room, place the bag on the floor, and resume her knitting. Sometimes she would let me open in my lap the heavy red album with the silver-plated corners. There was no longer any mystery attached to many of the photographs, but there were some over which Grandmother would sprinkle her reticent remarks: "One day, Ana Luisa, when you grow up . . ."

But she never told me anything: I had to grope about, a word here, a gesture there, and piece them together while I waited for her revelations. What had happened to Aunt Barbara, the beautiful almond-eyed aunt with the smile about to break into a grin had the photographer waited just a while longer? He hadn't. Her teeth remained hidden and so did everything else. I put my questions to Grandmother, who wrinkled her brow. "One day she went out to buy some lace and never came back. Dear Barbara was somewhat highstrung." Yes, I would learn all the facts about her when I grew up, not just about her but also about another mysterious aunt, Ofélia. "She drank poison mistaking it for Milk of Magnesia. She died a month after her wedding," Grandmother informed me in a dry tone. She would much rather talk about Grandfather, who wore a black frock coat and had a lock of plastered hair on his forehead. Always in profile, his hands resting on the silver head of a walking stick and his chin resting lightly on his hands, in a dreamy pose. He had died quite young, after falling off his horse. "This one was taken a week before the accident," she added, showing me Grandfather elegantly atop a horse, also in profile. "He was an upright man. May God keep him."

God must also have kept Uncle Maximiliano, with his malicious green eyes. "Everybody in our family has green eyes," murmured Grandmother, turning her water-green eyes to me. One of this uncle's eyebrows was raised much higher than the other, an expression that matched the ironic lips with their drooping corners, the photograph was the illustration of the poem that Grandmother had written down in purple ink: "*I know thee, world, and how well!* . . ." He had married an Englishwoman and had become one of the most powerful businessmen of his time. "He had character. He founded farms, cities."

I would turn this over in my mind. A founder of farms, well it could be, but a founder of cities? . . . Cities were something huge and very complicated. Was it possible for a single man to build all those things? And I would turn the page, in search of the bright-faced Englishwoman with her curls and her small teeth with the gaps between them. They had met on board a ship, during Uncle Maximiliano's return from Europe. "They had eleven children. They were extremely happy," Grandmother sighed, and with the tip of a fingernail she scratched the perforations that snaked along the sailor collar that the young woman was wearing. "What a pity, the worms are eating it . . ."

The dead had already been devoured. Now it was the turn of the photographs. Not even the ribbons tying Aunt Consuelo's hair had been spared. Only the almond-shaped eyes remained intact. I already knew that Aunt Consuelo had entered a convent, where she died. But why the convent? Grandmother put on a nostalgic air: "Vocation. Little Consuelo was so sensitive, she was always crying. A little saint she was. On her twentieth birthday she saw an angel sitting at the foot of her bed. On that day she announced to my parents: 'I'm going to become a nun.' She did look a bit like Little Saint Theresa."

When Margarida rebelled and decided to reveal the "rottenness" of my family, I was outraged. She said "rottenness" and this word hit me like a punch. "Rottenness" sounded much too rotten, it made me thing of carrion, of flies . . . If she had said *"potins"* as Grandmother would have, I wouldn't have minded so much. But Margarida didn't know any French. Neither did I. Words couldn't remain well-behaved: free like her, they were wild, reinless horses. Fearless.

"It's a lie, it's a lie!" I said, covering my ears. But Margarida went on relentlessly: Uncle Maximiliano had married the Englishwoman with the curls for her money, he was no better than a scoundrel. And Aunt Consuelo, well, Aunt Consuelo cried all the time because she missed having a man, she wanted a man not God or a convent or a sanatorium. What really counted was the first option. I reacted violently: how dared a boarder who worked for her room and meals, a child of poor parents brought up by my family as a member of the household, and a mulatta to boot, how dared she disparage my domestic idols? No, there couldn't be any of this filthy ambition and sex in the corseted hearts of the dead of the album. All of them wore corsets, even Aunt Consuelo, who had a wasp waist and small breasts pointing in two different directions, like my eyes do.

I was panic-stricken. And what did she mean by saying that my mother had been a Jew? . . . Margarida also had to stir up this: had anyone ever spared her feelings? Well, then better listen to this. I listened. I, the girl who had been so well trained to classify people according to two clear-cut groups, as though they were the material of a chemistry lab: good people and bad people. Good and Evil— capitalized—never mingled with each other. Sometimes the Devil would sneak into a house, and hiding himself behind a piece of

furniture, he would snoop to find out what was going on. But if
he happened to see an angel hovering about the ceiling, he would
put his tail between his legs, and crestfallen, he would harangue
in some other parish. That's how I used to think. That's how I
wanted things to be. Aunt Consuelo, lust-ridden, tossing about on
the hard bed in her cell, Uncle Maximiliano making babies and
living off the Englishwoman he didn't love, Aunt Ofélia killing
herself a month after her wedding. And my mother with her Jewish
name and her violin—but to what kind of family was I now being
introduced? Unusual, long-suffering people. Whom I would have
loved much more than the idealized images Grandmother had presented to me. But I became afraid when I discovered the fear that
other people could feel. I wanted heroes and heroines.

How could the fear that other people felt be greater than mine?
I was confused. Grandmother had taught me to believe in unadul-
terated beauty and kindness. There was Heaven. There was Hell,
but it was a very remote concept, romantically linked to the concept I had of beggars and criminals—a breed of grubby people,
condemned to eating out of the troughs with the pigs and to living
in prisons. To be remembered in the daily-recited Lord's Prayer.
And to be forgotten, as behooves unpleasant thoughts. "Mental
health!" warned Grandmother the day I refused to eat a steak because I felt sorry for the steer. I should think of butterflies when
eating steer and of steers while impaling butterflies—I had been
assigned by my teacher to display various specimens on a cardboard. Lepidoptera, I explained to Margarida, and she kept repeating the word, she loved learning new words. "I don't want a
vegetarian for a granddaughter, vegetarians are always morbid. Eat
up, steers were born to be eaten, if not by us, then by someone
else . . ."

I learned very early that promoting "mental health" meant doing
nothing to help those who had toppled down into the abyss. And
I used to imagine a rocky, black abyss, into which sinners plunged
themselves without any hope of rescue. However, no matter how
hard I tried, I was never able to visualize the bodies down there at
the bottom, and this fact set my mind at rest. And after all, wasn't
it possible for many of them to save themselves at the eleventh
hour by hanging on to a bush? To a rock? . . . Steers and people
could be saved by virtue of miraculous intervention, "miracles are
part and parcel of mental health," she had taught me. The only
requirement was to be worthy of a miracle.

The book which I used to keep hidden under the mattress had

a story about a woman who fell in love with a priest and was then turned into a headless mule every Friday, when she'd run about, frightening people. The metamorphosis was inevitable. Had there been a miracle then in Aunt Barbara's case?—the question immediately occurred to me the moment Margarida told me in a burst of fury that the beautiful lady never left the house to buy any lace, she left the house to meet a young priest. She bore him five children: had she had seven, the seventh child would have been a werewolf. How could it be possible, how? I shuddered at the thought of a huge headless horse, bucking down and down into a crater. I recalled Grandmother saying in a warning tone: "She was highstrung, rather unstable . . ."

I was also aware that my mother was never mentioned. Never. Unlike my father, whose intelligence and charm were often recalled under the slightest pretext, "He had a lot of charm!" I didn't know what charm was, but if my father had it then it had to be a good quality. And my mother? Why was she kept wrapped up in silence?

"It's a lie, Margarida. You've been telling me lies, nothing but lies," I kept repeating as I felt the broad, light-colored planks of the floor sway under my feet. I even threatened her with my clenched fists. "Shut up, shut up! That's enough, that's enough!" And I could still hear her shattered voice as it proceeded to shatter everybody. Despite being in a daze, I was able to notice that Margarida was turning darker and darker, Margarida, who had succeeded in making herself almost white-skinned while primping herself to meet her boyfriend. Her hair was bristling. Her lips were gray. She displayed her wonderful mettle, hurling herself at words with that same dispossession of a person hurling himself into a blaze. She also knew all about her own origins, no, she didn't have any illusions: they went back to her grandmother, black Ifigênia, who had starched and ironed my family's clothes ever since she was a young woman, the iron packed with embers—it was the starch age. When she became pregnant, Uncle Maximiliano was quickly shipped away to Europe, later to return with the Englishwoman with the curls. And equally speedy were the arrangements made for her to marry the family's foster son, an army sergeant fond of dancing and playing the guitar. She gave birth to a boy, who was almost white and had green eyes. The sergeant dropped out of sight and the boy died of pneumonia. "God's ways are wise!" Grandmother must have said. Ifigênia's second pregnancy was more peaceful, and the sergeant sometimes put in an appearance.

She gave birth to a girl, who thrived. "We'll christen her Florence," my grandfather, who enjoyed reading Florence Barclay's novels, had suggested. Grandmother vetoed the suggestion. "The idea! Such an aristocratic name for the poor little thing!" If he wanted to make use of novels, then why not *Isaura, the Slave*? Then Ifigênia began to waste away, feeling "a pain in her chest that went through her back," and Isaura was raised in an orphanage until she was old enough to work. She never did, though. When she was old enough to start working to make up for all the trouble she had caused the family, she got tuberculosis, as her mother had. At the sanatorium she fell in love with a Polish orderly and was discharged from the hospital when she became pregnant, but oh God, do all foster daughters have to end up as fallen women? The recovery from TB was short-lived though; she died a month after giving birth to the baby. "At her own convenience too," Grandmother must have said. It was spring and the garden was covered with tiny blue marguerites when the baby was brought home. "We'll call her Margarida," Grandmother decided. She took her to the orphanage (the Pole had simply disappeared) and on her tenth birthday, Grandmother brought her home: I needed an attendant and the new maid needed someone to help her with the starching and ironing. In the trunk that had belonged to the dead woman there was a picture of the Pole in his hospital uniform. Margarida pinned it on the wall in her bedroom. "Don't I look like my father?" she would ask me. When we quarreled I would tell her that she was Isaura's spitting image. "But you've never seen my mother!" she protested. To which I'd reply innocently that I had known her grandmother. Then she would crawl under the bed, where she lay crying and tearing her hair.

It was Saturday. After dinner she came to my room to borrow my eyeliner. "Quick, give me your black eyeliner, I want to do my eyes." I let her have it. It was at that moment, as she was eagerly primping herself for her first date, that her extraordinary beauty struck home to me. "But will Grandmother let you go?" I asked while drawing a vase with orchids. "She doesn't know, I'll just sneak out," Margarida whispered. And she entreated me to let her have some of my toilet water. Grandmother then entered the room. She took the knitting out of the bag. I lowered my eyes to the writing pad where I had sketched the orchids: early that morning I had informed Grandmother about this engagement, "Margarida is dating Doctor Peninha's son." Grandmother listened and asked me to taste some of the confection, did it need more sugar? She was

making guava paste. The recollection of the aroma of the crushed
guavas in the reddish copper boiler enveloped me again in their
spicy vapor. It was the smell of betrayal. "No, Margarida, you're
not going out with this young man. A white young man, from an
important family. It would be most irresponsible of me to consent
to this relationship. Come on now, wash your face and go to bed.
You'll thank me one day, just listen to me carefully, you'll still
thank me for having prevented you from going out with him."
Margarida fell on her knees, she pleaded, she tore at her face,
weeping loudly. "We love each other, godmother, we love each
other!" Grandmother got up impatiently: "It's no use insisting." I
got to my feet and in the mirror I saw my angular face. The squint
in my eyes. Margarida was still sobbing, lying on the floor. "You
witch! you witch!" she kept saying as soon as Grandmother left the
room, taking the bag with her. "She's a witch!" she screamed, stif-
fening her body and pounding on the floor with her clenched fists.
I stood staring at myself in the mirror. I'm not good, I thought.
I'm evil. I made a mean face and then smiled at myself. Friend and
confidante. Enemy and informer. Now I couldn't stop, I had to go
on until I was sure that the priest would deny me Communion. I
went back to my desk. The vase with orchids seemed hideous. I
tore up the sheet of paper. And I began to draw a flower on the
palm of my hand. Well, Margarida, why don't you try to find another boyfriend? This one can't possibly like you, as Grandmother
explained. Get one your own color, don't you think it would be
better?

She wiped her eyes, now blotched, on her skirt. She smoothed
down the head of hair that had bristled during her fit of despair.
Hoarse from crying, she spoke in a low voice: "You're her spitting
image. Exactly like her." She started off softly but she soon grew
excited, her voice thick, as it had sounded on the night when the
two of us had drunk almost half a bottle of cherry liqueur. I quickly
closed the door, "You're shouting, Margarida, Grandmother will
hear you!" But livid, and all fired up, she proceeded to lash out at
me. My Mother was a Jew.

"It's a lie! A lie!" I kept repeating. The same nausea that I had
experienced on Easter Sunday, when I had eaten up a huge chocolate egg. In the midst of this nightmare, I caught glimpses of Aunt
Consuelo, Uncle Maximiliano, Aunt Ofélia as they swirled by ...
Aunt Consuelo's habit was torn, she was dancing in tears, clinging
to a man. Aunt Ofélia was running around the bed, one hand
covering her breasts, the other her sex ("this aunt of yours had the

same madness, only in reverse, she loathed men"), and the husband pursuing her, let's cut out this nonsense, Ofélia, cut it out! I felt the Milk of Magnesia that she had drunk in one large gulp fizzing in my mouth. It's not magnesia, auntie, it's poison! Naked and beheaded, in came Aunt Barbara, half woman, half mare, I'm going out to buy some lace! I eschewed a black cassock and ran into my mother, who enveloped me in her black head of parched hair, exactly like David's, the Jew who owned the antique shop: "In Germany they are stepping on Jews as if they were cockroaches! ..."

I woke up at dawn. Margarida's voice was sounding again in the silence, saying that Grandmother hadn't attended her son's wedding because the young woman was a Jew: in Germany our little Sarah would have been disposed of by now. Stepping on Jews as if they were cockroaches ... But who told you all this? I asked, and in the dark Margarida's face looked infinitely sad. "I've learned about it, darling. There are many other things I know too. Many other things ..." I turned on the light. Of the night before, only a tiny spot caused by her tears had remained on one of the rosy planks of the floor. I began to tremble. My mother a Jew? ... But it was so terrible to be a Jew, everybody around me was always saying that it was terrible. "I like Blacks better," I once overheard Grandmother whisper to a friend. The friend then made a gesture which I couldn't quite see. Grandmother stroked me: "No danger of that! She's a Rodrigues, down to the way she walks!"

Now I could understand certain words. Certain silent pauses. In particular, I could now understand the persistence with which everybody pointed out my resemblance to my father. In fact, there was little I could remember about either of them: I had a notion that he was tall, strong, and fond of laughing. As for my mother, I vaguely recalled her pale eyes—could they have been blue?—her white, rather timid hands. Much sharper than the contours of her face was the scent from her hand cream, my cousin used the same cream, and suddenly her image surfaced sharply, exactly as I had last seen her, wearing a lilac-colored dress, the violin in her hand. Had she been beautiful? Surely not, but she must have been gentle and shy. Afraid of Grandmother. Afraid of my father. Her fear struck me more powerfully than her beauty, and with this component I tried to outline her profile. However, just like in my old jigsaw puzzles, there were some missing pieces and I wondered if in my eagerness to complete the picture I hadn't taken pieces from other puzzles. Sarah and Marcus. Sarah Ferensen.

They had died in a train crash. "But if it's no longer fashionable, nobody ever dies in train crashes anymore, why your son and daughter-in-law?" had wondered one of Grandmother's friends, an elderly woman with bluish teeth. I was struck by the perfection of her teeth and when I told Margarida about them, she burst into laughter: "They're false teeth, silly!" The woman had a reputation for being scatterbrained; however, her half-witted remark was indelibly printed on my memory, and so were her dentures. "But if it's no longer fashionable! . . ."

In a derailment. "They were found under the cogwheels, holding hands," Grandmother told me, "their bones had been crushed, but their faces were intact." Using these very same words, I reported the accident to Margarida. She listened without great interest, she already knew all the details. However, she was struck by the word *cogwheels.* She looked it up in the dictionary to determine its exact meaning; ever since she learned how to read, she had been in love with words: she would write down any words that were new to her and then hurry to the dictionary, which she had learned to use "like an intellectual," bemoaned Grandmother. "This poor girl is already acting like an intellectual, what with her mania of reading all the time, we'll have to put a stop to it before she starts getting ideas. I've warned you against kindling any illusions in this poor soul: the more educated she becomes, the more unhappy she'll be. I wish she had remained illiterate." I learned that Grandmother should have said *iron fittings,* not *cogwheels.* Under the iron fittings, holding hands.

Sarah Ferensen, a Jew. The F with a period after it: it wasn't Ferreira, it wasn't Fernandes, it was Ferensen. Half of Margarida's blood was Negro, but half of mine . . . I closed the window, closed my eyes, and pressed my face against the ice-cold windowpane. So it was true. The silence surrounding her name could now be accounted for. Her absence from the photo album with the silver-plated corners, "she hated having her picture taken." With my clenched fists I hit the befogged windowpane. With the tip of a finger I traced a J on the glass. I erased it. Would I have to follow Margarida's example and erase all traces of my mother, leaving only those belonging to my father? With four thumbtacks I would pin my father's photograph over the head of my bed, like Margarida had done with the Pole's. With three nails they had crucified Jesus, they could have chosen the thief. But they chose Him instead and for this reason they had been sentenced to wandering all over the earth, with no right to rest or peace. Craving for nothing but riches. I closed my hand over the tiny gold heart that I had taken away from Margarida.

The accursed half was obvious in her. And what about me? I examined my hands. Was it in my damp hands? In my hair? In my squint? I walked around the room. The sign must be in my evil half, in the half given to scheming, to wheedling, to betraying. But why was I always doing such things? "You're always so afraid. Why are you so afraid of everything?" Margarida had asked me the night we had drunk up the liqueur. Was it fear that made me sly? deceitful?

I went to see Grandmother, who was sitting in her golden chair, the needles clicking in and out of the tight mesh of the gray knitting, which unfolded between her fingers like a coat of mail. She had worn mourning ever since her husband's death: she had aged everything that could be aged in her and now she stood stagnant in time, the hair white, the skin lackluster under the film of violet-scented talcum powder. Unalterable, like the preserves that she prepared in the huge, large-mouthed jars. Lonely like the picture of her widowhood, the eyes watchful, the waist thin, the breasts squashed under the corset.

"Well? How's Margarida today? Has she calmed down?" she asked. "She has stopped crying," I replied. Grandmother smiled, if one could call a smile that slight drawing up of the skin on the left corner of her mouth, where three creases appeared, as precise as if carved in stone. A mineral-like smile, complete with talcum powder to dry out any fortuitous moisture. That's how we began all our dialogues, which consisted of short questions, followed by answers that were as short as the stitches knitting the network of accord. I compressed my lips. For the first time I was unwilling to talk, for the first time I was frightened by words, which were more ambiguous than centipedes with their dozens of paws seething every which way. Where would they lead me?

It was with a new emotion that I opened the photo album, now that I had seen the wrong side of the people in the photographs. For the first time the women in the album seemed as terror-stricken as I was. And why were they terror-stricken? Catching their breath. The fear in their eyes, in anticipation of—what? I wiped my damp hands on my dress. "The sweat in Ana Luisa's armpits is green," Margarida had once remarked as she washed one of my blouses. Fear was now sprouting green in between my fingers; my sweat, green, acquired the same sepia hue of the photographs, which kept adhering to each other obstinately. United in solidarity.

"So what's new, Ana Luisa?" Grandmother asked in her absent-minded manner. Would I have saved myself that morning if instead of satisfying her appetite for malicious gossip I had confronted her, demanding the truth—what about my mother? I want to know, Grandmother, tell me. I could have faced her. But I didn't consider myself her equal. The mere thought of the key question—was my mother a Jew?—made my face burn. I began to lose heart. I comforted myself with the thought that she would never reveal anything beyond what would be contained in the ambiguous phrasing of her reply, embodying a *yes* and a *no*. She would then make harsh remarks on the dangers of having strangers amidst our family, invading our privacy (she was aware that Margarida was my source) and she might even use the title of the book she had been reading to underline the irony, *"The dangerous relations* are the foster children!"* And to bring the episode to a conclusion with dignity, a reference to the grief that large families like ours had to go through. A lot of tradition, yes, but a lot of people as well. The perfect relations were perfect and the imperfect ones could only have been foreign or insane, obviously. Obviously.

"I've got some homework to do," I said. She still persisted, wasn't there anything new to tell her? I lowered my head and went into the garden. There I found Margarida, barefoot, watering the plants. On her washed face, her usual expression, somewhat colder perhaps. "Has this rosebush dried up?" I asked. She looked at me through the fan of the sparkling water pierced by the sunlight. "Too early to tell." Her voice seemed to be coming from far away. We were standing as close to each other as I had stood to Grandmother a moment before. Yet, if we were to stretch out our arms, we wouldn't be able to touch each other. I removed the chain from my neck and proffered her the small gold heart, "You lent it to me, Margarida, it's yours." She looked away, with indifference. It was as if I had offered her one of the pebbles under the soles of my shoes. "Keep it, I don't want it anymore." I considered asking for her forgiveness, yes, it was me, it was me who told on you but I'll never do it again, forgive me, Margarida, forgive me! Instead, I went back to my room. At lunchtime I could feel Grandmother's irritation: why did I have to chew so noisily? and why didn't I hold the knife properly, was this the way to hold a knife? I hid my hands in my lap and I don't know why I began to think of my mother holding the violin bow.

When Margarida came in with the coffee, I felt my eyes fill with tears: the three of us were alone now. I was overcome by a strong longing for the coffee of the day before, when the dead of the album were still happy. When my mother was still a sketch depicting a blond young woman named Sarah, who was fond of music. How easy to be engaging and garrulous! How easy to pretend! How easy life could be! To say nothing but what people wanted to hear, to do nothing but what people, beginning with Grandmother, expected me to do. The ease with which I strove diligently to win over friends—so strong in me the instinct to play these games, half schemes, half improvisations. Much later I was to learn that growing up meant scheming. I was just a girl. So how could there already be so much scheming inside me? I could no longer tell whether at any given moment I was being sincere or being crafty, such was the extent to which I had adapted myself to the social conventions. Margarida was often astonished, had I really meant it? Did I really think that young woman was beautiful, the one in the straw hat? When she called my attention to such things, I felt ashamed, yet in order not to lose face, I upheld the deception.

"It even seems that you gain something by saying things like that," Margarida would remark whenever she caught me. And wasn't I surely gaining something? With her outspokenness, Margarida gained everybody's rejection. I hadn't tasted rejection yet: I was the polite, generous girl, willing to beat the egg whites for the cakes, or to recite poetry at the social gatherings on Fridays, when Grandmother had her friends from the Red Cross over for one of her so-called "charity afternoons." They'd spend hours on end sewing for the orphanages and old people's homes, while the radio kept broadcasting news about the imminent outbreak of the second world war. "He's the man of the century!" Grandmother would say. She was referring to Hitler.

Although Grandmother was held in high esteem by all her guests, a couple of them would disagree: "Well, yes, but this racist mania of his is intolerable. The poor Jews, they also have the right to live, don't they?"

"Of course they do!" Grandmother would assent, casting a quick glance around her, suspecting that in such a diverse group there were bound to be some Jews. And she would quickly call me, let's put politics aside now, my granddaughter is going to recite. She would order tea to be served. She would turn off the radio. I would clasp my hands over my stomach, put my feet together and hold my head up. I would hold my head up. Two or three fairly short poems before the steaming teapots were brought in. When the clattering of the cups became audible, it was time for me to stop—

the cue was Grandmother's discreet clearing of her throat. Followed by a smile, "Good, darling, now go and get yourself a cup of tea!" I would say my polite good-byes to the ladies, without forgetting to say something pleasant to each and every one of them, often a passing remark praising some detail in the outfit they were wearing; from Grandmother I had learned the importance of praising a detail: the importance of a finish in a cuff, of a brooch, of a button . . . I would praise this button. And I would leave the room, pretending I didn't hear the remarks behind my back, what a delightful girl!

I had to be delightful. This need was already fear, but a fruitful, stimulating fear which made me love my fellow creatures, or rather, made them believe in this love. In exchange, I would earn their good opinion and in this opinion I found strength. It was what everybody expected of me. What Grandmother demanded from me. Now something had changed. But why? Had I lost my gift for dissimulation, for craftiness?

That evening Grandmother wanted to play chess after we finished our herb tea. I got the chessboard out. I opened the box and set the chessmen, the black ones were always mine. I was sure I was going to play badly. And live badly. One by one, I lost all my chessmen. Grandmother was annoyed, "Why don't you move this knight forward? You have to learn how to fight, my child. Come on, take the offensive!"

The white queen moved across the chessboard and trapped my king. I had no way out. "Checkmate!" she said. I opened my hands and suggested we play another game. Which she refused, saying that my heart was not on playing, it was plain boring this way.

I picked up my needlework. Ah, if only I could tell her about some event or other, and make her smile the way I used to be able to, she had always approved of my small talk, of my minor perversities. Now it was as if the needle with the red thread that was piercing the cloth in a zig-zag path had stitched my mouth shut.

"Imagine dating the son of a Court Judge, that's crazy! Has the girl taken leave of her senses? Everybody will hold this girl in derision," began Grandmother. It was as if we had just resumed discussing the matter. I held the needle suspended over the cloth. Derision. What did *derision* mean? There was a time when I would have asked Margarida to look it up in the dictionary. Too late now. "She's fond of him," I managed to say. "Fondness, nonsense! Reading all those books in the evenings has turned her head, all that slush about young women from poor families getting married to their rich cousins. I told you that this mania of forever reading would come to no good. I've warned you. Against kindling illusions in this poor soul. But I know what I'm going to do: I'm going to keep the books locked away in the bookcases, this should put an end to such nonsense."

"You've changed a lot," she remarked a few days later. We were in the garden. I was learning some grammar rules by heart. She was pruning a rosebush. I tilted my head over my shoulder in a vague, interrogative movement: "Have I?"

"I've done everything for you, Ana Luisa. The best schools, the best clothes. I've done everything I could. But I've noticed that you've changed. You're listless, you barely reply to my questions. It even seems that you've been avoiding me."

I sank my head to my chest, and listened silently to the bitter complaints she uttered while pruning the rosebush. The ruthless shears close-cropped the branches, which dropped to the ground, and they looked as lush as the ones that had been spared. How was she able to tell them apart? I stepped back. She would prune me like that too unless I gave her proof of my strength.

"Sometimes I even think that you're afraid of me. Why are you afraid of me?" she asked, softening her voice. I tilted my head again over my shoulder in a forlorn gesture of submissiveness. She didn't understand the fact that it was necessary to be fearless in order to justify fear. Before she went inside, taking the shears and the gloves with her, she remarked in an absent-minded way, as if she were discussing the garden: "Interesting . . . you look more and more like your mother!"

My face began to throb with the violence of my pounding blood rushing to it. I hid myself behind a book. Through my tears I could see the letters—lopsided—toppling down the page. Crushed.

Teatime. A couple of ladies in the charity group would still persist as I came in with the plates of cookies: "Come on, darling, won't you recite for us? Why don't you anymore?" I would shake my head, looking so ill-at-ease that it must have been a relief to them when reciting was left out of the program. There could be nothing delightful about this girl with the face of a banished monkey reciting poems about love, which was compared to a crystal vase, ah, if by accident a fan were to touch this crystal. "It's her age," Grandmother would explain when she thought I couldn't overhear her. "She's reaching adolescence, a really difficult time of life."

Their conversation. Domestic servants: getting more and more insufferable. Fashion: were women still wearing those heavily padded shoulders and tailored suits? The threat of war. The woman with the chestnut-brown hair kept attacking Hitler's politics. Most of them agreed with her, he was responsible for the general tension, heavens forbid, what if the second world war, which now seemed inevitable, were really to break out? Would we declare war? "Of course," cried out the woman in the white velvet beret. After swallowing her food, she was able to speak out. She put down her plate with the remains of cake: the very thought of her sons' possible conscription made her sleepless. She had three sons, did they realize what it meant?

My hand shook as I poured more tea into the cup of an elderly woman in a nurse's uniform, she was taking a nursing course at a nonprofit hospital. The conversation began to take its hateful course. It was like in that guessing game when I'd ask Margarida to find the bonbon that I had carefully hidden. She would grope about until she got near the hiding place and I would warn her: it's getting hot! hotter! it's red hot! . . .

Except that now the roles were reversed; the rules of the game were beyond my control. I asked Margarida to refill the silver teapot. It was the moment when the subject of the Jews usually came up. The Jews. The elderly woman in the uniform was going to trigger the attack, and Grandmother would have to back her. And I would have to leave the room right away, otherwise I would never again be able to hold my head up. She is going to start up and I'm going to leave right away. I do, slamming the door behind me to let everybody know that I'll never allow them to attack the Jews in front of me.

It was neither the elderly woman nor Grandmother, the perfect hostess slicing the cake and making her guests feel at home, but a young woman wearing a black sweater and a pearl necklace. "On this issue, I'd say that Hitler is right. It's outrageous. A Jew is a Jew. It goes without saying."

There was a burning in my throat, which felt dry, lacerated. I stiffened my body and put the teapot down on the table. And I stood there. For the second time I could have saved myself. I picked up the teapot and resumed serving tea.

"This slice is for you, my child. You can have a second helping if you want to," Grandmother said kindly. Her unexpected kindness touched me so much that I felt like screaming. She knows that I know, she knows. Except that there was a difference now: the attack had come from a stranger, indirectly someone had attacked her granddaughter and this attack affected her too: She had to side with me. And to a certain extent, to side with her son, who at the moment of his death held his wife's hand when they were trapped in the iron fittings of the train. I began to eat ravenously. I was also underneath the cogwheels. But alive.

That evening Margarida looked at me for a long time. There was some sorrowful attentiveness in her gestures. She stared at me in a way I couldn't fathom: "I have a new boyfriend, you can go and tell her. Do you want to know his name? Antonio."

I shook my head sadly, no, Margarida, never again, believe me. She took a clean nightgown out of the dresser and laid it out on my pillow. As she reached the door, she turned round and even smiled. Next morning, when I went to her room, I found it empty. On the dingy wall, the holes left by the thumbtacks, and the rectangular trace left by the photograph of the Pole.

Grandmother received the news calmly. But I could feel her anger coming loose from that false calmness. In an obscure way, I felt responsible for Margarida's escape. I cringed like a frightened animal.

"She must have run away, of course, with this student . . . what's his name?" she asked, snapping her fingers. With an impatient gesture, her hand grazed my shoulder. "It's obvious that you know but are unwilling to tell me, never mind, I'll take all the necessary steps. What a pretentious mulatta. Ungrateful to boot. Next time I'm getting a coal black girl, one imbued with the tradition of her race. Princess Isabel, right? I wish she were alive today to see what her liberal sentimentalities have led us into!"

The new maid's name was Joaquina. Grandmother finished knitting the gray coat and the war broke out. The war, I kept saying to myself. And I would look at the peaceful May sky with no clouds and no airplanes. And I would look at Grandmother, as she smiled sardonically at my aunts, who had dropped in one day, wearing the uniform of the Volunteer Women Working for the Anti-Air Raid Passive Defense. "Don't be ridiculous, for heaven's sake!"

"But if there is a raid—we have to get the population ready for it," Aunt Jane said as she took off her white gloves. She tucked them into her broad belt, which was fastened with a golden buckle. She ran her hands over her large breasts, squashed under the lead-gray tunic. Grandmother raised her eyebrows. Then she spoke with that restrained irritation of people dealing with small children: "There isn't going to be any air raid, Jane. And even if there is

one, what could two nitwits like you possibly do for the population? What, for heaven's sake?"

Thousands of Jews, their hands moist like mine, were being mas-
sacred. But everything was happening far away from me, a war in
some remote place; uselessly, the newspapers persisted in their
panic-ridden headlines about the horrors taking place inside and
outside cities. Uselessly, the radio kept broadcasting hourly reports
on resounding victories, defeats, ah, those voices spitting out truths
and lies rhythmically like machine guns. I began to abhor the newspapers. And to avoid the radio. I shut myself up in my room, with
my books. With my records. And I would read and listen to music.
I read nonstop. How terrible it was when I had to open my shell
and allow some invasion; how exasperating everything beyond my
door. I would run my hands over my familiar objects—my knick-
knacks, which held no surprises, nothing unexpected. The teddy
bear with its fur grown threadbare. The doll in its taffeta dress, the
old rose color now completely faded. I wanted to wear nothing but
worn-out shoes to which my feet had grown used to. And old
clothes in subdued colors which nobody would notice—oh God, if
only I could get into a crack in the wooden floor and there remain
forgotten by both people and gods!
    During my holidays I would bury myself in movie theaters.
Grandmother trusted me; she thought me incapable of committing
any foolishness, not so much because she thought me virtuous but
rather because she felt I was lacking in imagination. Thus I enjoyed
the relative freedom of coming and going, which merely provoked
remarks that weren't any more sarcastic than usual. Sometimes I
would watch three movies in a single day: then I would feel great.
Free. Other people's stories, whether on the screen or in books,
would enrapture me to such an extent that being wrenched off to
face the kind of reality that only made me suffer amounted to an
act of violence. Even Joaquina would startle me at times as she
came in and pulled me by the sleeve, she had some speech imped-
iment, "Lunchtime, Ana Luisa."
    I didn't go to clubs. I didn't have any friends. When I felt quite
lonely, I would go into a pastry shop and, without glancing around
me, I would stuff myself with pastry.
    Grandmother had long since given up any ideas of turning me
into a brave, spirited young woman. Into a bright one. "But why?"
she must have wondered sorrowfully. Why had I, after my promising beginnings, turned into such a slowpoke? She liked to use

this word, *slowpoke*. She lost faith in me, and it wasn't easy to forgive me for this. Not after having devised so many new incentives
to build up my character. Weary, she gave up: I was weak, which
to her amounted to a deficiency in the make-up of my character.
There was nothing to strengthen. The way I wore my hair irritated
her: couldn't I see that combing my hair back flat from the forehead like that and then fastening it at the back of my head could
only make my forehead, already broad, look even broader? It elongated my face, didn't it? And the habit of biting my fingernails, oh
God! Besides being unesthetic, wasn't it revolting to keep my fingertips inside my mouth? My thinness was also a favorite subject
of her onslaughts: "Ana Luisa, you're as flat as a board, darling,
maybe if you tried some special exercises, hm? The women in our
family have always had beautiful busts, I don't know who you've
taken after ..." Out of everything, only my squint was spared,
"Marcus had this same way of looking ..."

One evening—it was Christmas—I told her about my intentions
of specializing in languages. The tips of her fingernails were drum-
ming faintly on the wine glass and the sound of the crystal was as
cold as her voice as she remarked that my mother had had this
same facility in languages. "As a matter of fact, the Jews, generally
speaking ..."
She had been short-tempered since early morning, when she
learned that the Axis had suffered yet another defeat. "The British
are to be blamed! As they also were when we lost the ..." She
snapped her fingers nervously. When she couldn't come up with
references, she fell silent. We went into the living room, where the
Christmas tree was. The family had gathered there, the conversation intermingled with dried fruits, wine, and sarcasms which
Grandmother bandied with a group of relatives who loved and
hated each other with equal intensity. When Aunt Jane finally arrived, late, wearing her Volunteer uniform (she had been on duty
until then and hadn't had time to change), excitement bordered
on hysteria. Everybody was talking at the same time. It was necessary to shout to make oneself heard. "Lately, our assignment for
the evenings consists of patrolling the black-out zones," Aunt Jane
was explaining to her younger sister, who was interested in joining
the movement. "If we see any lights in a house, we have to rush
there and ask people to screen them. It's also against the law for a
man to light up a cigarette in the street; a simple match, even the
ember of a cigarette, can be seen from above!" Grandmother cut

her short, gripping her by the arm. "Who, Jane, who can see us from above?" Aunt Jane turned her hazel eyes to Grandmother: "Who? The bombers, darling, that's who, the bombers!" My cousins burst into laughter, which was so boisterous that my uncle had to drag them out of the room. They couldn't stop laughing.

After everybody left, I sat down on the floor cushion to eat my slice of turkey in peace. "Ana Luisa, why aren't you wearing your new dress? And look at your hair! ... Was it much too difficult to cut your hair in bangs? Why do you persist in being so unpleasant? And so ugly?" I would like to be beautiful, I replied. She started to pick up the gift wrappings that lay scattered about. She piled the empty boxes and the ribbons on a chair. "This is turning into polemics, child. Your negligence amounts to an attack on me." I tightened my stomach. My mother used to have stomach problems, the fainthearted always do. Do you think I'm unhappy just to upset you? I asked. She didn't hear me; she was talking to Joaquina, who had come in to tidy up the living room.

Once in my room, I let my hair loose and cut a short fringe across my forehead. The bangs came out crooked. I examined myself in the yellowish mirror. And if I were to get married? It would be a way of freeing myself, but then there would be the husband, and I would have to get rid of him. Unless I really loved him. But Grandmother had already warned me that it was most unusual for two people to get along well *in everything*. What she meant by *in everything* was sex. "Very few women enjoy it, my child. Men, yes. But women have to pretend to a certain extent, sex doesn't have the same importance for them. We have to fulfill our duties; everything else is superfluous. If there is pleasure, so much the better; but if not, well, that's all right, nobody has ever died because of it."

Nobody? I thought of the photo album. First, they'd take off the jewelry. Next, their dresses. Then it was time to take off the corset, its stays so stiff. So tight its laces. Obediently, they would lie down, ice-cold like the bedsheets, "nobody has ever died because of it." But the women were already dead.

On the following morning Grandmother interrupted her reading of the newspaper to talk about Margarida. "Well, it so happens that she hasn't run away with that student after all, but with the first bum she found standing on a street-corner, a social outcast, a Negro ... The police have asked if I want to do anything about it. Do what? Better leave things as they are. With a Negro, imagine.

To have raised a girl as if she had been my own daughter only to
have her deflowered by a Negro."

Virginity. According to her, young women fell into two main
groups: virgins, and nonvirgins. Margarida now belonged to the
latter group—one more direct attack against our family. The virgins would travel along a road strewn with flowers, with enough
oil in their lamps, whereas the young women in the other group—
the foolish nonvirgins—were destined to a road strewn with thorns.
Demoralized, they would end their days in loneliness, if not overtaken by some other terrible fate, which Grandmother didn't even
dare mention. She would raise a hand, and then shaking the outstretched hand prophetically, "I don't even like to think about
it . . ."

The battle of my marriage was about to start. The battle. Why
did she have to use such a pompous word? But there wouldn't be
any battle, for she had already made up her mind—I was to marry
early. I was expected to cooperate. "I want to see you safe before
I close my eyes forever," she kept telling me. And being safe meant
having a husband. The cruelty with which she referred to my un-
married aunts—*shelved,* she'd say. The contempt with which she
uttered this word, "It looks as if So-and-So has been *shelved.*"

I opened a drawer to store the length of worsted that she had
given me for a tailored suit. Then I leafed through the French
fashion magazine that had been placed in the box: beautiful fash-
ions, beautiful models. To get married. If there was love, great; if
not, well, it didn't really matter, the really important thing was not
to let the golden years slip by. "The splendor of youth is short-
lived. As an example, look at your Aunt Jane, who used to flit about
like a butterfly, just look at her now, she has even resorted to
wearing a soldier's uniform to make herself appear interesting, to
draw attention to herself, poor thing." The French fashion magazine was a warning: "You have to spruce yourself up, Ana Luisa!"
I kept resisting her. Yet why? Was it really just to annoy her? I
thought of my mother with her useless violin. And her useless
death. She bequeathed me a name—Ferensen—which I had learned
to disown. And this feeling of powerlessness. Of insecurity. The
war was already coming to an end, and from now on the Jews
would be left alone. But for how long? A pity my mother hadn't
lived long enough to tell me that I should hold up my head and
laugh at the fools. At all the smug people and their prejudices.
Why didn't she live long enough to tell me how beautiful, how
intelligent, how graceful her daughter was? Tears began to drop

on the fashion magazine, where they looked like droplets of quick-
silver as they slid along the slick pages, barely staining the satin
lingerie trimmed with lace. It had been convenient for her to have
died young, holding hands with the man she loved. But what about
me?

This one won't do because he's old and short-sighted, I thought
while attending mass on the first Sunday of the year. I stood smiling at the ceiling of the church, where angels fluttered amidst flowers. My thoughts were falling senselessly like the roses in the
garlands that were scattered amidst the clouds. I amused myself by
trying to figure out how the painter had managed to paint the
ceiling, where he had positioned himself—it must have been difficult. I gazed at an angel with chestnut-brown hair, like mine.
Cross-eyed, too. The angel and I exchanged a look of complicity.
Mass was now over and Grandmother hadn't shown up. She kept
preaching about the need to observe all the commandments, yet
she herself hardly ever observed any. She sometimes hinted that
between God and her there was some sort of direct access, some
secret understanding, which exempted her from the rituals. There
was no need for Joaquina to attend mass, either, but for different
reasons: "Duty before prayers," she would say. "Staying home in
order to do one's work is still the best way of pleasing God."

It was raining when I came out of the church. At that very moment Rodrigo came up to offer me his umbrella. From novels and
movies, I was already familiar with this easy formula of introducing
oneself, "Strange, isn't it, but it seems to me that we've known each
other for a long time!"

With me it wasn't just an impression; it was certainty. He came
up to me and offered me his umbrella. It was just as easy for me
to let myself be guided as it was for him to guide me. He spoke
loudly. He laughed loudly. Yet he wasn't vulgar. His gestures had
that same premeditated agility of a cat's.

There was affection in the way he held me by the arm, but also
a certain detachment, which would allow me to disengage myself,
if I so desired. I didn't. The blood rushed to my face when I looked
into his eyes. I felt sure we would become lovers.

"Did you go to mass?" I asked. His laughter was contagious.
"Me? . . . attending mass?" He wore a beautiful black raincoat, but
his umbrella, quite decrepit, was the cheapest possible kind.

We walked into a café. "I'm going to paint you exactly as you
look now wearing your red pullover, just a tiny bit cross-eyed," he

said, and then ordered a cognac. I ordered tea. "I'm a painter, but jazz is my real passion, I'll have my own jazz band one day."

A week later we were lying naked under his wool blankets, listening to his records. And as we made love passionately, I held back my tears, trying hard not to cry as I had done the first time. "If you feel like crying, go ahead and cry, Aninha, don't be ashamed of your tears ..." It's because I feel so happy, I told him, and he mounted me with the same eagerness with which he mounted his motorcycle, he had an Italian bike. "Well, then go ahead and cry, Aninha. With me you can do anything you feel like doing—you can cry, laugh, walk on a tightrope, have you ever tried walking on a tightrope? I have, it's quite easy really."

I told him about Grandmother. He listened attentively, but sometimes he would burst into laughter. Even when he was no longer laughing, his face remained lit up. "You're beginning to lose that way of acting as if you were buried under a ton of stones," he said. "And you no longer look around you, giving people the impression that you were running away from the police."

He was four years older than I was, and he was vaguely enrolled in some sort of pre-university course, and he painted, listened to jazz, and had just won a scholarship to study in Ireland. Why Ireland of all places? I wanted to know. He stood staring at me. His blond hair was rather long, which made people turn around to stare at him curiously, why would a young man wear his hair long like that? Hadn't he learned about the crewcut during the war years? His motorcycle—garish, different from all other bikes that were becoming a common sight then, was also a source of curiosity. He had delicate hands, with manicured fingernails.

"I'm a globe-trotter," he replied. "It's turned out to be Ireland, so Ireland it is! Will you go with me, Aninha? But first I want to finish your portrait ..." He would talk a lot about this portrait, which he had already started. And about the trips we would take together on his motorbike.

Deep in my heart I knew that there would be no portrait and no trip. But his enthusiasm cheered me up, and I would make plans. As long as we don't go to Germany, I said. I'm a Jew. At least half a Jew, I told him at lunch one day. He grabbed my hand: "If you promise to give me your share of pork I won't tell the waiter, I'll make any deal for a chunk of pork!" he said, filling my glass with wine, which he had taught me to appreciate. "Listen, Aninha, promise me that you'll never feel sorry for yourself again. That you'll never regard yourself as a pitiful thing. I don't know what will ever become of us, but no matter what happens, will you do this for me?"

I knew Grandmother's greatest flaws, which could be reduced to two: arrogance and avarice. I also knew that I had these very same flaws, without, however, possessing her courage. But only through love did I realize the extent of my own selfishness and meanness, a meanness due more to unhappiness than to anything else. Feeling terribly unworthy, I would confess to him, I'm evil, cowardly, I don't deserve you. He would smile: "You'll become wonderful the moment you start liking yourself. There was a time when I felt this way too, but it's over now. We're both very young, Aninha, as young as the steers that aren't even aware of their own strength ... The war has ended, there'll be guerilla warfare, for God's sake, everything is good, connected. That's life. The important thing is not to get tied down to anything, to keep your arms free to dance, to fight, to make love. Hm? what do you say to that, Ana Luisa Ferensen Rodrigues! You've got a beautiful name, don't you know? But come on now, get rid of these bangs, stop hiding yourself."

But I kept my forehead hidden and for two months I resorted to all kinds of ruses to hide my poor love from Grandmother. And above all, to hide my hope. Nowadays I wonder if she hadn't known all along about Rodrigo, from the very first day when I ran into him in the rain. She must have let me go on just out of curiosity, out of spitefulness. As she'd do when we played chess, always encouraging me to fight, "Come on, why don't you move this knight forward, what are you waiting for?" I'd take hold of my knight and in my naive show of independence, move it at a gallop across the chessboard. Then, as soon as she felt that I was overstepping, she would quickly make her move.

"Joaquina's making a chicken pie on Sunday. Why don't you ask this young man over for lunch?" she said one day when I got home from college earlier than usual because Rodrigo had been unable to meet me. The familiar sweat broke out, dampening my hands. I put away the scarf and the beret: even without looking at her, I could feel her gaze, now soft, upon me. But her kindness frightened me.

I don't know if he'll be able to, I began, and she cut me short:

"Of course he will, child. I must say that I don't like to see you meeting in the streets as if you were a poor, homeless housemaid. You have a family, a home, he'll be welcome here."

I threw myself at Rodrigo, hugged him tightly, kissed him on the mouth, the eyes, the hair, "Rodrigo, Rodrigo ... she's found out about us, I don't want anything to change, I don't ..."

A light-drenched Sunday. He mounted his motorcycle. I got behind him, clinging to his waist, oh God, don't let him go away, please don't. I nodded politely at an elderly couple who looked disapprovingly at us as they walked by. Rodrigo revved the engine. "Nazi Granny will be impressed by my elegance, look, a signature tie, a Jacques Fath, Aninha, Jacques Fath!"

The tie didn't go with his faded clothes or with his worn-out shoes, all tattered and with holes, very likely, in the soles. I recalled the first time we met. The black raincoat. The umbrella. I laughed amidst my tears. "But Aninha, what can she possibly do to us?"

She did. Even before having met him, she must have intuited that he was fickle and inconsistent. Carefree—that was the right word. Carefree. Such a fragile love couldn't last. Our first quarrel. I wanted to warn him of the dangers, the pitfalls, no Rodrigo, she can't possibly like you, all this politeness of hers is phony, there's something behind it, don't trust her. He became annoyed, was I paranoid or something? Nonsense, he was well aware that she was a dyed-in-the-wool member of the bourgeoisie, she was born this way and would remain so until the day she died, quite a type she was. He respected her type. He realized that he was the opposite of the man she had in mind as a prospective son-in-law, grandson, he corrected himself. As long as she remained charming, there was really no harm in her.

Her invitations to dinner were now almost daily. Good wine. Small gifts. She turned on her kindness. Her smiles came easily as she narrowed her eyes while the metallic needles proceeded along their winding path under the wool. "Our drummer is going to paint my portrait," she announced. I reacted. He doesn't have any money to buy the paints, Grandmother, he couldn't even finish my portrait. She stared at me innocently. "But I'm advancing him some money, darling, we've settled this matter." Furious, I went after him, you're not going to take money from her, are you? He was practicing the new drums he had gotten in exchange for his motorcycle. He made a graceful gesture to silence me, will you be quiet, please. I'm composing. The subject of Nazi Granny could wait. We had reached the point where we argued over almost anything—what was the source of this bitterness slowly leaking out? "You're a dusty petty bourgeois," he said laughing. I laughed with him, yet weren't there always the remains of some painful question, even after our long dialogues in which we calculated the future?

Calculations. Reconciliation was through lovemaking. Full. Complete. Without the former fervor.

And what about the portrait, Grandmother? When are you going to sit for it? I wanted to know, and in her lap, she spread open the green beret that she was knitting for Rodrigo. She made a remark about the color, it would look beautiful on his yellow-gold hair, the colors of the national flag. She stared at me.

"Ah, yes, I've asked him to postpone it until his return, I've been having migraine headaches lately. The portrait can wait." I didn't follow her. What was she talking about, whose return? She resumed her knitting. "But don't you know, child? He's leaving at the end of this month on that trip he had been planning—to Ireland, isn't it?"

I questioned him: why didn't you tell me anything, Rodrigo? And what about money? He poured himself some whiskey. He poured me some, too. "Granny offered me a loan, she thinks it's a way of getting rid of me. To buy paints, as she made a point of stressing. She handles things with great finesse."

You bet she does, I replied. I left him reclining against the cushions, looking as beautiful as an angel, as enraptured he listened to the jazz he loved.

The living room with its vague smell of altars. The tapestry with a leopard peering from amidst the trees. The piano. The photo album with the silver-plated corners—everything exactly as it was when I used to go there to listen to her stories about the selected members of the family—the ones who had lived and died in a state of perfection. The bag wasn't there. I went to her bedroom. I found her sitting up in bed, still wearing her daytime clothes. And suddenly, she struck me as being old. She asked if I had enjoyed the movie, was it a war movie? She made a disdainful sound with her tongue. Quite boring those plots, always showing how smart the Americans and the British were, whereas everyone else ... She turned off the radio, which had been playing Albinoni's *Adagio* softly. She wanted to know if I had received any news yet. I shook my head.

"Well, he wasn't really very dependable, was he?" she said. "But he certainly was charming. I'm glad you didn't nurse any dreams."

I did nurse dreams, I told her. But I wasn't ready to love. Him or anyone else. But now I know, at least I think I know. What I've lost in illusions I've gained in assurance.

"It didn't last, child."

I sat down on her red velvet chair. I squeezed the ball of green wool in my hand. Where was he now, he and his beret? His music? That it hadn't lasted didn't really matter. It had been love. Fleeting by, just as he did in the dream I had had the night before, when he appeared before me with an open umbrella, the very same one, but I never got to see his face, I merely guessed that the indistinct shape was him. He waved at me. And then vanished, leaving behind him the umbrella and the roar of the motorcycle—dust and sound, soon mingling with the engine noise of a highway truck. Yet it had been love. My self-criticism had been honed—never before had I been able to see myself so clearly as now, and with that kind of toughness that had caused Rodrigo to take me to task more than once: "Don't blow things out of proportion, Aninha, people are always better than they think they are." But even during the most crucial phases of my self-scourging, I had something that I had never had before—trust. Trust in myself, in other people; trust in God, whose existence I was unsure of, although I felt sure that He would never desert me. It was a love that lifted me up in the air and then shook me up and turned me inside out—I became resplendent. A revolution through love.

She held out her hand. Her skin had the same splotches of the photographs. I kissed it. Do you bear any grudges against me? None, Grandmother. As she saw it, she had won the game, and was now displaying compassion mingled with kindness. With sympathy. Her eyes kept telling me: come, darling. I'm here, I can help you. I'm just a bit tired, it was a tough game, I've aged a lot over the past two months. I need a respite, it was difficult, wasn't it?

Very difficult, I said.

"What's very difficult, Ana Luisa?" she asked, puzzled. "What are you smiling at?" Was I smiling then? I pressed her hand. Not until the following day, when I would come to her and announce, *I'm leaving*—not until then would she be able to understand my secret smile. No, not now. She had already had her tea, so let her have her victory sleep. She deserved it. After all the repressed anger and all the tears she must have choked back as she suffered the humiliation of knowing that we were lovers. And without being able to blow up—on the contrary, she had exchanged pleasantries, had poured out the wine, meekly, courteously, groping about like a blind woman, Grandmother whose eyes were so sharp. She deserved a night of truce.

"This business about this young man," she began, hesitatingly. "I never wanted to interfere, you know I didn't. And if I offered him the check it was because . . ."

It's all right, Grandmother, I know. I thank God for having had this love. She wanted to point out once more that if we really thought about it, Rodrigo had exchanged me for a trip.

"Everything I did or refrained from doing, Ana Luisa, was to keep you from being heartbroken, child."

But I'm not heartbroken, I replied.

She turned to me, shocked.

"You aren't?!...." Was I scatterbrained, even more open to ridicule than Margarida, who after all had been a mere foster child? I had behaved like a loose woman, hadn't I, and yet, didn't I have any compunctions about it? Any anguish? She attempted a smile. It was sad to see how this imitation smile crimped her face, which looked like an eroded stone. "He must be resigned to this fact too, you're both so very young, it's easy for you to forget."

It is, I agreed.

"It won't be long before you meet someone who'll really love you, a young man of character, right, child? He doesn't have to be rich, you are, everything I have is yours. A well-educated, polite, young woman like you ..."

I broke into laughter. It was time to prod me on, "Advance this knight!" she would command as we played one of those games that made me want to lose all my chessmen in order to hasten my defeat. "Come on, don't give up!" I pressed her hand. I knew that deep down she loved me but why was this bottom so deep? Deep down she wanted me dependent. Insecure. The horse now advanced naturally, without any thoughts of conquests—but what was there to conquer? After spitting out the bloodied bit, it began to trot away, ah, how beautiful my black horse, now free.

"You were laughing, Ana Luisa, why?"

Something funny crossed my mind. Nonsense.

"Your temperament has changed, child. Quite a lot, do you realize?"

She was uneasy, what could this change mean? A Jewish girl whom her lover had just ditched and yet cheerful? She was disturbed. She changed her position.

Don't be bitter, Grandmother. I've just discovered my sense of humor, isn't it great?

"Listen, Ana Luisa, you'll never hear me utter the slightest reproach. I just want to help you, that's all, I just want to help you."

But she was the one in need of help. I got up. It was strange to hear her voice, which seemed to come from within the photo album. And the album was in the bookcase. I pressed my eyes with the palms of my hands.

I know, Grandmother. I'm very grateful to you.

She drew herself up straight. She looked puzzled. Was I being ironic? I—of all people? She folded her arms as if she felt cold.

"No matter what happens, you'll always have my support. Even during those stormy days of your affair, although I knew what was going on, I never said a word, as you well know. I could have interfered, but I didn't. The mere thought of you riding that machine driven by that reckless young man was enough to make my heart pound. My own dear grandchild, her hair dishevelled, without a shred of modesty ..."

It's because I'm also a Ferensen, I interrupted her gently. The bad side, Grandmother.

She became flustered. Was her little Ana Luisa mocking her now? Wary, she faltered. Could something like this be possible? Had I really gotten rid of my old complex, had I? but how? Odd ... She clasped her hands over her breasts and tightened her mouth.

I drew closer. Are you feeling all right, Grandmother?

"This pain, child," she said faintly, smoothing down her chest.

I unbuttoned the collar of her dress. Since I had changed, she was bound to change her tactics, too: she would bring me round using death as blackmail. I got a whiff of the scent of violets.

Would you like me to take off your corset? I asked when my fingers touched the stiff stays.

"No, child. I'd feel worse without it."

I opened the window. The Milky Way was throbbing with stars. I inhaled the scent of the night: soon it would be dawn.

Translated by Eloah F. Giacomelli

Rubem Fonseca
(1925–   )

Born in Minas Gerais, the Brazilian Rubem Fonseca was educated
in Rio de Janeiro, where his family moved when he was seven. His
reluctance to grant personal interviews has made his background
something of a mystery, although he admits to having graduated
from law school and studied public administration in the United
States. Fonseca also worked for the state police, the power and light
company, and various newspapers before becoming a full-time
author. They were experiences that would seem to have informed
the violent, sometimes grotesque, often sexually explicit
underpinnings of his sophisticated urban fictions.

In 1963, Fonseca published his first collection of stories. Then in
1976, his *Feliz Ano Novo* ("Happy New Year") (1975), from which the
present story is taken, was banned by the federal censors for being
"offensive to morals and decency." Two years later, a letter of
protest against the measure (which was also applied to works by
Ignácio de Loyola Brandão and José Louzeiro) was signed by over a
thousand artists and intellectuals but, in Brasília, was refused by the
then minister of justice, Armando Falcão. Copies were also sent to
President Carter and to Senator Edward Kennedy, as well as to
leading newspapers and journals in the United States, all of which
produced little reaction abroad but in Brazil marked a turning
point in the transformation from military dictatorship to *abertura,*
or political "opening." Fonseca took the case to court and lost,
when the judge ruled the book to be not only "offensive" as
charged but also "an apologia for criminal behavior." The author's
immediate reaction was to write an even more violent and sexually

explicit collection of stories, which appeared in 1979. On appeal, the ban was finally lifted by the courts in November of 1989.

He has published in English translation two superb novels of crime and detection: *High Art* (1983) and the comic *Bufo & Spallanzani* (1985). His recent *Vast Emotions and Imperfect Thoughts* (1988) was an unprecedented bestseller in Brazil.

Lonelyhearts

I was working for a popular newspaper as a police reporter. It had been a long time since the city had seen an interesting crime involving a rich, young and beautiful society lady, deaths, disappearances, corruption, lies, sex, ambition, money, violence, scandal.

"You don't get crimes like that even in Rome, Paris, New York," the editor said. "We're in a bad period. But things'll change soon. It's all cyclical. When you least expect it, one of those scandals breaks out that provides material for a year. Everything's rotten, just right, all we have to do is wait."

Before it broke out they fired me.

"You just have small businessmen killing their partners, petty thieves killing small businessmen, police killing petty thieves. Small potatoes," I told Oswaldo Peçanha, editor-in-chief and owner of the newspaper *Woman*.

"There's also meningitis, schistosomiasis, Chagas's disease," Peçanha said.

"Out of my area," I said.

"Have you read *Woman?*" Peçanha asked.

I admitted I hadn't. I prefer reading books.

Peçanha took a box of cigars from his desk and offered me one. We lighted the cigars. Soon the atmosphere was unbreathable. The cigars were cheap, it was summer, the windows were closed, and the air conditioning wasn't working well.

"*Woman* isn't one of those colorful publications for bourgeois women on a diet. It's made for the Class C woman, who eats rice and beans and if she gets fat, tough luck. Take a look."

Peçanha threw me a copy of the newspaper. Tabloid format, headlines in blue, some out-of-focus photos. Illustrated love story, horoscope, interviews with TV actors, sewing patterns.

"Think you could do the 'Woman to Woman' section, our advice column? The guy who was doing it left."

"Woman to Woman" carried the byline of one Elisa Gabriela. *Dear Elisa Gabriela, my husband comes home drunk every night and . . .*

"I think I can," I said.

"Great. You start today. What name do you want to use?"

I thought a bit.

"Nathanael Lessa."

"Nathanael Lessa?" Peçanha said, surprised and offended, as if I had said a dirty word or insulted his mother.

"What's wrong with it? It's a name like any other. And I'm offering two homages."

Peçanha puffed his cigar, irritated.

"First, it's not a name like any other. Second, it's not a Class C name. Here we only use names that are pleasing to Class C, pretty names. Third, the paper only pays homage to whom I want it to, and I don't know any Nathanael Lessa. And finally"—Peçanha's irritation had gradually increased, as if he were taking a certain enjoyment in it—"here no one, not even me, uses a masculine pseudonym. My name is Maria de Lourdes!"

I took another look at the newspaper, including the staff. Nothing but women's names.

"Don't you think a masculine name gives the answers more respectability? Father, husband, priest, boss—they have nothing but men telling them what to do. Nathanael Lessa will catch on better than Elisa Gabriela."

"That's exactly what I don't want. Here they feel like their own bosses, they trust us, as if we were all friends. I've been in this business twenty-five years. Don't come to me with untested theories. *Woman* is revolutionizing the Brazilian press, it's a different kind of newspaper that doesn't run yesterday's warmed-over television news."

He was so irritated that I didn't ask just what *Woman* intended to do. Sooner or later he'd tell me. I just wanted the job.

"My cousin, Machado Figueiredo, who also has twenty-five years' experience at the Bank of Brazil, likes to say that he's always open to untested theories." I knew that *Woman* owed money to the bank. And on Peçanha's desk was a letter of recommendation from my cousin.

When he heard my cousin's name, Peçanha paled. He bit his cigar to control himself, then closed his mouth, as if he were about to whistle, and his fat lips trembled as if he had a grain of pepper on his tongue. He opened his mouth wide and tapped his nicotine-stained teeth with his thumbnail while he looked at me in a way that he must have thought fraught with significance.

"I could add 'Dr.' to my name. Dr. Nathanael Lessa."

"Damn! All right, all right," Peçanha snarled between his teeth, "you start today."

That was how I came to be part of the team at *Woman*.

My desk was near Sandra Marina's, who wrote the horoscope. Sandra was also known as Marlene Katia, for interviews. A pale fellow with a long, sparse mustache, he was also known as João Albergaria Duval. He wasn't long out of communications school and constantly complained, "Why didn't I study dentistry, why?"

I asked him if someone brought the readers' letters to my desk. He told me to talk to Jacqueline in the office. Jacqueline was a large black man with very white teeth.

"It's no good being the only one here who doesn't have a woman's name, they're going to think I'm a fairy. Letters? There aren't any. You think Class C women write letters? Elisa made them all up."

"Dear Dr. Nathanael Lessa. I got a scholarship for my ten-year-old daughter in a fancy school in a good neighborhood. All her classmates go to the hairdresser at least once a week. We don't have the money for that, my husband drives a bus on the Jacare-Caju line, but he says he's going to work overtime to send Tania Sandra, our little girl, to the hairdresser. Don't you think that our children deserve every sacrifice? Dedicated Mother. Villa Kennedy."

Answer: Wash your little girl's head with coconut soap and wrap it in curling paper. It's the same as the hairdresser. In any case, your daughter wasn't born to be a baby-doll. Nor anyone else's daughter, for that matter. Take the overtime pay and buy something more useful. Food, for example.

"Dear Dr. Nathanael Lessa. I am short, plump and shy. Whenever I go to the outdoor market, the store, the vegetable market, they rob me. They cheat me on the weight, the change, the beans have bugs in them, the cornmeal is stale, that kind of thing. It used to bother me a lot but now I'm resigned. God is watching them and at the day of judgment they will pay. Resigned Domestic. Penha."

Answer: God doesn't have his eye on anybody. You have to look out for yourself. I suggest you scream, holler, raise a scandal. Don't you have a relative who works for the police? A crook will do also. Get moving, chubby.

"Dear Dr. Nathanael Lessa. I am twenty-five, a typist and a virgin. I met this boy who says he really loves me. He works in the Ministry of Transportation and says he wants to marry me, but first he wants to try it out. What do you think? Frenzied Virgin. Parada de Lucas."

Answer: Look, Frenzied Virgin, ask the guy what he plans to do if he doesn't like the experience. If he says he'll dump you, give him what he wants, because he's a sincere man. You're not some gooseberry or vegetable stew to be sampled. But there aren't many sincere men around, so it's worth a try. Keep the faith and full speed ahead.

I went to lunch.

When I got back Peçanha called me in. He had my copy in his hand.

"There's something or other here I don't like," he said.

"What?" I asked.

"Ah, good God, the idea people have of Class C," Peçanha exclaimed, shaking his head pensively while he looked at the ceiling and puckered his lips. "It's Class A women who like being treated with curses and kicks. Remember that English lord who said his success with women came from treating ladies like whores and whores like ladies."

"All right. So how should I handle our readers?"

"Don't come to me with dialectics. I don't want you to treat them like whores. Forget the English lord. Put some happiness, some hope, tranquillity and reassurance in the letters, that's what I want."

"Dear Dr. Nathanael Lessa. My husband died and left me a very small pension, but what worries me is to be alone and fifty years old. Poor, plain, old, and living a long way out, I'm afraid of what's in store for me. Lonely in Santa Cruz."

Answer: Engrave this in your heart, Lonely in Santa Cruz: neither money, nor beauty, nor youth, nor a good address brings happiness. How many rich and beautiful people kill themselves or lose themselves in the horrors of vice? Happiness is inside us, in our hearts. If we are just and good we will find happiness. Be good, be just, love your neighbor as yourself, smile at the cashier when you go to pick up your pension.

The next day Peçanha called me in and asked if I could also

write the illustrated love story. "We turn out our own stories, not some translated Italian fumetti. Pick a name."

I chose Clarice Simone, two more homages, though I didn't tell Peçanha that.

The photographer of the love stories came to talk to me.

"My name is Monica Tutsi," he said, "but you can call me Agnaldo. You got the pap ready?"

Pap was the love story. I explained that I had just gotten the assignment from Peçanha and would need at least two days to write it.

"Days, ha ha," he guffawed, making the sound of a large, hoarse domesticated dog barking for its master.

"What's so funny?" I asked.

"Norma Virginia used to write the story in fifteen minutes. He had a formula."

"I have a formula too. Take a walk and come back in fifteen minutes; your story'll be ready."

What did that idiot of a photographer think I was? Just because I'd been a police reporter didn't mean I was stupid. If Norma Virginia, or whatever his name was, wrote a story in fifteen minutes, so could I. After all, I read the Greek tragedies, the Ibsens, the O'Neills, the Becketts, the Chekhovs, the Shakespeares, the Four Hundred Best Television Plays. All I had to do was borrow an idea here, another one there, and that's it.

A rich young lad is stolen by gypsies and given up for dead. The boy grows up thinking he's a real gypsy. One day he meets a very rich young girl and they fall in love. She lives in a fine mansion and has many automobiles. The gypsy boy lives in a wagon. The two families don't want them to marry. Conflicts arise. The millionaires order the police to arrest the gypsies. One of the gypsies is killed by the police. A rich cousin of the girl is assassinated by the gypsies. But the love of the two young people is greater than all these vicissitudes. They decide to run away, to break with their families. On their flight they encounter a pious and wise monk who seals their union in an ancient, picturesque, and romantic convent amidst a flowering wood. The two young people retire to the nuptial chamber. They are beautiful, slim, blond with blue eyes. They remove their clothes. "Oh," says the girl, "what is that gold chain with a diamond-studded medallion you wear on your neck?" She has one just like it! They are brother and sister! "You are my brother who disappeared!" the girl cries. The two embrace. (Attention Monica Tutsi: how about an ambiguous ending? making a nonfraternal ecstasy appear on their faces, eh? I can also change the ending and make it more Sophoclean: they discover they're brother and sister after the consummated fact; the desperate girl leaps from the convent window and creams herself down below.)

"I liked your story," Monica Tutsi said.

"A pinch of *Romeo and Juliet,* a teaspoon of *Oedipus Rex,*" I said modestly.

"But I can't photograph it, man. I have to do everything in two hours. Where do I find the mansion? The cars? The picturesque convent? The flowered wood?"

"That's your problem."

"Where do I find," Monica Tutsi continued as if he hadn't heard me, "the two slim, blond young people with blue eyes? All our models tend toward the mulatto. Where do I get the wagon? Try again, man. I'll be back in fifteen minutes. And what does Sophoclean mean?"

Roberto and Betty are engaged to be married. Roberto, who is very hard-working, has saved his money to buy an apartment and furnish it, with a color television set, stereo, refrigerator, washing machine, floor waxer, dishwasher, toaster, electric iron, and hair dryer. Betty works too. Both are chaste. The date is set. A friend of Roberto's, Tiago, asks him, "Are you going to get married still a virgin? You need to be initiated into the mysteries of sex." Tiago then takes Roberto to the house of the Superwhore Betatron. (Attention Monica Tutsi: the name is a pinch of science fiction.) When Roberto arrives he finds out that the Superwhore is Betty, his dear fiancée. Oh heavens! what a horrible surprise! Someone, perhaps a doorman, will say, "To grow up is to suffer." End of story.

"One word is worth a thousand photographs," Monica Tutsi said. "I always get the short end of things. I'll be back soon."

"Dr. Nathanael. I like to cook. I also like to embroider and crochet. And most of all I like to wear a long evening gown and put on crimson lipstick, with lots of rouge and eye shadow. Ah, what a sensation! What a pity that I must stay locked in my room. No one knows that I like to do these things. Am I wrong? Pedro Redgrave. Tijuca."

Answer: Why should it be wrong? Are you doing anyone harm? I had another reader who, like you, enjoyed dressing as a woman. He carried on a normal, useful, and socially productive life, to the point that he was selected a model worker. Put on your long gowns, paint your lips scarlet, put some color in your life.

"All the letters should be from women," Peçanha reminded.

"But this one is real," I said.

"I don't believe it."

I handed the letter to Peçanha. He looked at it with the expression of a cop examining a badly counterfeited bill.

"You think it's a joke?" Peçanha asked.

"It might be," I said. "And it might not be."

Peçanha put on his reflective look. Then:

"Add some encouraging phrase to your letter, like, for example, 'write again.' "

I sat down at the typewriter:

Write again, Pedro, I know that's not your real name but it doesn't matter, write again, count on me. Nathanael Lessa

"Shit," said Monica Tutsi, "I went to do your great piece of drama and they told me it was stolen from an Italian film."

"Wretches, band of idiots—just because I was a police reporter they're calling me a plagiarist."

"Take it easy, Virginia."

"Virginia? My name is Clarice Simone," I said. "What idiocy is this of thinking only Italian fiancées are whores? Look here, I once knew an engaged woman, a really serious one, who was even a sister of charity, and they found out she was a whore too."

"It's okay, man, I'm going to shoot the story. Can Betatron be mulatto? What's a Betatron?"

"She has to be a redhead, with freckles. Betatron is an apparatus for the production of electrons, possessing great energy potential and high velocity, impelled by the action of a rapidly changing magnetic field," I said.

"Shit! That's really a name for a whore," said Monica Tutsi admiringly, on his way out.

"Understanding Nathanael Lessa. I have worn my long gowns gloriously. And my mouth has been as red as tiger's blood and the break of dawn. I am thinking of putting on a satin gown and going to the Municipal Theatre. What do you think? And now I'm going to tell you a great and marvelous confidence, but you must keep my confession the greatest secret. Do you swear? Ah, I don't know if I should say it or not. All my life I've suffered the greatest disillusionment from believing in others. I am basically a person who never lost his innocence. Betrayal, coarseness, shamelessness, and baseness leave me quite shocked. Oh how I would like to live isolated in a utopian world of love and kindness. My sensitive Nathanael, let me think. Give me time. In the next letter I shall tell more, perhaps everything. Pedro Redgrave."

Answer: Pedro. I await your letter, with your secrets, which I promise to store in the inviolable reaches of my recondite consciousness. Continue this way, confronting aloofly the envy and insidious perfidy of the poor in spirit. Adorn your body, which thirsts for sensuality, by exercising the challenges of your courageous mind.

Peçanha asked: "Are these letters real too?"

"Pedro Redgrave's are."

"Strange, very strange," Peçanha said, tapping his nails on his teeth. "What do you make of it?"

"I don't make anything of it," I said.

He seemed preoccupied with something. He asked about the illustrated love story but took no interest in the answers.

"What about the blind girl's letter?" I asked.

Peçanha got the blind girl's letter and my reply and read aloud: " 'Dear Nathanael. I cannot read what you write. My beloved granny reads it to me. But do not think I am illiterate. I am blind. My dear granny is writing this letter for me, but the words are my own. I want to send a word of comfort to your readers so that they, who suffer so much from small misfortunes, may look at themselves in the mirror. I am blind but I am happy. I am at peace, with God and my fellow man. Happiness to all. Long live Brazil and its people. Blind but Happy. Unicorn Road. Nova Iguacu. P.S. I forgot to say that I am also paralyzed.' " Peçanha lighted a cigar. "Moving, but Unicorn Road doesn't ring true. You'd better make it Windmill Road or something like that. Now let's see your answer. 'Blind but Happy, congratulations on your strength, your unwavering faith in happiness, in good, in the people, and in Brazil. The souls of those who despair in their adversity should take nourishment from your edifying example, a flambeau of light in the darkness of torment.' "

Peçanha gave me the papers. "You have a future in literature. This is a great school we have here. Learn, learn, dedicate yourself, don't lose heart, work hard."

I sat at the typewriter:

Tesio, a bank employee, resident of Boca do Mato, in Lins de Vasconcelos, married to Frederica in his second marriage, has a son, Hipolito, from his first marriage. Frederica falls in love with Hipolito. Tesio discovers their sinful love. Frederica hangs herself from the mango tree in the back yard. Hipolito asks his father for forgiveness, leaves home and wanders desperately through the streets of the cruel city until he is run down and killed on the Avenida Brasil.

"What's the seasoning here?" Monica Tutsi asked.

"Euripides, sin and death. Let me tell you something: I know the human soul and don't need any ancient Greek to inspire me. For a man of my intelligence and sensitivity it's enough to look around me. Look closely at my eyes. Have you ever seen anyone more alert, more wide awake?"

Monica Tutsi looked closely at my eyes and said, "I think you're crazy."

I continued:

"I cite the classics only to demonstrate my knowledge. Since I was a police reporter, if I don't do that the cretins don't respect me. I've read thousands of books. How many books do you think Peçanha has read?"

"None. Can Frederica be black?"

"Good idea. But Tesio and Hipolito have to be white."

"Nathanael. I love, a forbidden love, an interdicted love, a secret love, a hidden love. I love another man. And he also loves me. But we cannot walk in the street holding hands, like the others, exchange kisses in the gardens and movie theaters, like the others, lie in each other's arms on the sandy beaches, like the others, dance in night clubs, like the others. We cannot get married, like the others, and together face old age, disease and death, like the others. I do not have the strength to resist and struggle. It is better to die. Good-bye. This is my last letter. Have a mass said for me. Pedro Redgrave."

Answer: What are you saying, Pedro? Are you going to give up now that you've found your love? Oscar Wilde suffered like the devil, he was ridiculed, tried, sentenced, but he stood up to it. If you can't get married, shack up. Make a will in each other's favor. Defend yourselves. Use the law and the system to your benefit. Be selfish, like the others, be sly, implacable, intolerant and hypocritical. Exploit. Plunder. It's self-defense. But, please, don't carry out any deranged gesture.

I sent the letter and reply to Peçanha. Letters were published only with his approval.

Monica Tutsi came by with a girl.

"This is Monica," Monica Tutsi said.

"What a coincidence," I said.

"What's a coincidence?" asked the girl Monica.

"The two of you having the same name," I said.

"His name is Monica?" Monica asked, pointing to the photographer.

"Monica Tutsi. Are you Tutsi too?"

"No. Monica Amelia."

Monica Amelia stood chewing a fingernail and looking at Monica Tutsi.

"You told me your name was Agnaldo," she said.

"On the outside I'm Agnaldo. Here inside I'm Monica Tutsi."

"My name is Clarice Simone," I said.

Monica Amelia observed us attentively, without understanding a thing. She saw two circumspect people, too tired for jokes, uninterested in their own names.

"When I get married my son, or daughter, is going to be named Hei Yoo," I said.

"Is that a Chinese name?" Monica asked.

"Or else Wheet Wheeo," I whistled.

"You're becoming a nihilist," Monica Tutsi said, withdrawing with the other Monica.

"Nathanael. Do you know what it is for two people to like one another? That was the two of us, Maria and I. Do you know what it is for two people to be perfectly attuned? That was us, Maria and I. My favorite dish is rice, beans, finely shredded kale, manioc meal and fried sausage. Guess what Maria's was? Rice, beans, finely shredded kale, manioc meal and fried sausage. My favorite precious stone is the ruby. Maria's, you guessed it, was also the ruby. Lucky number 7, color blue, day Monday, film Westerns, book *The Little Prince,* drink beer on tap, mattress Anatom, soccer team Vasco da Gama, music samba, pastime love, everything the same between her and me, wonderful. What we would do in bed, man—I don't mean to brag, but if it were in the circus and we charged admission we'd be rich. In bed no couple was ever so taken by such resplendent madness, was capable of such a dexterous, imaginative, original, pertinacious, splendiferous, and fulfilling performance as ours. And we would repeat it several times a day. But it was not just that which linked us. If you were missing a leg I would continue to love you, she would say. If you were a hunchback I would not stop loving you, I would reply. If you were a deaf-mute I would continue to love you, she would say. If you were cross-eyed I would not stop loving you, I would respond. If you had a paunch and were ugly I would continue to love you, she would say. If you were all scarred with smallpox I would not stop loving you, I would respond. If you were old and impotent I would continue to love you, she would say. And we were exchanging these vows when a desire to be truthful struck me, as deep as a knife thrust, and I asked her, what if I had no teeth, would you love me? and she replied, if you had no teeth I would continue to love you. Then I took out my dentures and threw them on the bed with a grave, religious, and metaphysical gesture. We both lay there looking at the dentures on top of the sheet, until Maria got up, put on a dress and said, I'm going out for cigarettes. To this day she hasn't come back. Nathanael, explain to me what happened. Does love end suddenly? Do a few teeth, miserable pieces of ivory, mean that much? Odontos Silva."

As I was about to reply, Jacqueline came by and said that Peçanha was calling me.

In Peçanha's office was a man wearing glasses and a goatee.

"This is Dr. Pontecorvo, who's a—just what are you?" asked Peçanha.

"A motivational researcher," Pontecorvo said. "As I was saying, first we do a survey of the characteristics of the universe we're researching, for example: who is the reader of *Woman*? Let's suppose it's the Class C woman. In our previous research we've surveyed everything about the Class C woman—where she buys her food, how many pairs of panties she owns, what time she makes love, what time she watches television, the television programs she sees, in short, a complete profile."

"How many pairs of panties does she own?" Peçanha asked.

"Three," Pontecorvo replied without hesitation.

"What time does she make love?"

"At nine-thirty P.M.," Pontecorvo replied promptly.

"And how did you find all this out? Do you knock at Dona Aurora's door in the housing project, she opens the door and you say, good morning, Dona Aurora, what time do you get it on? Look here, my friend, I've been in this business for twenty-five years and I don't need anybody to tell me what the Class C woman's profile is. I know from personal experience. They buy my newspaper, understand? Three pairs of panties . . . Ha!"

"We use scientific research methods. We have sociologists, psychologists, anthropologists, statisticians, and mathematicians on our staff," said Pontecorvo, imperturbable.

"All to get money from the patsies," said Peçanha with undisguised scorn.

"As a matter of fact, before coming here I put together some information about your newspaper which I believe may be of interest to you," Pontecorvo said.

"And what does it cost?" said Peçanha sarcastically.

"This I'll give you for free," Pontecorvo said. The man seemed to be made of ice. "We did a miniresearch on your readers, and despite the small sample size I can assure you, beyond the shadow of a doubt, that the great majority, almost the entirety, of your readers is made up of Class B men."

"What?" screamed Peçanha.

"That's right, Class B men."

First Peçanha turned pale. Then he began to turn red, then purple, as if he were being strangled. His mouth open, his eyes bulging, he rose from his chair and, arms spread, staggered like a crazed gorilla in Pontecorvo's direction. A shocking sight, even for a man of steel like Pontecorvo, even for an ex-police reporter. Pontecorvo retreated before Peçanha's advance until, his back against the wall, he said, trying to maintain his calm and composure, "Maybe our technicians made a mistake."

Peçanha, who was within a centimeter of Pontecorvo, underwent a violent tremor and, contrary to what I expected, did not pounce upon the other like a rabid dog. He seized his own hair forcefully and began tearing it out, as he screamed, "Comedians, swindlers, thieves, exploiters, liars, scum of the earth." Pontecorvo nimbly made his way toward the door, as Peçanha ran after him throwing the tufts of hair yanked from his own head. "Men! Men! Class B!" Peçanha snorted madly.

Later, after calming down—I think Pontecorvo escaped by the stairs—Peçanha, seated behind his desk again, told me, "That's the kind of people Brazil's fallen into the hands of—manipulators of statistics, falsifiers of information, con men with computers, all of them creating the Big Lie. But they won't pull it off with me. I really put that wretch in his place, didn't I?"

I said something or other in agreement. Peçanha took the box of El Ropos from the drawer and offered me one. We smoked and talked about the Big Lie. Afterward he gave me Pedro Redgrave's letter and my reply, with his okay, for me to take to the composing room.

On the way I saw that Pedro Redgrave's letter wasn't the one I had sent him. The text was different:

"Dear Nathanael, your letter was a balm for my afflicted heart. It has given me the strength to resist. I will not make any deranged gesture. I promise to . . ."

The letter ended there. It had been interrupted in the middle. Strange. I didn't understand. Something was wrong.

I went to my desk, sat down, and began writing the answer to Odontos Silva:

He who has no teeth also has no toothache. And as the hero of the well-known play put it, "There's never been a philosopher who could bear a toothache with patience." Besides, teeth are also instruments of revenge, as Deuteronomy says: an eye for an eye, a tooth for a tooth, a hand for a hand, a foot for a foot. Dictators despise teeth. Remember what Hitler told Mussolini about another meeting with Franco: I prefer having four teeth pulled. You're in the situation of the hero of that play *All's Well If Nobody Gets Shafted*—no teeth, no taste, nothing. Advice: put your teeth in and bite. If biting doesn't do the trick, try punching and kicking.

I was in the middle of Odontos Silva's letter when I suddenly understood everything. Peçanha was Pedro Redgrave. Instead of returning the letter in which Pedro asked me to have a mass said for him and which I had given him together with my answer about Oscar Wilde, Peçanha had handed me a new letter, unfinished, surely by accident, and which was supposed to come into my hands by mail.

I got Pedro Redgrave's letter and went to Peçanha's office.

"May I come in?" I asked.

"What is it? Come in," Peçanha said.

I handed him Pedro Redgrave's letter. Peçanha read the letter and, seeing the mistake he had committed, turned pale, as was his wont. Nervously, he shuffled the papers on his desk.

"It was all a joke," he said, trying to light a cigar. "Are you mad?"

"For real or a joke, it's all the same to me," I said.

"My life would make a novel . . ." Peçanha said. "Let's keep this between the two of us, okay?"

I wasn't sure what he wanted to keep between the two of us, his life making a novel or his being Pedro Redgrave. But I replied:

"Of course, just between the two of us."

"Thanks," said Peçanha. And he breathed a sigh that would have broken the heart of anyone who wasn't an ex-police reporter.

Translated by Clifford E. Landers

Paulo Emílio Salles Gomes
(1916–1977)

Born in São Paulo, Brazil, of a mixture of Brazilian and English ancestry, Paulo Emílio Salles Gomes was the son of a famous physician. In his teens he was politically active in the leftwing alliance that sought to overthrow the dictator Getúlio Vargas, who had come to power through a popular revolution in 1930 but, by 1932, had already consolidated considerable autocratic power. During the 1936 wave of repression that followed the failed communist uprising—inspired by Moscow, late in 1935—Salles Gomes was among the thousands of communist and leftwing activists and intellectuals arrested and detained without trial. In prison, he organized theatrical events and a "university" for instructing inmates both politically and intellectually. The following year he took part in a spectacular prison escape that involved tunneling into an adjacent building, an escape he nearly foiled by falling into a chicken coop.

Toward the close of 1937, Salles Gomes was absolved by the Tribunal on National Security but had already fled to France. There he studied with Henri Langlois at the French Cinémathèque, nurturing a passion for film that would lead to his writing (in French) a classic biography of Jean Vigo, published in 1957. Returning to Brazil in 1941, he worked as a film critic. He broke with the communist party in 1945, when the leader of the 1935 uprising, Luís Carlos Prestes, just released from prison, proposed that the party join with Vargas (who after flirting with the Axis powers had now resigned himself to the Allied cause) in a national reconciliation. In 1948, he was back in Europe to attend a World Peace Congress in Wroclaw, Poland (with Jorge Amado), and to

237

continue work on the Vigo biography. From Europe, he
contributed articles on film and literature to the various literary
supplements of Brazil.

He went on to organize several university departments of cinema
in Brazil and founded Brazil's own cinematheque. In the sixties,
Salles Gomes provided the intellectual and political inspiration for
the founders of the Brazilian *cinema novo* or "new cinema,"
including Nelson Pereira dos Santos and Glauber Rocha, who were
actively engaged in opposing the post-1964 military dictatorship.
He eventually married the novelist Lygia Fagundes Telles and in
the last year of his life published his only book of fiction, *P's Three
Women,* a tragicomic masterpiece of a cosmopolitan sophistication
unmatched in Brazilian literature since the works of Machado de
Assis.

Twice with Helena

If it hadn't been for my arthritis I would never have met Helena again. I realize it's inappropriate to begin a story of youth by alluding to arthritis, my own or hers, but the truth is that without this malady, our meeting in São Pedro thirty years later would never have occurred. She in Pacaembu and I in Alto dos Pinheiros, each moving in different circles, taking taxis or using our own cars, neither of us frequenting nightclubs or parties and neither in the limelight, the chances of our paths crossing were negligible, and indeed for three decades they never did, as if God had answered the ardent supplications I directed heavenward. Nevertheless, if one stops to think about it, a man and a woman who are both over fifty, arthritic, affluent, and living in São Paulo, would sooner or later be bound to turn up at the same time in Águas de São Pedro, the spa village where bourgeois and middle-class rheumatics reserve rooms in two or three principal hotels.

I didn't recognize Helena at first when I saw her. She was sitting beside Professor Alberto, taking the air in the small park decorated with colorfully painted plaster dwarfs. Him I recognized at once, in spite of his white hair and the modern glasses which had replaced the heavy tortoiseshell ones that used to grace his powerful nose. For years he was my mentor and close friend. The vastness of his knowledge and the way in which his intelligence could maneuver his accumulation of cultural data made me esteem the professor—when I was able to evaluate him—as the first genius I had ever met. The first and the only, I can say today as I enter old age and expect from those who are intelligent more than just multi-plicity of talents. Nobody ever liked me as much as the professor did. He thought me gifted, and from grade school on he lent me books, and thus oriented my reading. His diligence continued through my university days, when I naively tried to deepen my taste for letters, art and ideas that he had determinedly aroused in me. He took upon himself the formation of my basic ideas in all areas; he met and approved my girl friends, including my first more or less professional mistress. It was he who engineered a scholarship for me to study in Europe; it was he—who never trav-eled—who methodically organized the itineraries and the list of indispensable visits to be made: the section of the Montparnasse Cemetery where Baudelaire is buried, the exact number of the house on rue Monsieur le Prince where Auguste Comte lived, and the address of the Vatican Library of Milan where certain lesser known sketches of Leonardo da Vinci were kept.

To my mind of twenty, the professor's forty years made him a confirmed bachelor, and it was not without surprise that I received, in Paris, the letter announcing his marriage. During the two years that I had been abroad we had corresponded regularly, but with the passage of time I had sensed in my mentor's letters ever-growing doses of melancholy, as well as a decline in his fervor to cultivate me. I attributed this change in tone to the disappointment I must be causing him. My impartial love for culture was being replaced by a liking for politics, a discipline he found boring. Worse yet, I was inclined toward fascism, a movement for which Professor Alberto had only scorn, particularly after the appearance of integralism and the blow of the New State. The beginning of World War II hastened my return home, and it was with a certain apprehension that I went to meet him again, for the first time in his new house in Pacaembu that he had taken after marrying. I was curious to meet Helena, about whom I knew nothing more than her name, the professor's letters having been impersonal. But she was not there; she was spending some time in Campos do Jordão, he told me with a wide smile of welcome that I have never forgotten. For the next few weeks he hardly let me alone. I had come back from Europe much thinner, and this upset him greatly; he insisted that I see several doctors and have various laboratory tests. In spite of my excellent health I obeyed him without resis-tance; I reckoned that he, like so many others approaching old age, had become obsessed with illness and was including me in his obsession. My impatience with the meticulous slowness of the doctors disappeared upon seeing my friend's satisfaction at all the "negative" laboratory results. As for the rest, the discussions I had feared never occurred. When the names of Hitler or Mussolini entered the conversation—at my provocation—he would shake his head and change the subject. One day I caught him showing tolerance for the extremists, as we called subversives in those days. But he disarmed me at once, explaining that in politics, a liberal such as himself must tolerate everything, even a fascist, although he actually tolerated only one: me.

Three weeks after my arrival, the professor left to join his wife in Campos do Jordão, inviting me to go there for a few days. I made preparations to travel with him, but the idea didn't please him. He consulted a small calendar with close attention, asked what the date was, counted on his fingers and fixed the precise moment I should arrive, three or four days hence. I then realized that he wanted to make sure that I would be at his side on my birthday, which was close, and I thanked him for remembering it. But he affected surprise, as if he only that minute remembered a date he had never let go by unrecognized.

It was easy to locate the isolated cottage, surrounded by pine trees, in Umuarama. I didn't immediately identify the girl who opened the door as Helena; I never supposed the wife of my forty-year-old friend would be so young—and above all so lovely. But a contretemps awaited me. In response to an urgent message from his family, it seemed, the professor had left that very morning, not having had time to notify me, but he would be back within four or five days. Helena announced this quickly, without looking at me, as she stood in the doorway. Her timidity was contagious. Embarrassed, I replied that it was perfectly all right, I would stay with an aunt in Capivari and would come back in a few days to see if the professor had returned. I was about to shake hands with her, when I noted a certain tremor in her lips as she walked quickly back into the house. When she finally spoke, I couldn't understand her words. From her confused stammerings I could make out only a series of negatives, pronounced with agitation. I was perplexed and very ill at ease. Finally Helena, after a visible effort, managed to say that the professor had left explicit instructions that I install myself in the cottage and wait for his return. My constraint was as acute as hers. I resolved not to accept the situation that was being forced upon me, but Helena, controlling her nervousness, insisted that she could not let me go. She now spoke with surprising authority, though she still turned her great green eyes away from me—the only element in her behavior that had not changed since she had first opened the door. I must add that during the days I spent there, Helena never once looked at me. The first time she did so was thirty years later, in the garden with the plaster dwarfs. If I was reluctant to stay at their country house, it was because of the affliction that those shifting eyes caused me: the most beautiful eyes I had ever seen in my life, fixed always on something just to the left or right of my head. I agreed to stay only when she said that I would put her in a difficult position regarding her husband; he had insisted that I wait there for him. Much against my wishes, I took my bag to the bedroom she indicated. The cool afternoon was sunny, and with relief I accepted the suggestion that I take a solitary walk. Dinner, she told me, would be at seven.

During my walk through the woods, I couldn't stop thinking about my strange welcome. I alternately criticized and pardoned Professor Alberto, who was responsible for the uncomfortable situation. I couldn't figure out what type of woman Helena might be—what she, in her youth and beauty, could have found in the professor, an extraordinary man in so many ways, but already old and without any fortune to speak of. Nothing fit; the uncertainty of it all was disturbing. And those eyes that wouldn't meet mine!

When I went into the small dining room, Helena was waiting for me. She had dressed and combed with care, her hair piled high on her head, her long neck accentuated by a plunging décolleté gown such as one saw in American films. Her bare arms were firm and delicate. I observed that in addition to being beautiful, she was exceptionally seductive. A small fire flickered in the fireplace. She went to the kitchen various times, bringing a soup tureen, a platter with roast duck à l'orange, bottles of fine French wine. I realized, again embarrassed, that the house had no domestic employees; Helena did everything. At the same time, I took advantage of her walking back and forth to better appreciate her dress, which clung tightly to her hips. I reflected on how clothing styles had changed in my absence.

Dinner was enjoyable. In the beginning my hostess seemed stiff, but gradually her expression became more relaxed, helped perhaps by the wines, which she drank in the same quantity as I. The first time she laughed at my stories about Paris, I was dazzled. The row of fine, well-set teeth, with a tiny sliver of rosy gum visible above, constituted the final touch of desirability, and I put down my glass, suddenly feeling almost dizzy. My rapture was interrupted by a slight sensation of discomfort, and settling myself more comfortably in the chair, I perceived that I was in the midst of an erection. Perturbed, I began to talk about the professor, what he meant to me, how much I owed him, how I loved and admired him. Helena's mouth had been mobilized in the expectancy of more laughter, but it dissolved into a wan smile of approval when I mentioned her husband. Her eyes shifted from their usual point beyond me to focus on the wine bottle, which she lifted to fill our glasses to the brim. I, the recent European traveler, privately observed that to fill wineglasses to overflowing, as if one were drinking beer, was the Brazilian idea of hospitality, but I did not pursue this snobbish thought. I was dying to catch another glimpse of gum through her lovely lips, so I didn't bring up the professor again. Instead I went back to my Parisian anecdotes, with growing exaggeration and success. Several times Helena repeated her undulating trips to the kitchen. By the time I tasted the caramel pudding, the erection was no longer a bother. It was welcome. While a certain degree of drunkenness caused me ironic thoughts about the great liberal who tolerated everything, a shred of conscience pacified me with the thought that effectively I was doing nothing wrong. I offered to help Helena make the coffee and she giggled at my clumsiness. In truth, standing up, I felt clumsier than before. The undershorts and trousers of 1940 had a looseness that impeded one's either disciplining or liberating an erection. That gaze which avoided my face by moving from the top of my head to wander about the sides and lower parts of my body ran the risk of fixing itself upon a breach of manners capable of annulling the evening's enchantment. However, my scruples didn't last long; not that I overcame them, but I simply let myself be carried away on the succession of gestures, drinks, and laughter. After the coffee, Helena brought glasses and a bottle of very special champagne that I had once tasted on a visit to Reims. I was unaware that it could be purchased in Brazil, since even in Paris it was difficult to find and extremely expensive. When Helena asked me to open a second bottle, I thought about the professor's apparent increase in prosperity as I made an effort to remove the swollen cork. Helena's ever-shifting eyes had now acquired a new brilliance. It was this shine that made the idea of madness cross my mind when—after a motionless moment of silence—she resolutely advanced toward me and pressed her body against mine.

The room to which she led me was totally dark. This setting for our lovemaking remained in complete obscurity during the four days and nights that I spent with her in the cottage. Even when I sought her during full daylight, the refuge was always dark. Due to the un-scheduled urgency of our desire, I spent more time in that bedroom than anywhere else in Campos do Jordão, though I never actually saw a single object, fabric, or piece of furniture it contained. Outside it, I was hardly with Helena. The *toilette* and banquet of the first night were not repeated. Discreetly dressed, she served the meals, but did not sit down at the table with me. They consisted of substantial but simple fare: rare steaks instead of duck, and pitchers of orange juice in place of wine. She authoritatively imposed the distribution of my time: when not in the darkness or at the table, I went for solitary walks through the woods or rested in my room, which she entered only to bring me eggnogs made with an excellent cognac, the con-sumption of which she stood watching, like a severe and efficient nurse. Indeed, the sensation that pervaded me outside our amorous moments was precisely that of one who has escaped a grave disease and is experiencing the euphoric fatigue of convalescence. The word *fatigue* is appropriate. Not that Helena was exactly insatiable, but she worked hard to provoke my climax as fast and as often as possible. With her consent I shortened my walks through the woods in order to lengthen my rest periods.

On the first night I didn't notice her taking any precautions at all—in those days the Pill didn't exist—and, fearing her inexperience, I asked her about it. The voice that came from the shadows was ironic as she answered that she knew what she was doing and that her com-petence was certainly greater than mine in this area. As a matter of fact, we talked very little, in or out of the blackness of the wide mat-rimonial bed. I don't remember hearing her pronounce my name, which I appreciated, since I always found it ridiculous. Nor did we allude to the professor again, but in the drowsiness of the rest periods his image haunted my thoughts. I spent the small amount of energy I had left reflecting on him, Helena, myself, us. Our explosive passion justified everything: we must face the husband with loyalty.

Four days had passed. The cries of birds brought to the perma-nent night of the bedroom a sign of approaching dawn in the real world. The moment had arrived to tell Helena that we must make a decision. Her voice had never been so tranquilly docile as when she answered me. The decision had already been made. I would leave this very morning, because the professor would be back in the afternoon. She did not love me. It had been nothing more than a caprice she wished to experience; well, she had experienced it. She did not regret it but she considered it finished. She had never betrayed her husband before and did not expect to do so again. If she changed her mind, she would let me know. I was forbidden to attempt any contact with her or the professor. She would tell him that I had been disrespectful and that she had been obliged to send me away, thus justifying my definitive separation from them. I mustn't bother myself with moral questions; the option was clear: I must either lose the professor's good opinion of me, or destroy my friend. If I got up immediately, I would have time to shave, pack my bag, drink a glass of milk with some crackers, and catch the seven o'clock bus. The ticket with my seat number was in the drawer of the dresser in my room. The milk was in the refrigerator and the crackers in the cupboard, inside the tin with a parrot painted on it. She would not see me off. The good-byes had been said and she would stay in the bedroom until I was gone. Never had Helena talked so much. I followed all her instructions to the letter, including the crackers and milk. I left in such a daze that it was only upon arriving in São Paulo that I remembered it was my twenty-fifth birthday.

During the seconds that it took me to approach the old professor as he rose from the stone bench in the dwarf-decorated park, I relived thirty years' worth of feelings. At first, my love for Helena and my shame toward the professor had all been one, making me a miserable creature no longer interested in Hitler's victories, my work, women, or life itself. In the second phase, I thought sometimes of Helena, sometimes of the professor. When it was Helena's turn, the absurd hope of her seeking me once more—a possibility she herself had raised that morning when she had said good-bye—would inundate me. Thoughts of Professor Alberto, on the other hand, made my imagination take flight. I am convinced that it was because of him that I began to hate fascism. I tried to enlist in the army; I dreamed of dying a nationally recognized hero with my picture in all the papers so he would find out and would pardon me. As time passed, my ardor for Helena began to cool under the power of substitutes. But during those thirty years there was no shame, personal or national, that could rival that brought about by the image of the professor. At the very instant I bent over to shake his hand, shame invaded the deep wrinkles of my face with a red flush, juvenile and intact, as bright as the scarlet-tinted beret worn by the dwarf among the rosebushes. Upon closer inspection, I could evaluate the devastation of the old teacher's face; it was much greater than one would suppose for the seventy-odd years I ascribed him. If I recognized him in the park from a distance of several yards it was due to the growing twilight, which transmitted only his silhouette, familiar to me exactly because I hadn't seen him for thirty years and had thought about him daily. Meeting him suddenly in full light, I would have recognized him only with difficulty. As he spoke my name, he made a gesture as if to introduce Helena, whom I only then recognized. Unlike the professor, she had become harder to recognize from a distance; she was a shadow with its limbs folded up, intimidated by rheumatism. Her face, seen close up, was still smooth and much like its original, which time had blurred in my memory. Our hands barely touched, mutual reluctance augmented by arthritic precaution. She never stopped staring tranquilly at me the entire time, her eyes charged with investigation. As for the professor, his effusive expressions of the old fondness were marked by unconcealable signs of discomfort. I have forgotten what we said in the course of this brief encounter, except for a few surprising political allusions. At one point he affirmed that if he were the right age, he would be robbing banks and assaulting headquarters like ... His hesitation was provoked by Helena, who placed an arthritic hand on his shoulder. I looked more attentively at the old man's face, trying to figure out the meaning of this game, and to my alarm discovered delirium emanating from his eyes and causing his lips to twitch. The crisis was over quickly, but it drained the professor, who, after a moment of panting to catch his breath, proposed to Helena that they retire. I went with them along the street and across the small bridge, which had been named for a forgotten poet. We stopped before a hotel with an indigenous name: Jerubiçaba. The old man pointed to a tablet, where I read that "jerubiçaba" in the language of the Tupi Indians meant "loyalty." I once again felt the blood rush to tint my wrinkles, but he only commented, with the apparent fastidiousness of erudition, that the Tupi of the hotel corporation didn't inspire his confidence any more than the Latin of the local clergyman. He added that he was an assiduous frequenter of the chapel there in Águas, where an aged priest persisted in saying the mass the old-fashioned way. The reference to loyalty was not, evidently, directed against me, and this idea relieved me, but the relief didn't last. Frightened, I perceived that the professor was making ironic remarks to gain time: he intended to tell me something of grave importance, he announced. I waited, chilled. He reflected a little, looking at the ground, and began to speak in a voice so soft that to hear him I almost had to put my face against his. Removed a little from her husband's whispers, Helena took advantage of the opportunity and bade me farewell with a discreet movement of her head. The terrible hour of judgment, awaited for thirty years, had arrived. Helena's departure, however, left the professor almost helpless. He leaned on my arm with such force that for an instant I had the impression that he was going to attack me. Then quickly he calmed himself and his voice became clearer. As for me, this postponement of the execution gave me time to gather courage for the attitude I meant to take. I would hear everything without saying a word; at the end I would kneel before him and, if he didn't push me away, I would kiss his hand.

He began by saying in a calm voice that the time and place weren't right for the long conversation he intended to have with me, but that we could meet on the following day. Electrified with hope—his tone made clear the certainty of pardon—I managed to stutter some word of recognition for the grace placed within my grasp. Yet as he continued, his words again silenced me, not so much from penitence as from alarm at the completely unexpected direction he took. Speaking with an increasing clarity that seemed impregnated with despair, he said that he had committed a crime and had paid dearly for it. The punishment had been such that he could not conceive of anything worse. Even so, he hadn't found peace. He had gone back to the church of his childhood, was trying to confess and receive communion daily, but his nature made him rebel daily as well, wanting to escape his incommensurably cruel chastisement, in spite of its being deserved. He passed his days in weighing the crime and the punishment on the balances of an insane scale. The fortuitous encounter with me seemed predestined, he added in great exultation. The remark about the "insane scale" put me on my guard: suddenly it occurred to me that the professor might be mentally deranged and I prepared myself to hear him out patiently. This new possibility would explain his confident cordiality ever since our meeting in the park; moreover, it revived in me pricks of remorse which now became irresolvable, since the pardon of a lunatic would be meaningless. His next words demonstrated to me that he had guessed my suspicions. He said that he could understand my uneasiness, that the confused generalities in which he was speaking must make him appear to be the victim of some morbid delirium. But unfortunately this wasn't the case; he wasn't demented, the facts existed and they were unchangeable. On the following day I would find out about anything and could judge for myself. We agreed to meet in the little park at sunset. Excessively bright light was bad for him.

* * *

As I went slowly up the landscaped ramp leading to the Grand Hotel, my mind was racked with agitation, which had lasted through the night and was finally overcome only by fatigue in the wee hours of the morning. When I awoke, I was immediately assaulted by the anxiety of the evening before, and my tension increased as the hour of the meeting approached. Seated on the same bench as on the previous evening was Helena, alone. She was looking with interest at the remains of a plaster dwarf, only two small yellow boots contrasting with the green of the lawn. It had been toppled either by the wind or by some tourist insensible to the simple prettiness of the spa. She began by saying that the professor was not feeling well and had spent the day in bed; but that this wasn't the only reason he had failed to come. In truth, after meeting me again he couldn't find the strength to converse with me further. He had asked Helena to do it for him, to tell me everything, everything, and she was ready to carry out her mission to the letter. There were, however, a large number of details surrounding an important fact that she didn't know and refused to probe into. She insisted, moreover, that I let her speak without interruption, not only to make her task easier but also because she would exhaust the subject at hand to such an extent that no query could possibly remain unanswered.

All my earlier sentiments had now been replaced by such curiosity that for the moment the identity of Helena herself was forgotten. I believe the same thing happened with her: as soon as she began to speak, my personality dissipated, though her eyes never once left my face. She spoke slowly in an almost continuous stream, taking care to forget nothing, so methodical that she never needed to go back to fill in something she had already covered. Helena's somewhat declamatory manner of expressing herself held a literary familiarity for me, and as I tried to recall the name of the writer whom she resembled, I discovered that it was myself, the unpublished author of numerous writings in an old-fashioned, at times pompous, style. Her manner remained severe during the entire course of her narrative, and the ironies that occasionally sprang up were intrinsic to the facts she was relating, never calculated to provoke the affliction I again now felt.

"Alberto loved only three persons in his life. The first was you, and if you hadn't gone abroad and I hadn't come along, you would probably have been the only one. This was even more extraordinary because I doubt that anyone exists who has more love to give than he. I cannot explain why, but I know that his feelings for his parents and brothers never went beyond the requirements of convention. His so-called friends, from childhood, youth, and adulthood, were numerous but inconstant, and were merely companions for play, study, or conversation. This psychological block was undoubtedly profound but not insurmountable, since with only your reserve and directness you managed to strike home to his immense reserves of stored-up affection. From first making your acquaintance when you were in grammar school until you left for Europe, you were the center of his life. He never held anything back from you, he even found your name attractive. When we met, it was I who fell in love first; he had thoughts only for his absent friend. How he lamented not having a picture of you! I love my husband today as much as ever and I am jealous by nature. And so, during more than thirty years of loving him, you were the only person of whom I was ever jealous. I liked Alberto the day I met him and I began to seek him out under the most varied pretexts. I think that he was happy to have me for company because he found me an attentive listener interested in stories about you. He read your letters out loud and made long comments, omitting from the narrative, as I later found out, one or two more scandalous adventures. He would talk laughingly about your innumerable sweethearts, about your insistence on introducing them to him one by one in order to get his opinion. My jealousy was probably unbecoming, but it was thanks to you that he came to know me better and to like me. In my urge to separate him from you I precipitated things; we became lovers one morning and that very afternoon he started getting our marriage papers in order. The motive for his haste to marry was the desire that I get pregnant as soon as possible, which I at first found touching, but then I grew cool when he said he wanted our child to be a boy just like you. From that moment our lives began to darken. Months passed and I didn't get pregnant. In his pride he blamed me. Only after having me examined by countless specialists who unanimously confirmed my capacity to reproduce did he resign himself to submit to similar examinations. He went to a dozen doctors and as many laboratories. Finally, accepting the fact that he was sterile, he grew closer to me than ever before. In all our thirty years together, it was in this period that we were most united; our thoughts and our reactions were like those of one person. Only this incredible identification with each other could have made possible the madness to which we resorted. The first time Alberto expounded the plan to me, I reacted with

horror and ran crying to my confessor. I was and still am a Catholic; my religious beliefs have always been real in spite of their
simplicity, remaining so in the face of my husband's atheism and
even when I grew intellectually and became capable of knowledge,
reflection, and self-expression. My confessor had previously become angry with me on two occasions, the first when I gave myself
to Alberto before our marriage, the second for not persuading my
husband to marry in the Church. This time, he lost his temper and
shouted at me. According to him I was being induced by the devil
to challenge God's will directly and to commit a crime against my
neighbor. And if I became an accomplice in my husband's perverse
scheme, he said, there would be no more place for me in the Catholic church; *he* at any rate forbade me to mention it to him again—
within the confessional or without. But he didn't follow through
with this prohibition, continuing—with sorrow—to receive, hear,
and counsel me in the confessional, sacristy, and parish house,
even as late as last year when he died of old age. I discussed my
confessor's arguments with Alberto. With his usual clarity, he established a difference between the priest's two statements. He made
sarcastic remarks about believing in the possibility of human defiance of God, an idea which could only spring from the diabolic
sin of pride, a subject on which he rightly considered himself an
authority. He didn't jest, however, at the reference to the crime
against one's neighbor. That was the point he came back to again
and again during the weeks he spent persuading me. He easily
destroyed my poor arguments, since he was, in fact, the patient
and competent agency behind my line of reasoning. Today I can
see clearly the method he used. First, he isolated God, showing
him to be equally inaccessible to a believer or an atheist. Then he
concentrated on the crime against his neighbor, that neighbor, of
course, being you. For the sake of argument, he named himself the
criminal and you the victim, and asked who would be more seriously hurt. He deliberately began the debate on the vulgar level of
immediate appearances—he the cuckold and you the seducer. Next,
he contrasted his own painful frustration with the impetuous enjoyment of sex you had described to him so often in letters and conversations. His reflections progressed to higher and higher levels until
they reached a sphere of sublime spiritual values, which even today
I recall as moving. The gravest consequence for both of you would be
the mutual loss of friendship. Alberto analyzed how little this would
mean to you, whose life was replete with the love of family, friends,
and women; you who called forth affection by the simple act of living;

you who had revealed an incredible capacity for new beginnings. Then he would approach the matter from the opposite angle, outlining all you meant to him. The comparison was irresistible. You would be merely a bit inconvenienced by a broken friendship, whereas he would be making a true sacrifice. He explained to me the need for this sacrifice in terms of a newly adopted, sincerely believed system of metaphysics that denied the scientific naturalism he had always embraced: he was one of those men destined to have little in any area of life. A mysterious law denied such individuals as himself the right to accumulation or variety; these could only be achieved through substitution. The figure two was his quota of love in this world and had been filled by myself and you. The love for a child would demand the sacrifice of one of us, you or me. Indeed, he told me something for which I've only recently forgiven him: that if he had gotten me pregnant, he would have found it harmonious for me to die in childbirth and the quota to be filled by you and the child. This perverse temper was rare. The sentiment of our unity generally prevailed, and based on that, Alberto discarded the counterproposal I made of our adopting a child. It seemed essential to him that the child should emanate from at least one half of the single being we constituted. I don't need to say more, because the person exterior to us, indispensable even if temporary, could be no one other than yourself. I must admit that the dark side of my personality played a role in what happened: tangled with fears and scruples of all kinds, there was one element in this madness that always excited me—you would disappear forever from Alberto's life."

Without taking her eyes from me, Helena stopped talking for an instant. I didn't say anything and she proceeded.

"I don't believe it's necessary to explain in minute detail the project he had planned, since you are as familiar with its execution as I am. What made everything easier was the extraordinary knowledge he had of you. He had observed that the girls who most attracted you—in life, in illustrated magazines, or on the movie screen—all had one thing in common: when they laughed one could see the beginning of their upper gums. I was never the type who laughed much and when I did, I hardly opened my mouth. I had to submit myself to painful exercises in front of the mirror until I could force my aching muscles to wrinkle up my lip in the necessary position. The cinema, which he has always detested, was also useful. You would drag him to see films—only you could— and Alberto amused himself with your enthusiasm for hairdos that elongated the neck and dresses that unabashedly insinuated the curves of the body. Not since your departure for Europe had he set foot in a theater, but he began going again with me, guided by the photos on display, making me pay close attention to the actresses' gowns and way of walking. He completed the indoctrination with numerous copies of sensational magazines, most of them printed in English. We went to shops looking for yard goods; I myself took on the job of cutting and sewing because I couldn't bear the absurdity of ordering such a dress from a seamstress. I'm good at sewing but I had to remake that outlandish getup five times. The rehearsals were even longer, first in São Paulo and later in the setting of the cottage in Campos do Jordão. The dress rehearsal, extremely tiring, ended only an hour before you arrived. On that occasion, the diversity of Alberto's talents was once again manifested. I think he might have made a great director, and in the episode I'm recalling, the only obstacle that his creativity could not surmount was my incompetence as an actress. You undoubtedly found me an incoherent, restless, and capricious woman, when the character called for should have been above all welcoming and warm. Even so, what little I managed to do I owe to the pertinacity and—why not say it?—genius of my husband. The moment I came 'on stage,' when you rang the doorbell, I was overcome by such a fit of nerves that I almost gave up the whole thing. I marshaled all my strength, but I felt like an automaton about to fall to pieces. The failure of the opening scene altered the script and I was obliged to improvise. I'm aware that I came across badly, but at least I conquered the obstacle that almost caused the plan to fail: your unexpected decision to wait for Alberto's return at the home of your relatives in Capivari. I managed to control myself, but in order to carry out my job during four miserable, interminable days and nights I had to modify completely the character that had been composed with such care and imagination. I used very little of the long text he had written and which I knew by heart, having been obliged to recite it over and over again at the table, in bed, and during my leisure hours. You helped me a great deal at the first dinner when you talked the whole time, telling stories that I didn't hear, worried as I was with wrinkling my upper lip to show my gums when I laughed. In bed, silence was easier for me and I could dispense with the heavily erotic lines that Alberto had translated and adapted from special French books. The rest of the time, thank goodness, you agreed uncomplainingly to go for walks through the surrounding countryside or rest in the guest room. I can truly say that prior to the tragedy which befell us, that period with you was the worst of my whole life. It would have been totally unbearable if it hadn't been for your manner of submissively accepting the rules of the game without the slightest displeasure, even though I imposed them more authoritatively than I ever imagined I could. I feel that I'm probably attributing more merit than is due to myself and you, whereas it is only to Alberto that we owed the perfect development of the unhappy business. My poor and noble husband deserved that everything go well. The amount of attention he gave to ridiculously minute details will give you an idea of the determination, work, and expense he put into this. He knew what you most enjoyed eating and was greatly upset at not finding partridges and guinea hens available for that evening. He was saved by your letters from Europe, which he always consulted and in which you raved about *canard aux oranges*. The wines had been stored up for you long before the fatal night, but the champagne you wrote about on a picture postcard of the Reims cathedral was acquired with painful effort and considerable money. He was convinced that this champagne and no other must play a decisive part in that first dinner, the crucial chapter in the plot. In São Paulo, no wine dealer had heard of that brand; Alberto traveled to Rio in search of it, which was reasonable, but he extended his search all the way to Porto Alegre, having been led astray by mistaken information. He consulted wine connoisseurs to no avail and finally, disposed to go to any lengths, he tried the society editors. One of them informed him that a few dozen bottles of the famous brand were the glory of the wine cellar at the Jockey Club of Argentina. Alberto considered making the trip to Buenos Aires, but then he remembered that one of the wine experts he had consulted, a professor of literary theory, was planning to go there. This professor received him and the favor he asked with mild surprise, since he hardly knew Alberto. But as the man was amiable and sympathetic to anything concerning wines, he took it upon himself to carry out the difficult mission, which involved the bribery of an English maître d'hôtel, a venerable figure among the Buenos Aires upper crust. Yet in spite of this laborious acquisition of the champagne, it isn't the final example of his meticulousness, because it was mainly a shock tactic. Much subtler was the choice of the dessert. The duck and the wines were a direct appeal to your appetite and good taste, and effectively laid the groundwork for the maternal comforts of a homey pudding served in a wide dish. The function of the dessert was largely psychological; it was to provoke the subconscious mechanism of your memory, so vibrant as it was to sensual connotations. At first, Alberto had chosen figs, but back then they weren't as high quality as the ones they cultivate these days in Valinhos. This difficulty in finding decent figs was fortuitous because it led to an incomparably more refined solution. He was well aware of an affair you had had just before your trip to Europe, that woman with the bubbling laugh and the exposed gum who, according to your confidences, had had more powerful sex appeal for you than any other. You couldn't forget her, and your disappointment at finding out she had married was enormous. Several times Alberto had gone to restaurants with the two of you, and observed that she liked to vary the menu but that for dessert she always ordered caramel pudding. I think he was right to insist—in the face of my skepticism—that this dessert, humble in the eyes of most, must have acquired for you an emotional charge of the most explosive sort. When I gave him the complete report on the four days spent in the cottage, I conceded that the caramel pudding had been a more conclusive factor than the dress, the wine, or my gum to attract you to the kitchen when it was time for after-dinner coffee—in an acutely indiscreet state that would normally have constrained any well-bred person. But then, it would be inaccurate to say that Alberto and my preparations were inspired exclusively by the direct observation of life. We read and studied a great deal, especially Alberto, who single-handedly took on the foreign-language texts, an area in which I was never very strong except for Spanish and French. The erotic books taught us that a meal accompanied by fine wines is stimulating, but that repetition of such a repast is counterproductive. A large part of this reading was useless, since most of the material was devoted only to imparting the prolongation of stimuli to the limit of tolerance, refinements which had no practical use for our ends. As for us, we were always frugal with sex. Since our objective regarding you was simple, the innocent observation of nature sufficed, and it was in this area that I made my modest contribution. I am the granddaughter and daughter of farming people, and I spent my childhood in the midst of horses and cattle. I was amazed to read, in the Spanish translation of a Scandinavian book, the illustrated description of a method very much like the manipulations to which stallions are submitted to increase their breeding capacity while shortening the time required for their function."

This time Helena paused slightly longer. Her voice had become hoarse. She moved closer to be able to speak more softly. Her eyes had changed; they were not merely directed toward me, but were scrutinizing me closely, completely attentive to my presence.

"Alberto was terribly worried about your health. Certain passages from a letter in which you scoffed at the French doctors gave rise to his suspicion that you had contracted some venereal disease in Paris. But it wasn't only that which led him to subject you to so many examinations. From our own experience with doctors, we had learned that the proportion of sterile men is much higher than is commonly supposed. It was absolutely necessary that we be certain of your reproductive capacity, without which all our patient effort would have been useless and, worse, ridiculous. Once your virility was established, the days planned for our time together were chosen with precision. The only thing Alberto couldn't manage to remember was the rhythm of my menstrual flux. He underlined my dates on a small calendar that he consulted, slightly embarrassed, when he fixed the date on which we would meet in Compos do Jordão. He relaxed only when you reminded him that you would be celebrating your birthday with us. In spite of all our planning, we feared the intervention of some unforeseeable factor, and for this reason it was decided that when you and I parted, the possibility of further encounters would not be discouraged. We considered the possibility of having me look you up again—several times if necessary. It wasn't. Our son was born at normal term, exactly nine months, day for day, hour for hour, from the time you left the cottage. I am sure that if you had left one day earlier, the whole thing would have had to be done over. Starting from the instant that my pregnancy was confirmed, we never again mentioned your name. What's more, I know that during fifteen years he never even thought about you, which led me to believe in this strange theory of his quota of loved ones being limited to two. Yet the devotion and love with which he inundated my son's life and mine had such volume and force that it alone would have accelerated the transformation of the world, given the unthinkable hypothesis of one's being able to participate therein. As for myself, before we met I knew you exclusively through Alberto, a knowledge that had never had a visual reference. We had no pictures of you in our home, and to go forward with the task I had undertaken, it was essential that I not look at you. For the first few minutes, I had to watch myself, but afterward not seeing you became automatic. In bed, the darkness facilitated things, but I had other motives for choosing the dark. To kiss you without seeing you would be easier than an hour and a half spent avoiding your face over dinner, although I managed to do that on the first evening. If there were a technical necessity—say, if you had fallen into the category of the obsessive visual erotics classified by Kerner (an improbability according to my husband)—I would have turned on the lights in order to expose my nudity as long and as often as necessary. My sense of shame would not have been offended, since it had gone off with Alberto and only returned after you left. If I arranged the darkness, it was because I didn't feel I had the right to hide the small statues of Our Lord and the saints that always accompany me. At the same time, I couldn't tolerate their seeing or being seen by the stranger at my side. They had no part in all that; I always kept God rigorously out of the scheme, even to the point that during those days, I never once stopped saying my prayers. But I never asked for divine help to get pregnant. In short, because I didn't see you, you remained unknown to me in form, even in flesh, since I was always too busy concentrating on my work to feel your weight or penetration. You were an easily forgotten abstraction. I probably felt an unconscious need to blot you out completely. Later, when memory brought things back one by one, Alberto and I decided that if your death had indeed occurred, confirming your total disappearance, there might have been hope for us. He abandoned this idea at once, but I did not. In my mature years, I stopped agreeing unconditionally with all my husband's views, though I never failed to recognize his overwhelming superiority. We leaned in different directions according to the shadings of our temperaments, my husband's proud and self-castigating, mine much quieter. In our happy years, the result of this difference was to fuse us together in the joy of being parents. I would not know how to describe the happiness the child brought us. And it would be cruel to speak of it. From babyhood our child was an exact replica of all Alberto's good qualities, added to which he had a wonderful disposition, toward everyone and everything with which my poor husband never got acquainted. As an adolescent, he was talent and virtue incarnate—a beautiful young man. The darkening of Alberto's nature dates from this time. His face took on a look of diffuse apprehension and soon acquired the contours of premature old age. Since it was always he who took command of our conversations, I waited quietly, always fearing that he would actually reveal what was on his mind. His changed humor began to create crises, always heralded by his behavior at the table; he would stare fixedly at the boy to the point of embarrassing him.

Afterward, Alberto would get up in silence and spend hours in the library writing numbers or—what was worse—locking himself in the bedroom to cry. Our son possessed the somewhat ambiguous gracefulness that comes with puberty and, remembering our old readings about sex, I asked myself if what was bothering Alberto could be the fear that the boy was a homosexual. But the boy, whom I still regarded as a child, soon found a girl friend and began a relationship in keeping with the pattern of today's young people. Still Alberto remained tense and silent. As time went on, the boy spent less and less time at home. The university, the girl, his job, his numerous friends, a great many commitments that I knew nothing about, and finally the apartment that he rented with his girl friend, all prevented our seeing him often. He would have dinner with us on the occasions of his and our birthdays. I didn't complain, understanding how painful it must be for a young man like him to witness his father's inexplicable suffering. It was with the greatest dismay that I would examine the wastebasket, full of wadded-up pages: numbers, nothing but numbers arranged in the most varied compositions and accompanied by the plus or minus sign; devoid, however, of any arithmetic function. The calculations were of a sort that was beyond me. He read imported books with an obsession; they too were inaccessible to me due to their language and style. Although my preoccupation grew I never thought of forcing him to see a doctor, because I knew my husband was not mad. But he gave that impression, principally at our son's birthday parties and to such an extent that I thought about canceling these dinners. It was not necessary. On the day that he was twenty-five years old, the boy and his fiancée did not appear at the dinner that I had prepared with special attention and sadness, resolved as I was that it would be the last one. The approach of this birthday had brought on a stronger than usual crisis in Alberto: he withdrew into total silence, not even touching the meals that I took to him in bed. His going down to dinner was out of the question, which relieved me considerably. On this unfortunate night I went up to our bedroom to get ready, wanting to present an agreeable appearance to the young people. I was happy to hear Alberto's voice, although he spoke in a tone of panic. He said that *if* our son should arrive, he wanted to be told, but he didn't wish to see him that night; he should come back the next day. I wondered what this "if" might mean, and thought about it again when, much later, I was dining alone at the nearly untouched flower-adorned table. At a certain moment I perceived that Alberto had gotten up and was listening, panting, to the silence of the house. A few minutes later, I heard strange sounds and I ran to the bedroom where I found him with his eyes popping out of his head, in a state that appeared to be one of agony. During the following weeks I thought only of Alberto's survival and I did only one thing—fight for his life. The doctors could not diagnose his illness, and did nothing more than skeptically write prescriptions for trivial medicines. If he didn't die, it was because I didn't let him, and also because he didn't want to leave me. As soon as he grew better, I went to my son's apartment in Vila Buarque but the doorkeeper only knew that the young couple had moved some time before. I tried to find out more from the man, telling him who I was, that the father of the young man was very ill, and that I needed to inform him. Could he tell me of some neighbor or friend? I had to find out his new address. The man, who came from the Northeast, merely shrugged his shoulders; he could tell me nothing more. I returned home beside myself, but Alberto, who was emerging little by little from his fatigue and silence, asked me nothing. Now his convalescence was unexpectedly quick. He gained new energy and soon began to go out daily, on trips the purpose of which I never knew. He also started to worry a lot about me again, trying to calm me with respect to our son's disappearance. Then one day he told me that the boy had been arrested but added that I should not worry excessively, the arrest of young people had become commonplace. Yes, he had already taken certain actions; one must stay calm. Finally, with infinite caution, he told me that our son had died—on his birthday. It was Alberto's turn to take care of me and not allow me to die. His battle was far harder, because I had no scruples about dying and leaving him alone. When I had once again been restored to the world (though I was victimized by attacks of arthritis so painful that they actually diverted my thoughts) Alberto resumed his travels, sometimes spending months away from home. I'm certain he found out about everything, absolutely everything and, in keeping with his character, was only satisfied when he exhausted all the possible sources of information. I learned only that my son had been arrested under a false name— which I was never told—and that a few days later he died in prison. I never allowed myself to know more, and even during his most violent ravings, Alberto always respected my ignorance. On the two or three occasions such as last night when, already skirting delirium, he came close to forgetting himself, the touch of my hand was enough to make him stop. As I have never allowed myself any exercise of the imagination, I shall go to my grave knowing only that my son was arrested and that he died on the day he turned twenty-five. I made an exception in the case of his fiancée and asked questions. I learned that she also had been arrested and had lost her mind. One of her grandfathers is rich and she is now hospitalized in Switzerland, probably for the rest of her life, which I pray to God will be short. Alberto completed his mission and returned home; since then he has left only twice a year to accompany me here. Lately he has been attending the earliest mass of the day in the Perdizes parish. He has never again opened a book; he reads only inside himself, collecting material for his ceaseless reflections—he has never been so talkative. Before the tragedy he already considered himself to blame for everything, and he has not wavered from this fundamental belief. He arrived at it by elaborating in succession various theses which, removing the variations and combinations, can be reduced to two; one, already imagined before our son's death, and the other, which he definitively embraced. They boil down to the same thing: he committed a crime and his punishment was the death of the boy. What distinguishes one thesis from the other is the nature of the crime. The starting point was the old idea of the quota of people he had a right to love in this world, with the cipher two implacably present. He had gotten this notion from numerology, a science which, as usual, he later studied exhaustively. This worry, which as you know had such importance for us at the time we decided to provide ourselves with a child, disappeared during our son's first years and youth. Today I ask myself if what unleased Alberto's imagination wasn't an eventual resemblance he saw between our son and you. I have no way of knowing if the man I went to bed with in Campos do Jordão but never saw was like my son. These last two days I've been scrutinizing you, trying to figure out if my son, when he grew older, would have resembled you. But this is an absurd effort because he'll always be twenty-five years old until the moment of his second and final death, when Alberto and I leave this world. The part played by the figure twenty-five in the drama was decisive. In numerology, the combination between the two and the five can be fatal, and when Alberto remembered that you turned twenty-five on the exact day you made me pregnant, he never again stopped his research and calculations in the hope of seeing the invariably ill-fated omens annulled by some error. The coincidence of dates and ages, too incredible to be mere coincidence, strengthened Alberto's theory in my view. From then on, it wasn't hard to convince me that the crime denounced by my husband's numerological science had been committed above all against you. Alberto did not have the right to displace you, nor me for that matter, in his affection. We were irremovable and his love for us untransferable. Any disobedience whatsoever would directly violate the Great Law, which had marked and warned him with the one incontrovertible sign: sterility. Believing that he had the right to substitute another person as long as he respected the prescribed quota, Alberto cheated, with the added offense of designating to the person unfairly eliminated—you—the job of sowing the seed for the substitution itself. He trespassed even deeper into the forbidden zone. Through some sign I was unaware of, he became alarmed at the crime he had committed and thought about putting you back into the position you formerly occupied. But it was too late. The substitute—our son—was about to be born and, lost in the hellish maze, my poor and intrepid husband wished that through my death the quota to which he had the right would be filled by our son and you. Later, delirious with the hope that somehow the alchemy of life might be duped, he ardently hoped that you had died, so that the trinity composed of himself, our son, and me might not be altered. This notion led Alberto to abandon the first thesis that I not only accepted, but to which I remain faithful in spite of his persuasive dialectic and the chidings of my confessor. It was the first time my husband did not manage to break down my train of reasoning. This failure confirms his merit and ability as a teacher, for it seems to me almost miraculous that I should have been able to confront him, my own mediocrity being what it is. With the priest I had less trouble maintaining my position, since once I discovered I could not make him understand the duplicity of the universe, I kept his sphere of knowledge separate from my husband's. At any rate, it was the idea of trinity that led Alberto to adopt the position that he today defends. He sought to probe the nature of the contradiction between the three and the two. The possibility of a fusion between the three and the one seemed transparent to him. On the rare occasions that he attempted to find analogous terms for the Unrevealed Truth, he concluded with his usual optimism that there should be no reasons for its contradicting the Revealed Truth. If the three and the one attract each other irresistibly, the reciprocal revulsion between the two and the three is also uncontrollable. When he completed the deeper theoretical study of the problem, he believed he had found the key to the understanding of his destiny. He had erroneously interpreted the number two as his quota by ascribing to himself the faculty of loving and being loved by up to two people. In reality, he had the right to only one, since his pride—or more precisely his self-love—had already filled half of his quota from the start. It is not up to me to argue with him about this last idea, which offers no loophole. If I resist him it is because I am moved to tears by the overwhelming and fragile humanity Alberto emits, his heroically humane willingness not only to assume all the blame of the world but also, always, to restrict his own rights to life, defense, and protest. The conviction to which he has come has the merit, aside from all the others, of promoting the gradual pacification of his spirit. You and our son having been sacrificed, leaving only him and me, he now knows that I did not constitute still one more ponderous threat to the universal equilibrium. His rebelliousness has almost dissipated, and yesterday's episode was an exception that will not be repeated. It was caused by the impact of meeting you, a happening filled with potential consequences that we must not risk. If the reciprocal love between Alberto and you should be reborn, everything will start over again. Yesterday's meeting was the last one. My twenty-five days' cure has only begun, and Águas de São Pedro is too small for the three of us. I insist that you leave today. I want to make it clear that Alberto and I do not expect you to condemn or to absolve us, for you will understand that you have neither the authority nor the ability to judge. In order to protect us from any possible trick of fate that might take advantage of Alberto's fragile humanity, I shall say that you did not respect the gravity of the situation, that you mocked us for being two dithering lunatics. I must now hurry back to him; in these last few years I have never left him alone for so long a time. I realize that there are only two people in the world who deserve this sacrifice: the insane fiancée and yourself. Farewell."

Stunned by astonishment and emotion, I did not notice that Helena had left me. When I found myself alone on the bench, surrounded by dwarfs, I ran at once toward my hotel, crossing through the center of the lawn to gain time. The hillside there is steeper than near the driveway; I arrived at the front desk too breathless to talk and had to catch my breath before announcing that I was leaving and wanted my bill. The receptionist looked at me with surprise, without understanding what I was trying to say. I realized that in the last few hours I had misplaced the habit of speech, and I needed to concentrate for the words to resume their customary function.

As I drove back to São Paulo, the roads clear at that hour of the night, the amount of attention needed to drive the car did not interfere with the course of my thoughts. I at once abandoned the picture in my head of Helena's pathetic face and the tragic figure of the professor to fix instead upon the son that I had gained and lost in so short a time. The skeletal outline of his existence—birth, studies, love, battle, death, and martyrdom—threw an immense emptiness over me that only his memory could fill. The idea made me go back to the other interpreters of our drama. When I say "our" I am conscious of my pretentiousness, since I was hardly more than an extra. But I decided to prolong my part, since I could not commit the memory of my son to the custody of three insane people: one locked up in Switzerland, the other two calmly completing the cycle of their madness here in São Paulo. I decided to ask my son to save and enrich me, and thus I am prepared to do anything, even to seeing Helena and the professor again. As this isn't possible, I need to take maximum advantage of the weeks they will be staying in Águas de São Pedro.

Upon arriving home, I spent the rest of the night thinking about the situation and writing this narrative, which will be my defense if I'm caught housebreaking in Pacaembu. I am going there now, this morning, the twenty-fifth day of the month, on which I am completing my fiftieth year and commemorating for the first time the date of my son's conception and death. Barring some unforeseen event, I will not come back without at least a picture of him and some books I need to study. This accumulation of birthdays, the day of the month which I only now have noticed, and which multiplied by two equals the number of years I've lived, all of this tends to increase the agitation that has taken hold of the very depths of my being but will not impede my leaving for Pacaembu in two minutes, three at the most. To get there from Alto dos Pinheiros should take me twenty-five minutes. The possibility of recognizing and eventually being recognized by Helena's holy images is a matter of indifference to me.

To this document I sign my whole name instead of just the initial "P" that I customarily put before my surname. I am in fact called Polydoro, a favorable combination of five consonants and three vowels (whose relationship the new orthography alters), a clownish name given me in honor of an illustrious great-grandfather, a name that doomed my aspirations to harmony and elegance in a cruel and arbitrary world, the secret logic of which I have been ignorant of until today in spite of the rare opportunity afforded me: to know the great professor.

Translated by Margaret A. Neves

FOUR

Carlos Fuentes
(1928–   )

The Mexican Carlos Fuentes (actually born in Panama) spent his childhood in various capitals of Europe and Latin America where his father was posted as a diplomat. He attended school in Washington, D.C., during the late thirties and Santiago, Chile, in the early forties, where one of his classmates was José Donoso. Fuentes went on to complete a law degree in Switzerland. In the fifties he was back in Mexico, heading the department of cultural affairs at the ministry of foreign affairs.

He began his writing career in both fiction and journalism. His first work of fiction appeared in 1954, a Kafkaesque collection of short stories that focused fictionally on certain questions of Mexican identity also raised by Octavio Paz in his seminal essay *The Labyrinth of Solitude* (1950). Four years later Fuentes published his first novel, *Where the Air Is Clear* (1958), which through a variety of Modernist and cinematic techniques reaches back into Mexico's violent pre-Columbian, colonial, and revolutionary past. The result is an apocalyptic fresco of a Janus-like Mexico City of the fifties with one face glaring at an evidently ruinous modernity and the "other" face masking an equally dangerous, undeciphered past. In his next important novel, *The Death of Artemio Cruz* (1962), the focus is narrower, more subterranean, as the "spoils" of the Mexican revolution are mined from the fragmented consciousness of a dying victor. That same year Fuentes published a haunting tribute to Henry James in the form of a poisonous jewel of a novella entitled *Aura*, in which the specter of a repressed sexuality is Aztec rather than Victorian.

In 1963, he visited Eastern Europe, lived in Rome for a time, then settled in Paris as Mexico's ambassador to France. Fuentes has since held distinguished lectureships (Cambridge, Princeton), contributed to a wide range of European and North American newspapers, and collaborated in numerous educational television programs on the subject of Latin America. Some of his early stories have been collected in English translation in *Burnt Water*. His other translated novels include *The Good Conscience* (1959), *Holy Place* (1967), *A Change of Skin* (1968), *Terra Nostra* (1975), *Hydra Head* (1978), *Distant Relations* (1981), *The Old Gringo* (1985), and *Christopher Unborn* (1988). A new collection of short fiction, *Constancia and Other Stories for Virgins*, appeared in 1989.

The Doll Queen

To María Pilar and José Donoso

I

I went because that card—such a strange card—reminded me of her existence. I found it in a forgotten book whose pages had revived the specter of a childish calligraphy. For the first time in a long while I was rearranging my books. I met surprise after surprise, since some, placed on the highest shelves, had not been read for a long time. So long a time that the edges of the leaves were grainy, and a mixture of gold dust and grayish scale fell on my open palm, reminiscent of the lacquer covering certain bodies glimpsed first in dreams and later in the deceptive reality of the first ballet performance to which we're taken. It was a book from my childhood—perhaps from the childhood of many children— that related a series of more or less truculent exemplary tales which had the virtue of precipitating us onto our elders' knees to ask them, over and over again: Why? Children who are ungrateful to their parents; maidens kidnapped by splendid horsemen and re- turned home in shame—as well as those who happily abandon hearth and home; old men who in exchange for an overdue mort- gage demand the hand of the sweetest, most long-suffering daugh- ter of the threatened family . . . Why? I do not recall their answers. I only know that from among the stained pages came fluttering a white card in Amilamia's atrocious hand: *Amilamia wil not forget her good friend—com see me here wher I draw it.*

And on the other side was that sketch of a path starting from an X that indicated, doubtlessly, the park bench where I, an adolescent rebelling against prescribed and tedious education, forgot my classroom schedule to spend some hours reading books which, if not in fact written by me, seemed to be: who could doubt that only from my imagination could spring all those corsairs, those couriers of the tsar, those boys slightly younger than I who floated all day down a great American river on a raft. Clutching the side of the park bench as if it were the bow of a magic saddle, at first I didn't hear the sound of the light steps that stopped behind me after running down the graveled garden path. It was Amilamia, and I don't know how long the child would have kept me company in silence had not her mischievous spirit one afternoon chosen to tickle my ear with down from a dandelion she blew toward me, her lips puffed out and her brow furrowed in a frown.

She asked my name, and after considering it very seriously, she told me hers with a smile which, if not candid, was not too rehearsed. Quickly I realized that Amilamia had discovered, if discovered is the word, a form of expression midway between the ingenuousness of her years and the forms of adult mimicry that well-brought-up children have to know, particularly for the solemn moments of introduction and of leave-taking. Amilamia's seriousness was, rather, a gift of nature, whereas her moments of spontaneity, by contrast, seemed artificial. I like to remember her, afternoon after afternoon, in a succession of images that in their totality sum up the complete Amilamia. And it never ceases to surprise me that I cannot think of her as she really was, or remember how she actually moved—light, questioning, constantly looking around her. I must remember her fixed forever in time, as in a photograph album. Amilamia in the distance, a point at the spot where the hill began its descent from a lake of clover toward the flat meadow where I, sitting on the bench, used to read: a point of fluctuating shadow and sunshine and a hand that waved to me from high on the hill. Amilamia frozen in her flight down the hill, her white skirt ballooning, the flowered panties gathered on her legs with elastic, her mouth open and eyes half closed against the streaming air, the child crying with pleasure. Amilamia sitting beneath the eucalyptus trees, pretending to cry so that I would go over to her. Amilamia lying on her stomach with a flower in her hand: the petals of a flower which I discovered later didn't grow in this garden but somewhere else, perhaps in the garden of Amilamia's house, since the pocket of her blue-checked apron was often filled with those white blossoms. Amilamia watching me read, holding with both hands to the slats of the green bench, asking

questions with her gray eyes: I recall that she never asked me what
I was reading, as if she could divine in my eyes the images born of
the pages. Amilamia laughing with pleasure when I lifted her by
the waist and whirled her around my head; she seemed to discover
a new perspective on the world in that slow flight. Amilamia turning her back to me and waving goodbye, her arm held high, the
fingers moving excitedly. And Amilamia in the thousand postures
she affected around my bench, hanging upside down, her bloom-
ers billowing; sitting on the gravel with her legs crossed and her
chin resting on her fist; lying on the grass, baring her belly button
to the sun; weaving tree branches, drawing animals in the mud
with a twig, licking the slats of the bench, hiding under the seat,
breaking off the loose bark from the ancient tree trunks, staring
at the horizon beyond the hill, humming with her eyes closed,
imitating the voices of birds, dogs, cats, hens, horses. All for me,
and yet nothing. It was her way of being with me, all these things
I remember, but also her way of being alone in the park. Yes,
perhaps my memory of her is fragmentary because reading alternated with my contemplation of the chubby-cheeked child with
smooth hair that changed in the reflection of the light: now wheat-
colored, now burnt chestnut. And it is only today that I think how
Amilamia in that moment established the other point of support
for my life, the one that created the tension between my own ir-
resolute childhood and the wide world, the promised land that was
beginning to be mine through my reading.

Not then. Then I dreamed about the women in my books, about
the quintessential female—the word disturbed me—who assumed
the disguise of Queen to buy the necklace in secret, about the
imagined beings of mythology—half recognizable, half white-
breasted, damp-bellied salamanders—who awaited monarchs in
their beds. And thus, imperceptibly, I moved from indifference
toward my childish companion to an acceptance of the child's grace
and seriousness and from there to an unexpected rejection of a
presence that became useless to me. She irritated me, finally. I who
was fourteen was irritated by that child of seven who was not yet
memory or nostalgia, but rather the past and its reality. I had let
myself be dragged along by weakness. We had run together, holding hands, across the meadow. Together we had shaken the pines
and picked up the cones that Amilamia guarded jealously in her
apron pocket. Together we had constructed paper boats and followed them, happy and gay, to the edge of the drain. And that
afternoon, amid shouts of glee, when we tumbled together down

the hill and rolled to a stop at its foot, Amilamia was on my chest, her hair between my lips; but when I felt her panting breath in my ear and her little arms sticky from sweets around my neck, I angrily pushed away her arms and let her fall. Amilamia cried, rubbing her wounded elbow and knee, and I returned to my bench. Then Amilamia went away and the following day she returned, handed me the card without a word, and disappeared, humming, into the woods. I hesitated whether to tear up the card or keep it in the pages of the book: *Afternoons on the Farm.* Even my reading had become infantile because of Amilamia. She did not return to the park. After a few days I left on my vacation, and when I returned it was to the duties of the first year of prep school. I never saw her again.

II

And now, almost rejecting the image that is unfamiliar without being fantastic, but is all the more painful for being so real, I return to that forgotten park and stopping before the grove of pines and eucalyptus I recognize the smallness of the bosky enclo-sure that my memory has insisted on drawing with an amplitude that allows sufficient space for the vast swell of my imagination. After all, Michel Strogoff and Huckleberry Finn, Milady de Winter and Geneviève de Brabant were born, lived, and died here: in a little garden surrounded by mossy iron railings, sparsely planted with old, neglected trees, scarcely adorned by a concrete bench painted to look like wood which forces me to think that my beau-tiful wrought-iron green bench never existed, or was part of my ordered, retrospective delirium. And the hill ... How believe the promontory Amilamia ascended and descended in her daily com-ing and going, that steep slope we rolled down together, was *this*. A barely elevated patch of dark stubble with no more height and depth than what my memory had created.

Com see me here wher I draw it. So I would have to cross the gar-den, leave the woods behind, descend the hill in three loping steps, cut through that narrow grove of chestnuts—it was here, surely, where the child gathered the white petals—open the squeaking park gate and instantly recall ... know ... find oneself in the street, realize that every afternoon of one's adolescence, as if by a miracle, one had succeeded in suspending the beat of the surrounding city, annulling that flood tide of whistles, bells, voices, sobs, engines, radios, imprecations. Which was the true magnet, the silent garden or the feverish city?

I wait for the light to change, and cross to the other side, my eyes never leaving the red iris detaining the traffic. I consult Amilamia's card. After all, that rudimentary map is the true magnet of the moment I am living, and just thinking about it disturbs me. I was obliged, after the lost afternoons of my fourteenth year, to follow the channels of discipline; now I find myself, at twenty-nine, duly certified with a diploma, owner of an office, assured of a moderate income, a bachelor still, with no family to maintain, slightly bored with sleeping with secretaries, scarcely excited by an occasional outing to the country or to the beach, feeling the lack of a central attraction such as my books, my park, and Amilamia once afforded me. I walk down the street of this gray suburb. The one-story houses, doorways peeling paint, succeed each other monotonously. Faint neighborhood sounds barely interrupt the general uniformity: the squeal of a knife sharpener here, the hammering of a shoe repairman there. The neighborhood children are playing in the dead-end streets. The music of an organ grinder reaches my ears, mingled with the voices of children's rounds. I stop a moment to watch them, with the sensation, as fleeting, that Amilamia must be among these groups of children, immodestly exhibiting her flowered panties, hanging by her knees from some balcony, still fond of acrobatic excesses, her apron pocket filled with white petals. I smile, and for the first time I am able to imagine the young lady of twenty-two who, even if she still lives at this address, will laugh at my memories, or who perhaps will have forgotten the afternoons spent in the garden.

The house is identical to all the rest. The heavy entry door, two grilled windows with closed shutters. A one-story house, topped by a false neoclassic balustrade that probably conceals the practicalities of the roof terrace: clothes hanging on a line, tubs of water, servants' quarters, a chicken coop. Before I ring the bell, I want to rid myself of any illusion. Amilamia no longer lives here. Why would she stay fifteen years in the same house? Besides, in spite of her precocious independence and aloneness, she seemed to be a well-brought-up, well-behaved child, and this neighborhood is no longer elegant; Amilamia's parents, without doubt, have moved. But perhaps the new tenants will know where.

I press the bell and wait. I ring again. Here is another contingency: no one is home. And will I feel the need to look again for my childhood friend? No. Because it will not happen a second time

that I open a book from my adolescence and find Amilamia's card.
I'll return to my routine, I'll forget the moment whose importance
lay in its fleeting surprise.

I ring once more. I press my ear to the door and am startled: I
can hear harsh, irregular breathing on the other side; the sound
of labored breathing, accompanied by the disagreeable odor of
stale tobacco, filters through the cracks in the door.

"Good afternoon. Could you tell me . . . ?"

When he hears my voice, the person moves away with heavy and
unsure steps. I press the bell again, shouting this time: "Hey! Open
up! What's the matter? Don't you hear me?"

No response. I continue to ring, with no result. I move back from
the door, still staring at the tiny cracks, as if distance might give
me perspective, or even penetration. With my attention fixed on
that damned door, I cross the street, walking backward. A piercing
scream, followed by a prolonged and ferocious blast of a whistle,
saves me in time. Dazed, I seek the person whose voice has just
saved me. I see only the automobile moving down the street and I
hang on to a lamppost, a hold that more than security offers me
support as icy blood rushes through my burning, sweaty skin. I
look toward the house that had been, that was, that must be, Amilamia's. There, behind the balustrade, as I had known there would
be, are fluttering clothes hung out to dry. I don't know what else
is hanging there—skirts, pajamas, blouses—I don't know. All I see
is that starched little blue-checked apron, clamped by clothespins
to the long cord swinging between an iron bar and a nail in the
white wall of the terrace.

III

In the Bureau of Records I have been told that the property is
in the name of a Señor R. Valdivia, who rents the house. To whom?
That they don't know. Who is Valdivia? He is down as a businessman. Where does he live? Who are *you?* the young woman asked
me with haughty curiosity. I haven't been able to show myself calm
and assured. Sleep has not relieved my nervous fatigue. Valdivia.
As I leave the Bureau, the sun offends me. I associate the aversion
provoked by the hazy sun sifting through the clouds—thus all the
more intense—with a desire to return to the humid, shaded park.
No. It is only a desire to know if Amilamia lives in that house and
why they won't let me enter. But what I must reject is the absurd

idea that kept me awake all night. Having seen the apron drying on the flat roof, the apron in which she kept the flowers, I had begun to believe that in that house lived a seven-year-old girl I had known fourteen or fifteen years before ... She must have a little girl! Yes. Amilamia, at twenty-two, is the mother of a girl who perhaps dresses the same, looks the same, repeats the same games, and—who knows—maybe even goes to the same park. And deep in thought, I arrive once more at the door of the house. I ring the bell and wait for the labored breathing on the other side of the door. I am mistaken. The door is opened by a woman who can't be more than fifty. But wrapped in a shawl, dressed in black and in flat black shoes, with no makeup and her salt-and-pepper hair pulled into a knot, she seems to have abandoned all illusion or pretense of youth. She observes me with eyes so indifferent they seem almost cruel.

"You want something?"

"Señor Valdivia sent me." I cough and run my hand over my hair. I should have picked up my briefcase at the office. I realize that without it I cannot play my role very well.

"Valdivia?" the woman asks without alarm, without interest.

"Yes. The owner of this house."

One thing is clear. The woman will reveal nothing by her face. She looks at me, impassive.

"Oh, yes. The owner of the house."

"May I come in?"

In bad comedies, I think, the traveling salesman sticks a foot in the door so they can't close the door in his face. I do the same, but the woman steps back and with a gesture of her hand invites me to come into what must have been a garage. On one side there is a glass-paneled door, its paint faded. I walk toward the door over the yellow tiles of the entryway and ask again, turning toward the woman, who follows me with tiny steps: "This way?"

I notice for the first time that in her pale hands she carries a chaplet, which she toys with ceaselessly. I haven't seen one of those old-fashioned rosaries since my childhood and I want to say something about it, but the brusque, decisive manner with which the woman opens the door precludes any gratuitous conversation. We enter a long, narrow room. The woman quickly opens the shutters. But because of four large perennials growing in glass-encrusted porcelain pots the room remains in shadow. The only other objects in the room are an old high-backed cane sofa and a rocking chair.

But it is neither the plants nor the sparseness of the furniture that holds my attention.

The woman asks me to sit on the sofa before she sits down in the rocking chair. Beside me, on the cane arm of the sofa, there is an open magazine.

"Señor Valdivia sends his apologies for not having come himself."

The woman rocks, unblinking. I peer at the comic book out of the corner of my eye.

"He sends greetings and . . ."

I stop, waiting for a reaction from the woman. She continues to rock. The magazine is covered with red scribbles.

". . . and asks me to inform you that he must disturb you for a few days . . ."

My eyes search the room rapidly.

". . . A reassessment of the house must be made for tax purposes. It seems it hasn't been done for . . . You have been living here since . . . ?"

Yes. That is a stubby lipstick lying under the chair. If the woman smiles, it is while the slow-moving hands caress the chaplet. I sense, for an instant, a swift flash of ridicule that does not quite disturb her features. She still does not answer.

". . . for at least fifteen years, isn't that so?"

She does not agree. She does not disagree. And on the pale thin lips there is not the least trace of lipstick . . .

". . . you, your husband, and . . . ?"

She stares at me, never changing expression, almost daring me to continue. We sit a moment in silence, she playing with the rosary, I leaning forward, my hands on my knees. I rise.

"Well then, I'll be back this afternoon with the papers . . ."

The woman nods and in silence picks up the lipstick and the comic book and hides them in the folds of her shawl.

IV

The scene has not changed. This afternoon, as I write sham figures in my notebook and feign interest in determining the value of the dull floorboards and the length of the living room, the woman rocks, the three decades of the chaplet whispering through her fingers. I sigh as I finish the supposed inventory of the living room and ask for permission to see the rest of the house. The woman rises, bracing her long black-clad arms on the seat of the rocking chair and adjusting the shawl on her narrow, bony shoulders.

She opens the frosted-glass door and we enter a dining room with very little additional furniture. But the aluminum-legged table and the four aluminum-and-plastic chairs lack even the hint of distinction of the living-room furniture. The other window, with wrought-iron grill and closed shutters, must sometime illuminate this bare-walled dining room, devoid of either shelves or sideboards. The only object on the table is a plastic fruit dish with a cluster of black grapes, two peaches, and a buzzing corona of flies. The woman, her arms crossed, her face expressionless, stops behind me. I take the risk of breaking the order of things: clearly, these rooms will not tell me anything I really want to know.

"Couldn't we go up to the roof?" I ask. "That might be the best way to measure the total area."

The woman's eyes light up as she looks at me, or perhaps it is only the contrast with the shadows of the dining room.

"What for?" she says at last. "Señor ... Valdivia ... knows the dimensions very well."

And those pauses, before and after the owner's name, are the first indication that something has at last begun to trouble the woman, forcing her, in self-defense, to resort to a kind of irony.

"I don't know." I make an effort to smile. "Perhaps I prefer to go from top to bottom and not"—my false smile drains away—"from bottom to top."

"You will go the way I show you," the woman says, her arms crossed over her chest, a silver crucifix dangling over her dark belly.

Before smiling weakly, I force myself to realize that in these shadows my gestures are of no use, aren't even symbolic. I open the notebook with a creak of the cardboard cover and continue making notes with the greatest possible speed, never glancing up, taking down numbers and estimates for a job whose fiction—the light flush in my cheeks and the perceptible dryness of my tongue tell me—is deceiving no one. And as I cover the graph paper with absurd signs, with square roots and algebraic formulas, I ask myself what is keeping me from getting to the point, from asking about Amilamia and getting out of here with a satisfactory answer. Nothing. And yet I am certain, even if I obtained a response, I would not have the truth. My slim, silent companion is a person I wouldn't look at twice in the street, but in this almost uninhabited house with the coarse furniture, she ceases to be an anonymous face in the crowd and is converted into a stock character of mystery. Such is the paradox, and if memories of Amilamia have once again aroused my appetite for the imaginary, I shall follow the rules of the game, I shall exhaust appearances, and not rest until I have the answer—perhaps simple and clear-cut, immediate and obvious— that lies beyond the veils the señora of the rosary unexpectedly places in my path. Do I bestow a gratuitous strangeness on my reluctant hostess? If so, I'll only take greater pleasure in the labyrinths of my own invention. And the flies are still buzzing around the fruit dish, occasionally pausing on the damaged end of the peach, a nibbled bite—I lean closer, using the pretext of my notes— where little teeth have left their mark in the velvety skin and ocher flesh of the fruit. I do not look toward the señora. I pretend I am taking notes. The fruit seems to be bitten but not touched. I crouch down to see better, rest my hands on the table, move my lips closer as if wishing to repeat the act of biting without touching. I look down and see another sign near my feet: the track of two tires that seem to be bicycle tires, the print of two rubber tires that come as far as the edge of the table and then lead away, growing fainter, the length of the room, toward the señora . . .

I close my notebook.

"Let us go on, señora."

When I turn toward her, I find her standing with her hands resting on the back of a chair. Seated before her, coughing from the smoke of his black cigarette, is a man with heavy shoulders and hidden eyes: those eyes, scarcely visible behind swollen, wrinkled lids as thick and drooped as the neck of an ancient turtle, seem nevertheless to follow my every movement. The half-shaven cheeks, crisscrossed by a thousand gray furrows, sag from protruding cheekbones, and his greenish hands are folded under his arms. He is wearing a coarse blue shirt, and his rumpled hair is so curly it looks like the bottom of a barnacle-covered ship. He does not move, and the only sign of his existence is that difficult whistling breathing (as if every breath must breach a floodgate of phlegm, irritation, and abuse) I had already heard through the chinks of the door.

Ridiculously, he murmurs: "Good afternoon . . ." and I am disposed to forget everything: the mystery, Amilamia, the assessment, the bicycle tracks. The apparition of this asthmatic old bear justifies a prompt retreat. I repeat "Good afternoon," this time with an inflection of farewell. The turtle's mask dissolves into an atrocious smile: every pore of that flesh seems fabricated of brittle rubber, of painted, peeling oilcloth. The arm reaches out and detains me.

"Valdivia died four years ago," says the man in a distant, choking voice that issues from his belly instead of his larynx: a weak, high-pitched voice.

In the grip of that strong, almost painful, claw, I tell myself it is useless to pretend. But the waxen rubber faces observing me say nothing, and so I am able, in spite of everything, to pretend one more time, to pretend I am speaking to myself when I say: "Ami-lamia . . ."

Yes: no one will have to pretend any longer. The fist that clutches my arm affirms its strength for only an instant, immediately its grip loosens, then it falls, weak and trembling, before lifting to take the waxen hand touching his shoulder: the señora, perplexed for the first time, looks at me with the eyes of a violated bird and sobs with a dry moan that does not disturb the rigid astonishment of her features. Suddenly the ogres of my imagination are two solitary, abandoned, wounded old people, scarcely able to console themselves in this shuddering clasp of hands that fills me with shame. My fantasy has brought me to this stark dining room to violate the intimacy and the secret of two human beings exiled from life by something I no longer have the right to share. I have never despised myself more. Never have words failed me so clum-sily. Any gesture of mine would be in vain: shall I come closer, shall I touch them, shall I caress the woman's head, shall I ask them to excuse my intrusion? I return the notebook to my jacket pocket. I toss into oblivion all the clues in my detective story: the comic book, the lipstick, the nibbled fruit, the bicycle tracks, the blue-checked apron . . . I decide to leave the house without saying any-thing more. The old man, from behind his thick eyelids, must have noticed.

The high breathy voice says: "Did you know her?"

The past, so natural, used by them every day, finally shatters my illusions. There is the answer. Did you know her? How long? How long must the world have lived without Amilamia, assassinated first by my forgetfulness, and then revived, scarcely yesterday, by a sad impotent memory? When did those serious gray eyes cease to be astonished by the delight of an always solitary garden? When did those lips cease to pout or press together thinly in that ceremoni-ous seriousness with which, I now realize, Amilamia must have discovered and consecrated the objects and events of a life that, she perhaps knew intuitively, was fleeting?

"Yes, we played together in the park. A long time ago."

"How old was she?" says the old man, his voice even more muffled.

"She must have been about seven. No, older than that."

The woman's voice rises, as she lifts her arms, seemingly to implore: "What was she like, señor? Tell us what she was like, please."

I close my eyes. "Amilamia is a memory for me, too. I can only picture her through the things she touched, the things she brought, what she discovered in the park. Yes. Now I see her, coming down the hill. No. It isn't true that it was a scarcely elevated patch of stubble. It was a hill, with grass, and Amilamia's comings and goings had traced a path, and she waved to me from the top before she started down, accompanied by the music, yes, the music I saw, the painting I smelled, the tastes I heard, the odors I touched . . . my hallucination . . ." Do they hear me? "She came waving, dressed in white, in a blue-checked apron . . . the one you have hanging on the roof terrace . . ."

They take my arm and still I do not open my eyes.

"What was she like, señor?"

"Her eyes were gray and the color of her hair changed in the reflection of the sun and the shadow of the trees . . ."

They lead me gently, the two of them. I hear the man's labored breathing, the crucifix on the rosary hitting against the woman's body.

"Tell us, please . . ."

"The air brought tears to her eyes when she ran; when she reached my bench her cheeks were silvered with happy tears . . ."

I do not open my eyes. Now we are going upstairs. Two, five, eight, nine, twelve steps. Four hands guide my body.

"What was she like, what was she like?"

"She sat beneath the eucalyptus and wove garlands from the branches and pretended to cry so I would stop reading and go over to her . . ."

Hinges creak. The odor overpowers everything else: it routs the other senses, it takes its seat like a yellow Mongol upon the throne of my hallucination; heavy as a coffin, insinuating as the slither of draped silk, ornamented as a Turkish scepter, opaque as a deep, lost vein of ore, brilliant as a dead star. The hands no longer hold me. More than the sobbing, it is the trembling of the old people that envelops me. Slowly, I open my eyes: first through the dizzying liquid of my corneas, then through the web of my eyelashes, the room suffocated in that gigantic battle of perfumes is disclosed,

effluvia and frosty, almost fleshlike petals; the presence of the flowers is so strong here they seem to take on the quality of living
flesh—the sweetness of the jasmine, the nausea of the lilies, the
tomb of the tuberose, the temple of the gardenia. Illuminated
through the incandescent wax lips of heavy, sputtering candles, the
small windowless bedroom with its aura of wax and humid flowers
assaults the very center of my plexus, and from there, only there
at the solar center of life, am I able to come to, and perceive beyond the candles, amid the scattered flowers, the plethora of used
toys: the colored hoops and wrinkled balloons, cherries dried to
transparency, wooden horses with scraggly manes, the scooter,
blind hairless dolls, bears spilling their sawdust, punctured oilcloth
ducks, moth-eaten dogs, frayed jumping ropes, glass jars of dried
candy, worn-out shoes, the tricycle (three wheels? no, two, and not
a bicycle's—two parallel wheels below), little wool and leather
shoes; and, facing me, within reach of my hand, the small coffin
supported on blue crates decorated with paper flowers, flowers of
life this time, carnations and sunflowers, poppies and tulips, but
like the others, the ones of death, all part of a compilation created
by the atmosphere of this funeral hothouse in which reposes, inside the silvered coffin, between the black silk sheets, on the pillow
of white satin, that motionless and serene face framed in lace, high-
lighted with rose-colored tints, eyebrows traced by the lightest pencil, closed lids, real eyelashes, thick, that cast a tenuous shadow on
cheeks as healthy as in the park days. Serious red lips, set almost
in the angry pout that Amilamia feigned so I would come to play.
Hands joined over her breast. A chaplet, identical to the mother's
strangling that waxen neck. Small white shroud on the clean, pre-
pubescent, docile body.

The old people, sobbing, are kneeling.

I reach out my hand and run my fingers over the porcelain face
of my little friend. I feel the coldness of those painted features, of
the doll queen who presides over the pomp of this royal chamber
of death. Porcelain, wax, cotton. *Amilamia wil not forget her good
friend—com see me here wher I draw it.*

I withdraw my fingers from the sham cadaver. Traces of my fin-
gerprints remain where I touched the skin of the doll.

And nausea crawls in my stomach where the candle smoke and
the sweet stench of the lilies in the enclosed room have settled. I
turn my back on Amilamia's sepulcher. The woman's hand touches
my arm. Her wildly staring eyes bear no relation to the quiet, steady
voice.

"Don't come back, señor. If you truly loved her, don't come back again."

I touch the hand of Amilamia's mother. I see through nauseous eyes the old man's head buried between his knees, and I go out of the room and to the stairway, to the living room, to the patio, to the street.

V

If not a year, nine or ten months have passed. The memory of that idolatry no longer frightens me. I have forgotten the odor of the flowers and the image of the petrified doll. The real Amilamia has returned to my memory and I have felt, if not content, sane again: the park, the living child, my hours of adolescent reading, have triumphed over the specters of a sick cult. The image of life is the more powerful. I tell myself that I shall live forever with my real Amilamia, the conqueror of the caricature of death. And one day I dare look again at that notebook with graph paper in which I wrote down the data of the spurious assessment. And from its pages, once again, Amilamia's card falls out, with its terrible child-ish scrawl and its map for getting from the park to her house. I smile as I pick it up. I bite one of the edges, thinking that, in spite of everything, the poor old people might accept this gift.

Whistling, I put on my jacket and straighten my tie. Why not go see them and offer them this card with the child's own writing?

I am almost running as I approach the one-story house. Rain is beginning to fall in large isolated drops, bringing out of the earth with magical immediacy the odor of dewy benediction that stirs the humus and quickens all that lives with its roots in the dust.

I ring the bell. The rain gets heavier and I become insistent. A shrill voice shouts: "I'm coming!" and I wait for the mother with her eternal rosary to open the door for me. I turn up the collar of my jacket. My clothes, my body, too, smell different in the rain. The door opens.

"What do you want? How wonderful you've come!"

The misshapen girl sitting in the wheelchair places one hand on the doorknob and smiles at me with an indecipherable, wry grin. The hump on her chest makes the dress into a curtain over her body, a piece of white cloth that nonetheless lends an air of co-quetry to the blue-checked apron. The little woman extracts a pack of cigarettes from her apron pocket and quickly lights a cigarette, staining the end with orange-painted lips. The smoke causes the beautiful gray eyes to squint. She fixes her coppery, wheat-colored, permanent-waved hair, all the time staring at me with a desolate, inquisitive, hopeful—but at the same time fearful—expression.

"No, Carlos. Go away. Don't come back."

And from the house, at the same moment, I hear the high labored breathing of the old man, coming closer.

"Where are you? Don't you know you're not supposed to answer the door? Get back! Devil's spawn! Do I have to beat you again?"

And the rain trickles down my forehead, over my cheeks, and into my mouth, and the little frightened hands drop the comic book onto the wet paving stones.

Translated by Margaret Sayers Peden

Juan Rulfo
(1918–1986)

Juan Rulfo was born in a small Mexican village in the district of Sayula, a desolate land of wind, heat, and poverty in the western state of Jalisco. His characters are as timeworn as the land they inhabit, and when they are touched by the Mexican Revolution at all, it is as if by the obliterating god of some Greek tragedy.

Rulfo himself felt its wrath when his father was murdered in 1926, during the violent Cristeros revolt that pitted the Catholic Church against the Revolutionary state. His mother died when he was fourteen, whereupon he was sent by his relatives to an orphanage. In 1933, he moved to Mexico City, where he made his way by taking odd jobs while contributing to literary journals.

In the forties he wrote a novel that he subsequently destroyed. Then, in 1953, he published his only collection of stories, *The Burning Plain*, in which, together with a single novel, the haunting *Pedro Páramo* (1956), he achieved a lyrically dramatic concision unmatched in the modern Latin American narrative. Thereafter, he published only a few new stories and some television scripts, devoting his final years almost exclusively to his work as an archivist at the Indian Institute in Mexico City.

Luvina

Of the mountains in the south Luvina is the highest and the rock-iest. It's infested with that gray stone they make lime from, but in Luvina they don't make lime from it or get any good out of it. They call it crude stone there, and the hill that climbs up toward Luvina they call the Crude Stone Hill. The sun and the air have taken it on themselves to make it crumble away, so that the earth around there is always white and brilliant, as if it were always spar-kling with the morning dew, though this is just pure talk, because in Luvina the days are cold as the nights and the dew thickens in the sky before it can fall to the earth.

And the ground is steep and slashed on all sides by deep bar-rancas, so deep you can't make out the bottom. They say in Luvina that one's dreams come up from those barrancas; but the only thing I've seen come up out of them was the wind, whistling as if down below they had squeezed it into reed pipes. A wind that doesn't even let the dulcamaras grow: those sad little plants that can live with just a bit of earth, clutching with all their hands at the mountain cliffsides. Only once in a while, where there's a little shade, hidden among the rocks, the chicalote blossoms with its white poppies. But the chicalote soon withers. Then you hear it scratching the air with its spiny branches, making a noise like a knife on a whetstone.

"You'll be seeing that wind that blows over Luvina. It's dark. They say because it's full of volcano sand; anyway, it's a black air. You'll see it. It takes hold of things in Luvina as if it was going to bite them. And there are lots of days when it takes the roofs off

283

the houses as if they were hats, leaving the bare walls uncovered. Then it scratches like it had nails: you hear it morning and night, hour after hour without stopping, scraping the walls, tearing off strips of earth, digging with its sharp shovel under the doors, until you feel it boiling inside of you as if it was going to remove the hinges of your very bones. You'll see."

The man speaking was quiet for a bit, while he looked outside.

The noise of the river reached them, passing its swollen waters through the fig-tree branches, the noise of the air gently rustling the leaves of the almond trees, and the shouts of the children play-ing in the small space illumined by the light that came from the store.

The flying ants entered and collided with the oil lamp, falling to the ground with scorched wings. And outside night kept on advancing.

"Hey, Camilo, two more beers!" the man said again. Then he added, "There's another thing, mister. You'll never see a blue sky in Luvina. The whole horizon there is always a dingy color, always clouded over by a dark stain that never goes away. All the hills are bare and treeless, without one green thing to rest your eyes on; everything is wrapped in an ashy smog. You'll see what it's like— those hills silent as if they were dead and Luvina crowning the highest hill with its white houses like a crown of the dead—"

The children's shouts came closer until they penetrated the store. That made the man get up, go to the door and yell at them, "Go away! Don't bother us! Keep on playing, but without so much racket."

Then, coming back to the table, he sat down and said, "Well, as I was saying, it doesn't rain much there. In the middle of the year they get a few storms that whip the earth and tear it away, just leaving nothing but the rocks floating above the stony crust. It's good to see then how the clouds crawl heavily about, how they march from one hill to another jumping as if they were inflated bladders, crashing and thundering just as if they were breaking on the edge of the barrancas. But after ten or twelve days they go away and don't come back until the next year, and sometimes they don't come back for several years— No, it doesn't rain much. Hardly at all, so that the earth, besides being all dried up and shriveled like old leather, gets filled with cracks and hard clods of earth like sharp stones, that prick your feet as you walk along, as if the earth itself had grown thorns there. That's what it's like."

He downed his beer, until only bubbles of foam remained in the bottle, then he went on: "Wherever you look in Luvina, it's a very sad place. You're going there, so you'll find out. I would say it's the place where sadness nests. Where smiles are unknown as if people's faces had been frozen. And, if you like, you can see that sadness just any time. The breeze that blows there moves it around but never takes it away. It seems like it was born there. And you can almost taste and feel it, because it's always over you, against you, and because it's heavy like a large plaster weighing on the living flesh of the heart.

"The people from there say that when the moon is full they clearly see the figure of the wind sweeping along Luvina's streets, bearing behind it a black blanket; but what I always managed to see when there was a moon in Luvina was the image of despair— always.

"But drink up your beer. I see you haven't even tasted it. Go ahead and drink. Or maybe you don't like it warm like that. But that's the only kind we have here. I know it tastes bad, something like burro's piss. Here you get used to it. I swear that there you won't even get this. When you go to Luvina you'll miss it. There all you can drink is a liquor they make from a plant called hejasé, and after the first swallows your head'll be whirling around like crazy, feeling like you had banged it against something. So better drink your beer. I know what I'm talking about."

You could still hear the struggle of the river from outside. The noise of the air. The children playing. It seemed to be still early in the evening.

The man had gone once more to the door and then returned, saying: "It's easy to see things, brought back by memory, from here where there's nothing like it. But when it's about Luvina I don't have any trouble going right on talking to you about what I know. I lived there. I left my life there— I went to that place full of illusions and returned old and worn out. And now you're going there— All right. I seem to remember the beginning. I'll put myself in your place and think— Look, when I got to Luvina the first time— But will you let me have a drink of your beer first? I see you aren't paying any attention to it. And it helps me a lot. It relieves me, makes me feel like my head had been rubbed with camphor oil— Well, I was telling you that when I reached Luvina the first time, the mule driver who took us didn't even want to let his animals rest. As soon as he let us off, he turned half around. 'I'm going back,' he said.

" 'Wait, aren't you going to let your animals take a rest? They are all worn out.'

" 'They'd be in worse shape here,' he said. 'I'd better go back.'

"And away he went, rushing down Crude Stone Hill, spurring his horses on as if he was leaving some place haunted by the devil.

"My wife, my three children, and I stayed there, standing in the middle of the plaza, with all our belongings in our arms. In the middle of that place where all you could hear was the wind—

"Just a plaza, without a single plant to hold back the wind. There we were.

"Then I asked my wife, 'What country are we in, Agripina?'

"And she shrugged her shoulders.

" 'Well, if you don't care, go look for a place where we can eat and spend the night. We'll wait for you here,' I told her.

"She took the youngest child by the hand and left. But she didn't come back.

"At nightfall, when the sun was lighting up just the tops of the mountains, we went to look for her. We walked along Luvina's narrow streets, until we found her in the church, seated right in the middle of that lonely church, with the child asleep between her legs.

" 'What are you doing here, Agripina?'

" 'I came in to pray,' she told us.

" 'Why?' I asked her.

"She shrugged her shoulders.

"Nobody was there to pray to. It was a vacant old shack without any doors, just some open galleries and a roof full of cracks where the air came through like a sieve.

" 'Where's the restaurant?'

" 'There isn't any restaurant.'

" 'And the inn?'

" 'There isn't any inn.'

" 'Did you see anybody? Does anybody live here?' I asked her.

" 'Yes, there across the street— Some women— I can still see them. Look, there behind the cracks in that door I see some eyes shining, watching us— They have been looking over here— Look at them. I see the shining balls of their eyes— But they don't have anything to give us to eat. They told me without sticking out their heads that there was nothing to eat in this town— Then I came in here to pray, to ask God to help us.'

" 'Why didn't you go back to the plaza? We were waiting for you.'

" 'I came in here to pray. I haven't finished yet.'

" 'What country is this, Agripina?'

"And she shrugged her shoulders again.

"That night we settled down to sleep in a corner of the church behind the dismantled altar. Even there the wind reached, but it wasn't quite as strong. We listened to it passing over us with long howls, we listened to it come in and out of the hollow caves of the doors whipping the crosses of the stations of the cross with its hands full of air—large rough crosses of mesquite wood hanging from the walls the length of the church, tied together with wires that twanged with each gust of wind like the gnashing of teeth.

"The children cried because they were too scared to sleep. And my wife, trying to hold all of them in her arms. Embracing her handful of children. And me, I didn't know what to do.

"A little before dawn the wind calmed down. Then it returned. But there was a moment during that morning when everything was still, as if the sky had joined the earth, crushing all noise with its weight— You could hear the breathing of the children, who now were resting. I listened to my wife's heavy breath there at my side.

" 'What is it?' she said to me.

" 'What's what?' I asked her.

" 'That, that noise.'

" 'It's the silence. Go to sleep. Rest a little bit anyway, because it's going to be day soon.'

"But soon I heard it too. It was like bats flitting through the darkness very close to us. Bats with big wings that grazed against the ground. I got up and the beating of wings was stronger, as if the flock of bats had been frightened and were flying toward the holes of the doors. Then I walked on tiptoes over there, feeling that dull murmur in front of me. I stopped at the door and saw them. I saw all the women of Luvina with their water jugs on their shoulders, their shawls hanging from their heads and their black figures in the black background of the night.

" 'What do you want?' I asked them. 'What are you looking for at this time of night?'

"One of them answered, 'We're going for water.'

"I saw them standing in front of me, looking at me. Then, as if they were shadows, they started walking down the street with their black water jugs.

"No, I'll never forget that first night I spent in Luvina.

"Don't you think this deserves another drink? Even if it's just to take away the bad taste of my memories."

* * *

"It seems to me you asked me how many years I was in Luvina, didn't you? The truth is, I don't know. I lost the notion of time since the fevers got it all mixed up for me, but it must have been an eternity— Time is very long there. Nobody counts the hours and nobody cares how the years go mounting up. The days begin and end. Then night comes. Just day and night until the day of death, which for them is a hope.

"You must think I'm harping on the same idea. And I am, yes, mister— To be sitting at the threshold of the door, watching the rising and the setting of the sun, raising and lowering your head, until the springs go slack and then everything gets still, timeless, as if you had always lived in eternity. That's what the old folks do there.

"Because only real old folks and those who aren't born yet, as they say, live in Luvina— And weak women, so thin they are just skin and bones. The children born there have all gone away— They hardly see the light of day and they're already grown up. As they say, they jump from their mothers' breasts to the hoe and disappear from Luvina. That's the way it is in Luvina.

"There are just old folks left there and lone women, or with a husband who is off God knows where— They appear every now and then when the storms come I was telling you about; you hear a rustling all through the town when they return and something like a grumbling when they go away again— They leave a sack of provisions for the old folks and plant another child in the bellies of their women, and nobody knows anything more of them until the next year, and sometimes never— It's the custom. There they think that's the way the law is, but it's all the same. The children spend their lives working for their parents as their parents worked for theirs and who knows how many generations back performed this obligation—

"Meanwhile, the old people wait for them and for death, seated in their doorways, their arms hanging slack, moved only by the gratitude of their children— Alone, in that lonely Luvina.

"One day I tried to convince them they should go to another place where the land was good. 'Let's leave here!' I said to them. 'We'll manage somehow to settle somewhere. The government will help us.'

"They listened to me without batting an eyelash, gazing at me from the depths of their eyes from which only a little light came.

" 'You say the government will help us, teacher? Do you know the government?'

"I told them I did.

" 'We know it too. It just happens. But we don't know anything about the government's mother.'

"I told them it was their country. They shook their heads saying no. And they laughed. It was the only time I saw the people of Luvina laugh. They grinned with their toothless mouths and told me no, that the government didn't have a mother.

"And they're right, you know? That lord only remembers them when one of his boys has done something wrong down here. Then he sends to Luvina for him and they kill him. Aside from that, they don't know if the people exist.

" 'You're trying to tell us that we should leave Luvina because you think we've had enough of going hungry without reason,' they said to me. 'But if we leave, who'll bring along our dead ones? They live here and we can't leave them alone.'

"So they're still there. You'll see them now that you're going. Munching on dry mesquite pulp and swallowing their own saliva to keep hunger away. You'll see them pass by like shadows, hugging to the walls of the houses, almost dragged along by the wind.

" 'Don't you hear that wind?' I finally said to them. 'It will finish you off.'

" 'It keeps on blowing as long as it ought to. It's God's will,' they answered me. 'It's bad when it stops blowing. When that happens the sun pours into Luvina and sucks our blood and the little bit of moisture we have in our skin. The wind keeps the sun up above. It's better that way.'

"So I didn't say anything else to them. I left Luvina and I haven't gone back and I don't intend to.

"—But look at the way the world keeps turning. You're going there now in a few hours. Maybe it's been fifteen years since they said the same thing to me: 'You're going to San Juan Luvina.'

"In those days I was strong. I was full of ideas— You know how we're all full of ideas. And one goes with the idea of making something of them everywhere. But it didn't work out in Luvina. I made the experiment and it failed—

"San Juan Luvina. That name sounded to me like a name in the heavens. But it's purgatory. A dying place where even the dogs have died off, so there's not a creature to bark at the silence; for as soon as you get used to the strong wind that blows there all you hear is the silence that reigns in these lonely parts. And that gets you down. Just look at me. What it did to me. You're going there, so you'll soon understand what I mean—

"What do you say we ask this fellow to pour a little mescal? With this beer you have to get up and go all the time and that interrupts our talk a lot. Hey, Camilo, let's have two mescals this time!

"Well, now, as I was telling you—"

But he didn't say anything. He kept staring at a fixed point on the table where the flying ants, now wingless, circled about like naked worms.

Outside you could hear the night advancing. The lap of the water against the fig-tree trunks. The children's shouting, now far away. The stars peering through the small hole of the door.

The man who was staring at the flying ants slumped over the table and fell asleep.

Translated by George D. Schade

FIVE

THE CARIBBEAN

Rosario Ferré
(1938–   )

Rosario Ferré was born in Ponce, a town on the southern coast of Puerto Rico. She studied English literature at Manhattanville College, took a master's degree in Spanish and Latin American literature at the University of Puerto Rico, and obtained her doctorate at the University of Maryland.

She began her writing career in 1970, editing a Puerto Rican literary magazine and publishing fiction, poetry, and essays on literary and feminist topics. The magazine became an influential voice for young Puerto Rican authors, many of whom have since left their mark on the literary landscape of the island. After publishing her first book of stories in 1976, Ferré contributed a column of literary criticism to the newspaper *El Mundo* from 1977 to 1980. She also translated Lillian Hellman's *Scoundrel Time* into Spanish, and has fluently recast many of her own stories in a lushly baroque English prose. These latter include the novella and stories collected in *Sweet Diamond Dust* (1986), the title novella of which is a Rashomon-like tale of love and death that chronicles the decline of the island's sugar aristocracy at the turn of the century in the face of capitalistic intervention by North America. Ferré's critical works include studies of the fiction of Cortázar and of the Uruguayan Felisberto Hernández. A selection of shorter fiction may be found in *The Youngest Doll and Other Stories*. She has taught literature at a number of American universities and currently lives in Washington, D.C.

The Gift

No one expected Merceditas Cáceres, on the day Carlotta Rodríguez was expelled from the Sacred Heart, to hang her silk sash
from the doorknob, drop her medal of the Congregation of the
Angels in the alms box, and walk out through the schools' portico
arm in arm with her friend, head held high and without deigning
once to look back, with that gesture of paramount disdain so commonplace in those of her social class. Next to her through the half-
light of the entrance hallway went Carlotta, her huge body gently
swaying forward like a tame heifer's, her thick mask of makeup
running down her cheeks in furrows, hopelessly staining her white
blouse and the starched collar of her uniform with its varicolored
tears.

At that moment Merceditas was giving up, in the name of friendship, ten, perhaps twenty crowns of roses that already shimmered
like snowy rings at the bottom of the wardrobe where the nuns
kept the prizes to be awarded on graduation day, while Carlotta
went in pursuit of hers, that astonishing fan of golden peacock's
feathers that was very soon to gird her forehead like a crown. There
at the school's hallway she left behind, amid the rustling of blue
pleated skirts and starched white shirts, the many honors she had
so arduously worked for during her three and a half years at the
academy, the ribbons and medals that now would never shine on
her breast, while Carlotta went in quest of hers, of the bottles of
cheap perfume and of the flowered handkerchiefs, of the earrings
and bangles in gift boxes of garish velvet, which were to be so
lovingly presented to her by the members of her retinue on her

294

coronation day. Followed by her silver parade floats, she would walk a few days later down Ponce de León Avenue (as she would also do months later down the principal thoroughfares of Rio de Janeiro, New Orleans, and even Surinam), outfitted in her eighteen-karat gold robe and revealing, on the diamond-studded brim of her décolletage, her enormous dark breasts, sustained by a vision of the world that deserved, in the judgment of the venerable ladies of the Sacred Heart, the steaming torments of the cauldrons of hell.

The mango had been a present from Carlotta, who had brought it secretly into the school after spending the weekend at her father's house. She took it out of her pocket at recess and held it before her friend, balancing it in the palm of her hand.

"It was a present from the members of the carnival's committee at lunch today," she said, smiling. "It's of a variety called Columbus's kidney; sweet like a sugar loaf and soft like butter. Keep it; it's my gift to you."

Merceditas accepted the mango with a laugh and they walked together toward the small grove of honeyberries that grew at the end of the school's patio. It was their favorite haunt, because the shade of the trees provided a temporary release from the heat and also because the nuns rarely patrolled that part of the garden. Carlotta was describing the details of the lunch to her, all of which had had to do with the carnival's theme.

"Silver candelabra and plenas, cod fritters and Venetian table-cloths. You would have enjoyed the combination if you'd been there to see it. But what I really liked best was that the committee should have thought of that beautiful mango, Columbus's kidney, as an official gift. In the past, carnival queens were always presented with a jewel, be it a gold ring or a bracelet, on the day of their appointment."

Merceditas laughed again loudly, her head thrown back, thinking her friend was teasing her.

"It's called like that not in memory of Christopher Columbus's kidney, though, but of Juan Ponce de León's," Carlotta added. "He brought that variety of mango over from India, from a city called Columbus, and planted it himself on the island."

Merceditas looked at her friend and saw that, in spite of the historical blunder she had just made, she was speaking in earnest. "Then it's settled? You've accepted the appointment of carnival queen?" she asked.

"I'll be the first truly Creole queen in Santa Cruz, don't you think?" she said, rubbing her hand lightly over her dark cheeks. "Before queens were always so pale and insipid. If Don Juan Ponce de León should have seen me he would have picked me. Spaniards always preferred swarthy girls."

Merceditas tried her best to imagine her friend decked out in silk ruff, crown, and farthingale, but to no avail. Carlotta was too plump, and she lacked all the necessary social graces. It was precisely because of that, and because of her merry, candid disposition, that she had picked her as her friend.

"It's just that I can't picture you dressed up like a queen."

Carlotta smiled reassuringly and put her hand affectionately on her friend's shoulder. "Cleopatra was plump and rowdy, and you have to admit, from the pictures of her we've seen in the *Treasure of Youth,* that she never had hair as nice as mine."

Merceditas looked at her from the corner of her eye. It was true; her friend had a beautiful mane of hair that she had always admired, and which she wore carefully combed in heavy mahogany tresses, in compliance to the school's regulations. "Many visitors will come to town for the feasts," Carlotta added enthusiastically, "and if in the past we were famous for our tobacco and our coffee, in the future we'll be known everywhere for our carnival." They walked on together in silence, until they got to the wire fence that marked the end of the school's property at the edge of the garden. On the other side of the fence they could see the Portugués's stony riverbed, glinting in the sun like an unpaved highway.

"Aren't you afraid Mother Artigas may not like the idea of your carnival having to do with Juan Ponce de León? You know how finicky she is about historical matters."

"Whoever wants the sky must learn to fly," Carlotta answered, shrugging her shoulders. "I have no choice but to take the risk. And in any case, if Mother Artigas dislikes the idea of the carnival, you can be sure she'll have other reasons."

They finally heard the school bell ring and they parted company, walking toward the study hall building. Merceditas had dropped the mango in her skirt pocket; she could feel it swing there against her leg, and enjoyed its perfume of roses like an anticipated banquet. When she arrived at her seat she took it out surreptitiously and hid it at the bottom of her desk.

Merceditas Cáceres and Carlotta Rodriguez had become good friends in a short time. In truth, one couldn't find two students more unlike each other in the whole school. Merceditas came from a landholding family who owned some of the most fertile sugarcane valleys on the south of the island, as well as the mill after which she had been named. The Las Mercedes Sugar Mill was nearly as large as Snow White Mills, the huge sugar complex of the western town of Guamaní. She had been brought up by English governesses until she entered the Sacred Heart as a boarder; she had few friends and had always led a lonely life, having permission to leave the school only on weekends, when she was driven up the mill's slope in her family's limousine.

She had many cousins and relatives and had hardly had any contact with the people of the town. Inside the mill's compound there were several sundry and utility stores, a drugstore, medical offices, a swimming pool, and tennis courts where her cousins played daily with one another. Merceditas's shyness was in part the result of her not being used to talking to strangers, but it was also the outcome of the Cáceres's unpopular image in Santa Cruz. They had refused to belong to the local casino and *paso fino* club, for example; and their huge fortune had led them to feel a certain mistrust, and in some cases even disdain, of the townspeople. The latter responded in kind, and would never invite the Cáceres to the political and social activities that went on in their homes; an exile that the Cáceres undoubtedly welcomed, since they would seldom bend down to dealing with local authorities at the municipal level for the problems of their sugar empire, resorting always to the central sources of power on the mainland. When they were accused of having no patriotic spirit and of being citizens of nowhere, the Cácereses would laugh wholeheartedly, throwing back their blond heads (of which they were inordinately proud, attributing them to a German ancestor) and claiming that, in fact, the accusation was correct, as they considered themselves to be citizens of the world, and the only good thing about Santa Cruz was the highway that led to the capital.

Because of these reasons every Friday afternoon, when Merceditas left the Sacred Heart, she would lean curiously out the gray velvet-curtained windows of her family's limousine, observing the houses of the town attentively and wondering what life would be like inside. In spite of her great efforts to make friends with the classmates whom she knew lived in these houses, she had had little luck. It had only been on meeting Carlotta that she had for the first time felt appreciated for her own self, without her family name being in the least important. Carlotta's conversation, always peppered with jokes and mischievous innuendos, both cheered and amused her, and she found it especially interesting when she spoke to her of the town.

Carlotta, for her part, had discovered in Merceditas a valuable ally. Her presence in school, unthinkable a few years before, had been the result of the new outlook the nuns had been forced to adopt, when they discovered that the school's enrollment was only half full. It was an expensive academy, and the economic difficulties that even the most respectable families of the town had begun to encounter had forced them to begin to send their daughters to less exclusive establishments. The nuns had then altered their policy of admission, and for the last few years the daughters of the Acuñas, the De la Valles, and the Arzuagas had been obliged to share their top-rank education with the daughters of the Rodriguezes, the Torreses, and the Moraleses.

Among the latter Carlotta had always stood out for her friendliness, although the shade of her skin condemned her, even among the "new" girls, to a relative isolation. She was the first mulatto student to be admitted to the school in its half century of existence, and her recent admission had been talked about as something unheard of and radical even by the families of the "new." The surnames of the recent upcoming elite were still tottering insecurely in the social registers of the town, and this caused them to be undecided as to whether they should assume the canons of purity of blood that their peers, the old aristocratic families of Santa Cruz, had so zealously defended in the past. Thus they chose, in those cases that were unfortunately more obvious, to adopt a benevolent, distant attitude, which would establish the priority of the "mingled but not mixed."

It was true that Don Agapito Rodriguez's considerable assets had contributed greatly to the democratization of the admission requirements of the academy, so that now the venerable Ladies of the Sacred Heart would risk even the admittance of Carlotta Rodriguez to the school. Don Agapito was a small dry goods merchant who had recently struck it rich with a chain of supermarkets that had modernized the shopping habits of the town. In his establishments one could now choose all kinds of fruits and vegetables, as well as dairy and meat products brought from faraway towns or imported from the mainland, so that all the corner vegetable and neighborhood meat stores had been forced to close down. He was a widower, and his daughter was the apple of his eye. All of this added to the nuns' good fortune at having her with them. He had persuaded the owners of the town's food markets to provide the convent's modest daily staples, the dried beef, tripe, and pig's knuckles with chickpeas they so enjoyed, at half price; a visit to the town mayor, his second cousin, produced considerable savings in their electric bill; a call to Don Tomás Rodriguez, chief fireman and his uncle, yielded the promise that a modern water heater would soon be installed at the convent, the cost of which Don Agapito was willing to foot.

The nuns were congratulating one another for their wise decision in admitting Carlotta to the academy when they noticed that an unexpected friendship had begun to bud between her and Merceditas Cáceres. They always strove to be together—in the garden at recess; in the classrooms and in the dining room; and they had had the good luck to have been assigned neighboring beds in the boarding-student dormitory. At first the nuns were concerned that Merceditas's family might disapprove of such an intimacy, but they soon realized their fears were unfounded. The Cácereses spent their lives commuting from the island to the mainland in their planes and yachts, and Merceditas's friends were of little concern to them. The girls' friendship, on the other hand, offered the nuns the opportunity to make Carlotta feel accepted and loved at the school, thus partially allaying her loneliness. For Don Agapito, his daughter's friendship with no less than Merceditas Cáceres was undoubtedly a blessing from heaven. The school parents had traditionally attributed a great deal of importance to the social relations that were established between the girls at the school, since they often served as a base for favorable future business transactions, and in some cases even for unexpected betrothals. (Don Agapito might perhaps have been thinking of Merceditas's many brothers and cousins, in the case of Carlotta's possible future visits to the Cáceres home.) The nuns believed, in short, that the generous Don Agapito very well merited the friendship that had sprung up between his daughter and Merceditas; as to the Cácereses, who never cared a fig for the welfare of the town, and much less for that of the school, they deserved fully whatever harmful social consequences the girls' rapport might bring.

Having vanquished the obstacles to their friendship, the girls spent the year in happy camaraderie, and were waiting for the day when they would graduate together from the Sacred Heart. Merceditas had confessed to Carlotta that it was very important for her to graduate with as many honors as possible, because a high academic index would mean a scholarship, which would permit her to continue her studies at a university on the mainland. Her parents had made it clear that they would pay for her education only as far as high school, since at that time a profession was considered superfluous in a girl of good family.

Merceditas had nightmares every time she considered the possibility of having to stay buried at the mill's compound, married to a second cousin and enslaved to household chores, spending her free time running back and forth after a stupid ball on the family's green clay tennis courts, surrounded by equally green cane fields. She thought of Mother Artigas's offer to help her acquire a grant on the mainland as her only ticket to freedom, and because of it she had put heart and soul into her studies all year.

Carlotta, for her part, had no intellectual ambitions, but she knew that graduating from the Sacred Heart could open many future doors to her in town, and she thus tried to do her best. She knew that knowledge had a practical value, and she hoped, with her newly acquired training in mathematics and science, to help her father in his campaign to modernize the town. She admired Merceditas greatly, her dauntless daring in whatever project she undertook; and she looked to her as her saving Nike. All through the year Merceditas had taken her under her wing, and no one at school had ever dared call her a disparaging name, which might remind her of her humble origins.

Carlotta's good-natured ways, on the other hand, would act on Merceditas like a balm. She amused her endlessly with stories of Santa Cruz. She would describe the sunbaked streets one by one, shaded by groves of honeyberries and centuries-old mahogany trees, although a subtle ironic tinge would always creep into her voice when she talked about the nineteenth-century mansions of the patrician families of the town. She liked to point out that these houses, with white-washed façades heavily gessoed and hung with garlands, amphorae, and plaster cupids, reminded her of a row of wedding cakes just out of the oven and set on the sidewalk to cool. She also talked about the lives that went on behind their walls with a good-natured lilt of reproach, describing, without the merest hint of hate or resentment, how their inhabitants lived eternally in the half-light of respectability, hiding the fact that they were forced to live with much more modest means than those which the opulent walls of their mansions proclaimed to the world.

Thanks to Carlotta's stories Merceditas began to find out about the history of Santa Cruz. The old bourgeois families' proud stance before the economic ruin that the arrival of the troops from the north had provoked at the turn of the century seemed to her quixotic, but worthy of respect. The town's prosperity had hinged on the importance of its port, which had been praised by General Miles after his regiment of volunteers from Illinois had landed. It was blessed by a jetty and a deep bay, which had served as a stimulating rendezvous for commerce all during the nineteenth century, since it offered protection to the many vessels that sailed for Europe and North America, loaded with coffee, sugar, and tobacco.

The mountain range that surrounded the town to the north and to the west had been profusely planted with coffee and tobacco at the time, which the small landowners of the region would transport to the coast in mule trains, to be shipped abroad. Sugarcane, on the other hand, was grown in the lowlands, and it spread over the valley of Santa Cruz like a rippling green mane. Santa Cruzans were at that time a proud people, and they boasted that their coffee, tobacco, and sugar were famous all over the world for their excellent quality. They had, furthermore, made wise use of their bonanza, and with the revenues had built elegant theaters, plazas, loggias, a horse-racing track and a dog-racing track, as well as a splendid cathedral, whose towers could be seen gleaming arrogantly from far out at sea because they had been carved in silver.

All this began to change, and was still changing, with the arrival of the armies from the north. With the ruin of the tobacco and coffee plantations, the farmlands on the mountains were abandoned, and the trading firms that had dealt with them in town were forced to foreclose. Many of the criollo-owned sugar mills had then passed to form a part of the three or four super mills established on the island with the aid of foreign capital, as had been the case with Diamond Dust, the De la Valle family enterprise. Some of them, however, had managed to survive the crises thanks to their ingenuity, and such was the case of Las Mercedes Sugar Mill. More than twenty years before, the Cácereses had decided to build a rum distillery. At first it was no more than a rustic evaporating still, one of the many illegal contraptions that had sprung up by the hundreds in the back patios of the old mills of the valley. The Second World War had begun, and the veterans from Santa Cruz were returning home by the hundreds, armless and lame from its bloody battles, and looking for a magic balm that might make them forget their sorrows. It had been this sorry spectacle that had given the Cácereses the brilliant idea of naming their rum Don Quijote de la Mancha, as the islanders would immediately identify the beaten, half-starved gentleman on the label with the ravaged pride of their own country.

And it wasn't just amid the island's war veterans that Don Quijote's popularity became rampant; it also began to sell surprisingly well on the mainland. The inhabitants of the Metropolis had acquired a taste for the exotic rum produced by their colonies, and they felt inordinately proud of it. Don Quijote became proof that they were becoming internationally sophisticated: from now on, France could well have its Ron Negrita distilled in Martinique, and England its Tio Pepe packed and bottled in Dover, without worrying them in the least. They had their own Don Quijote, who would conquer the world from the lanky heights of his scrawny steed.

With the profits from the fabulous sales of their rum, the Cácereses built their family compound in the vicinity of the mill, turning it into a modern village. The houses all had swimming pools that shone like emeralds under the noonday sun, as well as manicured tennis courts. The atmosphere was refreshingly informal, in contrast to the stuffy customs of the town, where women would never be allowed to go out in pants "tight as sausages," as the Spanish priest used to shriek from the cathedral's pulpit on Sundays. While the women of the town were often overweight and never did any exercise, alternating between the church and the kitchen, where they were the fairy godmothers of their family's pampered appetites, at Las Mercedes women wore white shorts and tennis shoes, played badminton, skeet, and tennis, and would make a daily ritual of tanning themselves half-naked next to their pools.

During this same period Santa Cruz became a skeleton town, and quietly folded upon itself the exuberant flesh it had previously exhibited to the world. The magnificent buildings of yore, the theaters with Greek porticoes and the plazas decorated with fountains, had fallen into disrepair, so that they stuck out in the noon heat like the mysterious bones of a dream, monuments of a past whose practical use could only be guessed at by the townspeople. Sliding like shades at the back of their palatial houses, however, the old aristocratic families still survived, concealing their hurt pride and poverty behind their ornately decorated balconies.

This picture of Santa Cruz that Carlotta painted was a revelation to Merceditas, who had lived until then a sheltered life in the midst of her family's greenbacked cane fields. As she listened to her sitting next to the Grotto of the Virgin of Lourdes, or during their strolls through the school's garden, she was surprised at her love for the town. Carlotta's interest in the old aristocratic families was

mainly romantic in character. Like her father, she believed in progress and wanted to participate, once she had graduated from the
Sacred Heart, in the town's political and civic development. Don
Agapito was an active member of the board of directors of the
municipal hospital, as well as of the state penitentiary, and he
strove for progressive measures such as importing the latest cancer-
treating equipment with federal aid, or adopting a more humane
policy toward convicts. He was also manager of the Little League
baseball team and an influential member of the Chamber of Commerce and of the Lion's Club, from whose boards he always encouraged the admission of new, energetically active members, very
different from those aristocratic gentlemen who had been on the
board till then and who lived as recluses in their own homes,
dreaming of the glories of yore while the town went on dying
around them.

Only once a year did Santa Cruz allow itself to return to the
past, and it was at carnival time. As far back as anyone could remember, Juan Ponce de León's carnival had been the preeminent
social event of the town. King Momo, conga dancers, demons, and
ogres could change costumes but would always remain the same;
to take part in the carnival as one of these popular figures needed
no special voucher, no official investigation as to family and ancestors. When it came to the select company of Juan Ponce de
León's retinue, however, it was a different matter. To qualify for
the role of gentleman, with the right to wear a breastplate, plumed
casque, and foil, one had inevitably to be an Acuña, a Portalatini,
or an Arzuaga. In the specific case of the queen, the central figure
of the celebrations, the requisite of social decorum was considered
to be almost sacred. For this reason a committee of worthy citizens
was elected every year, who took pride in selecting an adequate
sovereign.

Once the court was assembled, after careful consideration of all
the candidates and a disputed voting campaign, the old aristocratic
families would throw themselves body and soul into the proceed-
ings, ready to astound once again the inhabitants of the town with
the pageantry of their timeworn riches. Every year they would pick
out a theme from colonial times, as for example the buccaneers of
Sir Francis Drake, who had once boldly roved the island's coasts;
or the tragic, unfortunate visit of Sir George Clifford, Count of
Cumberland, to the fortress of El Morro, where he had lost seven
hundred men before stealing the organ of the cathedral and the
bells of all the churches of San Juan; or, as in the case of Carlotta's

court, which was to be selected for the feasts of 1955, the heroic exploits of Christopher Columbus.

Perched as a child on her family's modest balustered balcony, Carlotta had been present at many of these carnivals. From it she had often admired the slow, stately carriages as they rolled before her house, heaped with calla lilies and roses and powdered with gold dust, on which rode the members of Juan Ponce de León's court, the children of the Acuñas, the Arzuagas, and the De la Valles, pitilessly distant in their disdain for the world and wrapped in their diamond-studded mantles like immemorial insects that anteceded history and defied the ravages of time.

Mother Artigas was wandering up and down the study hall aisle at sewing class, keeping watch of the rhythmic rise and fall of the girls' needles as they flew like tiny silver darts in their hands, when she suddenly came to a stop. She noticed an aroma of roses nearby and, joining her hands severely under her shoulder cape, she carefully scrutinized the faces around her. She noticed that Merceditas's cheeks had suddenly become flushed, and she walked slowly up to her.

"Would you be so kind as to open your desk top?" she asked with a smile, leaning attentively toward her, but taking care that the fringe of her veil wouldn't graze the girl's shoulder.

Merceditas felt tempted to look at Carlotta, but she controlled herself. She fixed her gaze on the heavy black beads of the rosary that hung from Mother Artigas's waist. She lifted the lid slowly, exposing the desk's contents: books, soap dish, folding glass, sharpened pencils, blue apron, white veil and black veil, neatly rolled next to each other. Mother Artigas reached into it with her hand, as though pursuing, with the sense of smell transferred to the tips of her fingers, the scent of the Columbus's kidney. Her sense of direction was accurate: she lifted the black veil and there it was, round and exuberant, giving off its secret perfume in all directions. She gave her a surprised look, a smile still playing on her lips.

"It was a present from Carlotta, Mother; the committee offered it to her on a silver platter at the luncheon where she was elected carnival queen. If you'd like to taste it, I'll slice you a piece."

She trusted that Mother Artigas would be lenient with her. She knew there was a law against bringing fruits into study hall, but it wasn't a serious offense.

"You did wrong to accept such a gift," whispered the nun haughtily. "Now you'll have to live with it until graduation day." And, turning her back on Merceditas, she walked rapidly away.

Mother Artigas's beauty had a great deal to do with the authority she wielded at the academy at the time. She had one of those translucent faces in which the lack of cosmetics emphasized the features' perfect harmony, and her exquisite breeding and courteous ways gave proof of her privileged upbringing. Tall and limber, she would appear in hallways and classrooms when it was least expected, and the students would all rise immediately and curtsy before her. Her black canvas half-boots, carefully dusted by the order's sisters at dawn, and her black gauze veil scented daily with lavender, seemed to be everywhere at all times, as her shadow could be seen gliding through the house like a mournful willow's.

In contrast to most of the other nuns, Mother Artigas had been born on the island, and because of her native upbringing it was considered she could deal more effectively than her companions with whatever problems of discipline the students might have, since she could understand them better. The girls were, after all, just ordinary misses from well-to-do families; but once they graduated their social status would become something very different, since as alumnae of the Sacred Heart they had the right to expect the highest respect and esteem of the town.

Most of Mother Artigas's companions had been born in far away foreign cities such as Valparaiso, Cali, and Buenos Aires. Their sad, polite manners, as well as their nervously fluttering eyelids, betrayed the reasons that had brought them to Santa Cruz, where they had taken refuge behind the solid colonial walls of their convent, trying to forget their own worlds in a small, anonymous Caribbean town. Under their tucked wimples they hid endless bitter disillusionments, romantic as well as economic, and their personal dramas were probably a symptomatic sampling of the difficulties Latin American patrician families were going through at the time. The landed aristocracy's tragic fate seemed to be sealed by industrial development, military dictatorships, and the gradual disintegration of a Latin American national consciousness among the new well to do.

Imprisoned in their memories, these nuns shunned an everyday reality that they found increasingly disagreeable, and they did their best to forget, through prayer and meditation, that they were living in a mediocre town inhabited by a people whose customs seemed so difficult to understand. Their entrance to the convent had been a hazardous enough ordeal, having had to raise two thousand dollars, the dowry one was obliged to bring to the altar as a bride of the Sacred Heart at the time, with great personal sacrifices. Once the wedding had taken place, they aspired only to the peace and forgetfulness they felt was their due, submitting without complaint to the strict rules of the convent, which required the virtues of silence, anonymity, and indifference to the world.

In their eyes, the girls that swarmed daily into their classrooms like restless swallows had neither face nor name, but were rather hosts of souls. They knew that, at any minute, they'd be forced to abandon them, since in obedience to the iron regulations of the Mother House in Rome, nuns were not allowed to remain in the same convent for more than three years. For this reason they saw them flock into their classrooms not as girls born in a particular country or educated in a specific cultural tradition, but as the daughters of all and of none; and they willingly surrendered the thorny duties of discipline and ethical instruction to Mother Artigas.

There was an additional circumstance that had conferred on Mother Artigas the mantle of authority in the nuns' eyes. It had been thanks to the generosity of the Artigas family, who thirty years ago had donated their old colonial palace to the Mother House in Rome, that the convent had been founded in Santa Cruz in the first place and that the privileged daughters of the town's bourgeoisie could study today at the Sacred Heart. Mother Artigas had an untiring amount of energy, and under her baton the school hummed like a well-trained orchestra. At dawn she'd already be standing at the kitchen door, ordering the sisters to baste, broil, and roast, with economy and wisdom, the simple fares that would be consumed at the convent during the course of the day. She'd also taken over the complicated duties of laundering and ironing the sacred altar linens as well as the girls' bed linen, taking scrupulous care that no fragment of the sacred host should fall carelessly among them; she personally supervised the starching of the nuns' dozens of veils and habits, ordering them to be dipped in lye once a month to prevent lice and vermin from multiplying inordinately, and hung out to dry on the roof under the noonday sun, so that from afar the convent often resembled Theseus's ship, with black sails unfurled by Caribbean winds. In short, she took care of everybody and of everything, and she would claim with pride that she did it all because the house was so close to her own heart.

Mother Artigas had had no difficulties in paying the dowry of two thousand dollars that made it possible to enter the order. Her family had been, and still was, one of the most powerful in the country, related to the De la Valles on her mother's side, and her parents had moved to the capital a long time ago. She had received an exceptional papal dispensation when she had taken her vows that exempted her from the cruel law of resettling every three years in a different country. To compensate she had promised herself, at the moment of becoming the bride of the Lord, when the priest was about to crown her head with the resplendent veil of chastity, to abide unfalteringly by the rest of the convent rules, casting off all human affection from her soul and tending only to that future moment of absolute happiness when she would be admitted into His embrace. She felt so deeply grateful for the privilege of remaining on the island that she swore she'd never fall victim to fond attachments, tendernesses, or endearments toward her fellow human beings, which became treacherous pitfalls of the will.

For this reason she regarded all display of emotion, all devoted attachments that might spring up among the girls, or between the nuns and the girls (the convent's sisters didn't count because they were of humble origin, and thus even though they cooked, ironed, and laundered, they were invisible to Mother Artigas), as a sort of scandal. In her eyes affection, devotedness, or even friendship were all suspect emotions that attempted against that sole union, perfect and irreversible, which would one day take place between the disciples of the Sacred Heart and their future husband on earth.

Since Mother Artigas had been named Corrector of Discipline, she had implanted a strict system of vigilance in the school. In every classroom, in every green-shuttered hallway, in every dusty path of the school's garden down which the students ambled at recess, she had posted an eagle-eyed, vigilant nun, whose black veil clouded all laughter and turned the girls' amicable conversation into frightened whispers. Her idea of discipline would change drastically, however, whenever she met Merceditas Cáceres, for whom she felt a special fondness. Merceditas had been a model student during her three and a half years at the school, and this made her inordinately tolerant and understanding toward her. Mother Artigas held high hopes for her, and she liked to supervise her studies personally. She had had an extensive education and had acquired more than one doctoral degree at foreign universities. She believed that women had an undeniable right to knowledge, having been unjustly barred from it by men for centuries, and the only obstacle that for a while had made her hesitate on her decision to enter the convent had been the clergy's traditional feminization of ignorance. She herself had at one time wanted to become a writer and had played with the idea of challenging the social and literary conventions of her world that condemned women to silence or, what was worse, to euphemistic, romantic verses, chock full of ruby bleeding hearts, cooing love affairs, and lace-flounced babies, but that hadn't the slightest notion of history, politics, or science. She had by now renounced her fantasy of a literary life, but had stuck to her guns in certain aspects of it even after entering the convent. She thus had always displayed the utmost disdain for the joyless writing of mystical nuns, whose ultimate role was submission, and she never encouraged the students to read a sacred book, be it the *Imitation of Christ* or *Lives of the Saints*.

Mother Artigas would spend hours with Merceditas poring over books and explaining to her the most difficult problems of calculus, philosophy, and linguistics. She always insisted to her that learning could be a higher goal than bearing children and that discipline was thus a necessary evil, because it taught people to forgo the comforts of the body and the pleasures of the senses for the good of the spirit. At these moments she insisted that the Greeks had only been half right, and that they would have saved themselves a lot of sorrow if their approach to life had been to have a Spartan mind in an Athenian soul. She therefore insisted that, in her future writing at least (Mother Artigas hoped that one day Merceditas would become a writer), she never accept the dictates of male authority and that, be it in politics, science, or the arts, she always looked to her own heart.

Mother Artigas, in short, believed that the only way women could dedicate themselves to the pursuit of knowledge was by forgoing human love and dedicating themselves to the divine order of things. She was an ardent soul, inspired by the zeal of her vocation, and she often talked to Merceditas about the spiritual advantages of deserving a destiny similar to that of the Princess of Clèves. Her tongue was soft as silk, and her protégée loved to listen to her when she talked of spiritual things, feeling from time to time the urge to follow in her footsteps. Mother Artigas talked to her then of the Sacred Heart's "burning flame, in which the believer must purify his soul, before arriving at the divine union with God," and she encouraged her to alternate her studies with frequent visits to the school's chapel, where there were always pious ceremonies going on. For Mother Artigas, religious indifference was the most dangerous sin, because it landed the larger part of humanity in hell. Merceditas tried to heed her counsel, and she made a conscious effort to take part in the frequent novenas, rosaries, and

benedictions that went on daily at the chapel. She even began going to communion at seven o'clock in the morning every first Friday of the month, because the nuns had assured her that whoever
managed to do so for nine months in a row was guaranteed salvation, but she found it more and more difficult to remember, and
when she arrived at the fifth or sixth month she inevitably forgot
about it, and found herself sound asleep in bed. This inexplicable
weakness became an obsession with her, and when the situation
had recurred half a dozen times she had to face the possibility that
perhaps she was not meant to be saved. Kneeling next to the other
students at her bench in the chapel, she would then listen desperately to their whispered prayers and fervid chants, letting herself
become faint under the clouds of incense and the perfume of the
lilies that thronged the altar, only to arrive at the conclusion, wiping her bloodless brow, that if salvation couldn't be earned by
doing good deeds but only by praying, she didn't stand a chance.
They could torture her knees all they wanted but not her mind,
because she couldn't stand being bored.

In spite of Merceditas's sincere admiration for Mother Artigas,
something in the nun had always made her keep her distance.
Perhaps it was the perfect beauty of her face or her exquisite manners at dinnertime, but the nun had always made her feel a certain
apprehension. Since Carlotta's arrival at the school a year before,
moreover, Mother Artigas had shown herself more reticent in her
expressions of affection, as though she resented the fact that Merceditas now had a close friend. For all of these reasons, during her
three and a half years at the convent Merceditas had hovered like
a moth around the nun's incandescent allure, feeling at times attracted and at times repelled by her presence.

Thus she wasn't really surprised at Mother Artigas's cold tone of
reproach on the morning she discovered Carlotta's mango hidden in
her desk. She kept quiet, and she did exactly as she was told. She laid
the fruit at an angle at the end of the writing table, so that the drops
of syrup that ran down its skin wouldn't stain the other objects that
were kept there. At first Merceditas didn't quite understand the extent of her punishment and she reveled in the fruit's aroma, which
seemed to her an unmerited reward. She would look at it from the
corner of her eye as she wrote her assignments, read, or sewed, secretly enjoying the fact that the mango reminded her of her friend,
and finding a funny resemblance between its heart-shaped, golden
silhouette and Carlotta's burnished cheeks.

The fact that Carlotta Rodriguez was elected carnival queen

didn't take anyone in Santa Cruz by surprise that year, with the exception of the nuns of the Sacred Heart. Don Agapito's influence had already spread to wider circles, and several of his friends had been elected committee members of Juan Ponce de León's feasts. Carlotta, on the other hand, had always dreamed of being carnival queen, and she jumped at the chance she was being offered. A few days after her appointment Don Agapito came to the convent and asked the nuns to give Carlotta permission to leave the school every afternoon from three to six, so she could attend to her carnival duties.

Once scepter and orb were held firmly in hand, Carlotta threw herself into the planning of the feasts. She met daily with her aides at the casino, from where she announced, as part of the updating of the celebration, that from then on the students of all public and private schools, and not only the children of the bourgeois families of Santa Cruz, could participate in the carnival ceremonies. Everything went well and a good number of boys and girls, many of them the children of Don Agapito's friends, had begun to turn up at the casino's door, asking to be admitted to this or that cortege, when Carlotta's enthusiasm for the celebrations began to make her feel the arrangements were inadequate, and that enough wasn't being done.

Set on giving the occasion an even greater luster and a truly international renown, she decreed that there be not just one, but three parade floats for her retinue to ride in, which were to be built according to the exact measurements of Christopher Columbus's galleons, the *Pinta*, the *Niña* and the *Santa María*, and which were to slide over a runner of blue silk that was to be laid down all along Ponce de León Avenue, bordering the harbors of the capital like a streak of ice next to a wind-tossed sea. She took it upon herself to supervise the opulent decoration of the costumes to be worn by her entourage, and she designed her own queenly robes herself, for which it would be necessary to melt several trunkfuls of coins worth a pirate's ransom. She ordered, on the other hand, to give the carnival a more popular appeal, that the orchestras play only guaracha and mambo, banishing the stiff cadences of the *danza* and the waltz to the depths of Lethe; and she commanded that the food that was to be served at the feasts should all be of Creole confection, perfumed with thyme, laurel leaf, and coriander, and braised in the ancient wisdom of kinki fritters gilded in lard. The coronation ceremony, which was to take place after the traditional two-orchestraed ball, would not be celebrated within the revered hall of mirrors of the casino but in the middle of the town plaza, where Carlotta had ordered her throne be set up.

When Carlotta's plans became known, Don Agapito's enemies, the old aristocratic families of the town, began to complain that the carnival was turning into a grotesque affair and that it was no longer the elegant social event that it had been in the past. Their dignity wounded because their children's surnames would not be paged out loud at the casino's doors at the beginning of the ball, and horrified to think that they would have to parade down Ponce de León Avenue in their jeweled attire, easy prey to street hoodlums and an envious rabble, they began to take them out of the corteges and forbid them to participate in the celebrations.

When Carlotta realized that her courtiers were abandoning her and that the carnival would have to be canceled if not enough young people participated in it, she immediately took action. She had the walls of the town plastered with edicts that announced that, from that day on, not just the children from the Sacred Heart, from Saint Ignatius's, and from the French Lycée were invited to the carnival, but *all* the young people of the town, whether they could afford to go to school or not. The very next day a motley crowd of suspiciously bedraggled courtiers and duennas began to mob the casino's doors, gentlemen and ladies decked out in cardboard cuirasses, tin-foil crowns, and crepe-paper trains who had begun to pour out of the town's ramshackle slums, as well as from its impoverished middle-class suburbs, and they were all admitted into Carlotta's court.

At the convent Mother Artigas had finally succeeded in a campaign to expel Carlotta Rodriguez from the Sacred Heart as soon as possible. She argued that Carlotta's behavior in the carnival's planned activities was an insult not only to the school but to the social class to which she so desperately wished to belong and for which she was carefully being groomed. The debate had been a prolonged affair, which had taken place behind closed doors in the impregnable secrecy of the cloister. At first the nuns had refused to listen to Mother Artigas's arguments because they were concerned with the adverse economic consequences they would have to face if Don Agapito were to withdraw his generous subsidy to the school. They reminded Mother Artigas that the world had changed drastically in the last ten years, and they insisted that the school's requirements for admission be flexible enough to accept the fact that Santa Cruz's society was in a state of flux, so that today's nobodies might be tomorrow's dons. They mistakenly believed, furthermore, that Mother Artigas's scruples against Carlotta were based on moral grounds, and that she had been scandalized by the daring design of her queenly robes, which had been recently published in the town newspaper, and thus they had tried to humor her out of her old-fashioned prudery, pointing out the fact that today the students of the Sacred Heart all wore plunging necklines at parties, innocently baring breasts and displaying their legs under the sweeping, bell-like crinolines of Luisa Alfaro and Rosenda Matienzo, the town's most fashionable designers.

Mother Artigas's arguments for expelling Carlotta, however, were devastating and final. She pointed out to her companions that Don Agapito's behavior in the feasts' arrangements had left much to be desired, and that he was indulging his daughter in an uncalled-for Asiatic splendor, spending an extravagant amount of money on her wardrobe and on her orphaned court. As a result of such excesses she had heard that his business, a chain of local supermarkets called The Golden Galleon, would soon be declared bankrupt. The nuns discussed between themselves, in frightened whispers, the ominous implications of such a scandal, and concluded that Don Agapito's economic ruin could bring about a serious loss of the academy's credibility in banking circles, as well as its eventual disrepute. Faced with these possibilities, the nuns voted unanimously to expel Carlotta Rodriguez from school. This was to be done as prudently as possible, as soon as Don Agapito returned from a trip abroad of several weeks. Carlotta would be sent home for a few days, with the excuse that the recent feverish round of activities had made her look peaked, extending her absence until it became final for reasons of health.

It's probable that nothing extraordinary would have happened and that Carlotta's expulsion would have gone practically unnoticed if it hadn't been for the striking metamorphosis she underwent at the time. She had always abided by the convent's rules in dress and appearance, so that when she walked in the study hall with her face smeared with makeup for the first time, the nun who was patrolling the hallways thought it was a joke. She quietly called her aside and asked her if she wasn't rehearsing for her role as carnival queen somewhat prematurely, and ordered her to go to the bathroom to scrub her face.

Carlotta obeyed without complaint and returned to her desk with face sparkling clean. But meekness could become, in her case, a powerful weapon, as is often the case with gentle souls. As soon as she found herself alone the next day at recess, she took out a stick of mascara, a lipstick, and a tube of heavy pancake makeup, and applied them generously to her face. Her features, shaded by the thick layers of paint, acquired a grotesque aspect that, as Carlotta later told Merceditas, laughing, was in character with the savage nature of the mestizo women with whom Juan Ponce de León probably fell in love. It was because she was their direct descendant that she painted her face with burnt coal, corozo nut oil, and the juice of the achiote seed, to test the courage of those not yet respectful of the island's way of life. She had piled her hair on top of her head in a wild cathedral of curls and thus ambled absentmindedly among the students, adorned with bracelets and necklaces that jangled on her white organdy blouse with heretic dismay.

Wherever Carlotta went there was laughter and fingers pointing her way, so that the school was in a constant turmoil. The nuns tried everything in their power to put a stop to this, but to no avail. Carlotta proved equally indifferent to rebuffs and reprimands, and continued smearing her face with paint and adorning herself like a harlot. Since her father was still away, moreover, she couldn't be sent home to stay. It was at this point that Mother Artigas decided to intervene, forbidding everyone in the school from talking to Carlotta, under pain of expulsion.

Finally exams were drawing near and Merceditas had begun to prepare herself in earnest. She needed to concentrate more than ever on her daily tasks in order to graduate with honors, but she found it difficult to accomplish. She was always keeping an eye on her friend, who would spend her days silently ambling down the school's corridors, naive and graceless as ever and with her face now disfigured by layers of horrid makeup, and it seemed to her Carlotta was trying to prove something she couldn't understand.

Although she didn't dare to defy Mother Artigas's prohibition by talking to her in public, Merceditas would always save her a space next to her at the dining room table and the chapel bench, and did her best to prevent the other girls from pushing her out of the school games at recess. Carlotta behaved as though nothing extraordinary was going on. She kept silent whenever she was ill treated and smiled good-naturedly at everyone, even when she was denied permission to go to the bathroom or to have a drink of water.

"I'd like to know why you're doing this, the point of the harebrained hairdo, of the stuff smeared on your face," Merceditas said to her one day when they were far enough away from the watch-nun not to be overheard. "Why the gypsy bangles, the whore's love beads, the floozie rings?" She was angry at her friend, but she didn't dare mention the rumors of expulsion that were flying around the school. She hoped Carlotta hadn't heard them, because she couldn't believe they were true.

Her questions went unanswered, and her friend's silence was magnified by the screams of the girls playing volleyball nearby. A shadow of resentment crossed Carlotta's face, but she soon got over her dispirited mood.

"As soon as Father returns from his trip I'll be going home," she said gaily. "You have no idea how many things still have to be done before my coronation! But I promise I'll come back to see you graduate."

Merceditas pretended she hadn't heard her. She had always thought that if Carlotta was expelled she'd leave school, but now she knew she didn't have the courage. She just couldn't leave after so many years of struggle. After all, Carlotta seemed to be taking everything in stride and not letting the disgraceful events get her down.

"If you come see me graduate, I'll go see you crowned," she said to her gamely, but without looking into her eyes.

Merceditas began to realize the full implications of Mother Artigas's delayed sentence around that same time, three weeks after it had been enforced. The fruit, which at first had so delighted her, had begun to turn color, and had passed from an appetizing golden brown to a bloody purple. It no longer made her think of Carlotta's smiling cheeks, but of a painfully battered face. Sitting before it during her long hours of study, she couldn't help being aware of the slow changes that came over its skin, which became thick and opaque like a huge drop of blood. It was as though the whole palette of colors in the passage from life to death had spilled over the fruit, staining it with cruel misgivings.

The thought of the fruit began to follow her everywhere, like the cloud of insects that flew about it at noontime, when the heat became unbearable. She'd think of it at recess, at breakfast and dinner, but when she saw it most vividly was before going to sleep at night, when she lay down on her iron cot at the dormitory. She'd look then at the ghostly reflections of the canvas curtains separating her sleeping alcove from that of Carlotta's, swinging heavily in the moonlit breeze; she'd look at the white pewter washbowl and at the water jug standing on the night table; she'd look at the black tips of the lookout's boots posted behind the breathing curtains, which reminded her of a snout in ambush, and she could hear, in the still of the night, the mango's slowly beating heart.

At that time Merceditas also began to notice a strange odor, whenever she walked into a classroom, or when she stood in one of the school's winding corridors waiting to be summoned by the nuns. It surprised her that she was holding her breath at breakfast, before the cup of fragrant hot chocolate the sisters served her every morning; when she knelt on her bench at the back of the chapel; even when she was taking a shower. It was an uneven smell, and it reached her at unexpected moments, when she was least thinking about it. Carlotta had noticed it, too, and had asked Merceditas if she knew where it came from, but she hadn't been able to answer. They had agreed, however, that it seemed to become stronger whenever a nun was nearby, as if the smell had a mysterious association with the morbid exuberance of their veils.

It was Carlotta's cheap perfume that brought Merceditas out of the dangerous melancholic state she was in, on the day Don Agapito was supposed to come to pick her up at the school. She stopped reading and looked at her friend in surprise. It was strictly forbidden to change seats at study hall time, but Carlotta behaved as if rules had ceased to exist. Made up and scented like a street tart, she sat at the desk next to hers and, instead of whispering, began to talk in a normal tone of voice. The lookout's furious glance and the neighboring students' mutterings left her unmoved.

"Are you coming to say good-bye? Father's downstairs waiting in the car, and everything's ready. I just have to go up to my room to get my suitcase. If you like, you can help me bring it down."

Her voice was steady but her cheeks were trembling slightly under the heavy coat of makeup.

"All right; I'll go with you," answered Merceditas, as she put away her book and swiftly lowered the lid of her desk, to prevent her friend from noticing its tomblike aspect. She went out to the corridor and Carlotta stayed behind a few minutes, to say good-bye to several of her classmates. She peered out sadly through the green-louvered windows at the courtyard, and wondered what Carlotta would do now that she wouldn't finish high school. She told herself that perhaps it wouldn't make much difference, and that knowing Carlotta, she'd probably find something in which to make herself useful in no time at all. Her friend lived in a world in which action was what mattered, action that eased other people's sufferings in particular; while she lived in a world of thought. All week she had dreaded the moment of saying good-bye, but now that it had come she felt almost relieved, convinced that her departure was for the better. She felt sad, and she knew she probably wouldn't see Carlotta again for a long time, but she welcomed the thought of having peace reign once more at the school, so she could go back to studying. Above all, she'd be free from the ominous feeling she'd had all week, that something terrible was going to happen to her.

They went up the spiral staircase together and quietly entered the senior dormitory on the third floor. Carlotta took her suitcase out from under the bed and emptied her drawers into it, stuffing in everything as fast as possible. She talked constantly about trivial matters, and her voice had a defiant ring to it, as though willfully breaking the silence that enshrouded the room. Carlotta's voice had a strange effect on Merceditas, who had been used to talking in whispers and walking on the dormitory floorboards always on tiptoe. She looked at what surrounded her as though seeing it for the first time: the heavy canvas curtains, now drawn back toward the walls to ventilate the room, revealed to her how near her own bed had been to her friend's, and hers to those of the other boarders. The night table, the water basin and the jug, the crucifix and the chamber pot, repeated again and again the length of the room as it reflected in a double mirror, made her feel everything was happening in a dream.

Talking and laughing at the same time, they picked up the suitcase between them and began the long trek to the school's main entrance on the first floor. Taking each other by the arm, they flew down the spiral stairs and, a few minutes later, were crossing the green-louvered dormitories of second and third year on the second floor. Once on ground level, they passed the laundry rooms and Merceditas saw the sisters bending over their ironing boards and cement sinks full of suds, pressing and scrubbing altar cloths and bed sheets; they passed the chapel and she saw several of her classmates kneeling in their benches and clouds of incense, monotonously repeating the same chants and prayers. She saw classrooms, corridors, cloisters, classmates all fly by as from a great distance. Carlotta walked calmly beside her, as though she had managed to rise above everything. She went on talking animatedly to Merceditas, and reminded her of the date when the carnival's feasts would begin. She had never mentioned the true reason for her departure, and she insisted she was grateful for the opportunity to devote herself entirely to her coronation duties.

They were walking now more rapidly, crossing through the galleries that opened onto the main classrooms, when Merceditas gave a sigh of relief. She hadn't even considered how she was going to feel after Carlotta had left and she would be without a single friend at the school, but she didn't want to think about that now. Her sole concern was that they hadn't met anyone hiding behind the classroom doors or lying in wait behind the corridor's shuttered

windows to fling insults at her as she went by. The girls were all
bent over their books or listening intently to their teachers, and
they didn't even turn around to look at them. She had almost
begun to believe her forebodings were wrong and that Carlotta
would finally be permitted to leave in peace, and she already saw
herself saying good-bye to her at the school's entrance hall, when
the smell reached her again. She stopped in her tracks and put her
hand on Carlotta's arm. They saw them at the same time, standing
together in a half circle and crouching under their somber veils,
obstructing the way to the door.

Mother Artigas stepped forward and disengaged herself from
the other nuns. Her feet slid softly over the slate-tiled floor, and as
she did so her gauze veil billowed around her like an overcast
cloud. Her face, framed by her wimple's snowy curves, seemed to
Merceditas more beautiful than ever, as though she were looking
out at her through a skylight. She was smiling, but her smile was
an icy wound on her face.

Merceditas let go of Carlotta's suitcase and warned her to put it
slowly on the ground. It was then that she noticed Mother Artigas's
long Spanish scissors, whose sparkling steel blades she had confused in the hallway's opaque light with those of the crucifix she
wore on her chest; and that she saw the second nun, half-hidden
behind Mother Artigas's headdress, take a firm step toward Carlotta, holding in her hands a white porcelain basin. Everything that
came later seemed to Merceditas to happen in a dream.

She saw Carlotta's silky curls begin to fall, still warm and perfumed, on the floor, and that Carlotta wouldn't budge; she saw
Mother Artigas's alabaster-white hands and arms, bare up to the
elbows for the first time, clipping her friend's head until she was
sheared like a sheep, and still Carlotta wouldn't budge; she saw her
take the sponge the acolyte handed to her and dip it in the pur-
plish foam of the basin, which had a pungent smell, and she still
wouldn't budge; she saw her wipe her face with it slowly, almost
tenderly, until the heroic features that Carlotta had drawn over
her own began to fade, erasing her lips and eyebrows, the eyelashes
she had so painfully glued to her lids one by one, her poppy-red
cheeks and her passion-flower eyes, and still she wouldn't budge.

Struck dumb like a statue, Merceditas listened to what Mother
Artigas was saying; to the stream of curses that flew out of her
mouth in whipping flurries, lashing her friend with a veritable
maelstrom of insults. She was screaming the dirtiest swear words
she had ever heard in her life, such as "Just who do you think you

are, you filthy nigger, you're not good enough to be one of the convent's cooks and you want to be carnival queen, stuck up on your throne like a mud-smeared blackamoor, like the glorified idol of the rabble's most vulgar dreams! Cursed be the day you first set foot in our school! Damn the very hour when they brought you here to be educated, dishonoring as you have done the holy image of our Sacred Heart!"

As she spoke Mother Artigas tore at Carlotta's uniform, ripping it apart with her nails while she rained slaps and cuffs at her bent head. Carlotta, who in her panic had kept the suitcase clutched in her hand, let go of it at last, and lifted her arms to protect herself from the shower of blows. The case fell open, spilling its contents all over the floor. Merceditas stared at the jumble of clothes, shoes, and books thrown at her feet and finally understood everything. She approached Mother Artigas slowly and stopped her next blow in midair. Mother Artigas turned toward her in surprise, not so much because she had intervened but because she had dared lay a hand on her.

"That's enough, Mother," she heard herself say.

Mother Artigas took two steps backward and looked at Merceditas with all the hate she was capable of. Carlotta stood between them, her head trounced like a billard ball and her blouse slashed in such a way that her bruised flesh showed through everyplace. She was crying silently, like a huge beaten creature. Merceditas drew near to her and slid an arm over her shoulders.

"You know what I'm thinking?" she said with a smile. "I appreciate your good intentions, but it really wasn't necessary. You didn't have to take my punishment home with you, because now we know for sure where the smell was coming from." And bending down, she searched in the huddle of clothes on the floor and came up with a stinking, ulcerated object, which dripped a mournful, tarlike liquid on all its sides.

"Here it is, Mother," she said, curtsying before Mother Artigas for the last time. "Here's your Sacred Heart. It's my gift to you."

Translated by the author

Reinaldo Arenas
(1943–1990)

Reinaldo Arenas has often been called the "enfant terrible" of Cuban letters, not only because of his baroquely dazzling and prolific output as a writer but also for his inexhaustible defiance in the face (and behind bars) of a fiercely dictatorial regime. Arenas was born in the rural Oriente province of Cuba and raised on a farm. He began writing as a child. He joined the revolution of Fidel Castro while still a young teenager and, two years after the triumph of the revolution in 1959, moved to Havana.

From 1963 to 1968, Arenas worked as a researcher in the José Martí National Library. In 1965, his novel *Singing in the Well* was awarded first honorable mention by a committee of judges headed by Alejo Carpentier. The first edition of the work, in 1967, was sold out in a week, but the novel was never to be reprinted in Cuba, though it went on to win the Prix Medici in France for the best foreign novel of the year in 1969. His second novel, *The Ill-Fated Peregrinations of Fray Servando*, was never allowed to be published in Cuba, and his subsequent manuscripts were periodically confiscated by the police. The novel appeared in Mexico, however, in 1969, in one of the many pirated editions of his works abroad.

In 1970, Arenas spent time in a forced labor camp intended to reeducate the youthful misfits of the regime, and there, on smuggled sheets of paper, he wrote the furiously inspired *El Central (A Cuban Sugar Mill)*. In 1972, a pirated edition of his short stories was published in Uruguay. He spent 1974 to 1976 in the infamous El Morro prison (where his merely *semi*-fictional Fray Servando had actually been confined two centuries earlier), but continued to smuggle manuscripts abroad.

319

As his works became more openly defiant of Castro, culminating in *Farewell to the Sea* (several times confiscated and rewritten, and finally published in 1982), the academic left outside of Cuba, who had earlier hailed him as heir to the great José Lezama Lima, began to drop him from their university syllabi. When he finally escaped Cuba through a bureaucratic blunder during the Mariel exodus of 1980, Arenas found himself to be as much a nonperson abroad (with the singular exception of France) as he had previously been at home. This situation was changing with the winds of glasnost when, in December of 1990, after a three-year struggle to complete two final novels and a memoir while suffering from AIDS, he committed suicide. Other works published in English translation include the novels *The Palace of the White Skunks* (1975), *The Graveyard of the Angels* (1987), and *The Doorman* (1988), as well as the two novellas *Old Rosa* (1966) and *The Brightest Star* (1971).

Bestial Among the Flowers

I

With Bestial, things were different. He could make his eyes change color; he ate quails raw; one time he told me, "Get down on all fours and I'll show you what'll feel good" (I ran off); he hated my grandmother, too, and he climbed way up in the coconut trees; he told me he knew how to fly; he'd fling cats up in the air and bust them; he talked; he took swims in the river and peed in the crock we kept the drinking water in. He knew how to read.

Without Bestial, things are the way it looks like they have to be. Nobuddy can't read or write a thing; Nobuddy doesn't climb up on the roof of the house or hold wasps' nests in their bare hands; Nobuddy's got no eyes (not even eyes that are just one color); Nobuddy doesn't eat lizards; Nobuddy doesn't say a word. Nobuddy's nobody.

When Bestial came, all of a sudden the house sort of shrank up, like a dog a person's about to take a stick to. My grandmother, who was out in the yard at the time weeding the marigolds, spit out a stream of yellow spit and walked into the front room. And my mother headed out to the well for water. He didn't look at me right away, and that bothered me, because I'd tried to pretend I hadn't seen him, and I'd finally managed to do it. The second he got out of the hands of the man that'd brought him (who disappeared that very instant), he went over to the coffee table where the kerosene lantern was just sitting there—it wasn't lit, I mean, because it was broad daylight—and he picked it up and dropped

321

it and smashed it to smithereens on the floor. My grandmother stood there with her mouth half open, like she'd been stunned by how quick that lantern had crashed and she couldn't quite manage to put her thoughts in order, but then she spit out another stream of yellow spit, and that got her control back; she walked over to Bestial and picked him up by the neck like he was a dead hen and held him up in the air for quite a while, just looking at him without even blinking, and then she set him down on the floor again and turned her back on him. "His name's Bestial," said my mother, who was coming in the door about then with the buckets full of water. And she went on talking about things with my grandmother; apparently the well had filled her in on everything. But then all of a sudden he looked at me, and I stopped hearing my mother. The minute he walked over to me I could see that his eyes were all different colors. "You've got a mother," he said, stopping and looking at me with so much disgust and scorn that I had to smile at him. And then he vomited. Then right away he looked at me again, but this time with unbearable love and understanding, like all of a sudden he'd seen a pimple full of pus and maggots on my face. And I saw a new sadness start coming over the house, a lot of it. "Mine I killed off a long time ago," he said, turning around and not looking at me anymore, and then he walked away leaving the filthy mess of vomit behind him. (He's a big liar, I thought, and the sadness started going down a little bit.) He went off to my room like he was annoyed about something. And my mother's voice took over my hearing again. "Angelina never cared about anybody but herself," she was saying. "She goes and hangs herself and leaves this stinking little mess on our hands, and *mean* to boot." "She did it on purpose to make our life miserable, I know she did," said my grandmother. "It's hard to believe she was my own daughter." "Well, if she set out to make our life miserable," said my mother, "she certainly managed to do it. That boy's a wild animal." *"Virgen santísima,"* moans my grandmother, "he'll set the whole house on fire!" "I wish he would," said my mother, "so we could get out of this damned infernal place." "Pig," my grandmother shot back at my mother, "all that ever comes out of that mouth of yours is blasphemy." And then they were at it—they started with just words but in a minute it was slapping and hair-pulling. But I went off to my room. Bestial had taken over my bed. He was snoring away, and he hadn't left so much as a corner for me to lie down in.

II

It was three days (and the nights with them) that we had to listen to those odd snores of Bestial's. Sometimes they were almost like arpeggios, but other times they were like chains that would suddenly start rolling or clanking along, and sometimes it was like the snoring was trying to imitate the cheeping of birds, but birds that I'd never seen or heard of, maybe birds on their deathbeds. The second day of having to listen to that snoring, my grandmother came into the room. It was when Bestial was imitating the grunting of a frog when a mink or something is trying to swallow it hind-end first. "I believe he's dying," she said. "Don't you wake him up." And she turned around and left again. The third day it was my mother that came in. Bestial's snoring by then was like a strange combination of the squeaking of the brakes on a train and a cuckoo. Also there was another sound sometimes, but I couldn't quite pin down what it was—it was one of those things he made up. "He smells like the very devil," my mother said, and she left holding her nose. For those three days, I never slept or took my eyes off him for a second; sometimes, so my mother wouldn't get too upset, I'd pretend to go off into the woods or the scrub. I'd leave the house, but then I'd run from tree trunk to tree trunk and slip back and climb in my window. My mother probably thought I was a mile away; I would hear her whistling outside there somewhere. Every once in a while I'd go over to the bed where Bestial was lying and I'd listen real close, trying to make out new sounds; early one morning it was a marvel—I heard something like bells ringing, or more like little bells jingling, tumbling over and over and falling, and then sort of falling apart, losing their clappers and everything; and then it would sound like they were just tumbling along like rocks, and plopping into the water.

But the third morning I didn't just get up and go over to the bed and stand there real quiet and scared looking at him and listening real real close to hear what I could hear—I reached out a hand, too, and I touched him, just with my middle finger, right on the end of his nose. That was when I heard footsteps coming fast through the grass out in the yard; it was raining. There was thunder and lightning with the rain, too, and it terrified the trees and made them whistle and drop off little branches. There was one clap of thunder after another after another, coming closer and closer, until the thunder turned into a bolt of lightning that struck right in the middle of the porch and burned the ivy vines to a crisp and blasted the front-room mirror to splinters. Bestial stopped snoring, opened his eyes, and jumped out the window straight into the storm. But first he said, "Let's go."

That was when you first started hearing my mother yelling, drowning out the rain and the storm and everything, but by then we were already sopping wet.

III

And suddenly, things were different. All that day and night, and all the next day, it never stopped raining. We spent the whole time out behind the tree trunks, or under the trees, or sitting up in the highest branches, or jumping out of the trees headfirst and at the very last second grabbing onto a skinny little vine that we always thought we were going to miss. Bestial would roll around in the leaves and slide on his belly through the loblollies and then run through the puddles of water that were so full they were practically lakes and he'd come out all wet and clean again. For a while we just walked, listening to the noise the rain made as it fell through the leaves, until we started hearing a truly deafening noise, like the rain was trying to bang its way right through a tin roof. Although I'd never gotten up the nerve to go all the way down there (because my grandmother said it was dangerous to get too close; she said it ate somebody for dinner every single day), I figured out that what we were hearing was the river, and I tried to tell Bestial. But he wasn't walking along beside me anymore, like he had been; he was already practically out of sight, running off to where that roaring, bellowing sound was coming from. By the time I got to the river, Bestial had already stripped off every stitch of his clothes and he was about to dive in. But the river wasn't what I thought it was going to be—a little stream of water flowing along under some lovely trees. No, it was a red-colored torrent of water, and the tallest trees you ever saw, pulled up by the roots, were floating down it like bobs on the end of a fishing pole. All of a sudden up on top of one of these buoy kind of things appears Bestial, yelling and waving his arms around, motioning for me to jump in too. I thought it over for a second. These other great big floaters came down the river, all rolling and tumbling in the current so fast you simply couldn't imagine it; up on one of them I saw a little white hen pop up, cackling like crazy, and trying to fly, but then I couldn't see her anymore for the rain. Then in the blink of an eye, which

I don't honestly remember, I'd taken all my clothes off and thrown them into the trees and started walking out to where the current was rushing along, and then I started feeling my feet sinking into this ice-cold mud that gave in at every step. Bestial's howling and whee-ing were his cries of victory at the deeds he was doing. I had my mind made up now; all I was waiting for was for him to look at me, but his eyes were going so fast that they didn't give me time to get ready. Then suddenly he leaped (probably to set me an example). He leaped for a noisy, rushing gang of trunks drifting crazily down the stream and sometimes stopping and making a big flurry of foam and spray and white water, and as Bestial and his yelling went floating through the air, all of a sudden it stopped. It was cut off like a person had taken a machete to it, and Bestial disappeared into the current. The gang of tree trunks went on roaring and rushing down the river, so fast it made your head swim. Then there came a row of uprooted naked-Indian trunks, all together and real shiny, that blotted out the top of the water. I stood there, running up and down the river with my eyes, but Bestial was nowhere to be seen. Now some fast gangs of tree trunks came by, as uninterested and nose-in-the-air as you please, and sometimes sort of zigzagging and jumping, spraying water all over my face. I sat down on a tree trunk and waited. When it started getting dark I realized I was naked; the current had carried my clothes away. Then all of a sudden it turned night—Bestial was not going to show up now. Dying of sadness and almost freezing to death, I started looking for the path back to the house. The sky still hadn't cleared off, but now the rain sounded tired, and now and again it let the shrieking of a bird interrupt it.

"Bestial drowned in the river," I said when I got home. By then it was pitch dark.

"*Virgen santísima!*" my grandmother said, without even listening to me. "He's come home naked! Come here, boy, I'm going to pull your ears off. Coming home naked like this. The very idea . . ."

"You goose," my mother was saying as my grandmother yakked. "Bestial's been in your bed asleep for hours already. Get in this house, we've been waiting for you so we could skin you alive."

She was so mad she looked calm.

IV

Skipping and dodging my grandmother's swats the best I could, I ran into my room, and there lay Bestial in my bed again, quiet and peaceful, snoring these short, delicate little snorts, but I couldn't stop to listen—my mother and grandmother were hot on my heels. I slammed the door in their face and bleated. I don't know whether it was the bleat or the door slamming, but one or the other woke Bestial up. "Open that door," he said. I tried to tell him what was in store for me if I did. But he calmly walked over to the door and opened it. My grandmother and my mother raised their hands and gave two slaps; he threw himself onto the floor before the slaps could get him, and then he took both women by the legs and pulled them out from under them. They landed in a heap, and before they could get up, he ran out of the house. And I was right behind him, pulling on my clothes as I went. It was late at night. All you could hear was the crickets and the whispering of the leaves talking to each other softly while the water dropped off them. Bestial walked out to the almond tree way at the far end of the yard, climbed up onto one of the highest branches in it, lay down on it, and started to whistle. What peculiar whistling. It was like the tired squeaking of little just-born mice. I stayed down by the foot of the tree; I was a little scared to climb up to the top, but I did whistle. As the whistling went on, things got lighter and lighter, until it was practically day, and I could see rising up out of the stand of crown-of-thorn plants a little sprout of happiness, and right away it started spreading and getting bigger and bigger and bigger (probably encouraged by the sound of the whistling), and by mid-morning it had spread all the way to the highest leaves up in the top of the almond tree. Bestial climbed down out of the tree. The two of us walked out through the pasture, stomping on the cowflops, which were still fresh, and flattening them out. When we'd walked for a long way we lay down in the grass and the cowflops; we opened our eyes as wide as we could and we lay there looking up. The happiness was still spreading. It had already risen up through the clouds and covered the house and spread out over the whole woods and scrub and everything, out all the way until your eyes didn't work very well anymore and the sky melted into the farthest hills. Then we went down to the canefield and cut ourselves a lot of new shoots and made ourselves a kite so big that neither one of us could handle it. And we took off, just lifted right up off the ground, hanging on to the end of the tail of the kite, and we floated up over the tops of the trees and the roof of the house, just like a poof of smoke, and down in the backyard my grandmother and my mother put their hands on their heads and shrieked in fear for our lives. All afternoon we wandered around through the sky, and when we landed (just about the same time the sun went down), we landed on the roof of the outhouse just as my grandmother, to the tune of fearsome cramps and terrible grunting, was easing her guts in it. The roof collapsed and my grandmother shot out like a scared chicken, yelling and cursing and with her skirt clutched up to her waist. We finally came to earth right over by the flowerbed where the marigolds were, all of them in flower. At that my grandmother got even scareder, and she ran over to us with her arms waving in the air, ready to tear us limb from limb. There was the most amazing mixture of terror and hate in her face, so amazing that for a second we just stood there gaping. But just as she was upon us, we took off—we jumped all the way over the thorny wild pineapple plants that she thought had our retreat cut off, and we ran off into the night.

V

With a moon that showed no more than the edge, and some-times seemed to have second thoughts and didn't show anything at all, we stayed out there hiding in the shadows and scrub. It must have been past midnight when Bestial finally stopped and gave a little sob and said in a voice that I thought seemed unusually soft, "Tell me about your grandmother." I started talking, and I'm not sure why, but my voice was awfully soft and low too. There was a lot the same in my grandmother and my mother. They were both brutal with their hands and in their gestures, and they both had the same way of using dirty words; they both walked the same way and they both wrung chickens' necks the same way; they both had the same way of kicking animals; and when they prayed they both had the same cowardly, wheedling way of praying. At dinner time, when my mother and my grandmother sat down at the two ends of the table, with the oil lamp in the middle, a person would say it was the same person, unfolded into two; when I talked to them I might have gotten mixed up myself if it hadn't been that my grandmother always got the end of the table the tablecloth reached to. Still, there was one difference between them, and it was enough of a difference to cloud over all the likenesses. My grandmother was rough and brutal, but she was cunning; my mother was brutal and stupid. In fact, my mother was nothing at all. She'd borrowed certain things she'd seen my grandmother do, the things that were easy to imitate, how rough she was in her gestures and the way she talked—because the rest of my grandmother was hidden way down deep, and it was a long time before I saw it, myself; that's why I never hated my mother as much as I did my grandmother. She, my mother I mean, was like a plot of land you could as soon spit on as plant a tree in. And on that little plot of land, all my grand-mother ever did was spit. That's why I hated her so much—hated my grandmother, I mean. I hated her like nobody else. Because she knew what was right and what was wrong, and she could have chosen between them. According to what some people say, back in the old days she'd been some sort of a witch, or a priestess in voodoo or something of the sort, and some people even said that she'd had relations with a crocodile that knew how to sing. But more than anything I hated her because she hated *me*. While I was just a bother to my mother, to my grandmother I was a worthless piece of garbage. And it was her opinion that counted. Everybody for miles around had respect for my grandmother, and even if nobody ever said hello or good-bye or kiss my foot to her, when she went walking down the road everybody peeked out their win-dows, and some people would even come out into their yards. I once heard somebody say that my grandmother knew how to read, and that she had a milk jug full of gold stashed away someplace in the hollow trunk of a ceiba tree. But of all the mysteries about my grandmother, the one that I liked to think about the most was the way she took care of that flowerbed full of marigolds. You had to see it for yourself—the attention she gave those flowers, which were the only ones for miles around. People say she had to bring in the dirt from I don't know how far away, just to make the flow-erbed, and that when she'd planted the seeds and watered them she lay down beside the flowerbed and she didn't get up again until they turned into tiny little green needles poking up out of the ground she'd spaded up and turned and crumbled till it was nice and soft for them. Every afternoon, my grandmother would make my mother go down to the well three or four times for water to water those marigolds with. But she wouldn't let *us* water them; she'd stand with the buckets off to one side of the flowerbed for a while, just looking at the flowers, and then she'd take the water and sprinkle it over them, real gently, with her hands, like a fine soft shower of rain. Then she'd get down on her hands and knees in the mud and clean all around the stalks of the plants, pulling out any tiny little weed or blade of grass that had come up during the day and cursing it. My mother would go into the kitchen and start serving up dinner; and I'd run off the porch, even before my grandmother ordered me to with that look in her eyes she had, and go pen up the calves. By the time I got back it would be getting dark already. The outline of my grandmother still hanging over the marigolds would be something wonderful then, and it would have the strangest effect on me; it looked like she was actually spilling right onto the flowers. The dark would make one single silhouette out of her and the flowers, like some strange kind of tree sentenced to grow upside-down, with its leaves and branches in the mud and the dark, dark trunk sort of fading out up into the sky. In a little while my grandmother would come into the kitchen; then we'd light the oil lamp and she would pass out the plates, with her hands still covered with dirt. There would invariably be a moth from the leaves outside stuck in her hair, and it would fall in the soup. Then the three of us would go out onto the porch and sit on the stools and face out into the night. In a while, as we sat, the smell of the marigolds would float in on a gust out of the dark. All three of us would breathe deep. And it would be almost a repayment for all the rest.

One night I decided I wanted to keep swallowing and swallowing that smell, so a little while after I went to bed, when my grandmother's snoring was well under way and I thought it was safe, I slipped out of the house as carefully as I could and I went out to the marigolds. I leaned over and put the tip of my nose to the flowers, and the smell was so strong I had to jerk my head up and take a few steps back; I knelt down a few feet away and squatted there real quiet, drinking it all in. Now the flowerbed started to stand out in the dark—it was like a whole swarm of tiny lightning bugs swarming up out of the ground. Because the flowers weren't just giving off that smell of perfume; they were giving off a bright glow too, of just the faintest shade of green. Each flower gave off shades of light according to its color; and suddenly I realized that it was like the ground was shooting off little bursts of fireworks. Just then, without knowing why, I looked around: like a bird with great motionless folded wings, there stood my grandmother, right behind me, wrapped in the darkness and a sheet. She stood there and held her eyes on me for a long time. On her face and all over her body I thought I could see some great sadness, though it might have been from the effect of the night. "Child," she said, "you go to your room and go to bed." And I went in and went to bed. When I got up the next morning I couldn't be sure whether it had been a dream or whether I had actually been out to the flowerbed with the marigolds in it. Which was why the next night I waited until everything was quiet and my grandmother was snoring so loud she was scaring the rats right off the roof, and then carefully, carefully, as careful as I could be, I went out to the flowerbed, leaned over the marigolds, and breathed deep. I loved that smell, but it was the same as every other night when it floated up onto the porch where we were sitting—not a bit stronger, not a bit unbearable. The wind shook the plants just like always and a wonderful coolness came over my face. But I didn't see any lights, just the color of the marigolds sort of tinting the fog a little bit, very very pale. By dawn I was tired of waiting, and I tried to get up, but I couldn't; somebody had laid a hand made out of earth on my head. "Child," said my grandmother, taking her hand off my head, "get to bed, now, and go to sleep." I got up, and when I looked at her I noticed there was an even more unbelievable sadness stuck to her body, all over her, that night. I stammered and stuttered a little, trying to say something to her, but she just put out her other hand made out of dirt and put it on my face and said, "I believe I'm going to have to kill you." I went right on to bed.

I woke up early, upset about all the little clods of dirt that had gotten in the sheet—that was proof that *that* night, at least, I hadn't been dreaming. After that, everything's been the same right down to like it is today, and I've been sort of gradually forgetting about that flowerbed—I was pretty disappointed by the marigolds, and I wasn't about to forget what my grandmother threatened—and I believe I've started being a lot like my mother.

All this was what I told Bestial, and then I started telling him about me and my mother, but apparently he wasn't interested because he broke in and said, with such a belly laugh it hushed every cricket and frog and owl in the night, "And how many husbands has that grandmother of yours had? Tell me about her husbands." But I couldn't tell him a thing. So we walked along in silence through the fields and the meadows, hunting sleeping quail by the light of the moon and eating them raw. The littlest ones, Bestial would pull the feathers off of without even wringing their necks, and then swallow them alive.

VI

It was a week before we went back home. We spent the whole time exploring the woods. In the afternoons we'd go down to the river and swim until all of a sudden (like always), night would come. Then we'd start trying to find out what the rocks that kept hiding their faces in the dirt were really trying to hide. Under one of them we found a nest some young scorpions had made on a rotten bird with its feet tied together with a black piece of ribbon. Bestial picked up the bird, scorpions and all, and one by one he picked the scorpions off and stepped on them and squished them. But he didn't eat them. He pulled the legs off the bird and threw it up in the air. "Your grandmother," he said as the bird dropped like a rock into the river, "does she leave the house much?" "Uh-huh," I said, "sometimes she goes out in the morning and doesn't come back till almost dark." "Ah," he said. And he ran off toward the arbor.

In the arbor the little hornets were singing as they ate the soursops; we stayed in the arbor a while, not doing anything, just listening to how that singing rang out, while once in a while a soursop that looked like it had pellet holes all over it would fall on our heads. Then we went over to where the big mattresses the bamboo plants made were lying on the ground and we lay down and watched the little figs drop off the strangler-fig vine and fall into the water. When we woke up, the sun had come out, and so had my mother and my grandmother, and there they were, standing right over us. My mother had her hands on her head and she was screaming and jumping up and down; my grandmother was calmer—she had a switch in her hand, and as she switched me with it across the eyes she said, "Listen to your mother crying, you little heathen, you get up and get on to the house." And she switched at me again, but I ducked my head and all she could do was switch me across the forehead. The two women grabbed me by the arms and lifted me up in the air and shook me like a cat and started carrying me home. I didn't resist, and even when they turned me loose I walked along calmly beside them. Bestial was over our heads, jumping from branch to branch through the mango trees and shaking the limbs so the rotten mangos would fall on us. My grandmother, who was walking along without saying a word, got furious when a green mango fell and hit her on the ear. "You're the devil himself, you damned child," she said to Bestial, and she spit at him. He was holding a wasps' nest in his hand at the time, and he laughed so loud and so strange that all the wasps fell out dead and landed on my grandmother's head. Still hanging on to the empty wasps' nest, and laughing out loud, he jumped down out of the tree and ran off toward the house. "That heathen's up to something," my grandmother said, changing color several times and running off after him. Once we were alone, my mother took advantage of the fact to yell several times as loud as she could and hit me. Then she started walking again and crying all the way, until finally she told me she'd almost died when she realized I hadn't come back home. The closer we got, the softer my mother's crying and yelling got, until by the time we came into the yard it was hardly bothering me at all. Then from the house we heard this piercing scream, and then a moan. I looked up at my mother, all excited, thinking she'd finally managed to do something interesting like make her yells burst way off out there away from her body. But I could tell from her expression that the noises weren't hers. So we both ran toward the house.

When we got there, everything was quiet. My grandmother was sitting on a stool in the dining room, smoothing out her dress and pulling on a shoe. I was about to say something, but she beat me to it, and as though my mother and I were two insignificant bugs she looked at us and said, "There's no dry kindling." Before I left with my mother to go out into the woods and find some dry kindling, I went into my room. Bestial was lying on my bed, peacefully snoring. Then I went out into the yard and stood looking at my mother walk away carrying the machete. Before I followed her I went over to the flowerbed with the marigolds in it. There was a flower pulled up by the roots lying on the muddy ground.

A few seconds later I was walking along beside my mother, out toward the woods.

VII

When the sun, melting down all over the fields, was lighting up just the tips of the top leaves on the palm trees, my mother and I came back, staggering under the load of dry kindling we'd picked up. My grandmother was standing over the marigolds with her arms crossed; she ordered us, without opening her mouth, to leave the kindling right there and go down to the well and get some water.

So we went.

Grandmother took the buckets and began to sprinkle the water on the flowers the way she always did. My mother went into the kitchen and served up the food. I went off to my room where Bestial was still snoring away. Plus it was already night.

VIII

Nighttime. The oil lamp sitting in the middle of the table and the four of us sitting around the oil lamp. When we'd finished eating, my mother gathered up the plates and carried them over to the sink. My grandmother, Bestial, and I went out and sat on the porch. The coolness of the evening floated up like it always did, and the uproar of the leaves and the jabbering of the crickets came with it. My mother, who'd finished washing the dishes and had put out the fire in the cookstove, dragged out a stool and sat down on it next to the three of us. All of a sudden we heard a noise that was different from the screeching of the crickets and leaves, and that didn't come from out of the dark, either; it was a very strange sound, which you couldn't compare with the mewling of a lost cat, although it was something along those lines: Bestial was singing. He was giving off that music that wasn't music or noise, quite, either, with his lips squeezed tight. All the other sounds had been frightened off, and all a person could hear was that whistling that wasn't whistling, taking over the whole night. That was when we got the first whiff of the marigolds, coming across the dark on just the slightest perceptible breeze. As the smell of perfume rose higher and higher through the shadows until it touched my head, and still went on rising, taking over the whole house, my senses had to divide up their work: some of them were tied up listening to that singing while others were pulled off toward that perfume and forgot about everything else. That was when I realized that the war between Bestial and my grandmother had been declared. I couldn't honestly imagine what kind of war it was going to be, or what kind of weapons they'd be using. But by the way the perfume was pulling on my senses from one side and the singing was pulling from the other, I realized that it was going to be a dirty, merciless battle and that it wouldn't be over till one of the two of them was eliminated for good. There was one second when the singing stopped, and all there was was the perfume, lording it over the whole night. But then right away it started fading. And like they'd been waiting for some order, the leaves and the crickets and other night animals started whispering and screeching again. We all walked into the front room, nobody saying a word. My mother and my grandmother went off to their rooms; Bestial and I went into ours. Without saying a word to each other, we crawled into bed.

Without the smell of the marigolds and without Bestial's singing, everything—I mean all the *things,* every little thing—seemed to sort of fade away into the peace and quiet, like they were following that order that makes them all disappear without really hurting them. My thoughts got quieter and quieter, too, so I could direct them the way I wanted them to go again. I put myself in the time that had elapsed since Bestial came into our house, and I stopped on the afternoon, or evening really, of that day I heard my grand-mother scream out and then moan. My mother and I ran into the kitchen again; I saw my grandmother sitting on that stool again. But this time, as though it had all been foretold beforehand, it wasn't only stretch out her hand and smooth down her skirt that I saw her do, I saw her a second before that with her hand lying down there, down there where her two legs came together, down under her belly. This time I didn't give my grandmother time to throw me off the track by running her hands down her skirt so she could pretend she'd been looking at the hem or something, much less let her drop one of her hands down to her shoe so she could pretend she was putting it on again; I just left my grand-mother's hand frozen there in that unmentionable area of her body; I looked at her face, and I discovered such an expression of pain on it, such terrible pain, that for a second I doubted the reliability of this second trip through the time that had passed. But the expression of pain went right away; her hand went down to the hem of her skirt, and then the time I'd seen played again was lying along on top of the time elapsed until the time re-played and the first time were the same. Then Bestial started snoring those strange snores of his. And there I was, in the present again. I won-dered if that snoring of Bestial's was real, or if this was another one of his tricks. But if it was, I said to myself, that would mean that he'd never gone to sleep, because he never sleeps without snoring. Could it be that he never sleeps, he just puts on that snoring so he can watch us without our paying any attention to the fact that he's there? But that's not possible either—during those first three days I never took my eyes off him, and I never saw him peek. Or could it be that he doesn't need eyes to watch other people with? I mean after all, he can make his eyes change color

anytime he feels like it. Maybe he really *doesn't* need them. He
might even be blind, or he might see out of some other part of his
body. But he *has* to need to sleep, or else that would mean that he
was already dead. Or doesn't he need to? Or could he actually be
dead? But then, supposing that he's dead or that he never sleeps,
his watching all the time would make sense when my mother and
my grandmother are in the house, but not when there's just him
and me. Or could it be that he doesn't trust me, either? But that's
impossible—we're friends, because I like him and he likes me. But
I guess it might be that even if I don't know it I'm part of the war,
too ... But I didn't want to go on scaring myself like that, so I
decided that the best thing to do was not think. While my mind
was going through all these convolutions I'd forgotten to pay attention to Bestial's snoring, and suddenly I noticed that he wasn't
in the bed anymore. The minute I realized that, I jumped out the
window and started tiptoeing and feeling my way through the dark
until I got almost over to the flowerbed with the marigolds in it;
there was this wonderful bright glow, all different colors, breaking
through the fog, like a tiny little rainbow down close to the ground.
And sort of swimming right in the middle of it, there was Bestial,
with his arms stretched out to the flowers, smiling. Just at that
second a huge animal with its fur standing up all over its body
loomed up beside the house, and it came panting and grunting
toward us, practically on all fours. It finally came into the glow
from the marigolds, and I saw that it was my grandmother and that
she was dragging an axe along behind her—her hair all tangled
and hanging down and her nightdress half off. I watched her lift
that axe up, huffing and puffing, and aim it right at Bestial's skull.
He was standing there looking straight in her eyes, and laughing
his head off. Then just as my grandmother was about to whack
him, Bestial, still laughing, grabbed one of the marigold plants by
the stalk and yanked it out of the ground, without once taking his
eyes off my grandmother. And that same scream echoed again, but
the calm and peacefulness of the night made it much much louder
this time. And I watched my grandmother gasp and breathe deep
and put her hand on that part of her body again, like it was that
part of her body, and not the flowerbed, that the flower had been
pulled out of. And then, as calm as you please, Bestial walked across
the flowerbed, while the colors and glow of the flowers moved
across his face. At one second when he was all lit up in blue I saw
that he wasn't smiling anymore, and when he finally stepped
through the last patch of orange glow, he looked very very serious

to me, almost exhausted. Just at that moment my mother appeared
around the corner of the house, carrying the oil lamp in one hand
and shading the flame with the other so it wouldn't blow out. Without any one of the three of them seeing me, I sneaked back to my
room and lay down and pulled the sheets up over my head. A few
seconds later I heard Bestial when he crawled in the window and
walked across the room. He was breathing hard when he sat down
on the edge of the bed, and then he lay down beside me. In two
seconds I could hear him snoring again.

IX

Morning came, and although I'd hardly slept a wink, I got up
early. The second I was sitting up on the edge of the bed, Bestial
woke up (or pretended to), opened his eyes, and got out of bed.
Then we went out to the woods to hunt lizards, and we slept up
in a coconut tree. We also went down to the river and jumped into
the water from way up where we'd been swinging on a vine. Everything seemed just like before: we'd swing from the thinnest little
branches and kill birds with a stick. That afternoon, after Bestial
caught some perch in his mouth and we'd eaten them raw, I told
him that my mother had confessed that she loved me and that if I
were to disappear or die or something she'd kill herself. "Kill her,"
he said to me, bringing a blade of grass up to his mouth to clean
his teeth with. "Kill her before she kills you." But that particular
day I didn't understand what he was trying to tell me, although he
didn't say another word all the rest of that afternoon, as though
he wanted to give me a chance to let what he'd said sink in. As the
sun was setting we turned back toward home again, but before we
got into the yard, Bestial went over to the well where my mother
filled up the buckets so my grandmother could water her flowers.
I saw that he was leaning way over the wellhead, so I leaned over
and looked in too, and we stood there looking at each other in the
bottom of the well till the night turned us completely dark and
blotted us out. Then Bestial walked out into the stand of prickly
wild pineapple plants and squatted down and started to cry. He
sobbed and sobbed. For a second I was confused; this person, I
thought, squatting down here at my feet and sobbing like a baby
can't be Bestial. Then I realized that it *was* Bestial, but that he
wasn't crying, he was just pretending to cry, and that that crying,
like the snoring, had some purpose behind it that I didn't know

about. Then finally I quit thinking anything, I just squatted down there beside him and, all of a sudden, I could hear myself sobbing too.

The sobbing of Bestial and me would get all twisted together and mixed up sometimes, and sometimes there would be one single rhythmic and harmonious sound that was almost like music. And at those moments we would be two poor, helpless, abandoned orphans, lost in the middle of a night that might not ever come to an end. Still, even at those times, I could feel that little tiny happiness that had started rising up out of the patch of crown-of-thorn plants and that by now had practically taken over the whole world. I could feel it mixed into the wind and floating off like smoke way up into the sky. And sure enough—when the two of us, both at the same time though neither one of us needed any signal to do it, when the two of us looked up at the sky, way way higher than the clouds, we could see it, way off among the stars.

In the glow of the night we walked to the house. When we got there, my mother and my grandmother had already eaten and gone out onto the porch to sit and rest. Bestial and I sat with them, but when the first gust of marigold perfume wafted up and blew in my nose, I stood up, went into my room, and got into bed and covered my face with the covers. But in spite of everything, I could still hear that singing of Bestial's that wasn't singing at all, and the smell of the perfume of the marigolds crept in under the sheets. Now they're starting to flash their weapons at each other, I thought; there'll be another battle tonight. So when around dawn sometime I heard my grandmother howling and I stretched out a hand and felt that Bestial wasn't in the bed, I wasn't mad or anything about what I had a feeling had happened, all I felt was this terrible new terror, and as it came over me I realized that I'd been part of the battle after all. Then I heard Bestial slipping into bed. I felt how cool and bright the morning was. The sun came up. Bestial stopped snoring. I got up and went out into the yard. My grandmother, lying on the ground beside the marigolds, was asleep with her hands covering the place the pain came from, protecting it. Her body would curl and shrink up now and again, and then stretch, like a garter snake that wanted to crawl away but that just stayed in the same place. "Let's go to the woods," Bestial said to me as he came out the kitchen door.

X

And we did.

XI

As the afternoon was finishing up we came back. Bestial was carrying three rats he had caught in the stand of prickly wild pine-apples and tied around his neck and a whole lot of spiders clutched in his hand like they were the roots of some kind of weed. I could see my grandmother in the yard, watching us (or maybe just watching Bestial) as we came up, with her eyes like the eyes of a scared dog, but one that's ready for you. My mother was coming up from the well with two buckets over her shoulder, walking patiently. She got to the flowerbed, set the buckets down beside my grandmother, and went off into the kitchen to finish fixing dinner. Bestial at the time was peeing in the crock we kept the drinking water in; he'd hung the rats up beside it. Then he turned around and walked right up to the cookstove where my mother was choking on the smoke, and he threw the spiders into the fire. The spiders ran around for a second when they landed on the red-hot cinders, but then their legs all shrivelled up and they burned to a crisp. "Jesus," said my mother, blowing on the firewood, her eyes all red. Then she gave Bestial and me our dinners and filled up another plate and walked out into the dusk to where my grandmother was still standing. She came back in, served herself, and peacefully started eating. Then I noticed that she had changed places at the table. She was sitting in my grandmother's place. I figured she hadn't realized it, so I went on eating. Meanwhile, night was filling up the sky behind the house, and you could hear the crickets chirping from out in the field, so clear that you'd have thought it had just finished raining and the air was so clean it didn't offer any resis-tance. And the racket kept getting louder. For a minute a person could hardly stand it. Then, like an announcement of their visit, the odor of the marigolds started slipping in through the windows, and within just a few seconds it was floating around the table. At that point I peeked out through the chinks in the dining-room wall, and my eyes had to struggle with the shadows and the dark, but I saw my grandmother hopping from one end of that flowerbed to the other like a hummingbird with so much work to do it would never get it all done. And in the wee hours of the morning my grandmother's screaming, changing rhythm and wiping out the screeching and whistling of the crickets, was the strangest sign of all that morning was about to break.

XII

I was out in the yard early, and I saw how my grandmother had begun to take the shape of an old tired bird. I thought and thought, and stood on one foot and then on the other, but I just couldn't work it out, and sometimes I felt so tired that I refused to let reason have any part of my mind, though I refused to give up, either. And the days went on, like a ring of slow vultures flying around and around in the sky, not really expecting to ever get anyplace in particular. My grandmother wouldn't set foot outside that flowerbed; she had my mother take her food to her, she stayed out there in the noonday sun (although sometimes she'd stick her head into the leafiest bunches of the marigold plants), she'd get soaked by the first rains of springtime and the hailstones that would sometimes take you by surprise. She finally gradually shrivelled up until all she was was a big old faded cockroach scurrying back and forth in the few plants there were, because the plants were starting to wither and shrivel up too, and all the care my grandmother gave them and all the water my mother brought them every afternoon as regular as clockwork from the well didn't seem to be doing a thing to save them. The moment finally came when all my grandmother was was this dried-out flowerstalk flung down there next to the poor rickety flowers. Still, every morning, the power of her screaming would tell me she wasn't beat yet.

And Bestial and I just went on living our lives like always: we'd still walk along on top of the briars, we'd still turn rocks over to catch scorpions and put them in our mouths and chew them up. And in the afternoons, just like it had been for I don't know how long, the river would be down there waiting for us, with its sparkling-shiny water that the little figs off the strangler-fig vine would be floating in. There was only one act that made the ceremonies of the days richer—just at dusk we would walk over beside the stand of prickly wild pineapples, down by the well, and we would cry. Then we'd go up to the house and when we got there we'd see my grandmother, in the day's last light, hopping exhaustedly like some sickly little elf from one end of the practically empty flowerbed to the other, still doing her job of guarding it, pointless as that was. Still, it was hard for me to accept her defeat. Remember, I told myself, she's a witch and a wizard-lady, and no one's ever learned whether she ever had a husband. It's not possible that she's given up without a fight, I said, because I hope you won't try to tell me that she's done a thing but wait for the attack, without trying to prevent it. Remember, too, that she once had what you might call a friendship with a crocodile that knew how to sing. Although that's not 100 percent sure, I went on to myself, contradicting myself. The truth is, I said, I don't believe there's any way out anymore. Although she might be planning something, you never know, she might have something up her sleeve yet, even if she looks pretty beat to me. Remember, she knows voodoo and everything else, and she's a witch, and nobody knows her birthday . . . Toward the end of December, my grandmother's body had shrunk up to almost nothing, you could hardly believe it, and she would take shelter in the dead leaves and mud of the flowerbed, like some kind of dying mole. Finally you could hardly make her out among the leaves and stalks of the plants, and she started making strange noises, like the wheezing of a cornered rat. And that day, when my mother and Bestial and I were sitting resting on the porch, at the edge of the dark that the night made, I almost had myself convinced that my grandmother wouldn't live to see another day. Still, just at the moment her scream seemed the tiredest, we got that wonderful smell of the marigolds. Then my mother coughed a little cough, walked over to the edge of the porch, and I saw her lift her two arms up from the blurry mass of her silhouette and stretch them out into the night. The smell had faded away by now, and the crickets, after their short rest, started gradually filling the night up again with their racket. My mother lifted her hands and covered her ears.

As my friendship with Bestial had grown and grown and grown, into something I'd never expected it to grow into, so big in fact that now we didn't even talk to each other, a terrible irrational hatred had started growing inside me toward my mother; but in the last few months that hate had not only taken on the shape of a big round red-hot coal sitting in the bottom of my stomach and sometimes jumping right up into my throat, it had actually started getting outside, showing up in certain ways outside my body—like in the way I'd clench my fists every time she walked by me with that tired owl-ly walk of hers, for instance, or in the way my eyes would shoot out sparks and my teeth would rattle whenever I'd see her blowing on the kindling to start a fire in the cookstove, or in the various plans I kept trying out to see if I couldn't kill her, though I never got anywhere—she'd always wake up just as I had her covered in alcohol but before I could light the match, or the food I had emptied a whole bottleful of strychnine into wouldn't set well with her, and she'd vomit it all up, or she'd see the bananaskins I laid all around the well so she'd slip and fall in and drown. But I didn't give up; and then, seeing her make some gesture that didn't belong to her, I would realize that my hate had grown so big that it had spread all over that house, even taking in the trees.

XIII

In the last dying dusk of April my grandmother had become no more than some blind ungainly insect groping through the dusty clods of the flowerbed, like she was trying to stumble across one of the few stalks that still stood, each one with its flower droopy and head down, like it was watching the last pitiful little hops of a dying bumblebee. My mother, leaning over the wellhead, never stopped hauling water up out of the well, and as she did she cried, while I methodically chunked rocks at her head to see if I couldn't crack her skull. The sun poured down on the limbs of the pine trees. Bestial was sprawled on the porch, flooding it with his whistling that wasn't whistling. And that's how night fell, with its worn-out screeching and racket. When my grandmother's shriek rang out like the short bleat of a frog, I could picture her putting those tiny scarred and bloody hands of hers on that unmentionable place where all the pain came from. My thoughts had all come to an agreement by now—and when they told me in the briefest and most official-sounding way that tonight would be my grandmother's last night, all I could do was nod.

But when the morning came and I skipped out in the yard, I looked over at the flowerbed where the last rickety stalk of the last emaciated little marigold plant stood, and what was my surprise to find my grandmother dancing around that marigold plant, first petting and touching it and then making these ungodly provocative gestures at it. Finally she gave a hop right out of the flowerbed and vanished like a dragonfly off through the high grass in the backyard. Bestial, who had been watching this whole ceremony from behind me, stood there for a second in total disbelief, but then his old cocksureness came back to him, and he pulled a piece

of wood off the eaves of the house and took off after my grandmother, to try to bust her wide open with that stick. But by now,
bucking like a wild dragonfly, she was already far out into the
scrub, and then she disappeared into the stand of wild pineapples.
"We've got to catch her," Bestial was saying, waving the stick around
and smacking at the wild pineapple plants. "We've got to catch
her." And he was kicking around through the rocks, growling, and
roaring as though he thought he could intimidate the plants that
were protecting her. Then he turned around and went in to the
cookstove and pulled out two sticks of burning firewood and set
fire to the stand of wild pineapple plants in three or four different
places. The fire flared, and then it started growing by the second,
and it was like the stand of wild pineapples was a flaming serpent,
writhing and then fading off in the wind. My mother came out
into the yard to watch all the animals and things run out of the
fire. Hundreds of singed birds hopped and flew out and headed
into the fields for safety. Among them we spotted the figure of my
grandmother, who was looking for protection from the fire, too;
she was shooting like a bolt of lightning across the burning grass
and weeds. But Bestial would not give up; with terrible war cries
he started pulling up the flaming wild pineapple plants and fling-
ing them into the four corners of the field. And then the fire began
in earnest; it was burning all through the fields and woods and
scrub and everything. There were the strangest cries I ever heard
that morning, and the strangest animals running and flying about,
too, with their shapes changing all the time and their shrieking
loud enough to burst your eardrums, and they would run out and
jump or fly up over our heads with the moths and butterflies and
ashes. Even rats tried to fly that morning, and lizards would jump
clumsily up in the air and then fall back down into the flames. And
then they would melt without a word. I watched a chicken with its
wings on fire fly by, scared to death, and fall like a meteorite right
on my mother's head, and at that my mother crossed herself three
times and ran and hid in the kitchen. The highest trees, the ones
I'd never been able to climb all the way to the top of, burst into
flame, and within seconds they were first columns of fire, and then
ashes, and then they'd blown away on the wind.

And then in the middle of that terrifying, wonderful brightness,
I began to think. This war, I told myself, is not being run by Bestial
or by my grandmother, either; it's being run by the marigolds, and
they're the only ones that know the rules of it. Because otherwise
Bestial wouldn't have had to invent all this fire and windstorm hell;

once my grandmother was gone, all he'd have had to do would be to walk over to the last remaining plant in the flowerbed and pull it up by its roots. So then it wasn't my grandmother that was guarding the marigold plants, it was them that were protecting *her* from the threat of Bestial. But for one short minute during the day they, the marigolds I mean, they would need to rest up from the exhausting watch they had to keep all night; and that would leave her, leave my grandmother I mean, totally unprotected, all she'd have would be her own strength, and *that* would be the minute Bestial would choose to go to the flowerbed and pick off the flowers. But all they would need, all the marigolds would need, I mean, would be one little second to get their strength back, which meant that Bestial would only have enough time to pull up one plant before he was repulsed again. So that means that both of them, my grandmother and Bestial both, were just doing the same shameful duty all soldiers had to do—because they were slaves to a higher power. That was what I was thinking, though I also had my doubts. After all, there was nothing that could prove it was true . . . Just as the fire was beginning to be the same all over, and the whole country around had turned into one huge monumental pyre, Bestial loomed up out of the flames like some triumphant demon. "She's got to be cracklings by now," he laughed, throwing a hot arm over my shoulders. And such a happiness bubbled up inside me: Bestial, after all these months, had spoken to me again.

XIV

But things didn't go quite the way Bestial pictured them: the next morning, my grandmother appeared, silhouetted like some raggedy elf against one corner of the house. She didn't look so much as singed, and she was dragging along behind her, with a stubbornness and determination that you knew would never, ever end, a book. We watched her drag it over to the flowerbed. She dropped it next to the stalk of that sickly droopy plant, and then hopped away. At that I turned toward Bestial, who had been looking for my grandmother all night long through the ashes and charcoal, and I saw on that immobile face of his the most incredible sadness I'd ever seen. So all that fire had been for nothing—my grandmother had come out of the ashes with a new mystery, and then vanished before our eyes. But why had Bestial just stood there without moving while my grandmother was coming toward us? My

mind wanted me to agree to study this some more, but I felt completely ridiculous, and I rejected all the new convolutions I'd have
had to follow. So, when it got dark and my mother and Bestial and
I sat out on the porch like we always did, watching some sparks
and burning brands flickering, out where the fire had been, I refused to think about anything, I just sat there and started waiting.
Finally it came time to go to bed, and we went into the house. And
even when Bestial stopped snoring and jumped out the window
into the sunrise, headed toward the flowerbed, I wouldn't give my
mind over to thinking, I just opened my eyes wide and jumped out
that window too and sneaked along over to the wall of the outhouse. I could see the marigold plant from there, with its single
flower—standing straight up now—surrounded by a glowing halo
that hovered around it like a crown. On the tree trunk was the lily,
shining bright. Bestial, his arms up to the elbows in the light, was
leaning over the flower. I watched him bend over until his face
was in the ring of shining light too. And then I pricked up my ears
as hard as I could so they'd be able to pick up my grandmother's
last scream from wherever she was out in the wilderness out there.
But just then Bestial lowered his bright face even further, and he
picked up the book in his glowing hands. He sat down in the
flowerbed, pulled the book over into the light from the plant, and
began to read.

At that my senses started banging in terror at the doors of my
thinking, like they wanted to knock it down. For a second I couldn't
bear the racket. But I covered my ears and refused to let them in.
The truth was, I had nothing to comfort them with.

XV

From that morning on, things moved so fast they made your
head spin. Before the sun was full up I went out into the yard and
I was shocked to see Bestial still squatting there reading in the
flowerbed; I walked over and spoke to him. But he didn't so much
as take his eyes off the book to look at me; you'd have thought he
didn't hear me.

I decided to stay there beside him all afternoon, but by nightfall
I was tired of calling him (sometimes as loud as I could), so I put
a hand on his shoulder. At that, I noticed that his body had lost
its tone—my hand sort of sank into his shoulder. I smelled my
fingers, and I thought (and now I was beginning to be almost ter-

rified) that I could smell the same perfume as the marigolds'. My mother came up from the well about then, and although my grandmother hadn't returned from wherever she had gone, my mother set the two buckets of water down next to the flowerbed; to my even greater shock, she started sprinkling water on that one plant, sprinkling it with her fingers, just like my grandmother did, so the water was like fine, gentle rain. She watered the whole flowerbed, even where not a single blade of grass grew. She sprinkled Bestial a few times, too. But he didn't even move to dodge the water.

I was so sad I didn't know what to do. I walked over to the porch and sat down on the stool, even if I hadn't even eaten yet. The night loomed up again over by one corner of the house. And it was just my mother and I sitting there in the middle of all those shadows, listening to the endless chirping and creaking of the few crickets that were still alive out in the ashes, and getting just the slightest whiff from the flowerbed on a gust of breeze from time to time. We just sat there like that, the two of us, in silence. But there was one moment that my hate for her got so big that it scared me. So I went to my room.

I lay there all by myself in the middle of a bed that kept getting bigger and bigger until I couldn't stand it anymore. Finally I got up and groped my way over to the window and jumped out into the dark. On tiptoe, I sneaked over to where Bestial was, and I sneaked up behind him, and I watched: he was as transparent as a windowpane, and one of his arms was completely dried out and buried in the ground. But he was still reading. And when I grabbed him by the neck and tried to get him up onto his feet, I noticed that his legs were stuck to the flowerbed and I couldn't get them loose. Then I looked close at the ground: the clods had started sort of wriggling, and once in a while you could hear them give off this just barely perceptible little shriek. A few seconds later my eye caught something—tiny green tips were beginning to push up out of the ground like little worms in the springtime, and then they were stalks, and then the stalks were putting out buds, and then the flowers opened and gave off such wonderful light and perfume that the night was almost drunk with it, and the night cowered back, and Bestial was wrapped in that halo of light and perfume, though he still had that book in his transparent hands.

During the day, Bestial's transparency gradually turned into millions of shades of green, like the colors of young sprouts. And by nightfall, when my mother started sprinkling water on his head and the flowers, a person could easily have mistaken him for some big, nice-looking lizard poking up out of the leaves. The only thing that told you that it was Bestial was the book he was still holding in his tiny hands. The next morning when the sun came up, I was not terribly surprised to see that his body had turned into a long slender stalk pushing up out of the ground, and that his arms were two bright shiny leaves, and that his head was getting soft and satiny like petals.

I stood up and started laughing out loud, and then I walked into my room. Lying in my bed, I discovered my face was sopping wet.

When the sun was up high, the flowerbed was richer by one marigold; it was exactly the same as the others, with exactly the same flower crowning the leaves. The book, which was still propped against the stalk, was all the testimony there was left that the plant was Bestial.

Then, out of the ashes and cinders and blackened stumps of the woods, my grandmother appeared. She rose up and walked across the morning to the flowerbed with grand, calm steps. I watched her, bathed by the morning brightness, plunge her hands into the marigolds like a thirsty horse dipping its muzzle into a clear quiet pool of water. With all her might she grasped the stalk the book was still leaning up against and with one tug she pulled the flower up by the roots. She raised her hand and held the flower in the air for a second, showing it to the sun. And then she brought it to her lips and with perfect aim she popped the flower in her mouth and swallowed it in one gulp.

Then she lay down on the ground. She smiled as she fell off to sleep in the pleasant shade of the marigold.

XVI

I picked up the book and walked with it for a long long way, across blackened gullies and rocks that were still hot. I finally came to the place that Bestial and I had run to, that night our friendship first started. The evening was an incredible violet. A swarm of hummingbirds, no doubt confused, were hovering over the tall cinders of burned grass. Some of the trees, black and crisp, had little charcoal limbs sticking out of them, drooping like fragile black icicles that any breeze that came along might blow away. For a second I stopped and breathed in the sharp smell of the boiled sap. There was a murmur of water, now perfectly familiar, way off in the distance, like somebody sobbing out beyond the last mounds of ash.

With my stomach full of the smell and the air, I started walking again, stepping on cinders and ash with every step. When my feet were practically up to their ankles in mud, I stopped. For a second I looked at that water that was now flowing along naked under the desert of ashes that was whirling up and gradually blowing away. And then I lifted an arm, cocked it back, and threw the book in the river.

XVII

And then the house sat in the middle of the night like a tiny lightning bug flickering way down at the bottom of an empty cistern. And there sat the three of us again, all looking just alike, in the dark I mean. The three of us, the way it had been before Bestial had made his appearance. And when the smell of the marigolds came through the night and swept across the porch, it felt to me like all the leaves were dropping off some great tall tree. In my room, the bed with its white white sheets seemed to be floating in the dark. I lay down and with my eyes open I started imagining the rats scurrying back and forth up on the roof. But in the morning I jumped up. I ran over to the window and in one hop I was outside in the yard.

And there I was again, standing in front of that flowerbed with its phosphorescent flowers. And I was sinking my arms into that rainbow-colored halo of light. And my hands, with a violence I never thought I was capable of, were pulling up the first plant. Then, just as I was raising it up in the air, pulling its roots free of the last little clods of dirt, I heard my mother from somewhere behind me, screaming that unearthly scream that came from some prehistoric time before anybody was alive, and I saw her put her hands down on that unmentionable part of her body.

Then I understood the words Bestial had said to me when I told him my mother had confessed that she loved me. But the words that ran easier through my memory were the ones he'd said to me that day when I was watching my grandmother writhing around in the flowerbed and he came out of the kitchen and came over to me and said, "Let's go out to the woods." And we did.

Translated by Andrew Hurley

Ana Lydia Vega
(1946–   )

Born in Santurce, Puerto Rico, Ana Lydia Vega began writing
poetry at ten under the influence of her father, a self-taught
popular bard from Coamo. In her adolescence, she devoured Nancy
Drew mysteries, which led to her first attempts at writing and to
her lifelong passion for reading detective stories. Vega graduated
from the University of Puerto Rico, where she eventually returned
to teach French language and literature. In 1969, she received her
M.A. degree from the University of Provence. At Montpelier, she
met her French husband, also an author, and went on to complete
her doctorate in 1978.

Vega's first stories were published in a collection she co-authored
with Carmen Lugo Filippi, in 1981. The following year her second
book of stories received the Casa de las Américas Prize, in Havana.
Vega's linguistically dazzling, parodic fictions with their perfectly
pitched humor continue to win her a growing international
audience (Juan Rulfo Prize, Paris, 1984; Pushcart Prize, New York,
1986). She lives in Rio Piedras and returns each summer to the
Pyrenees, where she does most of her writing.

I

Vilma's letter arrived like mouth-to-mouth respiration, a photo-finish so historically opportune that it plucked me out of one of those messes I seem especially called upon to get myself into.

I had just broken up with Manuel after our overnourished egos collided one too many times. My indifference to our classical separation trauma surprised even me when the chance arose for us to make up. Worse yet, I nearly wept for joy to learn that "the other woman" was none other than his lawfully wedded wife. I'd be hard pressed to say which of us outdid the other: I with my phony jealousy fit meant to soften the blow, or he as the contrite lover. They should have given him an Oscar for it. Best supporting actor.

I packed my bags and moved lickety-split to Rio Piedras. Got myself a closet that passed as a room, private bath and entrance. Not bad for the price and considering the laughably low wage I earn as a teacher. It was on Humacao Street, a land of insurgent student tenants, a place perfumed by the occasional fragrance of sewage overflow. Anyhow, I had a quite Woolfian room of my own in which to devote myself to writing, which is what really interested me. And I felt, if not happy, at least relatively worry-free.

It didn't last long, naturally.

In those days I was working on a half-documentary, half-detective sort of novel about a crime of passion that had happened a short time before in a middle-class condominium complex in Hato Rey. The notorious Malén murder had been milked by the yellow press for its particularly bloody character and its reactionary moral for hot-pussied women. The libretto was not especially novel: spurned macho discovers ex in wrap-around position with best buddy. Beneath the morbid wealth of details and the minute topography of the stab wounds, the message was pretty obvious: no matter how you slice it, women are no good.

I like to think that what got to me were the puritanical overtones of the coverage and not that grim curiosity that makes us stop on the highway and watch some poor fool's carcass being scraped off the pavement. At any rate, Malén's story hooked me but good from the moment I spotted her and her murderer's pictures together on the front page of the *Vocero*. She was very lovely, with wavy Lola Flores hair, lips lusher than lush, deep-set eyes. He was good-looking, too, with his knit brow and his satisfied expression, as of one who had done his horrid but ultimately justifiable duty.

Had chance not intervened, it would all have ended there—two pictures worthy of a better end, another run-of-the-mill tale of passion. However, as coincidence would have it—the thorny kind, rather like that of the murderer's name being Salvador—it all turned out to have happened in the same complex in which my mother rents. The poor woman was a veritable wall of wailing with her running lament about their jinxed building. First it was the baby who fell through the hole in the elevator, then it was the couple who did abortions and flushed the fetuses down the toilet, and now this woman—and how indecent a woman she was— walking the hall at night in the nude, a different man every day. It was bound to happen to her and finally had.

Thanks to this litany I learned all the rumors that her unemployed neighbors had filtered down, with a thousand editorial highlights thrown in: details that at once formed and deformed the macabre picture the paper had painted.

Malén and the ex-lover's friend had been listening to a record "cranked all the way up" when the murderer tried to "kick his way in" the apartment door. That may be why they failed to hear the metallic bang of the window over the hallway or, for that matter, his catlike descent into the darkness of the kitchen. They were "bare-ass naked" on the fold-out sofa in the living room, drinking beer and munching away at some *chicharrones* with typically after-the-act avidity. In walks their guest but he does not walk alone. Accompanying him this evening is a dagger with a seven-inch blade. In the time it takes her to realize what the murderer is on the point of doing, her traitorous friend bolts for the door, bye bye baby

and I don't mean maybe and I'll see you in the sunshine, honey.
Blows, insults, slashes. Malén plays dead, and hardly has to play at
all. The killer goes after the friend. Malén gets up as best she can,
staggers into the dimly lit hallway, paints the stairway down to the
next floor. Back from his futile search, Salvador sniffs out the trail
of the soon-to-be deceased while she searches for strength she
doesn't have to pound on the deaf doors in the hall. Knock, knock.
Nobody home, answers death.

Behold the rewards of the unvirtuous, declares the Condomi-
nated Wives Club, while United Unscrewable Macho Pigs note the
murderer's heroic candor in turning himself in the next day at the
Hato Rey police headquarters. I stuck her, he says, 'cuz she put out
for him, a corrupt, urban version of the ancient My Woman or
Nobody's. It goes without saying that no one asked why the guy
who hit fast-forward when he saw what tune was coming next didn't
have to spend a red cent on Band-Aids. Nor did anyone think to
recriminate the keep-me-out-of-this attitude of the spectators who
refused to open their doors when Malén came by on her final
errand. *Sí, sí, c'est la vie,* as they say in choice Puerto Rican French.

Little by little I gathered a respectable number of clippings and
witness accounts, mainly by talking to local gossips every time I
visited the cursed condominium to damage my laundry a little. A
simple tale of jealousy, I told myself, trying to play down my un-
wholesome fixation. Nothing really out of the ordinary about it,
and yet it was indeed out of the ordinary, with its world of vengeful
men and forbidden women, a world that, in some dark and twisted
way, is as intriguing as it is frightening.

So I began to weave the story—the novel—of Malén. With each
passing day the loose snippets of scenes got more and more mixed
up, and always there was something missing: the telling seam, the
one stitch that would suddenly render the pieces meaningful. I was
trying to cope with this when the sworn deposition given by my
neighbor, a housewife with a detective's chromosomes, temporarily
sliced through my concentration.

Doña Finí had been spoiling for war for several days. She had
her eyes trained on a "vagrant type" who was around the neighborhood all hours of the day and night, apparently in pursuit of
violable maidens. What really upset Doña Finí was that this street
stalker with wheels never seemed to take his eyes off the window
of my room, which, as fate would have it, faced the street. He
would even slow his car down noticeably, almost stopping as he
drew within a few feet of the obscure object of his putative desire.

Doña Finí was driving me crazy. No sooner would I get home from school, my toes curled in pain in the four-inch-high heels prescribed by elegance and my stomach ravenous for a Cuban sandwich to quell the boa constrictor inside, than she would bombard me with the fruits of her probes. Darlin', that is one low-down man, why I burnt the fried beans today just keeping an eye on him, I mean I clocked him, don't worry I'll send you a bill at the end of the month; here's how it went and you'd better listen up: he came by at seven, just after you left, then at ten-thirty, when I was changing Charlito's Pampers on the balcony; and then again at twelve o'clock when the noontime show was starting and Dani Rivera was in his sweet glory shouting let the people sing and dance, you know how he jumps around when he gets going, then back comes the phantom of the opera. Then he must have gone on break, got himself a bite to eat I guess, but he was back again at one, and again at two-thirty. And he went by just now, you didn't miss him by much, sweetheart, oh Mother of Mercy pray for us, someone has turned the face of shame loose in this country . . .

I confess I was secretly flattered by Doña Finí's revelations. I have never been overwhelmed by gentlemen callers. In university days my dear heart Vilma was the femme fatale, the man trap. I was one of those girls who wages her campaign on her wits. My brains would get me where my looks couldn't. Of course I made a show of blushing disgust at this hurricane alert to my alleged chastity, lest my neighbor's efficient reconnaissance go unrewarded. That whole week I reveled in my satyr's well-monitored suspense, never catching him in the act because of irregularities in my schedule during the school's tedious "activities month." Finally on Saturday, the first official day of summer vacation, I took courage and poked my nose out from behind the blinds, only to discover that what was happening here was *The Return of Manuel,* a film I had already sat through several times.

I was more bothered than disappointed. How in the hell had he found my new habitat? What right did he have to spy on me, and in the open daylight at that? Next he'd be going through my trash at midnight looking for wrinkled condoms for his album.

That is why I was so happy to get Vilma's letter, inviting me to spend three weeks with her in a village in the French Pyrenees free of charge. For this poor daughter of the tropics, it was the platonic ideal of the exotic. The one kink in the plan, she said, is that we will be staying in Paul's parents' house. She then proceeded to

describe in the most blissful language the Arcadian setting in which
I would be delivered of the Great Puerto Rican novel.

Although she had been in France for only five years, Vilma suffered from chronic homesickness. She corresponded with four university friends, among whom I, by papal proclamation, was her
favorite. Her elegiac letters were veritable questionnaires on what
she called "national gossip." As I was not much drawn to courtly
intrigue, I had to labor to slake her draculan thirst for the inside
stuff. I made do by filling manila envelopes with political opinion
clippings and even sent her *Claridad* regularly so that she could
stay, as she put it, "connected with the struggle."

I made an immediate decision, a rare thing in my life. I invested
my three years' worth of slave wage earnings in a super saver ticket,
stopped at Mami's for a week to throw my pursuer off track and
pacify Finí, and then crossed Columbus's pond, my portable Smith
Corona in one arm and the papers from the Malén case stuffed
under the other.

II

I arrived at night following a day and a half of globetrotting in
planes and trains. My Caribbean thermometer was not prepared
for the crisp air of the train station. It was all I could do to conceal
a soap-operatic quivering of the lips when greeting Paul in my
college-requirement French. To Vilma I was the ragamuffin Messiah come to visit.

What with the cold, the chit-chat, the drone of the motor and
the curves on the road, I believe I nodded off a few times. I don't
know if he was stubborn or just shy, but Paul hardly muttered a
word. He had his fun, though, speeding down that unlighted highway in the thick fog. Luckily, his parents were asleep when we got
there and I was spared another round of hellos. That would have
zombified me for good. Vilma had a nice, cozy room ready for me,
with a mountain goat's head mounted on the wall, the whole bit.
There was even a fireplace, no fire unfortunately, with blinding
copperware hung over it. Vilma was saving the master stroke, the
coup de théâtre, for last, and she presented it with great fanfare:
a handsome antique bureau. It was redolent of freshly applied
varnish and had innumerable little surprise drawers in it. Vilma
had had it specially restored for Carola Vidal, the writer. With a
capital W.

"If you don't hatch your novel here, then you're just plain sterile," she said, throwing a splendidly thick woolen quilt over my
double bed. And with that monstrous responsibility placed firmly
on me, she left me, my fatigue and my dreams to our ménage à
trois.

I arose early and threw the windows wide open. Our stone manor
lorded it over one end of the village in the heart of the Aspe
Valley, among gray and blue mountainsides camouflaged by the
clouds. I breathed deeply to purge my lungs of thirty years of San
Juan pollution, went and got the quilt and threw it over myself as
a stole. When I walked back to the window the post card panorama
was still there, but now it was dotted with folk characters. A flock
of little old ladies wearing black worked its way up a street that
the tall, narrow houses kept partially hidden from view. The perfectly synchronized tolling of a bell told me that they were going
to church. Realizing that it was Sunday, I felt a vague uneasiness
of bygone holy days and discarded obligations.

I looked at my watch, which was still on Puerto Rican time, and
cursed Greenwich Mean: I was six hours older. It was three in the
morning in Puerto Rico, and barring righteous arousal by car
alarms, shouting voices or gunshots I would still be snoring away.
But it was nine o'clock of a still morning in the Pyrenees, a place
in which—I could feel it so clearly and intensely—time was not
time as I knew it.

I stayed in my room for a while, unpacking my suitcase, arranging papers on the desk, and opening and closing drawers until I
heard the unmistakable sound of their highnesses awakening.
Shortly after that Vilma burst in, tactless as ever, shouting that the
cock had crowed and was I going to snore my vacation away and
a whole battery of signals that together spelled invasion.

"Get ready, Paul's parents are downstairs," she said with a certain mischievousness. She stood before the mirror of the huge,
military wardrobe next to the door touching up the part in her
hair. The old folks were indeed downstairs—he with his black *beret*
and his cane, she with her apron on and a coffeepot in her hand;
the two of them quite the archetypal via Chabrol provincial French
couple. I noticed that Vilma said good morning to him with the
obligatory assault to both cheeks, but not to her. I followed my
feminist instincts and did just the opposite—*mwah mwah* for
madam, a ten-horsepower handshake with tank-size smile for Mi-
sieur Beret. Both of them greeted me effusively, praising my long

black hair—a mop of ringlets—the hepatitis yellow of my skin and other Boriquan charms that will get a person out of a tight spot every time. In this exchange of bicultural pleasantries we had our *café au lait* and our oven-warmed *croissants*. Paul had failed to put in an appearance, and Vilma explained to me that he had gone fishing with his friends. I had already reconnoitered the displays of stuffed and mounted animals and weapons on the walls. So, an outdoorsman and tamer of wild game, was he? It seemed an appropriate pastime for Paul, one very much in harmony with his father's *beret,* his mother's apron, and the stone house in the mountains.

I offered to wash the dishes, to further pad my increasing lead with Paul's mother, but the offer, fortunately, was declined. Vilma dragged me to the door without allowing me so much as a quick trip to my room for a sweater. She had her spiel ready: you need the crisp mountain air, you'll warm up in no time. And I let myself be led away, like one of those shorn sheep you see crossing the village in the afternoon.

Mine was a short-lived innocence. Indeed, that first walk put a premature end to my vacation. Vilma confided to me what to a certain extent I had already guessed. Her marriage was going badly. She was even considering divorce, which is why she had requested the presence of *Madame Soleil* of the Caribbean. A confidante's is a thankless job. The more so with Vilma, whose insistence on "objectivity" and "critical distancing" I knew all too well. She was one of those people who go on talking for hours unaware of the exhaustion they cause in those who lie down, Gandhi-like, before the runaway train of their monologue.

The first two years were pure Hollywood bliss: the two students in Toulouse, Vilma discovering the "Old World," the romance, the wedding and the move to Bordeaux. Paul's first official act was to refuse to let her work, but that didn't hurt so much. The real problems began when he refused to respect her leisure time. She was not to speak to the downstairs neighbor and God help her if he got home and she was not in the kitchen stirring the soup with the big copper spoon given them by their Pyrennean ancients.

My whole contrived notion of *homo Galicus* crumbled to pieces. I had pictured them so sophisticated, so *evolués,* so Sartre and Beauvoir in the things that mattered . . . Vilma's husband made the vilest Puerto Rican macho look like a suckling babe. This Caucasian reincarnation of the Moor of Venice distrusted everyone and everything. Under the circumstances I wondered why he had authorized my discreet invasion of his universe. But that was not all. The Boriquan princess kidnapped by the evil boar hunter was suffering yet further vexation at the hands of the witch with the apron and the coffeepot, the very one who had treated me so courteously that morning.

"You're lucky you don't live with her," I said, as a kind of anticipated consolation.

Whereupon Vilma, her customary bravado broken, related to me the Hitlerian details of the persecution unleashed against her by her mother-in-law. Letters exchanged with Paul, telephone calls, flash visits to Bordeaux on the pretext of bringing kitchen knick-knacks ... the lady had never favored Paul's marriage to the Caribbean mammal, the plebian Josephine de Ceauharnais with the mestizo charms. And Madame Jocasta had "contacts" in the city who followed Vilma everywhere she went, relaying minute reports to the mother, who in turn submitted them to Paul for review.

It all sounded so strange, so conspiratorial, so Daphne du Maurier, that I had to wonder if my friend wasn't spinning a paranoid fantasy. Was she that far gone with homesickness? For obvious reasons, I said nothing. Anyway, her story—I offer this as one of the bedeviling ironies of the trade—absolutely fascinated me. All of the women of French film and literature driven to infidelity by sheer boredom went parading through my mind while Vilma Bovary persevered in her uncanny tale.

"Ironically, the least of my ordeals are these summers at the in-laws. At least here I can get around. I guess they feel more in control of the cage. Besides," she said, with thoroughgoing coyness, "there are no young people here."

"What about your father-in-law?" I asked, recalling Vilma's double kiss.

"The poor dear," she sighed with quiet eloquence.

And we continued our walk, arm in arm, along a highway that hid from us the bright insinuation of a river.

Paul arrived well into the afternoon. Or perhaps at night, for the day goes on there almost until ten o'clock with the same deceptive clearness. I know that we were already sitting at the table fishing vegetables out of the steaming soup while trading international courtesies with the in-laws. I felt pretty uneasy. After all, what Vilma had confided to me was not the sort of stuff that settles a person's mind. My senses grew extraordinarily sharp, unless it was the wine that Miseur Beret kept bountifully pouring for me with the wicked intention of getting me woozy. Anyhow, even the pictures and the stuffed boars in the kitchen seemed to be alive with the febrile indifference that signifying objects tend to take on.

When he entered it almost startled the spoon out of my hand. *Bonjour,* says Bluebeard, although, as I saw it, it was *bonsoir* that was called for. He kisses his mother, kisses Vilma, kisses his father and I thought I would have the honor but I was wrong. He extended his leather-gloved hand over the table to me. Then he went upstairs, excusing himself unintelligibly—Vilma had told me they sometimes spoke in Bearnese, the isolated dialect of the region— and dinner proceeded tensely and quietly. The *ratatouille* was delicious.

This time I did wash the dishes. Vilma dried and Madame swept. In that *pax domestica*—oh, the irony of it—I again found the quiet of the morning by the window. Only the three of us women, and the nine resounding clangs of the church bells.

Vilma bade me a tender good night at the top of the stairs. I took a long, hot bath, shivered as I dried myself, and sat down to correct—there would be no "hatching"—what few pages I had rewritten so far.

"Malén changes the record and lies back down. Nude, her dark skin flows under the blue lamp. Yes, she is quite nude and the music is pure punk, real greenhair, chain-around-the-neck punk. The telephone rings. It's Rafael and he is coming now, soon as the store closes, won't be long, bringing beer and Chinese food, don't cook nothin', baby, you don't want to smell like fried rice and don't put perfume on your neck either, it makes you taste bad. Malén says a soft OK, don't forget the egg rolls and the soy sauce and hurry, she is getting restless. Salvador has been watching her for three days now, following her all around in the car, peeing his name on the floor outside her apartment door, leaving puzzling messages. Fuck him, he interrupts, you're not his woman, that's all over, he don't sign checks for you and he got no mortgage on you, he don't scare me either but if he tries to I brought somethin' for special occasions, and he can file it right up his bottom drawers, OK goodbye now Malén, passion flower, sweet child, and then some heavy manly breathing that promises it all. Malén turns the record player off, regards herself, puts the radio on, lies back. She is nude and her skin glows under the red light. She is utterly nude and now they are playing an old bolero, an old Dipini bolero about forsaken love ..."

As I read in the pale light Malén slowly dresses herself in black, like a Truffaut dream.

III

The week crawled by with fattening meals, dishwashing marathons and clandestine rendezvous with my writing. I say clandestine because now that she had rediscovered our friendship, Vilma shadowed my every step. She would chase after me to the bathroom to confide yet another dreary little intimacy from her life with Paul. She told me, in fact, some deeply intimate things, things I wouldn't blurt out to my own shadow under torture. Her gift for storytelling forced me to listen with genuine interest, a source of guilt to me, for it was as if I were participating in some darkly obscene act despite myself. She realized this and drew the stories out, pausing at the awfullest moments so I would have to bare my indecent curiosity and ask.

"The first time he hit me I thought he was joking. I hit him back and he returned that one harder. I got scared, tried to run out of the room, he caught me, dragged me to the bed . . ."

Vilmic suspense. Then, just as I had pictured it, the story ends with him sticking it to her, as Freud forbid he shouldn't.

I didn't know whether to be scandalized or congratulate her, for she told me all this with a certain dubious winsomeness and with the strange enthusiasm of one who wants to frighten a child that wants to be frightened.

To Paul's discreet charm one could add that of his mother. Vilma told me—and this was not one of her darker secrets—that during one of their notorious fights at the in-laws' she tried to leave the room, only to find after unbolting the door that someone or something was blocking her way. Her evil husband found it all side-splittingly funny, as your common Gilles de Rais type might. Vilma swears she heard smothered laughter, undeniably female, on the other side of the door.

"Carola, I swear on my mother's grave it was the old lady."

Madam, that is, having a good laugh at what Paul was doing.

By the end of the week, my curiosity had diminished in inverse proportion to the anguish my friend's spectacular confessions were causing me. Worst of all was the effect it was having on my perception of everyday reality. Things became deformed. I would stammer when talking to Madame. Let Paul chance to walk into the kitchen and I would jump like a clown out of a jack-in-the-box. I couldn't look him straight in the eye. My only refuge was Miseur Beret, but a poor refuge he was. He spent most of his time watching television and the rest of it nodding beside the heater, the inevitable glass of red wine in his hand. Through all this Vilma adopted an attitude of total indifference, a kind of controlled calm which contrasted markedly with the atrocities she unloaded on me in industrial quantities whenever she caught me alone.

On Saturday I violated Swiss neutrality and boldly asked her to give me one God-blessed reason why they were still together. She had no answer.

On Sunday afternoon we went to Olorón-Sainte-Marie in the station wagon. Bluebeard at the wheel, Vilma next to him, Miseur Beret, the Witch of Snow White and your humble vacation martyr and the dogs all in the back. We drove all around the city—in my honor—and it was pure storybook medieval with its river bubbling across the main street and its surprise stairways, ideal for swordfights. Whole tribes of Gauls, grandparents and all, ambled, as did we, aimlessly, preceded by giant sheepdogs, and wandered into the open air cafés where idle, provincial youths of false worldliness ignored them.

We snacked on *chocolat viennois* with mouth-watering *russes* that Paul's mother ordered for me to try. Vilma ate nothing. She watched me through the steam of the hot chocolate as though amused. Madame was expatiating on the excellence of French pastry, a gospel truth which it was now my delight to confirm. Her husband, for his part, didn't hear a thing, absorbed as he was in unabashedly dunking his *russes* into his chocolate in what for me amounted to social sacrilege. Now and then even Paul would send a gentle, husbandly smile my way. Under the implacable eye of the trio, I dabbled the sugar granules off my chin while searching for something appropriate to say amidst such lavish but undeserved attention.

The Sunday ritual ended at seven in the evening, if one can call such brightness in the sky evening. Again we squeezed into the sedan for the trip back to our wuthering heights. Vilma chose to ride in the back and traded places with her mother-in-law. Her Puerto Rican hindquarters wedged me against the window. The conversation on the way back might have been that of any family anywhere in the world returning from a ritual outing. I found it hard to reconcile Vilma's tale of unbridled passions, a tale—or was

it a lifelong soap opera showing, to my despair, on all the channels—woven with third-worldly patience; hard to reconcile, that is,
with the kindly and hospitable people who were going out of their
way to please me.

Paul became talkative, pointing out sites of interest with great
regional pride. He would catch my eyes in the mirror with perfect
nonchalance, and I noticed as a result that his eyes were green and
not at all unattractive. After passing a bridge called Escot, he announced solemnly: we are now in Sarrance. A resting place on the
road to Santiago de Compostela, the village of Sarrance lay curled
against the highway overlooking the abyss of the valley. While Paul
waxed learned on the pilgrimage to Santiago, sending recondite
details to my foreign ears, Vilma grabbed my arm and pointed to
a sign which my humble understanding of French told me was an
inn. Then she whispered in my ear: that's where Maite lived; she's
the one who left her husband and children and ran away with a
garage mechanic.

Something in the intensity of her tone of voice made me turn
my head and lose myself in her dancing eyes.

On Monday the universal deluge burst upon us in a cold snap
made all the worse by a fog taken straight out of an English movie.
I was wearing two sweaters under a military jacket, two pairs of
thick stockings, woolen pants that Vilma had lent me, and still that
killer cold cut to the bone. A certain nostalgia for my island over
the seas was tapping at my heart. Had it not been for the fabulous
fire that Paul built for me, I believe I would have grabbed the
phone and arranged to catch the next flight out for the by now
folk-epically mythified Puerto Rico.

That day I got a respite. Paul was at home, which meant that
Vilma had to suspend her woman-to-woman siege. The fire enliv-
ened my fantasies. For a long while I watched it consume the logs
while turning my frozen story over in my mind. How should I
handle Malén's death? Who should I have tell it? The frightened
neighbor who wouldn't open the door? The jail guard who stands
in wide-eyed awe of the confessing murderer and his story? The
dime-a-dozen lover who, stinking of beer and nicotine, hears the
outcome of his last *soiree* over the radio? The medical student who
lifts the sheet and finds himself mesmerized by the bruised body
of a missing woman? Who would tell Malén's story? Who would
tell the truth if she was dead?

That night something odd happened. I remember that Vilma

had cooked the meal. Not without battling Madame's culinary mo-
nopoly, I might add. It was the twenty-fifth of July, the infamous
date of Puerto Rico's pseudo-constitution and of the even more
infamous Yankee invasion of our peaceful shores. Vilma decreed
rice and beans the supper fare in counter-commemoration of this
sorry day. She disappeared into the kitchen amidst a great percus-
sion of saucepans and stewpots, and emerged with two enormous,
deep bowls of half-caked white rice with Goya beans that I had
brought in my suitcase. This will hit them like a bomb, she said,
while, ever the professional, she placed our great national gruel
on the resigned plates of husband and in-laws.

The remark got me in the funny bone and the ensuing laugh
attack made history in the Pyrenees. Our howling grew louder with
each fateful raising of our forks. Looking back on it I have to admit
that it was an inexcusable breach of table manners. Vilma choked
and we had to pound her on the back several times. My guts ached
from trying to hold in the laughter. Both surprised and annoyed,
the elders regarded us with appallingly serious faces that only made
things worse. I had given up all hope of social redemption when
Paul's *ça suffit* resounded against the four stone walls like a rifle
shot from an expert hunter. A brutal pause. I speared two or three
beans in order to avoid looking at anybody, excused myself nice
and quietly and went upstairs to the library-living room, where all
of the heat in the house came from. I didn't want to lose an arm
in the explosion, if there was going to be an explosion.

Shortly after that, Paul came up. He sat on the sofa facing the
fire. I acted blithely unaware of him, keeping my eyes on the flames
dancing in the fireplace. We silently communed as the logs were
consumed. It was a brief but intense moment. There we were, he
and I, two perfect strangers joined through someone else's scheming and misery; I with a head full of truculent stories; he with who
knows what in his head. The two of us, uncomfortable and silent,
the fire our only excuse.

The next day I started a journal in a notebook full of old, still-
born stories. A substitute activity for the abandoned novel? A feeling that something important was going to happen? Intuition reads
its cards in braille.

IV

July 26

Still raining hours on end. Paul went to Pau. Mission unknown. Madame had me shelling tender beans (green beans, to her), a thankless job which nevertheless kept me busy. She made a heavenly *garbure,* just what we needed for the tyrannical weather and the lackluster mood. I think she may like me.

The cold makes Vilma nervous. She paces. Needs a victim. I let her into my room after lunch to calm her down. This household marks time by the gastrointestinal pace of its inhabitants.

She told me all about Maite's escape: the exemplary couple, the devoted husband, how the getaway sent a shock through the valley . . . I was stuffed to the gills with *civet de lièvre* and had to switch to automatic pilot and save the rest of the gospel according to Saint Vilma. Her stories—both her own and the ones she borrows—aren't very different from any lurid Mauriac novel.

Paul brought me two magazines from Pau and a *France-Dimanche.* Has Vilma perhaps spoken to him of my passion for the *fait divers?*

July 27

The rain is like a barbed-wire fence that keeps us indoors. Last night the people who rent the apartment above Paul's parents' garage came home. He is a doctor in Toulouse. She is quite unmistakably the doctor's wife. They have a six-month-old baby. It's nice to see new faces. They had linden tea with us. He speaks very good Spanish and I can detect Iberian impurities in his genealogy. Considerable charm. Vilma locked in on him, *bien sûr,* leaving the woman to me. I put the baby in my lap, jostled it abruptly to make the scene more decorous. It cried. Paul was watching, his face set in a suspiciously tender smile.

July 28

A letter from Mami. The island has come back to life and with it Malén, wearing fruit on her head and feathers on her behind. The murderer is in jail. He tried to kill himself but they stopped him. They found out he is from Barrio Jurutungo. I knew it, says my mother, righteous in her militant classism.

Salvador pursues me. Again I stalk the hallway of the ill-fated condominium with him. I see him stop at Malén's door. Hard music. The Persian blinds are broken. He forced them open himself the day Malén refused to open it for him. The blind is broken and

inside Felipe Rodríguez is singing the sorrows of a wounded macho.

I can hear Mami's enthusiastic voice: "Get some rest and make
the most of your chance to sightsee. France must be beautiful.
Socorro has been there and says it's wonderful. I only wish I might
have the chance that you got . . ."

Sweet, unsuspecting, and sixty.

July 29

The powers are not so deaf after all: the sun is out. Weakly, but
it is out. The Rousseaus want to go on a hike. Getting ready is a
scene: fresh bread and sausage for the sandwiches, regional cheese,
Bayonne ham, wine, water, fruit. The baby will stay with Paul's
parents, fortunately. I feel like the odd man out with these two
couples, like a referee who doesn't know the rules of the game. My
tennis shoes slide on the stones. Everybody else is wearing boots.

We take the back way out of the village. First there is paved
highway; then an ascending path. The bluish gray rooftops of the
white houses drop below us: color hides from sight here, as though
cowed by the uniformity of custom.

We discover a nest of promiscuous vipers in a hole in the rock
face. The men play it big and brave and tease them with a stick,
to the shrieking horror of Vilma and Madame Rousseau. I'm too
proud to utter a sound, though I fail to see the humor in all of
this. Vilma chews Paul out and Paul makes fun. Then I speak up
and the strongman sideshow ends. *En avant*

The wife, Paul and I walk in single file. Vilma's giddy laughter
and Rousseau's booming, virile voice reach us from above in a kind
of endless chatter. Paul goes on about wildlife: pathetic mountain
goats he has chased down, boars nearing extinction, enormous
bears that walk the roadways imposing respect, a whole *maquis* of
threatened species constantly in flight through the forests of the
region. I ask him why, then, does he hunt. He comes back down
the path with a long explanation laced from start to finish with
contradictions: hunting restores man's instincts, surrounds him
with his prey, victim and victimizer partake of their mutual animal
state, man relives a certain savory atavism and other pleasures of
the DNA. Madame Rousseau bestows a beatific smile of admiration
on him, but I am not convinced. It is killing for killing's sake. Yet,
the speech suits him well. It sounds like the Paul that Vilma has
portrayed. But does such a Paul exist?

July 30

Bad luck. Thundershowers again. I am sick with a ridiculous cold. My head is congested and my nose is red. I occupy myself by scribbling some nonsense on postcards Miseur Beret gave me. Old pictures of chubby women showing their black nylon stockings and their little, chicken-butt mouths. Funny that Vilma isn't using this chance to park herself in my cell. At night I find out *pourquoi:* she went shopping in Olorón with the Rousseaus. She gets back all excited— never lost the energy of her student-riot days—and is singing the praises of the doctor, she calls him Jean-Pierre now, while reviling the wife, who doesn't know her ass from page nine. You tell me, she says, how can she not know where Puerto Rico is. And, she adds, with a hint of pride in her smile, I think she is jealous.

July 31

... I watch through the blinds. Malén has returned from the dead, more radiant than ever. From her nude body there emanates an all-enveloping glow. She walks triumphantly through the transformed hallway and the doors open before her, oh Our Lady Malén, goddess of the passions of darkness. She walks straight ahead, heedless, disdaining doorways that so obviously beckon. A man comes near. I can't see his face. He caresses her buttocks, panting heavily as though stricken with pneumonia. She yields, sighs, moans, her hands slide up his back, shoulders, find his neck. And she squeezes, tenderly squeezes ...

Paul's mother brought me my breakfast in bed. I've got a bitch of a cold. I even feel the beginnings of fatigue in my chest, which means total regression to the wooden house of my childhood. Vilma wants Jean-Pierre to examine me with the stethoscope. I find it embarrassing; the man is on vacation. But she insists—nag, nag, nag. And she gets her way.

Doctor Jekyll asks me if I am asthmatic, taps the cold stethoscope here and there on breast and back. Vilma is leaning against the wardrobe, pelvis pushed out, sweater pulled tight, fire-engine red lips. I can spot the signals a mile away: professional manhunter and she's not hiding it. Jean-Pierre prescribes, diagnoses: I have the climate to thank for this. He lectures on the consequences of an abrupt adaptation to new climates. My antennae are up despite my cold and in the mirror I catch some unmistakable body language. Vilma, shockingly, lies down next to me. Jean-Pierre sits on the edge of the bed. They caress each other with their eyes. Oh my

God, I am thinking, they are going to have the orgy right here on the corpse of the helpless houseguest. My fantasy may be racing, but it is right on track. Vilma takes the stethoscope from his hands and examines herself in a splendid display of tropical tits. I open and shut my eyes. I am speechless.

August 1

I am better for the vaporizer but weaker for the antibiotics. My throat hurts. I'm all fucked up. I run into Paul on the way to the bathroom. I am wearing one of his mother's God-awful woolen nightgowns, an oedipal vision that appears to move him. *Pauvre petite,* he says, condescending to stroke my hair. *Malgré* my poor condition, I notice the stroke. Goose bumps, honorable withdrawal from the scene.

I slept all day long. Vilma brought me *crêpes* and a yogurt. I have a week left. I am beginning to count the days, like a prisoner.

August 2

Good weather looming. Patches of blue visible.

I feel flat-assed, which is no sin here but back home would cost me half of the fan club I've built up on the streets. Pale, too, which Mami, the diehard skin-lightener addict, would love.

The doctor's wife has been helping Paul's mother. Copper pans full of orange marmalade perfume the air. I sit on the stairs, flirting with a sunray. Surprise. Paul sits down beside me. Would I like to go to the post office, he proposes after the mandatory *bonjours*. I accept with the proper measure of shyness and courtesy. I go upstairs to get the postcards and a coat. When I come down Paul is starting the car. His mother is watching us—happens to be watching us?—through the window.

Our little outing proves costly. Paul wants to talk about Vilma. He tells me she has changed a lot, is reliving her adolescence, she lies, makes up stories. He tries to pick my brain: I know you two talk to each other all the time, you're old friends, she must have told you something, c'mon it's late, but I hold out, mutis, loose lips sink ships, clitoral solidarity to the end. We mail the letters in Bedous and he wants to stop somewhere for an *apéritif*. I feel unaccountably guilty for being out with Vilma's husband, though something tells me she is probably busy playing doctor in some solitary corner. Paul goes on about her: she never got used to it here, she's always nervous or in a bad mood and when she gets excited it's a forced, unnatural elatedness.

I look out the window to avoid having to reply. I wear an idiotic smile. Something sinister is going around and around in my head: "She lies, she makes up stories ..."

August 3

This emotional stirfry has me completely confused. It's a *huis clos* that would stump even Sartre's lame trio. Was this my own school-mate, the resolute lady with the twenty-eight-karat mind, first in our group to learn to drive a car, Miss Segurola of 1972? Had she turned donna Juana on me, a mythomaniac pouring poison in her supposed best friend's ears, and with all the *sangfroid* in the world?

This afternoon, as Vilma tormented us from her bubble bath with a fairly Freudian concert of old boleros (*Entrega total, Escandalo, A escondidas he de verte*—you name it) her mother-in-law came out to the garden to invite me in for a cup of tea, a British sort of urge which turned out to have strings attached. One of them a beauty. It so happened that Madame Rousseau had gone to Paul's mother with complaints: certain winks and giggles, certain beauty marks below the equator, tell me, *Docteur,* is it malignant or benign, and the worthy physician hadn't slept a wink lately with all this coming on going on, and the man is no light sleeper ... In short, your classical tale of jealousy, only this one was different in being very much justified. I could vouch from my own personal experience that the daughter-in-law in question really knew her stuff. Madame Jocasta didn't dare accuse Vilma in my presence and it's a good thing, because I don't know if I would have had the histrionics handy or the gumption on tap to stick up for her. She asked me to talk to her however and whenever I could without of course mentioning Madame's name ...

Multiple jeopardy: an undisciplined writer fresh from an amorous entanglement, held hostage in a house with a marriage nearing extinction, a friend and compatriot who is about to crack up or already has, a happy hunter happy to hunt down trapped tourists, a doctor with a roving stethoscope, a jealous, hung-up doctor's wife and an interventionist mother-in-law. Only the impassive Miseur Beret retains a semblance of psychological balance in this commune of free enterprise and open competition that Bertrand Blier would have given his life to film.

I should have said no. This was between Vilma and Paul, let the husband be housebound, let the wife mind her married life. But just like when you pay your taxes, you've got theory and you've got praxis. And I merely answered, with a studied meekness, that this was a very delicate thing, I don't know if I dare, I'm sure you'll understand ... And lest the vedette should emerge from her toilette, head wrapped in a big, knock-out Carmen Miranda towel turban, only to spot me brewing foul play with Mrs. Danvers, I gulped my tea down without stopping to think it might be poisoned and went back to the garden before the cock crowed thrice.

V

I don't know why I gave up on the journal. I guess you either live life or write about it. From here on it is I and not the journal speaking. And with the cool objectivity which distance affords.

I went to bed a little early that night, thanks to Paul's insistence that I play Scrabble in French with him and Vilma. Feeling like a Puerto Rican arraigned in a gringo federal court, I went up to my room and got in bed with Stephen King, my favorite stress pill. I don't know how late I stayed up reading. I fell asleep for what seemed like a short while, interrupted as I was by the annoying creaking of the stairs. I looked at the clock: it was three. The Miss Marple in me noted that the footsteps were going down the stairs and I soon heard the moldy scraping of the garden gate. The dogs did not bark: the nightwalker was someone they knew. I went up to the window to get a good look. Who would dare trifle with the raw Pyrenees summer at this uninviting, not-quite-dawn hour?

I had no time to apply Rouletabille's implacable logic. The figure's solemn gait betrayed her: Vilma, walking at night, alone, in baby-doll pajamas. Some ovary problem she has. Nocturnal rendezvous with the *promeneur solitaire*? That was a bit too much, even for someone willing to break the taboos of our little establishment. If she was planning to get down with the *docteur* mere minutes away from her snoring husband and his insomniac wife, then her goose was cooked, like well-done. There would be blood on the saddle and everywhere else. I pictured the scene: Vilma and Jean-Pierre, ancestrally splayed out in the alley between the two houses or rolling around on the dirty garage floor. Unmindful of the serpents in their glacial Eden, illuminated by the unwelcome light of the fireflies, they would fail to notice Paul as he crept toward them, rifle at the ready. In super slow motion, the noble cuckold collects himself and takes aim, awaiting the precise moment when they pull apart, whilst your humble servant silently witnesses, from her Hitchcockian vantagepoint, the end of Vilma.

But Vilma was not to meet such a bloody fate. She walked until she came to the forbidden garage. Then she stopped. Would she try to make her break in Paul's car? Would she leave Paul in his own parents' house, rubbing defeat in his face? And would she do it all—here was the most Machiavellian touch of all—dressed in a nightie?

I imagined the uproar, the five-star scandal to which the sound of the car going up the street would give rise. And as for me? I considered cloistering myself *per secula seculorum* there in the room of my vigilance. I would throw a vow of silence and a hunger strike in with the deal. Or I would seek asylum in the Puerto Rican embassy (wait a minute, what Puerto Rican embassy?) after a spectacular escape under cover of sheep's hide and in the anonymity of the herd that wound through the village every afternoon.

But as though in a Brian De Palma dénouement, Vilma did not make her break. She stood there for a relatively long time, treating the stars to a monologue. Then she did a languid about-face and returned to the confines of Nosferatu's castle.

Two days remained before my liberation. I arose late with rings around my eyes that seemed to sag to my knees. I spent an hour in the bathroom reading ancient *Nouvel Observateurs* and belaboring the constipation my "vacation" had earned me. Afterward I tried to repair the devastation with make-up.

I hadn't the slightest intention of finding myself alone with Vilma or her mother-in-law, and least of all with Paul. So I planned my magnificent descent for shortly before noon. Like a goddess *ex-machina* I confronted the profusion of exquisitries prepared, I suspect, in my honor. The perfect family picture: Papa, Mama, Baby. Vilma excused, "not feeling well." Her chair was empty and her plate face-down in mute testimony to the broken date. Then, the greetings began.

The three divine persons literally throw themselves on me, hailing me as the heroine of the *Résistance* that I am. Which is why I play the awaited one. I am a soft punching bag for their frustrations. They serve me, dote on me, spoil me. My fail-safe social docility has today earned me the title of new daughter-in-law: the replacement.

The rebel angel paces in her room. We eat as though oblivious to the subtle protest of the wood overhead.

In the afternoon I come upon the missing piece of the puzzle:

the doctor is gone. A giant *A LOUER* in the window of the empty apartment tells me what there is left to tell.

Vilma refused to come downstairs at all. I might have felt slighted had I not known what was going on. That night I fell into Paul's clutches as I tried to violate the intimacy of the marriage room. We crossed paths on the stairs. He had a tray full of rejected midnight snacks. I had a mooncalf face that said gosh I haven't noticed a thing.

"Is she better?" I said, assuming my role of neighborhood idiot.

"She refuses to eat," he said, playing the good-Joe husband.

I gave it one try. Can I see her? Better not. Maybe tomorrow. That "maybe" (that is, *peut-être,* since the scene was, after all, in French) was the unkindest cut of all. Did she actually intend not to come out before I was up and away? Now that was perfume with a petrochemical fragrance to it.

We couldn't stand there on the stairs forever watching that tray as if it were a body at a wake, so Paul asked me if I wanted to look at picture albums in the room with the fireplace. I must confess, in all honesty, that if there is anything I hate over and above all the petit bourgeois rituals that make up my pointless life, it is looking at family albums. But curiosity and perhaps a secret desire to return to the scene of our first ocular rapture twisted my arm into a perfect full Nelson.

The room was not the same without the fire. The walls looked dirtier, the upholstery on the lounge chairs bleached with age. The atmosphere was static, almost hostile in its *pax romana.* Paul returned with a voluminous tome. I sighed, bracing myself for the endless parade of chubby babies, virginal maidens in white and family clans trapped between either end of a sofa. Paul sat down beside me, redolent of rapidly splashed on after-shave, and placed the cumbersome thing on my lap. Without the slightest brushing motion, let me say in all truthfulness.

I began to turn the pages, offering the prolonged pause dictated by courtesy and the comments prescribed by the Association of Album Martyrs. But there was nothing standard about this album. Not content to overpopulate the walls with dead animals, Paul had gone to the extreme of taking pictures of the wretched victims of his exploits before, during and after they croaked. Mountain goats, wild boars, vultures, fowl of every social class and even a bear, ladies and gentlemen, in blatant defiance of laws enacted to protect all wildlife nearing extinction-by-shafting. The whole necrophiliac display appalled me. I tried to suppress all of my judgmental feelings about it. After all, it was almost normal that a hunter should wish to keep the unassailable proof of his prowess around like so many trophies. They are not people, they are animals, I told myself, struggling to accept the *fait accompli* of the massacre now opened before me, though deeply hurt within my environmental sympathies. By the seventh page I had used up my reserve comments and was wondering how in hell I was going to survive this zoological assault on my mental health. Oblivious to my trauma, Paul waxed prolix in his paleolithic epic narrative. I had to fight back a cry of joy when he turned the last page, but the joy stuck in my throat like rock salt when I saw the final outrage. Glossy, eight-by-ten, enormous in stark black-and-white: a mountain goat's head and, alongside the false, stuffed smile, cheek to cheek—it might have been a bizarre cliché out of a bolero—the mischievous face of Vilma, buggy eyes and stuck-out tongue.

I didn't dare look at Paul, who was blithely talking on. But I wasn't listening anymore. I felt stricken once more by doubt, as though by a blow from a hammer. In whose head was the truth filed away? Which one of them was the lesser of two evils? Which the greater?

I stayed awake most of the night, and when sleep finally knocked me out in the fifteenth round, I had no nightmares. I didn't need any.

The final day of my imprisonment, a Sunday, dawned brutally sunny. There was no mosquito-net fog typical of a Pyrenees morning. I heard Paul talking on the stairway with his mother and I heard them both go downstairs. I took ages to get dressed but then had to take my blouse off again. I had put it on inside out, an old, tried and true sign of inner strife. I took a blank sheet of paper and wrote in great big letters:

I'M LEAVING TOMORROW

I cut the paper and folded it, went out and slipped it under Vilma's door and knocked softly to announce my miniscule literary invasion. Sleeping Beauty did not acknowledge.

I followed the smell of true coffee down the stairs only to find that I had wasted my conspiratorial energies: there was the great Vilma, live via satellite, in all her Puerto Rican splendor, light years away from the depressing duet with the goat.

The old folks had gone to mass. Paul, in a burst of filial devotion, had accompanied them. Vilma was the contented, affectionate companion she had been on that cold night on which I arrived bearing fragrances from the island. We left our dishes in the sink, made some roquefort cheese sandwiches, filled a wine skin with red wine and marched out into the cold morning like a couple of schoolgirls. My friend was full of energy. She had a boundless vitality so frequent in my people, whose milk of life is misery.

"Get ready to pick up your feet," she said. "I've got ants in my pants."

And we walked and walked, singing *Verde Luz, Coño Despierta Boricua, Isla Nena* and a medley of other patriotic *apéritifs* for the return to the island. We went down to the river, stayed there quite a while remembering the crazy years and passing the wineskin back and forth. Vilma and Carola, laughing themselves silly, the way people will who feel either totally irresponsible or absolutely certain of tragedy. The violence of men and women seemed suspended. Its face, the face of a vampire subdued by the light of dawn, was hidden from us.

I acted on a happy notion: I proposed to Vilma that we return to Puerto Rico together. That is coming, she answered, in its own good time. The gravity of what she meant slowly seeped into my mind. Vilma was calm. She had the crushing tranquility about her of one who has made up her mind.

Miseur Beret was in charge of the soiree. In what amounted to a world record in loquacity, he told me every heroic twist and turn in the Second World War, while Madame, Paul and Vilma watched an old Marcel Carné film.

The night before is always a groove. I packed my suitcase and travel bag like a box of herbs for the Magi. That night I dreamt of French women who had their heads shaved for sleeping with Nazis.

The farewell was brief. I sat between two Arab workers en route to Morocco by way of Spain, and waved good-bye to Vilma through the window. Ever loyal to the precepts of his Manual of Western Civilization, Paul kept waving until the end. Vilma was more primitive about it and left before the train pulled out.

A veteran now of countless emotions, I dropped into my seat.

I anchored my eyes on the ambiguous countryside, as though awaiting a sign that will not appear.

At the border, I hustled to buy a Spanish newspaper while they switched cars.

VI

No fireworks, no military parades greeted me upon my return. It took me a few days to get used to breathing without eyewitnesses. Again I found myself in lockstep with my classes, as I went back and forth between my room and the school. My life was a worst-seller following its dull course. Doña Finí had nothing new to report.

Despite the mad pace, I couldn't stop thinking of Vilma. Her stylized image as the Latin madonna martyred my dreams. I finally stole a little time and wrote to her, a long letter full of questions, advice, everything I had not had the ovaries to tell her. It was my way of trying to allay with one stroke the succulent guilt complex I had been nursing since our departure.

Five, six weeks went by. Vilma never took this long to answer. Exile had made her prompt if nothing else. Were her feelings hurt? Had my postal impromptu disappointed her? Had she perhaps returned to Bordeaux? Surely they would forward her correspondence if that were the case ... I sent a note to the address in Bordeaux warning her of my other letter and asking her to acknowledge receipt.

My first letter came back in October. There, among my bills, was the envelope, soiled, tattooed with contradictory post office stamps, sticking jeeringly out of the mailbox at me. The phrase *DESTIN-ATAIRE INCONNU* traced in red over Vilma's name tightened around my heart with quiet foreboding.

Editor's Note

Early in December 1982, the author brought us the present manuscript, which we now publish as part of our *Textimonies* collection. On the thirty-first of the same month, while seeing the old year out with some friends, she died of a gunshot to the head fired through the window of her residence by an unknown party.

The publisher wishes to offer her wholehearted support to those organizations which have demanded a thorough investigation of this case.

Griselda Lugo Fuentes
EDICIONES SEREMOS

Translated by Mark McCaffrey

Gabriel García Márquez
(1928–   )

Born in a small Colombian town near the Caribbean ports of
Barranquilla and Santa Marta, Gabriel García Márquez spent his
childhood in the home of his maternal grandparents, the local
patriarchs, and rarely saw his parents. It was already the twilight of
the banana boom that had once brought hundreds of wealthy
foreign adventurers, the United Fruit Company, and waves of anti-
union violence to a now decadent model for the future author's
imaginary town of Macondo. The same year García Márquez was
born, a demonstration by restive banana workers ended in a
massacre by government troops. Yet by the time Márquez was old
enough to listen to his grandfather's stirring recollections, all that
was left of the town of Aracataca were its corruption and poverty,
and the ghosts of its oligarchical past.

At twelve, Márquez left for boarding school and then law school
in Bogotá, where he never completed his degree. Instead, his
studies were interrupted by the closing of the university in 1948,
occasioned by the nationwide outbreak of violence following the
assassination of a liberal presidential candidate. Though Márquez
reregistered at the University of Cartagena, his time was now
devoted more to a budding journalistic career and some
experiments in fiction published only in magazines. In 1950, he
returned to Aracataca with his mother to sell his grandparents'
house, a confessed turning point in his gestation as a writer.

He moved to Barranquilla and began writing his first novel, *Leaf
Storm,* a tentative mapping out of his imaginary Macondo. After the
book was published in 1955, Márquez left for Europe as
correspondent to *El Espectador,* finally settling in a hotel on the left

bank of Paris. There he wrote *No One Writes to the Colonel* (1962) and worked on *In Evil Hour* (1962). After travels through Eastern Europe as a reporter, Márquez returned to Colombia in 1957, where a year later he married.

With the victory of Castro's revolution in 1959, Márquez was sent to Havana to cover some of the trials of Batista's followers and returned to Bogotá to organize a branch of Prensa Latina, a press agency set up to counter the anti-Castro propaganda of the international agencies. In 1961, he moved to New York to work for the same agency, but, soon after the Bay of Pigs invasion, a power struggle within the agency led him to resign.

Márquez settled in Mexico and published a collection of stories, *Big Mama's Funeral* (1962). While he worked on film scripts and then for an advertising agency, he seemed to have exhausted himself as a writer. Then, in 1965, something happened in the way of an overwhelming rush of inspiration: he quit his job and with his wife's help spent the next eighteen months working six to eight hours a day on what would turn out to be a Latin American sensation—*One Hundred Years of Solitude* (1967), a fantastic family saga that overnight became the touchstone of "magical realism."

In 1982, Márquez was awarded the Nobel Prize and presently divides his time between Cuba, Mexico, and Spain. His other works include the novels *Autumn of the Patriarch* (1975), *Chronicle of a Death Foretold* (1981), *Love in the Time of Cholera* (1985), the short stories *Innocent Erendira* (1972) and a fictional re-creation of the life of the Latin American liberator Simón Bolívar, *The General in His Labyrinth* (1989).

The Last Voyage
of the Ghost Ship

Now they're going to see who I am, he said to himself in his strong
new man's voice, many years after he had first seen the huge ocean
liner without lights and without any sound which passed by the
village one night like a great uninhabited palace, longer than the
whole village and much taller than the steeple of the church, and
it sailed by in the darkness toward the colonial city on the other
side of the bay that had been fortified against buccaneers, with its
old slave port and the rotating light, whose gloomy beams transfig-
ured the village into a lunar encampment of glowing houses and
streets of volcanic deserts every fifteen seconds, and even though
at that time he'd been a boy without a man's strong voice but with
his mother's permission to stay very late on the beach to listen to
the wind's night harps, he could still remember, as if still seeing it,
how the liner would disappear when the light of the beacon struck
its side and how it would reappear when the light had passed, so
that it was an intermittent ship sailing along, appearing and disappearing, toward the mouth of the bay, groping its way like a
sleepwalker for the buoys that marked the harbor channel until
something must have gone wrong with the compass needle, because it headed toward the shoals, ran aground, broke up, and sank
without a single sound, even though a collision against the reefs
like that should have produced a crash of metal and the explosion
of engines that would have frozen with fright the soundest-sleeping
dragons in the prehistoric jungle that began with the last streets of
the village and ended on the other side of the world, so that he
himself thought it was a dream, especially the next day, when he

375

saw the radiant fishbowl of the bay, the disorder of colors of the Negro shacks on the hills above the harbor, the schooners of the smugglers from the Guianas loading their cargoes of innocent parrots whose craws were full of diamonds, he thought, I fell asleep counting the stars and I dreamed about the huge ship, of course, he was so convinced that he didn't tell anyone nor did he remember the vision again until the same night of the following March when he was looking for the flash of dolphins in the sea and what he found was the illusory liner, gloomy, intermittent, with the same mistaken direction as the first time, except that then he was so sure he was awake that he ran to tell his mother and she spent three weeks moaning with disappointment, because your brain's rotting away from doing so many things backward, sleeping during the day and going out at night like a criminal, and since she had to go to the city around that time to get something comfortable where she could sit and think about her dead husband, because the rockers on her chair had worn out after eleven years of widowhood, she took advantage of the occasion and had the boatman go near the shoals so that her son could see what he really saw in the glass of the sea, the lovemaking of manta rays in a springtime of sponges, pink snappers and blue corvinas diving into the other wells of softer waters that were there among the waters, and even the wandering hairs of victims of drowning in some colonial shipwreck, no trace of sunken liners or anything like it, and yet he was so pigheaded that his mother promised to watch with him the next March, absolutely, not knowing that the only thing absolute in her future now was an easy chair from the days of Sir Francis Drake which she had bought at an auction in a Turk's store, in which she sat down to rest that same night, sighing, oh, my poor Olofernos, if you could only see how nice it is to think about you on this velvet lining and this brocade from the casket of a queen, but the more she brought back the memory of her dead husband, the more the blood in her heart bubbled up and turned to chocolate, as if instead of sitting down she were running, soaked from chills and fevers and her breathing full of earth, until he returned at dawn and found her dead in the easy chair, still warm, but half rotted away as after a snakebite, the same as happened afterward to four other women before the murderous chair was thrown into the sea, far away where it wouldn't bring evil to anyone, because it had been used so much over the centuries that its faculty for giving rest had been used up, and so he had to grow accustomed to his miserable routine of an orphan who was pointed out by everyone

as the son of the widow who had brought the throne of misfortune
into the village, living not so much from public charity as from the
fish he stole out of boats, while his voice was becoming a roar, and
not remembering his visions of past times anymore until another
night in March when he chanced to look seaward and suddenly,
good Lord, there it is, the huge asbestos whale, the behemoth beast,
come see it, he shouted madly, come see it, raising such an uproar
of dogs' barking and women's panic that even the oldest men remembered the frights of their great-grandfathers and crawled under their beds, thinking that William Dampier had come back, but
those who ran into the street didn't make the effort to see the
unlikely apparatus which at that instant was lost again in the east
and raised up in its annual disaster, but they covered him with
blows and left him so twisted that it was then he said to himself,
drooling with rage, now they're going to see who I am, but he took
care not to share his determination with anyone, but spent the
whole year with the fixed idea, now they're going to see who I am,
waiting for it to be the eve of the apparition once more in order
to do what he did, which was steal a boat, cross the bay, and spend
the evening waiting for his great moment in the inlets of the slave
port, in the human brine of the Caribbean, but so absorbed in his
adventure that he didn't stop as he always did in front of the Hindu
shops to look at the ivory mandarins carved from the whole tusk
of an elephant, nor did he make fun of the Dutch Negroes in their
orthopedic velocipedes, nor was he frightened as at other times of
the copper-skinned Malayans, who had gone around the world enthralled by the chimera of a secret tavern where they sold roast
filets of Brazilian women, because he wasn't aware of anything
until night came over him with all the weight of the stars and the
jungle exhaled a sweet fragrance of gardenias and rotten salamanders, and there he was, rowing in the stolen boat toward the mouth
of the bay, with the lantern out so as not to alert the customs
police, idealized every fifteen seconds by the green wing flap of
the beacon and turned human once more by the darkness, knowing that he was getting close to the buoys that marked the harbor
channel, not only because its oppressive glow was getting more
intense, but because the breathing of the water was becoming sad,
and he rowed like that, so wrapped up in himself, that he didn't
know where the fearful shark's breath that suddenly reached him
came from or why the night became dense, as if the stars had
suddenly died, and it was because the liner was there, with all of
its inconceivable size, Lord, bigger than any other big thing in the

world and darker than any other dark thing on land or sea, three hundred thousand tons of shark smell passing so close to the boat that he could see the seams of the steel precipice, without a single light in the infinite portholes, without a sigh from the engines, without a soul, and carrying its own circle of silence with it, its own dead air, its halted time, its errant sea in which a whole world of drowned animals floated, and suddenly it all disappeared with the flash of the beacon and for an instant it was the diaphanous Caribbean once more, the March night, the everyday air of the pelicans, so he stayed alone among the buoys, not knowing what to do, asking himself, startled, if perhaps he wasn't dreaming while he was awake, not just now but the other times too, but no sooner had he asked himself than a breath of mystery snuffed out the buoys, from the first to the last, so that when the light of the beacon passed by the liner appeared again and now its compasses were out of order, perhaps not even knowing what part of the ocean sea it was in, groping for the invisible channel but actually heading for the shoals, until he got the overwhelming revelation that that misfortune of the buoys was the last key to the enchantment and he lighted the lantern in the boat, a tiny red light that had no reason to alarm anyone in the watchtowers but which would be like a guiding sun for the pilot, because, thanks to it, the liner corrected its course and passed into the main gate of the channel in a maneuver of lucky resurrection, and then all the lights went on at the same time so that the boilers wheezed again, the stars were fixed in their places, and the animal corpses went to the bottom, and there was a clatter of plates and a fragrance of laurel sauce in the kitchens, and one could hear the pulsing of the orchestra on the moon decks and the throbbing of the arteries of high-sea lovers in the shadows of the staterooms, but he still carried so much leftover rage in him that he would not let himself be confused by emotion or be frightened by the miracle, but said to himself with more decision than ever, now they're going to see who I am, the cowards, now they're going to see, and instead of turning aside so that the colossal machine would not charge into him, he began to row in front of it, because now they really are going to see who I am, and he continued guiding the ship with the lantern until he was so sure of its obedience that he made it change course from the direction of the docks once more, took it out of the invisible channel, and led it by the halter as if it were a sea lamb toward the lights of the sleeping village, a living ship, invulnerable to the torches of the beacon, that no longer made it invisible but made it aluminum every fifteen seconds, and the crosses of the church, the misery of the houses, the illusion began to stand out, and still the ocean liner followed behind him, following his will inside of it, the captain asleep on his heart side, the fighting bulls in the snow of their pantries, the solitary patient in the infirmary, the orphan water of its cisterns, the unredeemed pilot who must have mistaken the cliffs for the docks, because at that instant the great roar of the whistle burst forth, once, and he was soaked with the downpour of steam that fell on him, again, and the boat belonging to someone else was on the point of capsizing, and again, but it was too late, because there were the shells of the shoreline, the stones of the streets, the doors of the disbelievers, the whole village illuminated by the lights of the fearsome liner itself, and he barely had time to get out of the way to make room for the cataclysm, shouting in the midst of the confusion, there it is, you cowards, a second before the huge steel cask shattered the ground and one could hear the neat destruction of ninety thousand five hundred champagne glasses breaking, one after the other, from stem to stern, and then the light came out and it was no longer a March dawn but the noon of a radiant Wednesday, and he was able to give himself the pleasure of watching the disbelievers as with open mouths they contemplated the largest ocean liner in this world and the other aground in front of the church, whiter than anything, twenty times taller than the steeple and some ninety-seven times longer than the village, with its name engraved in iron letters, *Halálcsillag*, and the ancient and languid waters of the seas of death dripping down its sides.

Translated by Gregory Rabassa

Guillermo Cabrera Infante
(1929–   )

Born in the Oriente province of Cuba, Guillermo Cabrera Infante grew up in a poor family of militant communists who moved to Havana in 1941. He began writing in his teens and, in 1952, had his first encounter with censors (these, Batista's) over a story containing English profanities. A founder of the Cuban Cinematheque, he became the film critic (under the pseudonym "G. Cain") and eventually managing editor of the popular weekly *Carteles*.

After the Cuban revolution, Cabrera Infante helped to found the literary supplement to the previously clandestine newspaper *Revolución*. For two years he served as its literary editor, whereupon it was shut down "for lack of paper" by the cultural czars, who found it too "deviationist" editorially and condemned its role in the making of a controversial documentary (filmed by Infante's brother) on post-revolutionary Cuban nightlife. That year he also married his present wife, the actress Miriam Gómez, and published a book of short stories he later disavowed.

In 1961, Infante was sent to Belgium as cultural attaché. In 1965, he returned briefly to Cuba for his mother's funeral, then broke with Cuba definitively, renouncing his diplomatic post and eventually taking up permanent residence in London. That same year he won Spain's prestigious Biblioteca Breve Prize for a manuscript he would extensively revise (in part, with the inadvertently comic assistance of the Spanish censors) and finally publish in 1967—his masterpiece *Three Trapped Tigers*. By a spectacular mimesis of the vernacular and the vulgar (whose point of departure is the Roman twilight of Petronius's *The Satyricon*), the novel resurrects those lost Havana nights repudiated by the revolution.

In addition to working with his translators on the English and French versions that followed, Infante wrote several screenplays for Hollywood, including *Vanishing Point,* and translated Joyce's *Dubliners.* He also reworked some of the material he had stripped from the final *Three Trapped Tigers* into a devastating verbal fugue on Cuban violence perpetrated in the name of History from Columbus to Castro, which he titled *A View of Dawn in the Tropics* (1974). Then, in 1979, he published *Infante's Inferno,* a satirically erotic *bildungsroman* tracing the cinemato-sexual education of a slapstick Don Juan. His most recent work, written directly in English, is the anecdotal *Holy Smoke* (1985)—a comic disquisition on the cinematic, literary, and historical pleasures of the Cuban cigar.

The Phantom
of the Essoldo

"The Phantom of the Opera really existed"
G. Leroux

The L in London is for labyrinth: the city is indeed an enormous maze of names. Let me amaze you utterly, foreign visitor. I live in Gloucester Road, the one in South Kensington, postal zone SW7. But to hit my flat your taxi-driver must be as precise as a bombardier armed with a computing sight. (If you come by tube you'd better use a range-finder.) Alight barely three hundred yards to the right and you'll be completely off the mark: the street, the same street, is then called Palace Gate. That is if you're heading for Kensington Gardens. If you're river bound, Gloucester Road soon becomes Cranley Gardens and all of a sudden you are not in Cranley Gardens any more but in some other gardens, Elm Park Gardens—without even leaving the street where she lives. (She is of course the once and future love.) Then the road disappears abruptly. But does it? A Gloucester Road surfaces miles away across town, in East 10. There are other Gloucester Roads nicknamed successively Gloucester Road East 12, East 15, East 17, etc. Confused? You shouldn't be for there are further roads yet to come that, like Crookback Richard, are usurping the Gloucester title. They can be found hiding in Richmond (actually, in retribution there should be at least six Gloucesters in Richmond) and more of them in Croydon, Barnet and Twickenham— everywhere in London in fact. My God, the whole city is teeming with them! But by what other name can the road be as sweet as Gloucester?

We leave Number 53 one evening, any evening balmy enough,

382

turn left and only ten paces along Gloucester Road we are about
to cross Queen's Gate Gardens. There the smallest sign beneath
the street's name informs you: *"Leading to Queen's Gate Place,"* as if
this place were the center of nowhere. But a block later we will
come again to Queen's Gate Garden: a street in a mirror maze.
Today's London has become a version of Marienbad last year:
"Once more I walk along these corridors, through these halls,
across galleries in an immense edifice." We are not walking any
more on the pavement as hard as the real for the metaphysician,
but traversing a garden in the form of a solid square: a block of
flats. Perhaps this illusion is a mirage induced by so many rich
Arabs, or just Arabs, living in the luxury apartments: we are, don't
you forget it, in Saudi Kensington. Rolls and Bentleys parked by
the kerb must be another shape for the faithful camels of yore.
Made of glass and steel and chrome they sit still in their stolid wait
and their drivers, now called chauffeurs, do the ruminating in front
of the steering wheel. The desert, said the repetitious authoress of
the *Alf Layla wa Layla,* is a vast labyrinth made of sand: all space.
But then time is the sand in the hourglass' twin deserts: constantly
filling, endlessly emptying.

  Now we are facing the thick fog of fumes and the incessant fog-
horn of heavy traffic: here's Cromwell Road! To cross it is to brave
an endless stream of cars, taxis, trucks, motorbikes, bicycles and
vans—vain vanitas! But it also means to go across Harrington Gardens and those other gardens, Stanhope, and another gardens,
Wetherby Gardens, aligned to the right—and yet straight is the
path. Hereford Square and Brechin Place must be left behind before we come to Old Brompton Road, a Cronos of space: old does
not mean an expression of endearment here. (To think that we've
only walked a few blocks can give you vertigo.) Onslow Gardens is
not far from Ensor Mews, an enclave that is a homage to the Bel-
gian painter of masks and death's heads at a fancy-dress ball: life
as a kermesse, a fleshmass. Evelyn Gardens, which name could
mean pleasant in Dublin but in London is a confusion of noise
and smoke: Fulham Road ahead! Cross now and stay on the theo-
retically sunny side of the street, Elm Park Gardens: so many gardens and so few flowers. We reach now Elm Park Road, not to be
confused with Elm Park Road, N. 21. We turn left safely and then
right wisely—and we are in Old Church Street, with Mulberry Walk
and Mallord Street on our right darkly. And then, at last! it's the
beginning: King's Road! King's Road! King's Road! *Son et Lumière*

Bros. Sweetness and electric lights are a flowing stream that, unlike time and the river, flows both ways: up and down the road of life. Heraclitus has been proved wrong here: we can bathe more than once in the river of night for the sky is full of faces and neon dawns occur late at night and in the early morning: night had many names in Latin but Petronius, who lived by night, never had such profusion of nightlife. Invisible spiders weave the light in incandescent cobwebs. Wash your face in a nightwatch for electric night is here! Finally *l'éblouissement* of the fantastic façade that in crummy daylight is only brickwork and brown paint. The front, a-gleaming, makes us wade the stream, the street, to attain our goal, our gaol: *The Essoldo.* Night is about to become again aurora.

After buying the two tickets, or the same ticket twice, and about to go in, I looked up at a sign above painted with white light. Half of a sign rather: the odd end that said *alma.* Soul in Spanish perhaps? Or Alma Mahler Gropius Werfel in person, *die lustige Witwe?* Black is the colour of my true love's brown eyes in the dark. But nothing isolates twin souls more than darkness: it's the scalpel for Siamese siblings. Dark is the grave. So's a cinema hall when all the lights are out. Harrods said: "When you enter a cinema you enter another world." But when the cinema is dark—

"Damn it! We're late again. Damn!"

Souls so lost so suddenly.

"But the picture has just started!"

"Says who?"

"The usherette, that's who."

"Hush the usherette!"

"She should know."

"Usherettes, dear, can't tell a moving picture from a swinging door. Can't you see the movie's almost over?"

"But it has just started! Look at everybody at it."

"What do I look at?"

"The actors. They're all expectant! The movie's just begun."

"Not for me. Credits are not the menu but my main course."

"Look—"

"If I don't see the credits the movie might as well be over. At least if it's over I'd be able to catch the end credits, plus the cast."

"But dear—"

"Can't you see I won't be able to tell who's who?"

"Dear—"

"Who's the villain, who plays the lead?"

"Look, dear—girls."

"What?"

"Girls."

"Where?"

I looked all over the stalls.

"Up there."

"Which balcony?"

"On the screen, dearie. One hundred girls and a man—"

"My God! Deanna Durbin in reverse."

My dream at last come true! To drown in a lake of legs! Ahah! A soul at sea. There and then I stopped missing the tall buildings, the searchlights, the coloured beams—the fanfare! All slightly Art Deco—Pop Art Deco. The logo in the shape of things to come. The art of the 20th Century. Vitaphonefare. *Le cinéma parle: Ce soir-là, qui était celui les directeurs démissionnaires de l'Opéra, donnaient leur dernière soirée de gala.*

I've never been able to catch the name of anyone I meet for the first time. Those resigning managers of the Opera, for example, M. Devine—M. Polyakov? Are those their real names? To guess a Polish name! Like an astronomer I must rely thus on the stars. But this time, you see, there were no stars. Not even a starlet. For the first time I had to learn their names from scratch, Winslow Leach, Swan, Phoenix—she who's not a screamer but a singer and dances so gracefully, so beautifully, it's a pity that she should sing. But at least, true to her name, she doesn't die. Not really anyway. Swan has no other name. His past is a mystery but his person is already a legend, like Gloria Swanson. He brought the blues to Britain and Liverpool harmonies to America. He made a group famous, the Juicy Fruits. Now he's looking for the sound of the spheres, to inaugurate his own Xanadu, his own Disneyland, his music palace—the *Paradise!* He is also the head of Death Records. Its label is black, its logo a dead canary.

Let's come back to Phoenix: we must always come back to her, for she is a frequent Phoenix. She's from Arizona, has a fine contralto, eternally starry eyes and a puckered mouth, always about to smile. Though she is tiny she dances with a vigorous, petulant grace that is animal yet tamed. She looks like a child: a beautiful brat about to be spoiled by Swan and fame, in that order. She dances away amidst music and movement and graceful gestures. "It's magic!" proclaims the billboard under her face: pretty baby. But it's all Swan's ways, who looks like a *reductio ad absurdum:* Robert Redford as an ageless midget. He is in fact a dwarf older than Doc and Grumpy put together but he looks like Dumpy, the perverted urchin, a lecherous leprechaun, Tom Thumb up. Somewhere in his mansion—his house is his castle—he has a video tape with his picture in glorious Technicolour that ages and dry rots in his place, while his face is as spotless as his white gloves. He is, you'll never guess it, Mephisto Gray!

The movie begins with a rock group jerking, twisting, shaking, rattling and rolling more than swinging not to mention singing. Ah, aah, aah, yah, yah, yaaah! She waddy, oh shee waaaddy wadddy, ah, ah, aha, waddadddadaddy! Coocooocoook! Two gloved hands clap discreetly—and everybody in the rehearsal applauds wildly. Swan is pleased—or so it seems. He vaguely hears what his gopher is saying, complaining of some unfaithful wife and crying for revenge—suddenly; "Listen!" says Swan.

It is Winslow Leach at the piano singing his pop serenade: the future Phantom of the Popera. He is young but ungainly, gaunt, gauche, blond and balding and wearing thick eyeglasses to hide his bulging eyes: he is ugly but not yet a monster. He will become hideous eventually and will be forced to wear a mask. His cantata is now telling the story of Faust, he who sold his soul. Winslow's first bars at the piano sound very like an organ. When the gopher posing as a talent scout comes in to interview Winslow the latter informs him that his composition is a cantata on the theme, you've guessed it, of Faust. The scout asks him business-like: "What label's he on, Mac?"

Swan and his gopher and the Castro—the Castro is a castrato convertible, a rock singer with a high-pitched voice and an imposing physique. He pumps iron and belts out songs. But the part he plays is the one Winslow wrote for Phoenix to start with. The Castrato is a true singing capon, not Nelson Eddy. Very much like everybody else, capons are born to die but their death is almost never hair-raising. But the Capon's death will give you goosepimples. He is killed by Winslow Leach with a real death ray: a neon lightning! It's a sign of the times. The gopher too was shot by Winslow. Swan in turn was killed by time and the devil. So many villains and nobody left to hate! I would like to have somebody up there to really abhor. But there is none! I have only myself to hate. Wait a second! There is one. Such unperson is called Angelo Kuchachevich zu Schluderparcheru. Is he really? When he is Herbert Lom he is capable of saying, whispering rather this: "It's the will, Madeleine. The will that lives on!" From the underworld or the nether regions he mutters thus and you instantly know the meaning of the phrase "love that lives forever," as you know the meaning of the word forever—and even the meaning of the word love.

I must. Must you? Yes! I must get up and go, *now*. Though I hate to. I hate getting up in the middle of the movie. But I must go. Now!

watch for the ghost

It was little Jammes—the girl with the tip-tilted nose, the forget-me-not eyes, the rose-red cheeks and the lily-white neck and shoulders—who gave the explanation in a trembling voice:

"It's a ghost!" And she locked the door.

Superstitions

Sorelli was very superstitious. She shuddered when she heard little Jammes speak of the ghost.

"Have you seen him?"

"As plainly as I see you now!" said little Jammes whose legs were giving way beneath her, and she dropped with a moan into a chair.

Thereupon little Girty—the girl with eyes black as sloes, hair black as ink, a swarthy complexion and a poor little skin stretched over poor little bones—little Girty added:

"If that's the ghost, he's very ugly!"

"Oh, yes!" cried the chorus of ballet girls.

Ghosts

"Bah!" said one of them, who had more or less kept her head, "you see the ghost everywhere!"

And it was true. For several months, there had been nothing discussed at the Opera but this ghost in evening clothes who stalked about the building, like a shadow, who spoke to nobody, to whom nobody dared speak and who vanished as soon as he was seen, no one knowing how or where. As became a real ghost, he made no noise in walking. People began by laughing and making fun of this spectre dressed like a man of fashion or an undertaker. But the ghost legend soon swelled to enormous proportions among the corps de ballet.

After all, who had seen him? You meet so many men in dress-clothes at the Opera who are not ghosts. But this dress suit had a peculiarity of its own. It covered a skeleton. At least, so the ballet girls said. And, of course, it had a death's head.

"He is extraordinarily thin and his dress-coat hangs on a skeleton frame. His eyes are so deep that you can hardly see the fixed pupils. You just see two big black holes in a dead man's skull. His skin, which is stretched across his bones like a drumhead, is not white, but a nasty yellow. His nose is so little worth talking about that you can't see it side-face—and the absence of that nose is a horrible thing to look at. All the hair he has is three or four long dark locks on his forehead and behind his ears."

"The Opera ghost!"

"The Opera ghost! The Opera ghost!"

"The Opera ghost!"

Kindness to ghosts

Richard said: "But after all, it seems to me that you were much too kind to that ghost. If I had such a troublesome ghost as that, I should not hesitate to have him arrested!"

"But how? Where?" they cried, in a chorus. "We have never seen him!"

"But when he comes to his box?"

"We have never seen him in his box."

"Then sell it."

The ultimatum

MY DEAR MANAGERS:

So is it to be war between us?

If you still care for peace, here is my ultimatum. It consists of the four following conditions:

  1. You must give me back my private box; and I wish it to be at my free disposal from henceforward.

  2. The part of Margarita shall be sung this evening by Christine Daae. Never mind about Carlotta. She will be ill.

  3. I absolutely insist upon the good and loyal services of Mme. Girty, my box-keeper, whom you will reinstate in her functions forthwith.

  4. Let me know by a letter handed to Mme. Girty, who will see that it reaches me, that you accept, as your predecessors did, the conditions in my memorandum-book relating to my monthly allowance. I will inform you later how you are to pay it to me. If you refuse, you will give *Faust* tonight in a house with a curse upon it.

Take my advice and be warned in time.

                                          O.G.

"What's OG?"

"Opera Ghost."

"I see."

Horse sense

"Eleven," said the head riding-master.

"Twelve," repeated Richard.

"Eleven," repeated Lachenel.

"No, the acting manager told me that you had twelve horses!"

"I did have twelve, but I only have eleven since Cesar was stolen."

"Has Cesar been stolen?"

"Cesar the white horse in the *Profeta?*"

"There are no two Cesars. There are *no* two Cesars and he's been stolen!"

"How?"

"I don't know. Nobody knows."

"But after all, M. Lachenel, you must have some idea."

"Yes I have," M. Lachenel declared. "I have an idea and I'll tell you what it is.

"There's no doubt about it in my mind."

He walked up to the two managers and whispered:

"It's the ghost who did the trick!"

Richard gave a jump.

"What did you see?"

"I saw, as clearly as I now see you, a black shadow riding a white horse that was as like Cesar as two peas!"

"And did you run after them?"

"I did and I shouted. But they were too fast for me and disappeared in the darkness of the underground gallery."

Marche funèbre

The papers of the day state that there were numbers wounded and one killed. The chandelier had crashed down upon the head of the wretched woman who had come to the Opera for the first time in her life, the one whom M. Richard had appointed to succeed Mme Girty, the ghost's box-keeper, in her functions! She died on the spot and in the morning, a newspaper appeared with this headline:

TWO HUNDRED KILOS ON THE HEAD OF A CONCIERGE

That was her sole epitaph!

"LATPG."

Will of the whisper.

"What?"

"Look at those pretty girls."

What was she talking about? On the screen there were only two ugly men talking of royalties.

"I don't see any pretty girls, only two angels."

"Angels? What angels?"

"*Agents.* They're talking points."

"I don't mean up there but right next to me."

I spied with my little eye. In fact, out of the corner of my right eye, through a glass clearly, framed by my tortoiseshell armature, beyond her body: I saw no girls but two women. Not bad. I turned a little as if to talk with my Constance about Swan and saw they were a brunette and a blonde. The blonde was taller—or perhaps had a longer spine: *une blonde d'Ingres*. Or bigger buttocks to sit on: *steatopygia*. The brunette had a nice profile but already on its way to going witch. They were cosily watching the movie. A fine arrangement. But better the shadows than ordinary flesh. I returned to the show.

Lon Chaney moved with a studied languor, as if stealth became sloth. Thus through the sewers of Paris did Chaney walk. Ah Alonzo! How you suffered and pained and pined—and never complained. All he said was: "If I am a Phantom it is because man's hatred made me so!" Or more privately to Christine: "You shall stay to brighten my toad's existence with your love." As you have seen he signed his communiqués modestly "OG," when he could have written dramatically *The Phantom*. Claude Rains was playing the "Lullaby of the Bells" while Susanna Foster listened. But she didn't pay any attention, really. She seemed to have only overheard the bells. As to her own singing, her style of delivering a song could be called mere wishful singing. Oh Susanna! Meanwhile, in England, Herbert Lom grieved with howlings for all the wrongs done to him by several music critics he demoted to reviewers. Howlers and errata!

Chaney's makeup was so horrid, so repulsive and so frightening that no picture was released to the public before the motion picture opened. His horrendousness was so insulting to the eye then (before Hiroshima, before Auschwitz, before the horrors of modern warfare) that the movie was first shown to war veterens. Claude Rains had too fine a head to be a true monster from the inner world: *les égouts de Paris* were too disgusting for him, *un monstre délicat*. Even his mask was elegant, designed to highlight his British chin, which vanished more than receded in *The Invisible Man* leaving only his accent as an unseen stiff upper lip. Herbert Lom had a disturbing way of looking off screen when there was nobody there, as if trying to read his cue card and at the same time keeping his leading lady in focus. The mad man-made monster was London Chaney, Herbert Lomdon or both, Herbert Lom Chaney, as if Rains never came. But behind the mask, Czech or American, there always will be the hideous face of the real Lon Chaney, whom even the wolf-man called his senior: with his true mask of scar tissue, his eyes all orbs and his teeth, his teeth! Eech! How to describe them? His ghost gums alone could give pyorrhea a bad name. (Is that why dentists call it now periodontal disease? An innocuous name for a sickening illness.) But at a given moment, ladies and gentlemen, he comes down—no, he *descends*—the grand staircase of l'Opera in full colour, though it all has been tragic black and white before. If only you could see him in his cape (black and crimson), his costume of a Spanish grandeur and his be-jewelled mask—and how all of a sudden all around him instantly become a masked ball, a masque, a fancy-dress party! He was, as it were, the man who invented the carnival.

The fancy dress·ball

The ball was an exceptional affair, given some time before Shrovetide, in honour of the anniversary of the birth of a famous draughtsman; and it was expected to be much gayer, noisier, more Bohemian than the ordinary masked ball. Numbers of artists had arranged to go, accompanied by a whole cohort of models and pupils, who, by midnight, began to create an enormous din. Raoul climbed the grand staircase at five minutes to twelve and did not linger to look.

Raoul leaned against a door-post and waited. He did not wait long. A black domino passed and gave a quick squeeze to the tips of his fingers. He understood that it was she and followed her:

"Is that you, Christine?" he asked, between his teeth.

The black domino turned round promptly and raised her finger to her lips, no doubt to warn him not to mention her name again. Raoul continued to follow her in silence.

He could not help noticing a group crowding round a person whose disguise, eccentric air and gruesome appearance were causing a sensation. It was a man dressed all in scarlet, with a huge hat and feathers on the top of a wonderful death's head. From his shoulders hung an immense red-velvet cloak, which trailed along the floor like a king's train; and on this cloak was embroidered, in gold letters, which everyone read and repeated out loud, "Don't touch me! I am Red Death stalking abroad!"

Christine was pouting, almost crying.
"But you promised to let me go free if I behaved."
"Did I?"
"Yes! You promised."
"I did no such thing."
"You promised."

"I refuse to remember."

"You promised!"

"Ma chère, my *trahison d'être* is more powerful than your *raison d'être."*

Phantom by daylight

"I have never seen him by daylight ... it must be awful! ... Oh, the first time I saw him! ... I thought he was going to die."

"Why?"

"Because I had seen him!"

The masher, ma chère

"Suddenly a hand was laid on mine ... or rather, a stone-cold, bony thing that seized my wrist and did not let go. I cried out again. An arm took me round the waist and supported me. I struggled for a little while and then gave up the attempt. I was dragged toward the little red light and then I saw that I was in the hands of a man wrapped in a large cloak and wearing a mask that hid his whole face. I made one last effort; my limbs stiffened, my mouth opened to scream, but a hand closed it, a hand that felt on my lips, on my skin ... a hand that smelt of death. Then I fainted away.

"When I opened my eyes, we were still surrounded by darkness. A lantern, on the ground, showed a bubbling well. The water splashing from the well disappeared almost at once, under the floor on which I was lying, with my head on the knee of the man in the black cloak and the black mask. He was bathing my temples and his hands smelt of death.

"I made no movement and let myself go. The black shape held me up, and I made no effort to escape. A curious feeling of peacefulness came over me and I thought that I must be under the influence of some cordial. I had the full command of my senses; and my eyes became used to the darkness, which was lit, here and there, by fitful gleams. I calculated that we were in a narrow circular gallery, probably running all around the Opera, which is immense, underground. We slipped across the noiseless water in the bluey light then we were in the dark again and we touched shore. And I was once more taken up in the man's arms. And then, suddenly I was silent, dazed by the light. ... Yes, a dazzling light. I was in the middle of a drawing room that seemed to me to be decorated, adorned and furnished with nothing but flowers both magnificent and stupid, because of the silk ribbons that tied them to baskets, like those which they sell in the shops on the boulevards. In the midst of all these flowers stood the black shape of the man in the mask, with arms crossed and he said, 'Don't be afraid, Christine; you are in no danger.' It was the Voice!

"I had, no doubt, to do with a terribly eccentric person, who, in some mysterious fashion, had succeeded in taking up his abode there, under the Opera house, five stories below the level of the ground."

"More than the story of my life this reads like the story of my escapades—my scurriculum vitae!"

The monster she would love to hate

"The terrible thing about it is he fills me with horror and I do not hate him. How can I hate him? Think of him at my feet, in the house on the lake, underground. He accuses himself, he curses himself, he implores my forgiveness! . . . He confesses his cheat. He loves me. He lays at my feet an immense and tragic love . . . He has carried me off for love! . . . He has imprisoned me with him, underground, for love! . . . But he respects me; he crawls, he moans, he weeps! . . . And when I stood up, Raoul, and told him that I could only despise him if he did not, then and there, give me my liberty . . . he offered it . . . he offered to show me the mysterious road . . . Only . . . only he rose too . . . and I was made to remember that, though he was not an angel, nor a ghost, nor a genius, he remained the Voice . . . for he sang. And I listened . . . and stayed! . . . That night, we did not exchange another word. He sang me to sleep."

His Name is Erik

"When I woke up, I was alone, lying on a sofa in a simply furnished little bedroom, with an ordinary mahogany bedstead, lit by a lamp standing on the marble top of a Louis-Philippe chest of drawers. I soon discovered that I was a prisoner, and that the only outlet from my room led to a very comfortable bathroom.

"I felt sure I had fallen into the hands of a madman. I felt inclined to laugh and to cry at the same time.

"This was the state of mind in which he found me. After giving

three taps on the wall, he walked in quietly through a door which I
had not noticed and which he left open. He had his arms full of
boxes and parcels and arranged them on the bed, in a leisurely
fashion, while I overwhelmed him with abuse and called upon him
to take off his mask, if it covered the face of an honest man. He
replied serenely, 'You shall never see Erik's face.'

"I was very angry, slammed the door in his face and went to the
bathroom. . . . When I came out again, feeling greatly refreshed, Erik
said that he loved me, but that he would never tell me so except
when I allowed him and that the rest of the time he would be devoted to music. 'What do you mean by the rest of the time?'

"Erik did not eat or drink. I asked him what his nationality was
and if that name of Erik did not point to his Scandinavian origin.
He said that he had no name and no country and that he had taken
the name Erik by accident.

"After lunch, he rose and gave me the tips of his fingers, saying
he would like to show me over his flat; but I snatched away my hand
and gave a cry. What I had touched was cold, and at the same time,
bony; and I remembered that his hands smelt of death. 'Oh forgive
me!' he moaned. And he opened a door before me. 'This is my
bedroom, if you care to see it. It is rather curious.' His manners, his
words, his attitudes gave me confidence and I went in without hesitation. I felt as if I were entering the room of a dead person. The
walls were all hung with black, but instead of the white trimmings
that usually set off that funeral upholstery, there was an enormous
stave of music with the notes of the Dies Irae, many times repeated.
In the middle of the room was a canopy, from which hung curtains
of red brocaded stuff, and, under the canopy, an open coffin. 'That
is where I sleep,' said Erik. 'One has to get used to everything in
life, even to eternity.'

Unmasked!

"Then I saw the keyboard of an organ which filled one whole side
of the walls. On the desk was a music book, covered with red notes.
I asked leave to look at it and read, *Don Juan Triumphant.* 'Yes,' he
said, 'I compose sometimes. I began that work twenty years ago.
When I have finished, I shall take it away with me in that coffin and
never wake up again.' 'You must work at it as seldom as you can,' I
said. He replied, 'I sometimes work at it fourteen days and nights
together, during which I live on music only, and then I rest for years
at a time.' 'Will you play me something out of your *Don Juan Tri-*

umphant?' I asked, thinking to please him. 'You must never ask me that,' he said, in a gloomy voice. 'I will play you Mozart if you like, which will only make you weep; but my *Don Juan,* Christine, burns.'

"Erik's black mask made me think of the natural mask of the Moor of Venice. He was Othello himself. Suddenly I felt a need to see beneath the mask. I wanted to know the face of the voice, and with a movement which I was utterly unable to control, swiftly my fingers tore away the mask. Oh, horror, horror, horror, horror!

"If I lived to be a hundred, I should always hear the superhuman cry of grief and rage which he uttered when the terrible sight appeared before my eyes. . . . You have seen death's heads, when they have been dried and withered by the centuries, and perhaps, if you were not the victim of a nightmare, you saw his death's head at *Perros.* And then you saw Red Death stalking about the last masked ball. But all those death's heads were motionless and their dumb horror was not alive. But imagine, if you can, Red Death's mask suddenly coming to life in order to express, with the four black holes of its eyes, its nose, and its mouth, the extreme anger, the mighty fury of a demon; and not a ray of light from the sockets, for, as I learned, later, you cannot see his blazing eyes except in the dark."

Tuisez-vous, Raoul!

"I fell back against the wall and he came up to me, grinding his teeth, as I fell upon my knees, he hissed mad, incoherent words and curses at me. Leaning over me, he cried, 'Look! You want to see! See! Feast your eyes, glut your soul on my cursed ugliness! Look at Erik's face! Now you know the face of the voice! I'm a very good looking fellow, eh? . . . When a woman has seen me, as you have, she belongs to me. She loves me forever. I am a kind of Don Juan, you know!' And, drawing himself to his full height, his hand on his hip, wagging the hideous thing that was his head on his shoulders, he roared, 'Look at me! I am Don Juan Triumphant!' And when I turned away my head and begged for mercy, he drew it to him, brutally, twisting his dead fingers into my hair."

"Enough! Enough!" cried Raoul.

"Oh, be quiet, Raoul, if you want to know!"

Christine stayed with her mouth open, agape: she was not aping Marilyn Monroe, though she too was a fake blonde. She was ready to go on with her story.

The continuing story of OG

"Then he hissed at me. 'Ah I frighten you, do I? . . . I dare say . . . Perhaps you think that I have another mask, eh, and that this . . . this . . . my head is a mask? Well,' he roared, 'Tear it off as you did the other! Come! Come along! I insist! Your hands! Your hands! Give me your hands!' And he seized my hands and dug them into his awful face. He tore his flesh with my nails, tore his terrible dead flesh with my nails. . . . 'Know,' he shouted, 'know that I am built up of death from head to foot and that it is a corpse that loves you and adores you and will never, never leave you! As long as you thought me handsome, you could have come back, but now that you know my hideousness, you would run away for good. Oh mad Christine, who wanted to see me! . . . When my own father never saw me and when my mother, so as not to see me, made me present of my first mask!'

"He had let go of me at last and was dragging himself about on the floor, uttering terrible sobs. And then he crawled away like a snake, went into his room, closed the door and left me alone to my reflections. Presently I heard the sound of the organ. It intoxicated me; and I opened the door that separated us. Erik rose as I entered, *but dared not turn in my direction.* 'Erik,' I cried, 'show me your face without fear! I swear that you are the most unhappy and sublime of men; and if ever again I shiver when I look at you, it will be because I am thinking of the splendour of your genius!' Then Erik turned round, for he believed me, and I also had faith in myself. He fell at my feet, with words of love . . . with words of love in his dead mouth . . . and the music had ceased . . . He kissed the hem of my dress and did not see that I closed my eyes."

The Phantom's Identi-Kit

"I had occasion to go to the dressing room and, remembering the lesson he had once given me, I had no difficulty in discovering the trick that made the wall with the mirror swing round—to catch the monster stooping over the little well, in the Communists' road and sprinkling the forehead of Christine Daaé, who had fainted. The white horse which had disappeared was standing quietly beside them. I showed myself. It was terrible. I saw sparks fly from those yellow eyes. (In this connection, I may say that, when he went out in the streets or ventured to show himself in public, he wore a pasteboard nose, with a moustache attached to it, instead of his own horrible hole of a nose. This did not quite take away his corpse-like air, but it made him almost, I say almost, endurable to look at.)"

I prefer, though, Christine's own version as told some time later. Memory looms longer from afar. She confronted the Phantom in his lair, using the vanity of all builders as she had read in Ibsen.

"Do you like it here?"

The Phantom looked at her askance, to ask once:

"How do you mean?"

"Do you live in this *place*?"

But she didn't mean to be rude, of course. She managed to make *place* sound like *home,* as one sometimes mispronounces haven and it sounds more like heaven. It was difficult, this turn of word. But, after all, she was an opera singer, used to phrasing.

"I don't live, I *dwell* here," said the Phantom curtly—or was it courtly? "This is my abode. But in fact to dwell here is to live in the place of excreta."

"What do you mean?"

"I mean what I say. Excreta. There's no secret about excreta. There's no such thing as secreta, is there? What in a delusion of a grandee I sometimes call my picture palace is actually an underground building of shit. The famed canals, my black Venice, are in fact sewers. I truly deserve the Order of the Ordure! Here I dwell, *ma petite,* and dream and develop my philosophy: mere schemes to go on living after death. You can call it all, if you like, my *mystique de la merde.* It's all right with me. Moreover, I love the label. I like alliterations, you see. *Mal de merde,* speaking like a skipper."

"But you do lead a virtuous life."

"I suppose I do. But I have a vice, though. Punning. It's my only vice but I'm truly addicted. Do you know *Les Exploits de Rocambole?*"

"Rock and ball? What is it? A new dance? I'm afraid I don't know it."

"That's a good one! Well, Rocambole was to be a pallbearer in an Irish funeral. Somebody asked him if he was a griever and he answered: "No, I'm only here for the bier." Why don't you laugh? That was a wake of a pun. Here, let me show you."

He advanced toward her, his arms outstretched.

"Give us a kitsch."

She stepped back physically as if repelled aesthetically. The

Ghost felt the rejection in his very soul. Underneath his mask he should have been blushing—but bones don't blush. To cover for the embarrassment he looked at the ceiling, at the walls, as if surveying the place. He opened his arms in an all-embracing gesture. More than the Grand Old Man of the Opera he looked just like a madman.

"Don't you like the romantic grandeur of my *carcere?* A gaol with fall, as it were! Look at the dramatic expression I've given to my *Lebensraum,* how I've placed the *Sturm* next to the *Drang.* This is the representation of architecture transformed into the architecture of drama and imprisonment: a penitentiary for one under the Opera! Pure Piranesi."

"I see," said Christine politely.

"Do you really? It's getting dark in here."

The Phantom giggled.

"Excuse me but that was a joke."

Christine didn't even smile.

"Dostoievski, my colleague, once said that ideals have consequences. Today, tonight rather, I know better than the good old Dosto. I know that idols have consequences."

Christine remained silent. It was obvious that she didn't understand. She looked around instead, at the dark high ceiling. The Ghost noticed it.

"This most excellent canopy is a copy of an Art Deco marquee. It used to bear a motto: 'More stars than there are in heaven.' If you look closely you'll see that the stars have been painted, painfully, one by one. Some say it's not functional. A case of sour Gropius, no doubt."

"It's beautiful!"

"To me it's more than that: it's life. A foul and pestilent congregation of fumes."

"Why do you say that?"

The Phantom seemed to manage a smile somehow in the dark and under his mask.

"Give me your hand."

"Here."

"Where?"

"Here."

"Damn this place! Your hand, your hand, woman!"

"But here it is!"

"That's better. Now I can smile and also, with a little help from a joke, even laugh today. Though I'll be a grave man tomorrow."

"But you can be grave today if you want to."

"I know. I'm already grave but will I live tomorrow?"

"Tomorrow's another day," said Christine with conviction.

"Will I leave?"

"If you wish you can live forever."

"You misunderstand me—or rather you misspell me. I said, will I *leave?*"

"We all die, you and me both too."

"But my dear, that was another pun about the Will to Live!"

"We all die, you and me too."

"You said that before."

"Did I?"

"Yes, I'm afraid you're repeating yourself."

"How boring!"

"Not necessarily. You can bore me stiff if you want."

"If I do then we will die together."

"Good girl! I hate doing things by myself. Love and death are never good if done all alone."

"Aren't you confusing living with something else?"

"Like what?"

"Masturbation, if you pardon the expression."

"As the wounded egg said, *Poché!*"

"What do you mean by that?"

"That I am touched, that you moved me. In other words, I've been wounded by your arrow, Christa."

"My name is *Christine.*"

"Oh Christ!"

"Please, don't swear."

"Christ, in a crisis, you can call me what you want; the Phantom, the Ghost. Whatever. I'll call myself as if you were my owner, Christie's." The Phantom uttered a guffaw. "This is ridiculous! It's beginning to sound like an auction. Going, going, gone!"

Christine started to cry.

Quit stalling. Firmly I managed to leave my stall seat. I *had* to.

He is always seen pointing away at a thing unseen. Is he trying to tell us something or merely calling our attention away from his deformed face? Ah, the touchiness of monsters! I saw him once sitting at the organ, a big brute by Cavaillé-Coll, turning away on his stool, his chest cut out by lighting from the windchest, emerging from the enormous console with the manual keyboard, his tiny dancing feet still on the pedal-board, facing the multitude of pipes and reeds (actioned by the old Sticker-Backfall-Tracker mechanism instead of by Pneumatic Action), an affair all shiny brass and polished mahogany and ivory plus ebony on the keyboard. The player was transformed into another organ of the organ in spite of his frock-coat and his elegant but cumbersome crimson cloak, erect while remaining sitting, his right arm outstretched, his bony hand pointing again at the unseen off screen, his head crowning his back and red bulk. His head, his skull, his death's head of a face: teeth bare, lips parted and dry and crumbling like those of a living mummy come back from the dead after the twenty odd years when this movie was made. For, you see, it was Cagney as Chaney.

The present Phantom is the last in the dynasty, which he pronounces die nasty. He has an eerie voice, uncanny and forceful, and it comes from beyond the grave and into the funny phone. The name behind the name is Winslow Leach: wins low, win slow. Leach is just leech mispelt. The mockingbird beneath the bird mask is Winslow being mocked by a bird, a dead bird, a mute canary. Apart from the ancestral red cape, he actually has the head of a bird: an osprey, a bird of prey, a falcon-like bird. Though Winslow himself has been prey to scoundrels, exploiters and, funnily enough, ironic art leeches.

I pulled the heavy curtains rudely apart under the sign that said GENTLE—obviously half of it.

"What happened?" asked I, coming back as if coming to.

"Christine rode an albino stallion through the sewers."

"Which proves that you can take a white horse anywhere."

But she didn't get it. She simply did *not* get it. Women! Christine curled her lips.

"You wear a mask to hide your ugliness but your behaviour is hideous and yet you don't cover it with silk."

The Phantom bowed excessively, almost mockingly.

"I've been wounded by your arrow again. Twice. It is not, I vouch, Cupid's Bow, Clara."

"My name is Christine, if you please!"

"Good God, Chris, you certainly are a stickler for names! Can't you see the man is dying?"

"Who is?"

"I am, Chrissie. I am the man. But I'll never be your man. I'm grateful to you though. I couldn't sleep before I met you and your love made a zombie of me. I'll be awake even in death. It's love, Christine. Love that lives on!"

"What do you mean I helped you?"

"Allow me, please, a last Latin pedantry. *Amor vincit omnia,* except of course, *insomnia!*"

From somewhere (from above but not from heaven: *l'Opéra probablement*) came music and a voice singing "Una furtiva lagrima," from *L'Elisir d'amore,* by Gaetano Donizetti. Born Bergamo 1797, died there 1848, composed some sixty operas, had the gift of tune and knew how to write for singers.

"Ah, *il mio amico Mario!*"

"Sorry but I don't speak Spanish."

"But that's Italian. It means, Mario my friend, ah!"

"Does it hurt?"

"It's just an inversion. We villains are somewhat affected to a turn of phrase or two."

"Who's *we?* Your friends?"

"I have no friends. Not any more. We're not a gang, if that's what worries you."

"Oh but no! By no means—"

"In the last act, *mignonne,* villains are always left to fend, and feign, for themselves, utterly and hopelessly alone. Alone!"

OG hummed a bar or two from "Alone," aping Allan Jones on the pier. Villains are also good at parody and imitations. The Phantom smiled broadly, then laughed aloud as if singing the lead in *Pagliacci: ride, ride!* Obviously *A Night at the Opera* did a lot of harm to *l'Opéra* and to the Phantom's myth. Since then opera and the book have never been the same. OG sighed.

"I have no friends! That is, I have no friends left. Or right for that matter."

"Pray tell me, why do you do it then?"

"Do what?"

"All those things at the Opera."

"That's my *modus operandi.*"

He looked at her intently. She didn't move a muscle.

"*Castigat ridendo* but I don't see you laugh."

"I don't see you laugh either."

"That's on account of the mask. I'm a good punster though."

"Puns are the lowest form of wit," said Christine as if quoting.

"That's Addison's Disease."

"Which disease?"

"*Whose.* A girl is more beautiful when she knows her grammar."

"Who's disease?"

"That's better. Addison's. The man who established that last law of low comedy. But, as you can see, I'm an outlaw."

"Anybody can see that!"

"That, my sweet, is what I like about masks. Wear one, even a simple taffeta affair, and you are no longer a law-abiding citizen. A vulgar handkerchief over your mouth and the visit becomes a holdup. But if I go *larvatus prodeo* it's not because I'm a criminal. Morally, that is. I'm pure. Even more so because I live, literally, in the gutter. The urban turd, more than the Turbaned Turk, is my next-door neighbour not my mortal enemy. This is, for me, an everyday occurrence. It was a fart of life since I was a boy. I tried hard to study metaphysics but my father kept breaking wind. Wit can get no lower, *ma p'tite.*"

Christine took her hand to her nose and closed her eyes, mockingly. Suddenly the Phantom uttered a cry:

"I'm dying, Opera, dying!"

He fell to the floor, hurting himself with the base of a pillar. But his mask hid his pain with a pun. Was he really dying? The Phantom, with his thick Latinate accent, exclaimed as if indicting the fateful more than faithful girl:

"Keeler!"

Christine was aghast.

"Me?"

"Yes, you! You're killing me with love. Not with your love but with your lack of love, my unrequited love: this one-sided love of mine."

"Then you must be a romantic."

"Yes, you can call me a romantic. But you'll call me better if you call me an incurable romantic. Such is my sickness! I didn't get it by myself though. My father did. He gave it to my mother, the scoundrel. She passed it on to me in turn, the saint, unknowingly. Chancroid is the name. Not my mother's name but the name of the disease. Incurably hideous, hereditary, obscene. He could have been treated with potassium iodide, a cure available since 1834. He could, the fiend! Needless to say, he didn't. He gave it to my mother and she very soon had a ghost in her belly. Jingle belly, jingle belly! *Imagine, quand mon père, Louis, ne m'a jamais vu et quand ma mère, pour ne plus me voir, m'a fait cadeau, en pleurant, de mon premier masque!*"

But Christine didn't have a word of French. The Phantom saw it in her wide, English blue eyes.

"Oh, pardon my French! I couldn't help it."

"It's all right. I understood some."

"Did you really?"

"A pitty poor."

Did the Phantom smile? *Sait-on jamais.*

"You see, my dear, when in distress or fear or moved by passion one usually reverts to the mother tongue as if to mother."

"I understand."

"But not French, surely!"

"No, not French. I understand what you say in English about emotions and things."

"Do you?"

"Yes!"

"Then you'll understand me! For that's what I am: emotions and things covered by a mask."

He fainted dramatically.

"Has he died yet?" asked a voice in the dark.

"Not yet."

"He's always doing the dying," said the voice in the darkest.

"In different versions."

Her monster's voice

I recognized the voice of the monster.

"The requiem mass was not at all gay," Erik's voice resumed, "whereas the wedding mass—you can take my word for it—is magnificent! You must take a resolution. I can't go on living like this, like a mole in a burrow! *Don Juan Triumphant* is finished; and now I want to live like everybody else. I want to have a wife like everybody else and to take her out on Sundays. I have invented a mask that makes me look like anybody. People will not even turn round in the streets. You will be the happiest of all women. And we will sing, all by ourselves, till we swoon away with delight. You are crying! You are afraid of me! And yet I am not really wicked. Love and you shall see! All I wanted was to be loved for myself. If you loved me I should be as gentle as a lamb."

Suddenly the silence in the next room was disturbed by the ringing of an electric bell.

"Somebody ringing! Walk in, please!"

A sinister chuckle.

"Who has come bothering now? Wait for me here. I am going to tell the siren to open the door."

Heavy steps sounded slowly behind the wall, then stopped and made the floor creak once more. Next came a tremendous sigh, followed by a cry of horror from Christine, and we heard Erik's voice:

"I beg your pardon for letting you see a face like this!"

Another sigh, deeper and more tremendous still, came from the abysmal depth of a soul.

"Why did you cry out, Christine?"

"Because I am in pain, Erik."

"I thought I had frightened you."

"Erik, unloose my bonds . . . Am I not your prisoner?"

"You will try to kill yourself again."

"You have given me till eleven o'clock tomorrow evening, Erik."

The footsteps dragged along the floor again.

"After all, as we are to die together . . . Talking of death I must sing his requiem!"

Erik sang like the god of thunder, sang a Dies Irae that enveloped us as in a storm. And the voice changed and transformed distinctly grated out these metallic syllables:

"What have you done with my bag?"

Curious women: Curiouser

"I don't like curious women. You had better remember the story of Blue Beard and be careful . . . Come, give me back my bag! Give me back my bag! . . . Leave the key alone, will you, you inquisitive little thing?"

The Phantom as interior decorator

"What's the matter Christine? You're not going to faint, are you . . . as there is no one there? . . . Here . . . come down . . . there! . . . Pull yourself together . . . as there is no one there! . . . But how do you like the landscape?"

"Oh very much!"

"There, that's better!"

"Yes it's like the Musée Grevin . . . But I say, Erik . . . there are no tortures there! . . . What a fright you gave me!"

The Phantom was ominously silent.

"Did you design that room? It's very handsome. You're a great artist, Erik."

"Yes, a great artist, in my own line."

"But tell me, Erik, why did you call that room the torture-chamber?"

"Oh it's very simple. First of all, what did you see?"

"I saw a forest. Trees."

"And what is in a tree?"

"Birds."

"Did you see any birds?"

"No I did not see any birds."

"Well what did you see? Think! You saw branches! And what are the branches?' asked the terrible voice. 'There's a gibbet! That is why I call my wood the torture-chamber! . . . You see it's a joke. I never express myself like other people. But I am very tired of it! . . . I'm sick and tired of having a forest and a torture-chamber in my house and of living like a mountebank, in a house with a false bottom! . . . I'm tired of it! I want to have a nice, quite flat."

The Greatest ventriloquist in the world

"My dear little Christine! . . . Are you listening to me? . . . Tell me you love me! . . . No, you don't love me . . . but no matter, you will! . . . Once, you could look at my mask because you knew what was behind . . . And now you don't mind looking at it and you forget what is behind! . . . One can get used to everything. Plenty of young people who did not care for each other before marriage have adored each other since! You could have lots of fun with me. For instance, I am the greatest ventriloquist that ever lived, I am the first ventriloquist in the world! . . ."

The wretch, who really was the first ventriloquist in the world, had already begun to play the ventriloquist.

"Erik! Erik!" said Christine. "You tire me with your voice. Don't go on, Erik! Isn't it very hot here?"

"Oh yes," replied Erik's voice, "the heat is unendurable!"

"But what does this mean?"

"I'll tell you, Christine dear: it is because of the forest next door."

"Well what has that to do with it? The forest?"

"Why, didn't you see it was an African forest?"

And the monster laughed so loudly and hideously, that we could no longer distinguish Christine's cries! We heard nothing except the monster's laughter, and the monster himself can have heard nothing else. And then there was the sound of a body falling on the floor being dragged along and a door slammed, and then nothing, noth-

ing more around us save the scorching silence of the south in the
heart of a tropical forest!

Scorpions and grasshoppers

"Christine," I cried, "where are you?"

"By the scorpion."

"Don't touch it!"

"If, in two minutes, mademoiselle, you have not turned the scorpion, I shall turn the grasshopper, and the grasshopper, I tell you,
hops jolly high!"

"Erik," cried Christine, "do you swear to me, monster, do you
swear to me that the scorpion is the one to turn? . . ."

"Yes, to hop at our wedding."

"Ah, you see! You said, to hop!"

"At our wedding, ingenious child! . . . The scorpion opens the
ball . . . But that will do! . . . You won't have the scorpion? Then I
turn the grasshopper!"

"Erik!"

"Enough!"

"Erik! I have turned the scorpion!"

Ghost opera

The Persian at once felt who his singular visitor was and ordered
him to be shown in. It was the ghost, it was Erik!

He looked extremely weak and leaned against the wall, as though
he were afraid of falling. Taking off his hat, he revealed a forehead
as white as wax. The rest of the horrible face was hidden by the
mask.

"Where are Raoul de Chagny and Christine Daae?"

"I am going to die . . ."

"Come, my good man! You've done enough dying to last you a
lifetime."

"Of love. . . . . . . I am dying . . . of love . . . That is how it is . . . I
loved her so! . . . And I love her still. . . . . . . and I am dying of love
for her . . . If you knew how beautiful she was . . . when she let me
kiss her . . . It was the first time . . . I kissed her alive . . . and she
looked as beautiful as if she had been dead! . . ."

"Will you tell me if she is alive or dead?"

"I tell you that I am going to die . . . Yes, I kissed her alive . . ."

"And now she is dead?"

"She was waiting for me . . . waiting for me erect and alive, a real, living bride . . . as she hoped to be saved. My mother, my poor, unhappy mother would never . . . let me kiss her . . . She used to run away . . . and throw me my mask! . . . Nor any other woman . . . ever, ever! . . . Ah, you can understand, my happiness was so great I cried. And I fell at her feet, crying . . ."

And Erik fell into a chair, choking for breath:

"Ah, I am not going to die yet . . . presently I shall . . . but let me cry! Listen to this . . . While I was at her feet . . . I heard her say, 'Poor, unhappy Erik!' And she took my hand! . . . I held in my hand a ring, a plain gold ring which I had given her . . . which she said she had lost . . . and which I had found again . . . a wedding-ring, you know . . . I slipped it into her little hand and said 'There! . . . Take it . . . Take it for you . . . and him! . . . It shall be my wedding present . . . a present from your poor, unhappy Erik . . . I know you love the boy . . . don't cry any more! . . .'

"I went and released the young man, and I made Christine swear to come back one night when I was dead, crossing the lake from the Rue Scribe side, and bury me in the greatest secrecy with the gold ring, which she was to wear until that moment . . . I told her where she would find my body and what to do with it . . . Then Christine kissed me, for the first time, herself, here on the forehead . . ."

The monster resumed his mask and collected his strength to leave.

That was all. The Persian saw Erik to the door of his flat, and Darius helped him down to the street. A cab was waiting for him. Erik stepped in, said to the driver:

"To the Opera."

And the cab drove off into the night.

Phoenix! What about Phoenix? All about Phoenix. Some call her Phoneys because she was the only one to survive the carnage on stage. Quite a falling-off was there! But Phoenix will die too eventually. She will be born again and then she will live for some time and die again—to be born once more, intermittently immortal. *Ave Phoenix!* For she is art, just like Christine in the book and in this tale with a tail. The Phantom is the artist, the artist as outlaw. He is a man capable of selling his soul to the devil himself to see his art come to life. The devil is, as usual, a crafty impresario: he knows all the ropes, including the hangman's. The Phantom would sell his story to anyone, even to a lesser devil, in exchange for attaining art: major art. But his art is now a majorette, Phoenix, who might kill him to reach stardom. Such an artist was OG and now Winslow Leach. So, in a way, was Swan. He made everything devilishly baroque but at the same time possible: he was the devil as entrepreneur. Phoenix is the medium, the Greek bird with gifts. Art for the Phantom was a séance under the Opera: a season in Hades.

About the plot and its dénouement—it's Winslow, *du côté de chez Swan*, who discovers his employer's compact with Satan Inc. Therefore his own contract with Swan, signed not in phony red ink but in true blood, is evil and valid. It's not void: it's *the* void. Pallid Winslow aborts a majorette conspiracy. He flies from the wings to expose Swan on stage when he is about to espouse Phoenix. He shows him for the devil that he is: he was planning to *assassinate* her! (Now that she is famous she cannot be merely killed.) The murder would be sensational: to be transmitted live as she dies on stage during the ceremony, a mockery performed by the gopher, then the scout, now costumed as a bishop, with instant replays. But Knight moves in mysterious ways and he checkmates the Bishop by deflecting the hitman's bullet. It's Bishop who dies on stage in this chequered plot. Winslow kills Swan by simply unmasking him: he is the oldest dwarf on earth who suffers from terminal leprosy, syphilis and stage fright in that order. It all happens right there in front of the audience of teeny-boppers and whinny-poppers: pop gone berserk! Applause, cheers, chanting, rock and roll as Rocambole puns while Phoenix discovers, contrite but still under contract, the good side of Winslow. She rises in tears to the occasion. Deformed Winslow tries dying on stage: going, gone, dead as the Bird. He is the Phantom of the Pop Opera. End of music, end of the show.

"Ah, that's perfect casting!"

"The girl is good, yes."

"No, no, the Cast, the List of Characters, the Credits."

"Oh!"

"I knew you'd love it."

Give me some lights: away!

"The perfect picture! All myth and music and a garland of girls in a forest of feathers. Pure Pop! Much art with no matter. Tinted tinsel. Empty but beautiful—just like a scarlet starlet!"

Lights, lights, lights!

"What's the matter?"

"Aggravation."

"Between who and who?"

"Those girls next to me."

"Are they molesting you?"

"No, but they are much vexed."

"Ah ha! They should have started sooner."

Come, some music! Come the recorder!

They were playing the Queen's perfunctorily.

"If they like not the comedy, why then, belike they like it not, perdy?"

"Apparently they've lost something."

Perdido then. I looked at them now in the soft light and sweet music, for they had stopped playing "God Save the Queen" and were broadcasting some bossa nova of old from behind the crimson curtains and the screen. The girls revealed themselves as plain or ugly or plain ugly. Shadows in the hall can be deceiving.

"As far as I can see they didn't exactly lose their virginity."

"Please! They've really lost something. Ask them what it is."

"Why don't you ask them? Woman to woman."

"Please, *please!"*

I addressed them as if they were self-stamped envelopes.

"Have you lost something?"

"Purse," said the fake blonde and it sounded more like Perse. The tall brunette, nodding rapidly, looked as if she had lost her lips with her purse. They started looking again, everywhere in the house. What could they have in that handbag—Miss Prism's manuscript?

"Let's help them," said my cinemagoer. "They seem to be at a loss."

"For words."

"Please!" This seemed to be her only word for tonight but it was astounding how much it did express. Or was it her? "Let's give them a hand."

"Isn't one finger enough?"

"For God's sake!"

Reluctantly, I started looking. But she went vehemently further down the aisle in her quest. I joined her in the first row. Suddenly she stooped—to retrieve the lost handbag from under a seat. Or from the dark rather. How in hell did she—? She showed the apparel to me. It was an ordinary handbag, neither big nor small, plain and rather old. It was definitely mousey but it wasn't even hideously kitsch or campy or corny. It certainly wasn't an *objet trouvé.*

"Tell them you found it."

"Why don't you tell them?"

"It will be best if you told them."

"I'll tell them but *you* found it."

"All right."

"It's here!"

I shouted and she lifted the handbag in one hand for the other women to see. It wasn't terribly heavy, so she waved more than wielded it. The two women (I couldn't possibly call them girls any more: not with my present knowledge) rushed over. They were no angels. One of them almost snatched the purse from my constant nymphet's hands. Rude Ruth. The other opened the handbag, rummaged into it and out of it came a cry:

"It's *empty!*"

It was the girl not the purse crying.

"It's gone! Everything is gone! Money, compact, address book. Everything! Even my pack of *Camels!*"

"Are you sure?" asked the other. Instead of answering the blonde girl turned her handbag upside down—and nothing came out of it. How much surer can you be? She cried:

"Gone!" which in her modified Cockney accent sounded like a gong. Pity she wasn't Thai. Then she began to cry, to weep real tears, searing cries, sobs and chokes: a woman crying just like a woman. Then sudden silence came from between the proscenium arch and the screen: the music had stopped at last! But not her crying. We were alone in the theatre.

Alone, except perhaps for the Phantom. I had no doubt that he was the purse-snatcher. With this knowledge, feeling like an accessory after the fact, I started to leave the house. She came behind me, then the ugly brunette and the ugly blonde brought up the rear. Somewhere in the basement the Phantom was looking, for cover for the night. Night for day for him.

Outside there was the blinding light of the bulbous canopy and for a moment night had a thousand eyes, some of them watery. Then darkness came to us abruptly: the marquee lights were out. Even the name above the marquee was dark and all I could make out of the sign was the E and then to guess the SS. OLD and the O of course had all disappeared in the blackout. But the two girls remained. One of them still crying, the other still devoutly consoling, or counselling, her friend. My consistent companion was distressed by the spectacle the two women were making of themselves. Or was it perhaps moved by their devotion in adversity?

"Why don't you give her something?"

That was she.

"Me?"

"Yes you."

"Why don't you?"

"It's your money."

"But it's you who have it."

Like royalty, and the Beatles at the time, I never carry cash. Not in London, anyway. In New York I used to keep some in easy pockets to feed muggers on grass, alas. In Barcelona, that gaudy city of Gaudi, I used to pocket some coins for beggars who pack a gun.

"All right," I gave in or rather up. "How much do I give her?"

"You better ask her how much she lost."

"Just like that?"

"Just like that."

"And what if she says five hundred?"

"Don't be silly!"

I approached the crying and consoling couple to consult with them.

"How much money have you lost?"

She looked at me. Through tears darkly, I suppose.

"All I had! That's how much."

"How much is that in pounds?"

They looked at each other. Then the brunette answered:

"Ex quid."

The two words came across like one: squid.

"How much is X?"

They looked at each other as if solving an equation.

"Ten. Ten quid. A ten-pound note."

I turned to my generous gerund: *amando*. Now *dando*. She had already opened her handbag and fished out a ten-pound note. Crispy bill. It was only then, when I saw in the dark the new note gleaming, that I knew that we had made a mistake. The inconsolable lady had lost a ten-pound note—exactly like the one we were handing her. To a foreigner all ten-pound notes look alike: there's the queen, there's the number 10, there's the Bank of England and there's the rub. But it was too late. The girl, obviously a habit with her, had already snatched the bill from her, my, our hands, the crisp note flying away from us like a nighthawk back to her nest with a fresh quarry.

"Thanks," was all she said, as if we were paying her back some outstanding bill. All of a sudden, as an afterthought, she asked me:

"Are you an Arab?"

"I wish I were."

"A person then?"

"Of course I am a person! Though I was once an unperson."

"I mean Eyeranian."

"You mean to ask if I am from Iran."

"Yes."

"I caint say I am cause I ain't I'm not a Persian nor an Arab. Not even an Iraquois."

"How come you're so generous with money?"

"I'm a giver, you see. Though an Indian giver. Here's my card. You can return the money when you can. I'm always in."

"I thought you were a Persian."

Her insistence was baffling. Had she mistaken me for the Phantom's closet, or closest, enemy? His dearest rival, his semblable, his equal? I decided it was time to say good bye.

"Time to say good bye."

"I think so too. Good bye."

"Good bye."

"Good bye."

Both of them turned around to walk away, not before the brunette unpursed her lips into a thin smile. I must confess that I have never liked women with lips like a level line: thin lips are deceiving, just like the horizon. I stayed there on the pavement by the building, under the dark canopy of the Essoldo. I saw them climb into a gleaming, white, dashing two-seater sports car. The make was Morgan but she didn't let me deduce the improbable from the impossible.

"I think we met a mistake."

Malaprops can also be props.

"Me too. It's all too pat, pal."

"Surely they saw through it all."

"Through what all?"

"Can't you see? We were sitting next to them—"

"They came in *after*, remember?"

"They came after us all right. Suddenly they were right there, next to us with all those vacant seats around us. Then one misplaces her purse during the show. So we help her find it—in the most incredible place: the first row! She discovers then that her handbag is empty and there's ten pounds missing. Exactly ten pounds! And exactly the amount you gave her out of your gracious heart: a ten-pound note. Can anybody call it a coincidence?"

I was about to call it what she couldn't—but she motioned off with her angry head and said:

"They're kissing!"

"Probably good night." I didn't even bother to turn.

"I know good night kisses, buster, and this ain't a goodnight kiss!"

"Then it's good night till it'll be morrow."

"What's that supposed to mean?"

"The Tragicomedy of Juliet and Juliet. Let's go!"

We turned to cross King's Road, a dead river, and back into the lab. Lab is short for labyrinth. We came back the hardest way: *per aspera* but without the stars. Nor the moon late at night. When I was about to fetch my key and open the door, she discreetly pulled my arm: my left elbow.

"Look!"

"What?"

Like all shortsighted men I want to know what to see before looking at it: precisions.

"The girls."

"What girls?"

"The girls at the movies."

I thought she was pulling not my arm but my leg.

"You mean Marilyn Monroe and Jane Russell?"

"Come on! The girls at the Essoldo."

I wasn't kidding her. They really looked like British versions of Jane Russell and Marilyn Monroe. At least they did under the fully-lit marquee, bathed in the glare of the five minutes of fame they enjoyed as they cried and pleaded for money, while at the same time looking somewhat guilty: a slight case of swindle. Or were we the ones who seemed to be the guilty party? Now, seated in their white Morgan, a car that looked a lot like Cesar, the white horse in the underworld of the Opera, they appeared more miffed than mysterious. It was then, I believe, when I realized that I would never get my money back. It was there that I concocted my motto: "Writing well is the best revenge." It was there and then that I first thought of writing a story in which I would tell everything about that odd pair (were they au pairs?) the opposite way of Hemingway: to tell it like it wasn't.

Lastly, later, with my bunch of papers in hand, I once more went over to the Ghost's vast literary domain: the huge fictive edifice which he had made his kingdom and it was now my own—the ten-pound Opera. Of course, dear reader, I haven't told all. The perfect moviegoer never sees and tells. Even if he tells the plot, he never reveals the end. But for my own end I must quote a *graffito* I saw, *in passim,* as I was travelling on the Piccadilly Line, at Convent Garden station. It said, blurred by the double speed (speed-writing, speed-reading), but very visible:

Alejo Carpentier
(1904–1980)

The Cuban Alejo Carpentier was born in Havana of French and Russian émigré parents. They spoke French at home and, upon their return to Europe in 1914, settled in his father's native France. Carpentier went back to Cuba in the twenties to study architecture and music. There he helped to found the Cuban Communist Party and, in 1927, was arrested for his opposition to the Machado dictatorship. During the forty days he spent in jail, he worked on his first novel, later disavowed: *Ecué-Yamba-O* (1933), a superficial exploration of Afro-Cuban traditions among the poor of the island written according to the tenets of socialist realism.

Upon his release from prison in early 1928, he escaped to France with the help of the poet journalist Robert Desnos, who lent Carpentier his passport and papers. In Paris, Desnos introduced the young author to André Breton and the surrealists. Two years later, Carpentier sided with Desnos in the latter's pro-Soviet break with Breton. It was also in Paris that he met the Guatemalan author Miguel Angel Asturias, whose work on Central American pre-Columbian mythology was to influence his own writings.

With the outbreak of the Second World War, he returned to Cuba, where he began researching a book on Cuban music and writing the stories that would be collected only much later in *The War of Time* (1958). In the meantime, his reading of Spengler's cyclical interpretation of history and a chance visit to Haiti in 1943, in the company of the French theatrical director Louis Jouvet, provided the inspiration for his very different second novel, *The Kingdom of This World* (1949), with its now historic prologue

416

outlining Carpentier's faith in the special destiny of Latin America and the aesthetic implications of its peculiar cultural heritage.

He wrote two more novels while living in Venezuela, where he had settled in 1946. Then in 1959, following Castro's victorious revolution, the author came home to Cuba, where he worked for the State Publishing House while completing his baroque masterpiece *Explosion in a Cathedral* (1962). Treating the advent of the Enlightenment and the ideas of the French Revolution in the New World, the novel—with its twin leitmotifs of the printing press and the guillotine—may be read as a meditation on the dangers inherent in all revolutions as they begin to confront the temptations of dictatorship.

In 1966, Carpentier settled definitively in Paris, where he was posted as cultural attaché to the Cuban embassy. He died of cancer in 1980. Other translated works include the novella *The Chase* (1956) and the novels *The Lost Steps* (1953), *Reasons of State* (1974), and *The Harp & the Shadow* (1979).

Journey Back
to the Source

I

"What d'you want, Pop?"

Again and again came the question, from high up on the scaffolding. But the old man made no reply. He moved from one place to another, prying into corners and uttering a lengthy monologue of incomprehensible remarks. The tiles had already been taken down, and now covered the dead flower beds with their mosaic of baked clay. Overhead, blocks of masonry were being loosened with picks and sent rolling down wooden gutters in an avalanche of lime and plaster. And through the crenelations that were one by one indenting the walls, were appearing—denuded of their privacy—oval or square ceilings, cornices, garlands, dentils, astragals, and paper hanging from the walls like old skins being sloughed by a snake.

Witnessing the demolition, a Ceres with a broken nose and discolored peplum, her headdress of corn veined with black, stood in the back yard above her fountain of crumbling grotesques. Visited by shafts of sunlight piercing the shadows, the gray fish in the basin yawned in the warm weed-covered water, watching with round eyes the black silhouettes of the workmen against the brilliance of the sky as they diminished the centuries-old height of the house. The old man had sat down at the foot of the statue, resting his chin on his stick. He watched buckets filled with precious fragments ascending and descending. Muted sounds from the street could be heard, while overhead, against a basic rhythm of steel on stone, the pulleys screeched unpleasantly in chorus, like harsh-voiced birds.

The clock struck five. The cornices and entablatures were depopulated. Nothing was left behind but stepladders, ready for tomorrow's onslaught. The air grew cooler, now that it was disburdened of sweat, oaths, creaking ropes, axles crying out for the oil can, and the slapping of hands on greasy torsos. Dusk had settled earlier on the dismantled house. The shadows had enfolded it just at that moment when the now-fallen upper balustrade used to enrich the façade by capturing the sun's last beams. Ceres tightened her lips. For the first time the rooms would sleep unshuttered, gazing onto a landscape of rubble.

Contradicting their natural propensities, several capitals lay in the grass, their acanthus leaves asserting their vegetable status. A creeper stretched adventurous tendrils toward an Ionic scroll, attracted by its air of kinship. When night fell, the house was closer to the ground. Upstairs, the frame of a door still stood erect, slabs of darkness suspended from its dislocated hinges.

II

Then the old Negro, who had not stirred, began making strange movements with his stick, whirling it around above a graveyard of paving stones.

The white and black marble squares flew to the floors and covered them. Stones leaped up and unerringly filled the gaps in the walls. The nail-studded walnut doors fitted themselves into their frames, while the screws rapidly twisted back into the holes in the hinges. In the dead flower beds, the fragments of the tile were lifted by the thrust of growing flowers and joined together, raising a sonorous whirlwind of clay, to fall like rain on the framework of the roof. The house grew, once more assuming its normal proportions, modestly clothed. Ceres became less gray. There were more fish in the fountain. And the gurgling water summoned forgotten begonias back to life.

The old man inserted a key into the lock of the front door and began to open the windows. His heels made a hollow sound. When he lighted the lamps, a yellow tremor ran over the oil paint of the family portraits, and people dressed in black talked softly in all the corridors, to the rhythm of spoons stirring cups of chocolate.

Don Marcial, Marqués de Capellanías, lay on his deathbed, his breast blazing with decorations, while four tapers with long beards of melted wax kept guard over him.

III

The candles lengthened slowly, gradually guttering less and less. When they had reached full size, the nun extinguished them and took away the light. The wicks whitened, throwing off red sparks. The house emptied itself of visitors and their carriages drove away in the darkness. Don Marcial fingered an invisible keyboard and opened his eyes.

The confused heaps of rafters gradually went back into place. Medicine bottles, tassels from brocades, the scapulary beside the bed, daguerreotypes, and iron palm leaves from the grille emerged from the mists. When the doctor shook his head with an expression of professional gloom, the invalid felt better. He slept for several hours and awoke under the black beetle-browed gaze of Father Anastasio. What had begun as a candid, detailed confession of his many sins grew gradually more reticent, painful and full of evasions. After all, what right had the Carmelite to interfere in his life?

Suddenly Don Marcial found himself thrown into the middle of the room. Relieved of the pressure on his temples, he stood up with surprising agility. The naked woman who had been stretching herself on the brocade coverlet began to look for her petticoats and bodices, and soon afterward disappeared in a rustle of silk and a waft of perfume. In the closed carriage downstairs an envelope full of gold coins was lying on the brass-studded seat.

Don Marcial was not feeling well. When he straightened his cravat before the pier glass he saw that his face was congested. He went downstairs to his study where lawyers—attorneys and their clerks—were waiting for him to arrange for the sale of the house by auction. All his efforts had been in vain. His property would go to the highest bidder, to the rhythm of a hammer striking the table. He bowed, and they left him alone. He thought how mysterious were written words: those black threads weaving and unweaving, and covering large sheets of paper with a filigree of estimates; weaving and unweaving contracts, oaths, agreements, evidence, declarations, names, titles, dates, lands, trees, and stones; a tangled skein of threads, drawn from the inkpot to ensnare the legs of any man who took a path disapproved of by the law; a noose around his neck to stifle free speech at its first dreaded sound. He had been betrayed by his signature; it had handed him over to the nets and labyrinths of documents. Thus constricted, the man of flesh and blood had become a man of paper.

It was dawn. The dining-room clock had just struck six in the evening.

IV

The months of mourning passed under the shadow of ever-increasing remorse. At first the idea of bringing a woman to his room had seemed quite reasonable. But little by little the desire excited by a new body gave way to increasing scruples, which ended as self-torment. One night, Don Marcial beat himself with a strap till the blood came, only to experience even intenser desire, though it was of short duration.

It was at this time that the Marquesa returned one afternoon from a drive along the banks of the Almendares. The manes of the horses harnessed to her carriage were damp with solely their own sweat. Yet they spent the rest of the day kicking the wooden walls of their stable as if maddened by the stillness of the low-hanging clouds.

At dusk, a jar full of water broke in the Marquesa's bathroom. Then the May rains came and overflowed the lake. And the old Negress who unhappily was a maroon and kept pigeons under her bed wandered through the patio, muttering to herself, "Never trust rivers, my girl; never trust anything green and flowing!" Not a day passed without water making its presence felt. But in the end that presence amounted to no more than a cup spilled over a Paris dress after the anniversary ball given by the Governor of the Colony.

Many relatives reappeared. Many friends came back again. The chandeliers in the great drawing room glittered with brilliant lights. The cracks in the façade were closing up, one by one. The piano became a clavichord. The palm trees lost some of their rings. The creepers let go of the upper cornice. The dark circles around Ceres's eyes disappeared, and the capitals of the columns looked as if they had been freshly carved. Marcial was more ardent now, and often passed whole afternoons embracing the Marquesa. Crow's-feet, frowns, and double chins vanished, and flesh grew firm again. One day the smell of fresh paint filled the house.

V

Their embarrassment was real. Each night the leaves of the screens opened a little farther, and skirts fell to the floor in obscurer corners of the room, revealing yet more barriers of lace. At last the Marquesa blew out the lamps. Only Marcial's voice was heard in the darkness.

They left for the sugar plantation in a long procession of carriages—sorrel hindquarters, silver bits, and varnished leather gleamed in the sunshine. But among the pasqueflowers empurpling the arcades leading up to the house, they realized that they scarcely knew each other. Marcial gave permission for a performance of native dancers and drummers, by way of entertainment during those days impregnated with the smells of eau de cologne, of baths spiced with benzoin, of unloosened hair and sheets taken from closets and unfolded to let a bunch of vetiver drop onto the tiled floor. The steam of cane juice and the sound of the Angelus mingled on the breeze. The vultures flew low, heralding a sparse shower, whose first large echoing drops were absorbed by tiles so dry that they gave off a diapason like copper.

After a dawn prolonged by an inexpert embrace, they returned together to the city with their misunderstandings settled and the wound healed. The Marquesa changed her traveling dress for a wedding gown and the married pair went to church according to custom, to regain their freedom. Relations and friends received their presents back again, and they all set off for home with jingling brass and a display of splendid trappings. Marcial went on visiting María de las Mercedes for a while, until the day when the rings were taken to the goldsmiths to have their inscriptions removed. For Marcial, a new life was beginning. In the house with the high grilles, an Italian Venus was set up in place of Ceres, and the grotesques in the fountain were thrown into almost imperceptibly sharper relief because the lamps were still glowing when dawn colored the sky.

VI

One night, after drinking heavily and being sickened by the stale tobacco smoke left behind by his friends, Marcial had the strange sensation that all the clocks in the house were striking five, then half past four, then four, then half past three.... It was as if he had become dimly aware of other possibilities. Just as, when exhausted by sleeplessness, one may believe that one could walk on the ceiling, with the floor for a ceiling and the furniture firmly fixed between the beams. It was only a fleeting impression, and did not leave the smallest trace on his mind, for he was not much given to meditation at the time.

And a splendid evening party was given in the music room on the day he achieved minority. He was delighted to know that his signature was no longer legally valid, and that worm-eaten registers and documents would now vanish from his world. He had reached the point at which courts of justice were no longer to be feared, because his bodily existence was ignored by the law. After getting tipsy on noble wines, the young people took down from the wall a guitar inlaid with mother-of-pearl, a psaltery, and a serpent. Someone wound up the clock that played the *ranz des vaches* and the "Ballad of the Scottish Lakes." Someone else blew on a hunting horn that had been lying curled in copper sleep on the crimson felt lining of the showcase, beside a transverse flute brought from Aranjuez. Marcial, who was boldly making love to Señora de Campoflorido, joined in the cacophony, and tried to pick out the tune of "Trípili-Trápala" on the piano, to a discordant accompaniment in the bass.

Then they all trooped upstairs to the attic, remembering that the liveries and clothes of the Capellanías family had been stored away under its peeling beams. On shelves frosted with camphor lay court dresses, an ambassador's sword, several padded military jackets, the vestment of a dignitary of the Church, and some long cassocks with damask buttons and damp stains among their folds. The dark shadows of the attic were variegated with the colors of amaranthine ribbons, yellow crinolines, faded tunics, and velvet flowers. A picaresque *chispero*'s costume and hair net trimmed with tassels, once made for a carnival masquerade, was greeted with applause. Señora de Campoflorido swathed her powdered shoulders in a shawl the color of a Creole's skin, once worn by a certain ancestress on an evening of important family decisions in hopes of reviving the sleeping ardor of some rich trustee of a convent of Clares.

As soon as they were dressed up, the young people went back to the music room. Marcial, who was wearing an alderman's hat, struck the floor three times with a stick and announced that they would begin with a waltz, a dance mothers thought terribly improper for young ladies because they had to allow themselves to be taken round the waist, with a man's hand resting on the busks

of the stays they had all had made according to the latest model
in the *Jardin des Modes*. The doorways were blocked by maidservants, stableboys, and waiters, who had come from remote out-
buildings and stifling basements to enjoy the boisterous fun.
Afterward they played blindman's bluff and hide-and-seek. Hidden
behind a Chinese screen with Señora de Campoflorido, Marcial
planted a kiss on her neck, and received in return a scented handkerchief whose Brussels lace still retained the sweet warmth of her
low-necked bodice.

And when the girls left in the fading light of dusk, to return to
castles and towers silhouetted in dark gray against the sea, the
young men went to the dance hall, where alluring *mulatas* in heavy
bracelets were strutting about without ever losing their high-heeled
shoes, even in the frenzy of the guaracha. And as it was carnival
time, the members of the Arara Chapter Three Eyes Band were
raising thunder on their drums behind the wall in a patio planted
with pomegranate trees. Climbing onto tables and stools, Marcial
and his friends applauded the gracefulness of a Negress with gray-
ing hair, who had recovered her beauty and almost become desirable as she danced, looking over her shoulder with an expression
of proud disdain.

VII

The visits of Don Abundio, the family notary and executor, were
more frequent now. He used to sit gravely down beside Marcial's
bed, and let his acana-wood cane drop to the floor so as to wake
him up in good time. Opening his eyes, Marcial saw an alpaca
frock coat covered with dandruff, its sleeves shiny from collecting
securities and rents. All that was left in the end was an adequate
pension, calculated to put a stop to all wild extravagance. It was at
this time that Marcial wanted to enter the Royal Seminary of San
Carlos.

After doing only moderately well in his examinations, he attended courses of lectures, but understood less and less of his master's explanations. The world of his ideas was gradually growing
emptier. What had once been a general assembly of peplums, dou-
blets, ruffs, and periwigs, of controversialists and debaters, now
looked as lifeless as a museum of wax figures. Marcial contented
himself with a scholastic analysis of the systems, and accepted everything he found in a book as the truth. The words "Lion," "Os-

trich," "Whale," "Jaguar" were printed under the copper-plate engravings in his natural history book. Just as "Aristotle," "St. Thomas," "Bacon," and "Descartes" headed pages black with boring, close-printed accounts of different interpretations of the universe. Bit by bit, Marcial stopped trying to learn these things, and felt relieved of a heavy burden. His mind grew gay and lively, understanding things in a purely instinctive way. Why think about the prism, when the clear winter light brought out all the details in the fortresses guarding the port? An apple falling from a tree tempted one to bite it—that was all. A foot in a bathtub was merely a foot in a bathtub. The day he left the seminary he forgot all about his books. A gnomon was back in the category of goblins, a spectrum a synonym for a phantom, and an octandrian an animal armed with spines.

More than once he had hurried off with a troubled heart to visit the women who whispered behind blue doors under the town walls. The memory of one of them, who wore embroidered slippers and a sprig of sweet basil behind her ear, pursued him on hot evenings like the toothache. But one day his confessor's anger and threats reduced him to terrified tears. He threw himself for the last time between those infernal sheets, and then forever renounced his detours through unfrequented streets and that last-minute faintheartedness which sent him home in a rage, turning his back on a certain crack in the pavement—the signal, when he was walking with head bent, that he must turn and enter the perfumed threshold.

Now he was undergoing a spiritual crisis, peopled by religious images, paschal lambs, china doves, Virgins in heavenly blue cloaks, gold paper stars, the three Magi, angels with wings like swans, the Ass, the Ox, and a terrible Saint Denis, who appeared to him in his dreams with a great space between his shoulders, walking hesitantly as if looking for something he had lost. When he blundered into the bed, Marcial would start awake and reach for his rosary of silver beads. The lampwicks, in their bowls of oil, cast a sad light on the holy images as their colors returned to them.

VIII

The furniture was growing taller. It was becoming more difficult for him to rest his arms on the dining table. The fronts of the cupboards with their carved cornices were getting broader. The Moors on the staircase stretched their torsos upward, bringing their torches closer to the banisters on the landing. Armchairs were deeper, and rocking chairs tended to fall over backward. It was no longer necessary to bend one's knee when lying at the bottom of the bath with its marble rings.

One morning when he was reading a licentious book, Marcial suddenly felt a desire to play with the lead soldiers lying asleep in their wooden boxes. He put the book back in its hiding place under the washbasin, and opened a drawer sealed with cobwebs. His schoolroom table was too small to hold such a large army. So Marcial sat on the floor and set out his grenadiers in rows of eight. Next came the officers on horseback, surrounding the color sergeant; and behind, the artillery with their cannon, gun sponges, and linstocks. Bringing up the rear were fifes and tabors escorted by drummers. The mortars were fitted with a spring, so that one could shoot glass marbles to a distance of more than a yard.

Bang! . . . Bang! . . . Bang!

Down fell horses, down fell standard-bearers, down fell drummers. Eligio the Negro had to call him three times before he could be persuaded to go to wash his hands and descend to the dining room.

After that day, Marcial made a habit of sitting on the tiled floor. When he realized the advantages of this position, he was surprised that he had not thought of it before. Grown-up people had a passion for velvet cushions, which made them sweat too much. Some of them smelled like a notary—like Don Abundio—because they had not discovered how cool it was to lie at full length on a marble floor at all seasons of the year. Only from the floor could all the angles and perspectives of a room be grasped properly. There were beautiful grains in the wood, mysterious insect paths, and shadowy corners that could not be seen from a man's height. When it rained, Marcial hid himself under the clavichord. Every clap of thunder made the sound box vibrate, and set all the notes to singing. Shafts of lightning fell from the sky, creating a vault of cascading arpeggios—the organ, the wind in the pines, and the crickets' mandolin.

IX

That morning they locked him in his room. He heard whispering all over the house, and the luncheon they brought him was too delicious for a weekday. There were six pastries from the confectioner's in the Alameda—whereas even on Sundays after Mass he was only allowed two. He amused himself by looking at the engravings in a travel book, until an increasing buzz of sound coming under the door made him look out between the blinds. Some men dressed all in black were arriving, bearing a brass-handled coffin. He was on the verge of tears, but at this moment Melchor the groom appeared in his room, his boots echoing on the floor and his teeth flashing in a smile. They began to play chess. Melchor was a knight. He was the king. Using the tiles on the floor as a chessboard, he moved from one square to the next, while Melchor had to jump one forward and two sideways, or vice versa. The game went on until after dusk, when the fire brigade went by.

When he got up, he went to kiss his father's hand as he lay ill in bed. The Marqués was feeling better, and talked to his son in his usual serious and edifying manner. His "Yes, Father's" and "No, Father's" were fitted between the beads of a rosary of questions, like the responses of an acolyte during Mass. Marcial respected the Marqués, but for reasons that no one could possibly have guessed. He respected him because he was tall, because when he went out to a ball his breast glittered with decorations; because he envied him the saber and gold braid he wore as an officer in the militia; because at Christmas time, on a bet, he had eaten a whole turkey stuffed with almonds and raisins; because he had once seized one of the *mulatas* who were sweeping out the rotunda and had carried her in his arms to his room—no doubt intending to whip her. Hidden behind a curtain, Marcial watched her come out soon afterward, in tears and with her dress unfastened, and he was pleased that she had been punished, as she was the one who always emptied the jam pots before putting them back in the cupboard.

His father was a terrible and magnanimous being, and it was his duty to love him more than anyone except God. To Marcial he was more godlike even than God because his gifts were tangible, everyday ones. But he preferred the God in heaven because he was less of a nuisance.

X

When the furniture had grown a little taller still, and Marcial knew better than anyone what was under the beds, cupboards, and cabinets, he had a great secret, which he kept to himself: life had no charms except when Melchor the groom was with him. Not

God, nor his father, nor the golden bishop in the Corpus Christi procession was as important as Melchor.

Melchor had come from a very long distance away. He was descended from conquered princes. In his kingdom there were elephants, hippopotamuses, tigers, and giraffes, and men did not sit working, like Don Abundio, in dark rooms full of papers. They lived by outdoing the animals in cunning. One of them had pulled the great crocodile out of the blue lake after first skewering him on a pike concealed inside the closely packed bodies of twelve roast geese. Melchor knew songs that were easy to learn because the words had no meaning and were constantly repeated. He stole sweetmeats from the kitchens; at night he used to escape through the stable door, and once he threw stones at the police before disappearing into the darkness of the Calle de la Amargura.

On wet days he used to put his boots to dry beside the kitchen stove. Marcial wished he had feet big enough to fill boots like those. His right-hand boot was called Calambín; the left one Calambán. This man who could tame unbroken horses by simply seizing their lips between two fingers, this fine gentleman in velvet and spurs who wore such tall hats, also understood about the coolness of marble floors in summer, and used to hide fruits or a cake, snatched from trays destined for the drawing room, behind the furniture. Marcial and Melchor shared a secret store of sweets and almonds, which they saluted with *"Urí, urí, urá"* and shouts of conspiratorial laughter. They had both explored the house from top to bottom, and were the only ones who knew that beneath the stables there was a small cellar full of Dutch bottles, or that in an unused loft over the maids' rooms was a broken glass case containing twelve dusty butterflies that were losing their wings.

XI

When Marcial got into the habit of breaking things, he forgot Melchor and made friends with the dogs. There were several in the house. The large one with stripes like a tiger; the basset trailing its teats on the ground; the greyhound that had grown too old to play; the poodle that was chased by the others at certain times and had to be shut up by the maids.

Marcial liked Canelo best because he carried off shoes from the bedrooms and dug up the rose trees in the patio. Always black with coal dust or covered with red earth, he devoured the dinners of all the other dogs, whined without cause, and hid stolen bones under the fountain. And now and again he would suck dry a new laid egg and send the hen flying with a sharp blow from his muzzle. Everyone kicked Canelo. But when they took him away, Marcial made himself ill with grief. And the dog returned in triumph, wagging his tail, from somewhere beyond the poorhouse where he had been abandoned, and regained his place in the house, which the other dogs, for all their skill in hunting, or vigilance when keeping guard, could never fill.

Canelo and Marcial used to urinate side by side. Sometimes they chose the Persian carpet in the drawing room, spreading dark, cloudlike shapes over its pile. This usually cost them a thrashing. But thrashings were less painful than grown-up people realized. On the other hand, they gave a splendid excuse for setting up a concerted howling and arousing the pity of the neighbors. When the cross-eyed woman from the top flat called his father a "brute," Marcial looked at Canelo with smiling eyes. They shed a few more tears so as to be given a biscuit, and afterward all was forgotten. They both used to eat earth, roll on the ground, drink out of the goldfish basin, and take refuge in the scented shade under the sweet-basil bushes. During the hottest hours of the day quite a crowd filled the moist flower beds. There would be the gray goose with her pouch hanging between her bandy-legs; the old rooster with his naked rump; the little lizard who kept saying *"Urí, urá"* and shooting a pink ribbon out of his throat; the melancholy snake, born in a town where there were no females; and the mouse that blocked its hole with a turtle's egg. One day someone pointed out the dog to Marcial.

"Bow-wow," Marcial said.

He was talking his own language. He had attained the ultimate liberty. He was beginning to want to reach with his hands things that were out of reach.

XII

Hunger, thirst, heat, pain, cold. Hardly had Marcial reduced his field of perception to these essential realities when he renounced the light that accompanied them. He did not know his name. The unpleasantness of the christening over, he had no desire for smells, sounds, or even sights. His hands caressed delectable forms. He was a purely sensory and tactile being. The universe penetrated

him through his pores. Then he shut his eyes—they saw nothing
but nebulous giants—and entered a warm, damp body full of shadows: a dying body. Clothed in this body's substance, he slipped
toward life.

But now time passed more quickly, rarefying the final hours.
The minutes sounded like cards slipping from beneath a dealer's
thumb.

Birds returned to their eggs in a whirlwind of feathers. Fish con-
gealed into roe, leaving a snowfall of scales at the bottom of their
pond. The palm trees folded their fronds and disappeared into the
earth like shut fans. Stems were reabsorbing their leaves, and the
earth reclaimed everything that was its own. Thunder rumbled
through the arcades. Hairs began growing from antelope-skin
gloves. Woolen blankets were unraveling and turning into the
fleece of sheep in distant pastures. Cupboards, cabinets, beds, cru-
cifixes, tables, and blinds disappeared into the darkness in search
of their ancient roots beneath the forest trees. Everything that had
been fastened with nails was disintegrating. A brigantine, anchored
no one knew where, sped back to Italy carrying the marble from
the floors and fountains. Suits of armor, ironwork, keys, copper
cooking pots, the horses' bits from the stables, were melting and
forming a swelling river of metal running into the earth through
roofless channels. Everything was undergoing metamorphosis and
being restored to its original state. Clay returned to clay, leaving a
desert where the house had once stood.

XIII

When the workmen came back at dawn to go on with the demolition of the house, they found their task completed. Someone
had carried off the statue of Ceres and sold it to an antique dealer
the previous evening. After complaining to their trade union, the
men went and sat on the seats in the municipal park. Then one of
them remembered some vague story about a Marquesa de Capellanías who had been drowned one evening in May among the arum
lilies in the Almendares. But no one paid any attention to his story,
because the sun was traveling from east to west, and the hours
growing on the right-hand side of the clock must be spun out by
idleness—for they are the ones that inevitably lead to death.

Translated by Frances Partridge